McAlister's Allegiance

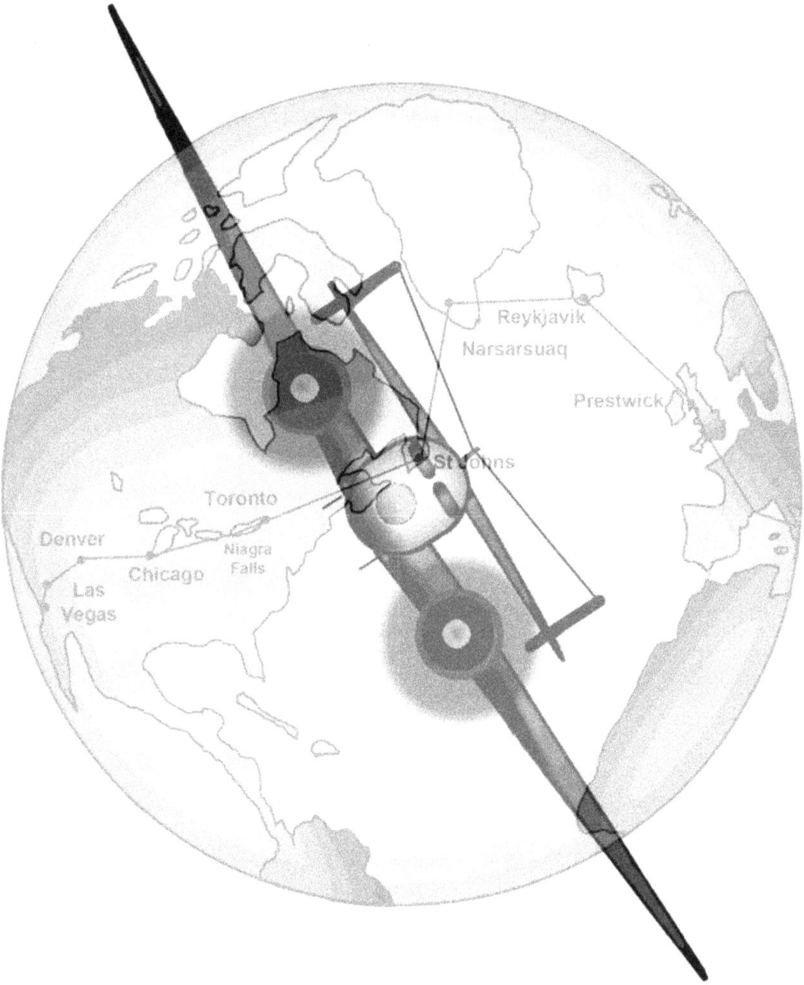

Richard Marman

Cover illustration, design and graphics by Richard Marman

Books by Richard Marman
Published by Abela Publishing

<u>The McAlister Line</u>
(In historical order)
McAlister's Trail
McAlister and the Great War
McAlister's Way
McAlister's Hoard
McAlister's Siege
McAlister's Allegiance
McAlister's Spark

<u>Web and Wave Illustrated Adventures</u>
(For children of all ages)

A Tale of Two Turtles
A Whale's Tale

<u>Illustrated for Rita Hayward</u>

Hannah Meets a Dragon

<u>Illustrated for Elle Burton</u>

Martha the Aeronaut

This book is dedicated
to my wife Judy
and my daughters
Sally and Elizabeth

Acknowledgements

I'd like to especially thank my wife Judy and my daughter Sally for their help in following the progress of the manuscript and making sure it kept going in the right direction. Thanks to Sheila Yong and my sister, Lesley for their feedback and initial proof reading and Judy Bandidt for the final goal-keeper's edit. Thank you to Wing Commander John 'Trackless' Millsom for DC-3 aircraft technical support. Finally cheers to John Halsted for being so enthusiastic about this series.

Glossary

Abyssinia	Present day Ethiopia
Air America	The CIA's personal airline
A First	First class honours degree achieved in British universities
A-1 uniform	Military parade dress uniform opposed to battle dress
APB	All points bulletin — an urgent police message requiring all recipients to respond
ARVN	Army of the Republic of Vietnam
ASIO	Australian Security and Intelligence Organisation
AVGAS	High octane aviation gasoline — petrol for piston-engine planes
Battle Dress	Serviceman's workday uniform
BBC	British Broadcasting Corporation
BEA	British European Airways
Big Red One	First Infantry Division, US Army
Biltong	South African name for beef-jerky
Bint	Girl
Blue-Lamp	Four-sided blue light at the entrance to British police stations
BOAC	British Overseas Airways Corporation — later to merge with BEA to form British Airways
DZ	Drop zone for paratroops or airborne cargo — pronounced 'dee-zed'
CASEVAC	Casualty evacuation — medivac (medical evacuation) is the term used today

CAT	China Air Transport — the forerunner of Air America
C-46	Curtiss Commando twin engine transport plane
C-47	Redoubtable twin engine transport plane also known as the Sky-train, Dakota (Dak), DC-3 and *Gooney-Bird*
C-in-C	Commander in chief
Check Point Charlie	Major crossing point between East and West Berlin during the Cold War
CIA	Central Intelligence Agency — US version of ASIO
Comfort Woman	Women and girls conscripted as prostitutes for the IJA
Cracker	Originally a white farmer or labourer — often used as a derogatory term by coloured Americans for whites
Crate	Aircraft
Customers	CIA operatives who travelled on CAT planes
DFC	Distinguished Flying Cross — RAAF and RAF award for bravery
DPD	Dallas Police Department
DORA	Defence of the Realm Act — British security legislation
DRV	Democratic Republic of Vietnam (North Vietnam)
Dry-Lease	Chartering a plane, but supplying your own crew
ETA	Estimated time of arrival
Fard salaf	Islamic mandatory worship
FBI	Federal Bureau of Investigation

Formosa	Present day Taiwan
Fox-mike	Frequency modulated (FM) radio
GBH	Grievous bodily harm
GIs	US troops
GONO	*Groupement Opérationnel Nord-Ouest* – Group of Operational Forces North-West i.e. the French Union Force at Dien Bien Phu
Grunts	American infantrymen
Janbiya	Arabian dagger
Jim Crow Laws	Coloured segregation laws in the USA
Judies	Teddy boys' girlfriends
KGB	*Komitet Gosudarstvennoy Bezopasnosti* – Committee for State Security – Russian equivalent of ASIO only meaner
Ki	Abbreviation for kilo when referring to heroin – pronounced 'kee'
KKK	Klu Klux Klan – Racially motivated secret organisation endorsing white supremacy in the USA
Limey	American term for the British – thought to have derived from 'lime-juicer' because lime-juice was part of 18th and 19th Century British sailors' daily food ration to prevent scurvy
LZ	Chopper landing zone – pronounced 'ell-zee'
MAAG	Military Assistance Advisory Group. US Special Forces operatives assigned to train the South Vietnamese military
MBE	Member of the Most Excellent Order of the British Empire – Prestigious British award for service to the nation

MG	Machine gun
MI-6	Secret Intelligence Service — British equivalent of the CIA & ASIO
MO	Medical officer
MP	Military Police
MPD	Montgomery Police Department
NCO	Non-commissioned officers — corporals, sergeants and warrant officers
NSW	New South Wales, Australia
Pentatonic Scale	Musical scale consisting of only five notes Oriental music is based on major scales while blues and rock-and- roll use minor scales
Perry	Pear cider
PFC	Private first class — GI equivalent to a lance-corporal
Pitot tube	Hollow pipe attached to an aircraft fuselage to measure forward air speed
Pommy	Australian term for the British
POV	Point of view
PR	Public relations
PSP	Pierced Steel Plating — interlocking perforated steel plates that formed a runway or road surface — also known as Marsden Matting
Quid	One pound sterling — Standard British currency until decimalisation on 15 February 1971
Readies	Cash — ready money
Red Caps	Military police
RLA	Royal Laotian Army
RLAF	Royal Laotian Air Force
RVN	Republic of Vietnam (South Vietnam)

S-55	Medium lift Sikorsky helicopter sometimes referred to as S-19 — Danny has used the designation S-55 throughout
Simi	Kikuyu machete
Sitrep	Situation report
Spooks	CIA agents
Tanganyika	Present day Tanzania
Teddy Boys	London Dandies of the 1950s and 60s
Torri-Rouge	Literally 'Red-Earth' the main airstrip at Dien Bien Phu
Tuskegee Red Tails	WWII fighter squadron manned by black airmen
Uncle Ho	Ho Chi Minh
Viet Cong	South Vietnamese Communists
Viet Minh	North Vietnamese Communists
Wet-Lease	Chartering a plane including its crew
WAC	**US** Women's Army Corps
WHO	World Health Organisation

Prologue — Merimbula NSW

My name is Zach McAlister, but if you've read my previous stories you already know that. In 2010 after my Nan died, I started to spend school holidays with my Grandpa Danny on his property near Merimbula. If you've never heard of the place, it's on the New South Wales coast close to the Victorian border.

Grandpa and I hadn't seen much of each other before that and at first it was a bit awkward until I discovered a bunch of neat stuff in his 3-bay shed. There were all kinds of things he'd collected throughout his life. He called them his artefacts. He'd collected photos, postcards and made pencil and watercolour sketches of things he'd seen along the way. Some of them are looking a bit tatty now, but he's scanning them and transferring them to electronic albums and collages. He's getting pretty handy with Photoshop now.

One intriguing item was a circular badge surrounding a lone-star emblem inscribed with the words: *Texas Rangers*. We'd often sit on his front veranda in the evening playing Scrabble and he'd tell me about his life back in the 'good-old-days' during the 1950s.

Grandpa likes to fix things too – tinkering, he calls it. I think I remember telling you he owned an impressive three dial Seiko wrist-watch from way back in the sixties when big watches and super-bikes were all the rage. The strap had broken years ago, but rather than just buy a new one, Grandpa had fitted the watch into a silver case and attached a chain so now it looked like one of those fob pocket-watches you see in western movies. He liked to do stuff like that.

Back then Grandpa had a girlfriend called Angela – well not exactly a girlfriend – their relationship seemed to run pretty hot-and-cold from what he told me. It made me curious though and, with the help of *Google,* I contacted Angela. She's a hot-shot doctor in England, but dropped everything and flew out to see Grandpa.

Angela never married or had any children, but was happy to move in with Grandpa and they've been together ever since. She doesn't appear to be in any hurry to return to London, which is fine because I know Grandpa really likes her and so do I. She's surprisingly down-to-earth for a high-flying famous doctor. My dad isn't too pleased about the situation and refers to Angela as 'that woman', but he's got a downer on a lot of things. I think he calls her even worse names when I'm not around. My mum is much less judgemental. She and Angela get along just fine.

Angela carries a metre-long white pole around, which seems a bit odd, but it has great sentimental value to her. Grandpa says she's cracked open a few skulls with the pole during their adventures together, so for a doctor, Angela is not above a spot of GBH if she feels the need.

What puzzled me was why they lost contact with each other for so many years, leaving Grandpa to marry Nan and raise a family in rural NSW. As a young man, he'd been a pilot and flown throughout South-East Asia, but had given that life away when he settled down with Nan. Well, sort of given it away. Grandpa had hinted that he was called upon to do work for Colonel Ted Serong and Brigadier Charles Spry from time to time.

Although Colonel Serong was an Australian, he was in thick with the CIA while 'Silent Charles' Spry was the head of ASIO. Grandpa had met both men back around 1950 and it appeared he had qualities the two military officers could exploit.

Grandpa's arch-mate at the time was Mad Monty, an Afro-American bush pilot who was always getting in and out of scrapes. The other major influence on Danny was his dad, George, who'd gone troppo while fighting the IJA on the Kokoda Track. George never returned to Australia, but set up house on an island in the Bismarck Sea with a Japanese ex-comfort woman called Mayu. Meanwhile Grandpa's mum married another bloke in Rockhampton. Grandpa Danny had little to do with his mum, but inherited some family memorabilia and a little cash when she died. If you haven't read them yet, you can find out how it all happened in my earlier stories.

'What happened between you and Grandpa?' I asked Angela one evening.

We sat on the veranda while Grandpa prepared dinner. He's a ripper cook and has taught me loads about preparing food. Angela described herself as 'rubbish-in-the-kitchen' so she's happy to let Grandpa cook while she washes the dishes afterwards which she says is a good deal because the dish-washer does all the work. She's never had to spend much time in the kitchen. She was a drop-dead gorgeous woman and had no trouble getting dates and being wined and dined by the rich-and-famous at the finest restaurants.

'Stubbornness would probably be the best way to describe it,' she replied with a sigh of regret. 'No, it was more than that. You see Danny and I just had different things we needed to do with our lives. I have always loved your grandpa, Zach, even as a teenager when I was often totally confused emotionally. Living half-a-world apart didn't help matters. We actually didn't spend a great deal of time together, which was just as well because when we did, we always ended up in a heap of trouble.'

'You should be happy about that,' Grandpa said, through the kitchen window.

'How's that?' I asked.

'It stands to reason, doesn't it? If I'd married Angela then I wouldn't have met your Nan, we wouldn't have had your dad and he wouldn't have married your mum and had you.'

'That's creepy,' I said.

'Not really,' Angela replied. 'It's all chance isn't it? I mean out of all the millions of people in the world and all the random encounters most people find someone special in the end.'

'I guess I got lucky twice,' Grandpa added.

'Didn't you want to have children, Angela?' I asked.

'I've thought about it sometimes, but I suppose I was so tied up with my work, romance just passed me by – until now.'

'You're going to stay then?' I suggested uncertainly.

Angela reached forward and squeezed my hand.

'I think I've worked long and hard enough, don't you?' she whispered. 'I love it here and I love Danny. I think I'm ready to take things easy now.'

'Have you told Grandpa yet?'

'Oh, I'm sure he already knows. He might act like a big lummox sometimes, but he's pretty sharp deep down.'

You can't imagine how pleased I was to hear the news. Angela had moved into Grandpa's bedroom as if it was the most natural thing in the world. What my dad would make of it was anyone's guess, but then it wasn't his life, was it? I was just happy that Grandpa wasn't alone anymore.

'I don't want you to think that I'm taking your Nan's place or yours for that matter,' Angela said.

I looked at her blankly. I hadn't given it any thought and she must have read my thoughts by my puzzled expression.

'You have a special relationship with your grandpa, Zach. I don't want to come between that. Please keep coming to see us whenever you like. You have no idea how much Danny values your company.'

It was then that I made up my mind to move to Merimbula when I finished school. I had no idea what I wanted to do, but I reckon I could turn my hand to most things. It was a quality most McAlisters seemed to have.

'But you have to tell me how you and Grandpa broke up. It can't have been easy for him. He kept your letters, you know ...' I stopped, wondering if I'd said something indiscreet.

Angela smiled and I'm sure she blushed slightly.

'They were a bit mushy sometimes,' she admitted.

'Please tell me about it. I mean you were thousands of miles apart. I'm surprised you met at all.' I said, realising I'd used Grandpa's old Imperial measurements.

'It all came about because Angela offered me a job,' Grandpa added as he joined us with a beer in hand. 'Dinner's brewing in the oven. It'll be ready in an hour — Danny's super non-PC beef casserole with mashed spuds and greens from the veggie-patch.'

Grandpa liked 'blokey' food.

'Sounds wonderfully hearty, darling,' Angela said sincerely. She wasn't one of those fussy, *I-don't-eat-red-meat*, females. Or worse still a vegan. 'Now come and tell Zach about our African adventure before dinner.'

'It's not quite as simple as that,' Grandpa said cautiously. 'Anyway, it sure didn't start anywhere near Africa – the other side of the world in fact.'

He was right and it actually took him a lot longer than that, especially as Angela kept adding her bits to the story. But I finally wheedled the truth out of them. It turned out to be an adventure that spanned four continents with twenty thousand miles of knocks, spills, physical and emotional cuts and bruises along the way.

Grandpa used a bunch of jargon, so once again I have included a glossary. Make sure you check it out before you get started or keep it book-marked so you can whizz back to it if you come up against something you don't understand.

Part 1 — Indochina

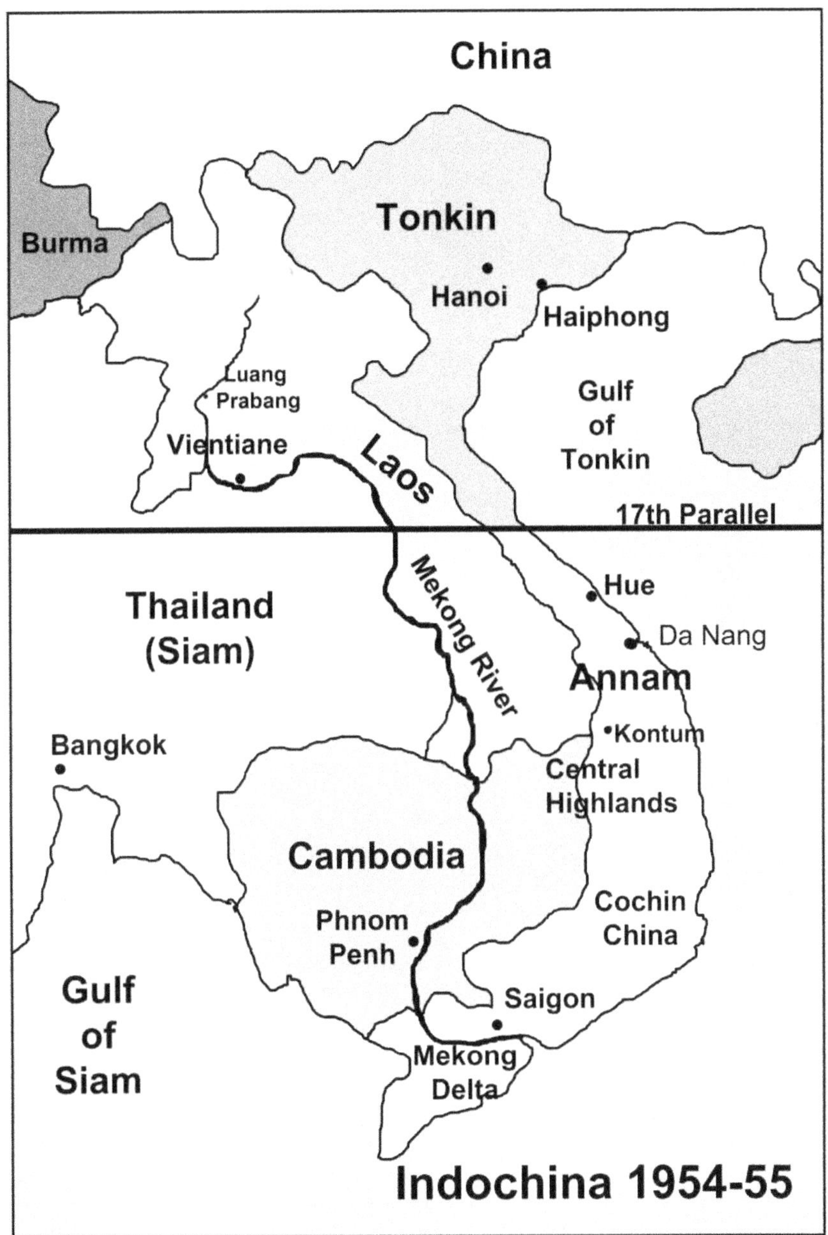

Chapter 1 — Back to Work

'Whatya planning to do now, Danny?' Monty asked as they sat in the shade of the palms on a beach where they'd been surfing and spear-fishing. Danny's dad George had built a shack on the north-east tip of *Kago Ailan*, where he kept his surf boards and fishing tackle. Whenever Danny visited his dad he liked nothing better than to spend quality time with him at the shack. On this occasion Mad Monty and George's live-in girl-friend, Mayu, had joined them.

They all took a break and enjoyed a barbeque lunch. George had brought along a brilliant new invention by the Malley's Refrigeration Company called an *Esky* that kept their beer deliciously cold when covered with ice cubes.

Danny's fractured leg had set well and he was back to his normal healthy self. The leg was broken when Danny was pitched into a tunnel by a mortar blast on the last day of the Dien Bien Phu siege. As an Australian, Danny had been spirited out of Indochina by Colonel Ted Serong to avoid any embarrassment to the Federal Government. Serong detested politicians, but he was a patriot of chauvinistic proportions.

Angela had also been whisked back to England by M1-6 agents to avoid diplomatic awkwardness between the British, French and emerging North Vietnamese Governments. She immediately resumed her medical studies at Guys Hospital. Danny received occasional letters, but they carried mixed signals. Angela was the master-exponent of complex emotional thinking.

When they weren't surfing, Danny and Monty rode an ex-military 1942 Indian Scout 500cc motorcycle up to the airfield where repairs to his beloved Grumman *Goose* were almost complete. George had restored the bike, which had been abandoned as *cargo-cult* salvage when US forces left the island after WWII. Both Danny and Monty thought they were becoming proficient riders although George described them as 'adequate'.

Monty had done the final tinkering with the *Goose* during his leave. He'd arranged with his pal Dave Bradley to fly the plane back to Lae when it received its airworthiness certificate. Dave who was an ace mechanic and now owned Monty's old firm *Alabama Aviation,* had done the lion's share of the restoration while Monty was aboard flying for CAT.

'I think I'll stay with CAT for now,' Danny replied, although Monty was less sanguine for once.

'You know CAT had been dubbed the "most-shot-at-airline-in-the-world", don't ya?' he warned. 'General Chennault still has *Customer* contracts in Vietnam,'

Customers were CIA operatives who used CAT as their own airline and were taking a close interest in the recent affairs of

Vietnam. In all fairness when it looked like CAT was going to be donated to the Communist Chinese in an appeasement gesture after the civil war, Chennault sold the airline to the US Government and everyone believed the CIA picked up the tab. Under those circumstances the agency felt justified in using CAT planes whenever it felt like it.

'That should have quietened down now the French are pulling out of Indochina. There's been a big conference in Geneva. I've heard they've chopped the country in half along the 17th parallel. Commies to the north – good guys to the south.'

'And how long do you think Uncle Ho will keep his word?' George asked. 'He'll be itching to send his blokes south before the ink is even dry on the treaty.'

Monty nodded sagely and took another gulp of beer. He actually had his own troubles closer to home. You see *home* was the problem. Monty had parked himself in Lae at the end of WWII and stayed in his shack by default, becoming part of the establishment. He'd bought a beach-hut and owned *Alabama Airlines* which provided a vital service for the highland and island communities.

Now that the shack had been burnt to oblivion by local bad-arse, Crazy Al, and the airline sold to engineer Dave Bradley, Monty could no longer lay claim to either of those assets. Dave had immediately offered Monty and Danny jobs if they wanted, but it wasn't as simple as that.

Monty's residency status was in doubt.

His passport was due for renewal and that meant a re-entry stamp from the Australian Immigration Department. Previously while he'd been in the US Army Air Corps, the Australian authorities were only too happy to oblige, but that was nearly ten years ago and things had tightened up considerably since then. To make matters worse, Monty was not only an alien national, he was black. He felt Aussies didn't like foreign black people wandering around the country wherever they pleased.

Normally his pals, Ted Serong and 'Silent Charles' Spry would have gone into bat for him. Serong was surprisingly influential for a mere lieutenant-colonel and Spry was of course head of ASIO. Unfortunately Ted Serong was off somewhere in Indochina or maybe the States — he travelled a lot — while Brigadier Spry had his hands full with the impending Royal Commission into what was becoming known as 'the Petrov Affair'.

Vladimir Petrov was a mid-range Soviet official who'd been posted to Canberra a few years earlier. Before his recall to Moscow, Petrov decided he'd seek political asylum and it was up to Spry to broker the deal. Petrov promised information and Spry promised immunity. Prime Minister Robert Menzies was happy to oblige as a defecting commie would be a feather in his political cap at a time when Communism was the most feared threat to Western democracy.

The plan would have gone off without a hitch except Petrov's wife, Evdokia couldn't make up her mind whether she wanted to stay or go back to Russia. Her dithering gave KGB agents enough time to frog-march her onto a plane at Mascot airport. When the plane stopped to refuel at Darwin it appeared Evdokia had a change of heart and wished to stay with her husband after all.

She was lucky because Spry ordered his ASIO stalwarts to rescue Evdokia and fly her back south where she and Vladimir went into hiding until the dust settled. Just as Spry and his people patted themselves on their collective backs, a photo of Evdokia being manhandled onto the plane at Sydney Airport splashed across the front pages of the national dailies. The press blew the story into a sensation far beyond its diplomatic worth.

The Australian Labor Party opposition accused Menzies of concocting the affair to enhance his chances in the upcoming election – which it did. The Russians withdrew their diplomatic mission from Canberra and insisted that Australian do the same in Moscow. So the press and opposition bayed for a Royal Commission of Inquiry to see what mileage they could make of it all.

Subsequently Charles Spry had his hands full to ensure that ASIO weathered the storm without egg on its face.

The upshot was that it looked unlikely that Monty would be able to remain on Australian soil, which included New Guinea. A driving factor in this decision was that Monty and Danny no longer owned a plane. Their precious *Gooney-Bird* was a total wreck on an airstrip near Hanoi and the North Vietnamese weren't going to give it back even if it could be fixed. Monty and Danny were pretty well cashed after Dave Bradley had finalised *Alabama Aviation's* sale and they'd divvied up the profits. Danny also had his back-wages from CAT and the RAAF safely stashed away in his Commonwealth Bank account.

Monty wasn't particularly keen to start another business venture just yet. So the decision was really made for him. Despite his misgivings, working for CAT seemed the best option especially as recently bullets had stopped flying quite as thickly. Flying for CAT provided a comfortable income while Danny and Monty waited to see what turned up next.

When they returned to George's bar in *Kagotaun*, Monty radioed Dave Bradley to book their flight back to South-East Asia.

*

Bob Rousselot, CAT's chief pilot, met them when they landed at Taipei International Airport.

'Welcome back,' Rousselot grinned, which was encouraging — he didn't smile much. Rousselot was one of those square jawed, handsome Americans in a Rock Hudson, Cary Grant sort of way. He was generally all business and this was no exception.

He hustled Danny and Monty into the back seat of a waiting car before getting in beside the driver. The man behind the wheel turned out to be Felix Smith who'd persuaded Monty — and therefore Danny by default – to join CAT in the first place.

'Howdy,' Felix beamed as he drove them to their hotel. 'Nice to see you again. There are a couple of guys waiting at the bar who'd like to have a word. Old buddies of yours, I believe.'

Danny badgered Felix and Rousselot for the identity of their 'old buddies', but they wouldn't say.

'It's OK, Danny,' Monty said. 'Let 'em have their little joke. Goddammit, it's not often we see Bob in a good humour.'

Danny and Monty checked their bags at reception and left a team of bell-boys to take it to their rooms while they headed for the bar. Two of the bar-stools were occupied by men in army fatigues. Both drank glasses of lager, but took their time about it.

'Blow me down,' Danny said. 'Captain White and Captain Black!'

The two men — one Caucasian and the other Afro-American as their names suggested — swivelled on their stools. Both men grinned and looked genuinely pleased to see Danny. That was because on many occasions Danny had flown the chopper that took them into harm's way during covert operations in Korea. They'd always completed their missions and Danny had always brought them back safely.

'Actually it's Major White and Major Black, now,' White said with some pride, indicating to the gold oak-leaf emblems on his collar. He had a point too. Normally after a war the military downsized dramatically. Servicemen were more often than not either retrenched or demoted to their pre-combat rank. To be promoted at all was remarkable.

'Congratulations,' Danny said genuinely, shaking both men by the hand. 'This is my pal, Monty Montgomery.'

'Oh, we know all about Monty,' Major Black said with a grin, but then the majors seemed to know all about everything in Danny's opinion. 'It seems you two are a good team and that's what we need. We've wet-leased a *Gooney-Bird* from CAT and we've especially asked for you two to crew it. That OK with you, Bob?'

'You're the *Customers* who're paying the bills, so you're welcome to these two outlaws.'

'Sorry to hear about Long Li,' Major White said as if he'd guessed Danny's sense of loss. The Singaporean had been Danny's friend and crewman, but was now missing in Indochina after the fiasco at Dien Bien Phu.

'He was still alive when I was casevaced to Hanoi,' Danny said. 'If anyone can survive out there, it's Long Li. I haven't given up on the little bastard yet.'

'How about you buy us a beer and tell us what the job is,' Monty suggested.

'We're going touring,' Major White beamed.

'Cool,' Danny said. 'When do we start?'

'Tomorrow we fly to Saigon.'

Bob Rousselot assigned Danny and Monty a C-47 from the CAT fleet which the *Customers* had leased pretty much indefinitely. CAT's chief pilot instructed Danny and Monty to act as co-captains, each doing pilot-in-command and co-pilot duties on alternate days. They didn't require a loadmaster as Major Black and Major White insisted they were quite capable of closing the plane's cabin door for themselves.

Bob Rousselot left after he'd briefed Danny and Monty, explaining a car would transport them to the airport the following morning. The two majors melted away into the night almost unnoticed soon afterwards. Melting away was one of their special talents. Danny and Monty had no idea where they slept – or indeed if they slept at all.

'Now there're a couple of weird dudes,' Monty said as he ordered another round.

'All I know is they're true guts-men,' Danny replied. 'The trouble is they have a knack of getting into hot water and we're going to be right in the thick of it with them.'

They finished their beer and decided to stroll through the nearby streets which remained a seething mass of humanity for most of the night. 'Suck in the atmosphere' was how Monty put it.

They selected a noodle stall and tucked into some tasty dishes, although Monty suggested they shouldn't investigate the ingredients too closely. The streets were abuzz with cyclists, hawkers, gawkers and the emerging transport-of-choice, motor scooters. Taipei's population, as with the rest of Formosa, had increased dramatically with the influx of refugees fleeing from persecution in Mainland China.

'Nice to be back..?' Monty suggested.

'I thought I'd had enough of South-East Asia after Dien Bien Phu,' Danny admitted, 'but this place does get under your skin, I guess.'

'Yeah, like leeches,' Monty suggested, but he seemed happy enough to be back at work.

When they arrived at the plane the following morning, Major White and Major Black were already there. They'd secured two pallets to the tie-down points along the fuselage. The pallets were loaded with crates and a variety of parcels, sacks and metal containers. Monty and Danny tossed their grips into a spare corner. They'd bought a ukulele each, because guitars were just too big to travel with. Danny and Monty still enjoyed jamming together and found the little Portuguese-Hawaiian instruments were surprisingly versatile if you took the trouble to explore their complexities.

'What's in that lot?' Danny asked Major Black.

'Sorry, Danny. If I told you, I'd have to kill you.'

'Yeah, yeah, very funny, major. Just tell me how heavy it all is so I can calculate the weight-and-balance sheets.'

Major Black gave Danny an estimate. Neither American CIA officer had ever mentioned their first names and Danny had the impression it was how they wanted things to stay. Maybe they didn't want to get too close to people in their precarious line of work, although both men appeared to be good friends.

Both Danny and Monty were happy to get back to flying and slipped into the task as if they'd never been away. They were both experienced C-47 pilots, taking the controls with ease. The flight to Vietnam was uneventful. Tan Son Nhat airport remained much as Danny remembered from almost a year earlier, although most of the French military planes were nowhere to be seen. CAT, US military and civil aircraft were parked together under a heavy GI and Marine guard.

Saigon was building up to the upcoming Tét celebrations. It was the biggest religious festival of the Vietnamese calendar, embracing cultural, religious, artistic and culinary aspects of local life. It was a golden opportunity for a hard working, and often oppressed population to let their collective hair down. Nevertheless the languid colonial atmosphere had deserted the city. A sinister uneasiness pervaded the boulevards, parks, market-stalls, public buildings and hotels. The *laissez-faire* French dominance was replaced by sombre uncertainty.

A staunch Catholic, rather recluse individual, Ngo Dinh Diem had been appointed as prime minister. No one actually knew by whom. Some suggested Diem was backed by American Secretary of State, John Foster Dulles, while others thought the militarily powerful Nhu family was behind the selection.

North Vietnam became a democratic write-off when the Communists took control. They began a series of murderous reprisals ending in countless thousands of deaths before Ho Chi Minh finally saw the futility of eliminating North Vietnam's entire population and stopped the purges. Meanwhile droves of Catholic and Buddhist refugees poured south, hoping life would be safer there. They were in for a big disappointment.

Communist terrorists were already infiltrating southern communities. The insurgents needed food and shelter and the best way to get it was to summarily execute several village leaders and take what they wanted, as well as recruiting or conscripting anyone they chose.

South Vietnam was a basket-case of racial enclaves and cultural diversity. Prime Minister Diem was ruthlessly subjugating these factions into a national 'sameness'. Buddhists were especially dissatisfied by Diem's strong 'pro-Roman-Catholic-anti-everyone-else' stance, fervently discriminating against all other ethnic factions.

Danny and Monty, accompanied by the two majors, booked into the Continental Hotel where Danny and Long Li had met author Graham Greene before heading to Dien Bien Phu. They checked in and decided to enjoy the evening before beginning their task.

Whatever that is, Danny thought.

The four men each carried a 1911 Army Colt automatic pistol in a holster strapped to a webbing belt. The belts were also fitted with a pouch containing spare magazine clips. Saigon wasn't the sort of town where you roamed around unprotected.

Theoretically the French military still controlled South Vietnam. The Geneva peace agreement gave them until April 1956 to leave the country entirely. In truth after Dien Bien Phu, they'd pretty well lost interest. The surviving French Union forces captured by the Viet Minh had all been repatriated after suffering terrible privations as POWs. The French troops quite rightly felt betrayed and abandoned by their government and frankly, Prime Minister Diem was welcome to the place. He could just duke it out with terrorists and outlaw gangs all by himself.

As they sat at a street side table facing the Rue Catinat, Danny, Monty and the two majors watched the frenetic preparations. The key, bustling Saigon thoroughfare was about to undergo a name change to Tu Do Street now that the French were leaving town. Store fronts and restaurants were adorned with bright banners, lanterns and colourful bunting. Red was a popular colour. Maybe Tét would buck everyone up and return the city to its past exuberance that reminded Danny of a Wild-West frontier town with rickshaws, push-bikes and motor scooters instead of horses.

Amid the cheerful chaos, a troupe of orange-robed monks marched towards them, forming a circle in the centre of the boulevard right in front of the hotel. Passing cyclists, pedestrians and motorists simple steered around the group. Danny had seen monks like these many times before, thinking they spent too much time praying and begging and not enough time actually doing anything — like getting a job.

This group did have something in mind however. It was unlikely they'd selected Danny and his companions as their target audience, but simply decided on a central and populated part of town to make their statement.

One of the monks moved to the centre of the circle and sat cross-legged on the street. His colleagues handed him a jerry-can before leaving in formation back the way they'd come. Before Danny, Monty or the CIA agents could react, the monk doused himself with the entire jerry-can's contents. The four men were suddenly alert as the stench of petrol wafted towards them. Danny was appalled to see the monk pull a box of matches from his robe. He opened the box, removed a match and struck it as calmly as if he was lighting a cigarette.

In a whoosh of fire that blasted a heat-wave hundreds of feet, the monk was engulfed by flames and reduced to a grotesquely charred corpse in seconds. He remained silent throughout the entire ordeal. As the flames subsided the black silhouette remained upright before slowly leaning sidewards and toppling over.

'Bloody hell,' Danny whispered. 'What was that?'

'A protest,' Major Black replied grimly.

'Shit, what's wrong with a placard..?'

Chapter 2 — Saigon Mayhem

'Welcome to the new Vietnam, Danny,' Major White said. 'We're here to find what makes the country tick now the French are leaving. So far the president has shown no interest in Indochina, but that's kinda changed now. Everybody is skittish about the domino principle. We're here to find out what makes these people so fanatical they're prepared to do what we've just seen. We're gonna try and work out what will happen next and what we have to do about it.'

'And just what in blue blazes did that prove?' Danny asked as they watched a crowd gathering around the monk's corpse, which now resembled a shapeless block of charcoal exuding a sickly, pungent smell of petrol fumes and burnt flesh.

'Got our attention, I guess,' Monty replied uncertainly.

'Well, he's not going to do that again,' Major Black observed. 'C'mon, let's get some dinner.'

'I've sorta lost my appetite,' Danny said.

'You saw worse than that in Korea and I imagine Dien Bien Phu was no picnic. There's nothing you can do, or could have done, Danny. We'll find a table inside and at least have another drink.'

But right about then the street gangs arrived and trouble really started.

On the surface, Saigon had seemed a content enough city, provided the Viet Minh left its residents alone. In reality it was a seething hot-bed of factional irritation and violence. While the French remained, their colonial police had been able enforce order. The guillotine had been a sinister disincentive to miscreants. The French certainly didn't hesitate to use it and it appeared that Prime Minister Diem's regime planned to follow suit.

Maybe so, but now France's harsh stability no longer existed, Saigon's underworld gangsters were out for vengeance – against each other and anyone who simply got in the way. One of the largest outlaw gangs was the Binh Xuyên which, with connections to the ARVN and Saigon Police Force, was spoiling for an all-out fight with any authorities who still didn't agree with them.

At first the bystanders appeared stunned and just stared at the blackened human mess lying on the Rue Catinat. Within a few minutes a water buffalo, drawn cart rattled incongruously into view. A single, ancient man in peasant dress sat on the cart although the buffalo seemed to be finding its own way. The cart stopped beside the burnt corpse and the old fellow clambered from his perch to inspect the priest's remains.

Who he was or who had summoned him remained a mystery. He pulled a large shovel from the cart. It seemed that he was about to scoop the body onto the cart and take it away. This led to an instant discussion between the groups of the people standing around. Everyone had an opinion about the priest's disposal.

'Looks like someone don't reckon that old guy's showin' proper respect,' Major Black commented.

'At least he's not just going to leave the poor bugger there,' Danny replied.

As the debate became more animated and the volume rose, the crowd broke into sections while others streamed in from side alleys until several hundred young men filled the Rue Catinat. It was quite clear that the mob represented several factions who were not on particularly good terms with one another.

Scuffles broke out almost immediately, escalating into an all-out street brawl within minutes. Danny was amazed when knives, machetes, pistols and even AK-47 rifles appeared as blood started to flow. Half a dozen rioters were instantly cut and trampled underfoot when shots rang out. Others fell, the victims of knife wounds and machete cuts amid screams of horror, terror and rage.

A spray of wayward slugs hammered into the Continental Hotel's facia, sending Danny and his companions diving for cover. Tables, chairs, cutlery, crockery, glassware and pot-plants scattered and crashed onto the pavement and street. As usual Monty didn't hesitate. He drew his 1911 Army Colt automatic pistol and from behind the cover of an upturned table, fired a full clip into the crowd.

'Hold it, Monty,' Major Black warned. 'They ain't after us.'

'Just discouraging 'em from trying.'

'Shooting will only draw attention to us...Oh shit!'

It was too late.

Major Black peeked over the pile of debris that had once been a sidewalk cafe. Monty's gunshots hadn't gone unnoticed, especially as a couple of the nearest rioters were writhing on the Rue Catinat nursing bullet-wounds. Men started pointing towards the Continental Hotel, which meant they were pointing at Danny and the others.

'Time to high-tail it outa here,' Major White yelled.

'Where?' Danny replied in dismay.

'The police station might be a good start.'

Danny had no idea where that particular sanctuary might be, but Monty and the majors were already on their feet and heading away from the crowd as fast as they could. Danny wasted no time following them. Sadly the crowd wasted no time either. With a collective howl of rage and indignation they charged after the four fugitives. Pedestrians and cyclists dashed helter-skelter ahead as they tried to avoid being pushed aside or trampled underfoot. It seemed many of Saigon's citizens weren't aligned to the street gangs and simply wanted to stay out of the way.

Taxis screeched to a stop and there were several collisions followed by a tirade of abuse. While Danny and his companions kept to the side-walks, the mob surged over and around the stalled vehicles. The screams, bellowing and general uproar were phenomenal, yet Danny barely remembered hearing anything.

Monty and the majors were some distance ahead and pulling further away. Although Danny was back to full health for flying status, and he had experienced no difficulty surfing provided he took it easy, sprinting full tilt down an uneven street was another matter. Soon the constant jarring on his newly-healed bone took its toll. His leg began to ache abominably which slowed him down to a point where the enraged crowd would easily overtake him.

Fortunately Monty sensed that Danny was lagging. He stopped and turned to see the danger. The yelling mob was about to swarm over Danny. Monty snapped another clip into his pistol-butt and levelled the weapon. Major Black and Major White joined him.

The three men steadied before firing several well aimed shots into the leading rioters. Each shot hit a target as men tumbled to the ground while those following tripped over the fallen victims. The crowd milled around in confusion which gave Danny time to reach his companions. By then he was limping badly.

'How far to Central Police Station?' Danny gasped.

'Too far,' Major White replied. 'You won't make it with that leg.'

'You go on. I'll take my chances in the back alleys.'

'It don't work that way,' Major Black insisted. 'We don't leave folk behind.'

Taking advantage of the crowd's indecision, the four men headed away. However, it didn't take the mob long to reorganise. Maybe not exactly reorganised, but the rioters certainly resumed the chase, although more cautiously at first. Gradually they regained their courage and broke into a howling run once more. Danny, Monty and the majors were forced to adopt a staggered retreat.

Using the cover of shop-front bric-a-brac, they moved on steadily. Monty and the majors took turns to act as rear-guard, firing off a few rounds to deter pursuit. Sure it slowed the crowd for a few seconds, but it didn't take long for a few ringleaders to rev up the rabble's courage once more.

As they reached a cross-roads, Danny realised four men against hundreds were never going to achieve a successful outcome. He had no idea where they were or which way to go and the crowd was only yards away.

'Not far now,' Major White said encouragingly, although Danny peered in dismay as the Central Police Station was still nowhere in sight.

They stood panting outside a corner cafe. It seemed Major White hesitated for a second as he took his bearings in the baffling labyrinth of streets, alleys and buildings that all looked the same to Danny.

And then disaster struck.

Suddenly there was a massive uproar as the streets filled with people coming from all directions.

'Where the hell did they come from?' Monty said.

'How the blazes did they know we were here?' Danny added.

Both points were moot. What mattered was that Danny, Monty and the majors were trapped behind some road-side tables once more. They were no better off than they'd been at the Continental Hotel — less so in fact because the crowd was now twice its original size. To make matters worse the cafe proprietor had quickly slammed the doors shut and bolted them from inside.

Undaunted, Major White grabbed one of the cafe chairs and smashed it through the front window before the owner could pull the shutters down. Monty fired a couple of shots as the four men clambered through the window, kicking shards of glass and wooden framework aside as they went.

'Where's the back entrance?' Major Black yelled at the cafe-owner who quaked in fear. He didn't answer, but dived behind his serving counter.

'That way!' Danny yelled, noticing that patrons and cafe staff bolted for the rear exit.

They followed the fleeing locals as angry rioters pounded on the cafe door and clambered through the shattered window.

Danny led the way although his leg was now throbbing painfully. They ran through the kitchen where abandoned woks sizzled over blazing wood fires. Pots, pans and chinaware clattered and smashed as the fugitives forced their way forward with no regard for the damage and destruction along the way.

Someone — no one remembered who — toppled a vat of cooking oil as he dashed past. The oil sprayed onto one of the cooking fires and erupted into a fireball. The entire kitchen was ablaze before Danny and his companions reached the door. They burst out into a garbage-littered back alley followed by a wall of flame that engulfed half the restaurant and blocked the pursuers' path.

Rioters scrambled back through the cafe window and the door that now lay in ruins where the crowd had smashed it down. Suddenly more people surged onto the scene, but they were not there to chase troublesome foreigners. They wanted to douse the fire before it caught hold and destroyed the entire city block. The original mob didn't care. They raced away still howling for blood.

Meanwhile Danny and his companions sneaked away. Major White led, poking his head around corners to ensure the coast was clear. Finally they reached a wide boulevard that he recognised as close to the Central Police Station. He grinned and gave a 'thumbs-up'.

'I reckon we've made it,' he grinned, which was just as well because they were running short of ammo.

'Where the bloody hell are the police when you want 'em?' Danny lamented.

'If they were smart, they probably dived for cover like everyone else,' Monty said.

'Those gang-bangers have most likely paid the cops off anyway,' Major Black observed.

The open, tree-lined street appeared quiet enough, so the four men confidently strode onto the pavement. The avenue was eerily quiet. There were no pedestrians, cyclists or vehicles of any kind on the street. That should have been a dead giveaway. Saigon streets were never empty.

They had only gone a few paces when to their horror they saw the way ahead fill with angry gangsters. They turned only to see a hundred more bellicose locals swarming behind them. Their escape was completely blocked in both directions.

Both mobs advanced cautiously, but there was no mistaking their intent. The gangs had formed an uneasy, mutual alliance against a common enemy. Men snarled and yelled abuse as they brandished clubs, knives and machetes. In truth you couldn't really blame them. Monty had started it by firing into the mob, causing injury and possible death. They had virtually destroyed a local eatery and endangered an entire city block.

Monty should have lain low, minding his own business, but that wasn't his style, was it? Although the South Vietnamese were as yet ambivalent about an American presence in their country, it was possible the crowd mistook Danny and his companions for detested French servicemen who still lingered before the final Gallic exodus.

And no Vietnamese — northern or southern — was prepared to show the ex-imperialists any mercy whatsoever.

As the crowd inched closer on both sides, Monty loaded his last clip while the majors cocked their weapons. Danny, who also carried a Colt 1911 automatic pistol realised he hadn't even drawn the weapon, but now was a good time to do so. The four men backed against a ten-foot stone wall that was impossible to scale. Individuals dodged behind the trees lining the street in an effort to stay under cover, but they were forced into the open as they advanced.

'Let 'em get close enough so every shot counts,' Major White growled through clenched teeth in grim determination. 'Maybe if we drop enough of 'em, the others'll get discouraged.'

The mob behind now formed a solid wall and was gaining confidence by the second. The people ahead were more fragmented, but advancing steadily. When the crowd surged forward, three events occurred in quick succession.

A disciplined volley of shots rang out, the echoes rattling through the streets of Saigon. The solid crowd stopped dead in its tracks, while the mob on the other side broke into two groups that moved to either side of the road. There were so many of them they were forced to squeeze together to make way for a Jeep that came slowly forwards. Flanking the vehicle was a platoon of US Marines and GIs.

The driver was a man about sixty years old. His grey hair was a military crew-cut style although he wore an open-necked shirt and linen pants instead of a military uniform.

The mob may have been prepared to rip four individuals to shreds, but they were reluctant to take on thirty well armed and well trained troops.

The Jeep pulled up beside Danny and his companions.

'Get in,' the driver growled.

To Danny's surprise, Major Black and Major White — who deferred to no one in his experience — meekly obeyed. Monty joined the majors in the rear seats while Danny sat beside the driver. The driver calmly executed a three-point turn and drove away at slow speed. The restless mob jeered, hissed and booed as the Jeep passed, but allowed the vehicle through.

The American platoon followed with their M-16 rifles cocked and ready.

As the mob faded behind them, Danny heaved a sigh of relief and his leg stopped aching so badly. Even Major Black and Major White looked reassured and Monty beamed at their good fortune.

'I reckon we'll park you guys at the Embassy until the heat dies down,' the driver drawled. 'You know, you were lucky I have snitches all over town. One of my guys rang the embassy yelling that four Yanks were in trouble, so I thought I'd better go look-see.'

'Fine by us, General,' Major White said. 'Thanks for calling out the cavalry.'

General?

'I reckoned I might need some back-up. I know you two — or should I say I know *of* you two,' the general said addressing the majors, 'but who are these guys?'

'Monty Montgomery late of the Tuskegee Red Tails, now with CAT.'

'Ah, one of Chennault's boys, eh? What about you, young fella?'

'Danny McAlister, sir. I'm with CAT too.'

'He's a shit-load more than that, general,' Major Black added.

'Pleased to meet you,' the general greeted, extending his right hand while he steered the Jeep with his left. 'You don't sound American to me.'

'Aussie, sir.'

'Long way from home, aren't you? What brings you here?'

'Wrong place at the wrong time, sir. It's something that happens to me a lot.'

'You can tell me all about it over supper. We're holdin' a bit of a soirée tonight. I'll send one of my guys to collect your gear. You CAT fellas are still staying at the Continental, I guess?''

'Yessir.'

'By the way, I'm Joe Collins,' the general announced.

Chapter 3 — Madame Nhu

'Lightning Joe' Lawton Collins was a guy to have on your side. He was a true fighting general, who'd played his part in beating the IJA out of the Solomon Islands. After a bout of malaria he was reassigned to the European theatre. He commanded the 7th US Army Corps which stormed Utah Beach on D-Day and kept pace with General George Patton's 3rd Army as it smashed across France, Belgium and into Germany.

After the war, Joe Collins served as the US Army's chief-of-staff until President Eisenhower posted him to Saigon as America's ambassador.

After a short drive, Lightning Joe pulled up at a building at a crossroad. Danny was surprised to see the embassy was a rather ungainly triangular, six-storey art-deco structure at 39 Hàm Nghi Boulevard close to the river and not far from Rue Catinat. Apparently the Americans did not yet feel the need to surround themselves with a high-walled bastion. That option was still a decade away, although a squad of poker-faced, well-armed US Marine stalwarts guarded the entrance.

'We're having important guests for dinner,' Lightning Joe announced, 'so you boys had better scrub up.'

'We didn't exactly come prepared,' Monty confessed.

'No problem,' the general declared with largess, but didn't elaborate.

The embassy wasn't particularly impressive. There was no massive entrance hall with a crystal chandelier, merely a modest reception area with a desk occupied by a severe young woman wearing black-framed spectacles. She assigned Danny and Monty a room on the third floor while the two majors occupied another room a few doors along the hallway.

A well-appointed bathroom served each floor. Soap, towels, toothpaste and brushes, shaving sticks and razors all lay neatly on a shelf above the wash-basin. Several bath robes hung on hooks behind the door. Danny was pretty sweaty and unpleasant after all the running around in the tropical heat, so he felt much better after a shave, shower and clean teeth. It seemed that the embassy staff were used to unexpected and hygienically doubtful visitors arriving and were ready and well equipped to accommodate them.

When he returned to his room his luggage was already there – Lightning Joe was indeed living up to his name. A tuxedo, dress shirt, bowtie and shoes lay on both beds. It appeared that the embassy staff members were also used to unexpected guests turning up without proper evening attire.

'Do you know how to tie a flaming bow tie?' Danny asked Monty when he returned from the bathroom.

'Not a whole lotta call for a tux in Alabama or New Guinea,' Monty confessed.

The tuxedoes fitted well and both Danny and Monty felt they were able to take on the diplomatic dignitaries if it wasn't for the embarrassing bow-tie issue. Monty tried to tie his own and then Danny's, but made an absolute hash of it both times. After a good deal of frustration and cursing they were still no further ahead when they heard a knock at the door.

When Danny opened the door he was greeted by a woman whose hour-glass figure was stunningly evident in a shimmering satin evening gown. Danny stood transfixed and then recognised the stern secretary from the main desk. Her hair now swirled elegantly to her shoulders and Danny was unsure whether he'd have recognised her except that she still wore her black-rimmed glasses. Now she smiled engagingly and didn't seem so officious after all.

'The general told me to give you about half-an-hour,' she said with a pleasant mid-Atlantic accent as she expertly fixed Danny's bow tie. She then saw to Monty's.

'The general thinks of everything, doesn't he?' Danny suggested.

'That's what embassy staff are paid to do,' the secretary replied. 'Diplomacy can be so touchy. Everything has to be just right.'

She surveyed her handy-work and appeared satisfied that Monty and Danny would pass muster.

'Why, you two gentlemen look so dashing, I'm sure you'd quite melt any girl's heart,' she said mimicking a southern belle with a coquettish wink. 'The general is expecting us in the reception room on the first floor. If you will be so kind as to accompany me, we'll meet him there.'

I wouldn't mind accompanying you anywhere, Danny thought, but it was hardly the time or place.

She explained she was Lightning Joe's *girl-Friday,* which meant her duties included receptionist, personal secretary, coffee and cigarette-girl, errand-boy, staff liaison, secret agent and anything else the general thought up. She spoke French, German and several Vietnamese dialects fluently and possessed a thorough knowledge of the nation's history and culture.

Not just a pretty face then...

'My name is Emily,' the secretary announced.

'I know,' Monty said smugly.

She eyed him suspiciously.

'I pay attention,' he grinned.

'Well bully for you, Captain Montgomery,' she said in a tone that could have meant anything although she continued to smile sweetly.

When they entered the reception hall, Major Black and Major White were already there. They too were smartly dressed in tuxedoes, each bristling with a colourful row of miniature medals honouring their daring exploits during WWII and Korea. Colonel Serong had told Danny he was entitled to wear the Korea Medal and UN Service medal (Korea), but it seemed the RAAF were unable locate him, so he'd have to apply for them when he got the chance.

Lightning Joe was similarly resplendent. He stood beside a man about the same age wearing plain military A 1 uniform. Although the stranger's shoulder epaulettes bore two stars of a major general, his chest was conspicuously lacking any military decorations.

'Captain Montgomery and Captain McAlister,' Emily announced, using their CAT titles rather than military rank of lieutenant. As Monty and Danny were no longer serving officers, Emily was scrupulously correct.

'Welcome, gents,' Lightning Joe said, 'I hope you found everything you need.'

'Sure thing, General,' Monty said, eyeing Emily with intent.

Monty's lechery probably didn't go unnoticed, but Lightning Joe let it slide.

'I'd like you guys to meet "Iron Mike" O'Daniel.'

Major General John 'Iron Mike' O'Daniel was another hard-nosed all-American hero. He'd been wounded and decorated for courage under fire during WWI. In WWII he led the US 3rd Infantry Division through North Africa. His men spear-headed the Anzio and Salerno landings before pounding their way through south Europe, reclaiming it from the Nazis, mile after bloody mile. He'd also served with distinction in Korea.

His many awards included the Distinguished Service Cross, Silver and Bronze Stars and Purple Heart, but he rarely chose to wear them.

Lightning Joe Collins and Iron Mike O'Daniel were probably the most capable American generals of WWII and represented a lot of high-priced help to be hanging around a tin-pot backwater like Vietnam.

'May I get you gentlemen a drink?' Emily asked, reverting to yet another of her multi-tasking roles.

'A martini, please,' Monty said eagerly, remembering that their evening's aperitif-hour had been so dramatically interrupted.

'A beer will be fine, thanks,' Danny said as Monty gave him *the eye.*

'What..?'

'Ain't you got no class?' Monty hissed.

Apparently beer was considered the beverage-of-choice for the unwashed masses while rich-and-famous sophisticates preferred cocktails or neat spirits. Emily appeared unfazed and returned with a frosty martini for Monty and handed Danny a glistening tall lager-glass, perfectly poured with a half-inch creamy head. You had to give it to the Yanks — they knew how to serve beer *cold*.

'I hope Carlsberg is to your taste, Captain McAlister,' Emily said. 'I understand Australians prefer lager.'

Her duty done, Emily excused herself to see how the supper arrangements were progressing.

'I hear you started a bit of a fracas down on the Rue Catinat tonight, Captain,' Iron Mike said, staring at Monty through steely, penetrating eyes.

'Sorry about that, General. I sorta got trigger-happy.'

'It probably worked out for the best. You took the mob's minds off their own differences. They'd most likely have done a lot more damage if they'd gotten stuck into each other. I've got my boys and a battalion of ARVN infantry patrolling Saigon's streets right now. Things seem to have quietened down. The embassy staff should be able to settle any ruffled feathers tomorrow.'

Danny wondered who Iron Mike's boys were, but didn't have time to ask.

'It won't matter in the long run,' Lightning Joe added. 'Something else will set 'em off again soon enough.'

'I hear you've made yourself useful to our two spooks here, Danny,' Iron Mike said, indicating the majors.

'I've had that honour,' Danny said with a grin. 'They just naturally get into trouble.'

'You too, I gather.'

'I survived the Hook in Korea and Dien Bien Phu. I guess I have an *un-charmed* life for getting into scrapes, but a *charmed* life getting out of them.'

'You were lucky to survive the march north and POW camps. I understand only half those guys made it home.'

'I was lucky I *didn't* go on the march north. Major Grauwin, the French Union's chief MO arranged for me to be casevaced to Hanoi as soon as the Viet Minh allowed flights in and out of *Torri-Rouge.*'

'You poor bastards were sold out,' Iron Mike opined. 'It all got too hard and the French Government just gave up. They simply couldn't see sense.'

'What do you mean, General?' Danny asked.

'It ain't any secret,' Iron Mike said, 'I'm here with the MAAG — Military Assistance Advisory Group. MAAG's had half a battalion of special trained experts here for a couple of years trying to get the ARVN some decent training. We've met nothing but opposition from the French generals. Those idiots were dead against giving the South Vietnamese any military autonomy. Look where it got 'em. The local troops are first-class, but their high echelon is made up of opportunists, toadies and downright criminals. Now our job is a hundred times more difficult.'

'Half a battalion is only around three hundred men,' Danny said. 'That doesn't seem very many to me.'

'You're right, young fella,' Lightning Joe said. 'I reckon we're going to have to commit at least an army corps sized ground force or just pack up and go home. I take it you're headed up country soon?'

'We go where the majors tell us, sir,' Danny said cautiously. He was in a room with two of America's finest combat officers and two very secretive spooks, who were no slouches when it came to warfare either.

He'd already noticed there were no French or Vietnamese officials present that evening, but that was about to change.

All heads turned to the door as Emily returned accompanied by a Vietnamese woman. She was immaculately dressed in a fitted knee-length satin dress, accompanying jewellery and patent leather stilettos. Her hair had been meticulously styled. Danny's assessment was:

- Age — 30ish.
- Beautiful — perhaps.
- Pretty — definitely.
- Alluring — certainly.
- Enchanting — absolutely.
- Dangerous — undoubtedly.

'Gentlemen — Madame Nhu,' Emily announced.

'I am sorry to be late, General Collins,' Madame Nhu said as she extended her hand. Lightning Joe to Danny's surprise, bowed slightly and lightly kissed her fingers.

Classy, Lightning Joe!

The general introduced Madame Nhu to everyone in the room although she knew Iron Mike well.

'I regret my husband has been called away to Hué,' Madame Nhu apologised. 'He has received reports of insurgent unrest and has been forced to investigate, but I have his full authority to represent South Vietnamese interests.'

That was pretty well true. Her husband, Ngô Dinh Nhu, was Prime Minister Diem's brother. Nhu ran a secret police force and was a serious wheeler-dealer behind the political and military scenes. He and his wife were considered by many to be the true power-houses of Diem's regime. Madame Nhu was renowned for beguiling diplomatic heavy-weights and heads-of-state.

She graciously accepted the glass of champagne that Emily offered. It seemed that the American delegation was familiar with Madame Nhu's taste.

'Thank you, Emily,' the Prime Minister's sister-in-law said with sincere warmth before mixing easily with the men in the room, charming each one in turn. Even the two majors seemed captivated. She looked straight into the eyes of whoever she conversed with. It didn't seem like shallow pretence to Danny, but genuine interest. She spoke fluent French, but deferred to English as there were only Americans in the room apart from Danny.

'I must commend you, Danny,' Madame Nhu said. 'You seem very young to be in this illustrious company.'

'I agree, Madame Nhu,' Danny stammered slightly. 'Monty and I sort of got swept up here by events.'

'How intriguing. You must tell me all about your mysterious sweeping.'

'You bet, Danny has plenty of interesting tales to tell,' Monty added.

'Oh, indeed?' Madame Nhu stared wide-eyed, resting her hand on Danny's arm. 'How intriguing. You must sit next to me at supper and tell me all about yourself.'

She turned to Lightning Joe.

'I'm sure you won't mind if I monopolise this charming young man, will you General?' she beamed.

Lightning Joe gave her an *I'm-pretty-sure-you'll-do-whatever-you-want-anyway* shrug.

Emily announced that supper was ready.

'I trust you have some American delights for me to savour, General Collins,' Madame Nhu smiled charmingly.

'Yes, ma'am,' Lightning Jack beamed in reply. 'Just as you like 'em.'

'Excellent. I always enjoy your hospitality and charming company.'

They sat at a circular table handsomely laid with silverware and crystal. Madame Nhu took Danny's arm and made a fuss of sitting next to him. Monty ensured he found a place beside Emily who appeared to have abandoned her administrative duties and accepted a glass of wine from one of the two Vietnamese waiters.

The entrée was a salad that Danny now realised American's ate before the main course, which they mysteriously called the 'entrée' – *go figure* as Monty would say. The main course consisted of hamburgers, chips that the Americans called French-fries, pinto-beans in a tomato and chilli sauce and green beans. Considering the abundance of gourmet French and Oriental cuisine available Madame Nhu loved the novelty of basic American short-order food. She was enjoying herself immensely. Danny got the impression she didn't get an opportunity to let her hair down often and found the company of such down-to-earth men refreshing.

She was astounded that Danny had seen combat in Korea and been trapped at Dien Bien Phu.

'*Mon cher*,' she cooed. 'You are a true hero.'

'Then I'm in good company. I think there are a bunch of brave men in this room right now, Madame Nhu,' Danny replied modestly. 'Monty flew resupply missions into Dien Bien Phu right up to the last day.'

'Well said, Danny,' Madame Nhu declared. 'Emily dear, I propose a toast.'

She stood and raised her glass while Emily followed suit.

'To these brave men,' Madame Nhu said. 'They are the hope for Vietnam.'

Both women drank earnestly before sitting once more.

'Thank you, ladies,' Lightning Joe replied graciously.

By now Danny's beer glass was empty and the wine waiter hovered around nervously.

'He's wondering if you'd like to refresh your glass, *mon cher*,' Madame Nhu whispered in Danny's ear, 'but he's not sure about the beer.'

'That's OK,' Danny said, feeling a bit of a lunk. 'I learnt to drink red wine from the Ities when I was cane-cutting in North Queensland.'

That led to a discussion about the time Danny ran away from *St Ursicinus* Catholic School to escape the abuse meted out by the Christian brothers in general and Monsignor Desmond Slaughter and Sister Gertrude in particular. Both Desmond Slaughter and Gertrude had since gone to the judgement of their Maker.

Good riddance to them and may they rot in hell.

The waiter sighed with relief and poured Danny a Shiraz. Being born and bred under French influence the waiter knew that wine with supper was how things should be. What he made of the hamburgers was anyone's guess. Perhaps Madame Nhu and Lightning Joe had conspired to tease the pseudo-French kitchen staff with their choice of evening menu. Whatever the chef thought, he'd produced excellent burgers.

Having learnt Danny was Australian, Madame Nhu quizzed him insatiably for knowledge about the country. She stored knowledge away, and was interested in just about every subject. As the evening progressed, Madam Nhu showed no signs of becoming bored, indeed she had settled in for the night. Danny worried about the following day when they were supposed to fly the majors on their mission up country, so he stuck to iced water, which Emily assured him had been boiled.

Finally Madam Nhu checked her diamond-encrusted gold wrist-watch and yawned.

'General, do you mind terribly if I impose on your hospitality tonight so we can start our discussions tomorrow morning.'

'Certainly, Madam Nhu,' Lightning Joe replied, nodding to Emily.

'I'll ensure your suite is ready, ma'am,' Emily said as she rose to make the preparations. It appeared the woman who was to become known as Vietnam's First Lady often stayed overnight. For such a well-known VIP, Madam Nhu travelled with a surprisingly small entourage. She was accompanied by a single maid, chauffeur and two heavy-duty minders. The embassy staff had no trouble accommodating such a small party.

Everyone retired shortly after midnight.

After finishing his nightly ablutions and dressed only in a bath-robe, Danny was surprised to find Emily waiting for him in the corridor.

'Come with me, please, Danny,' she said simply.

'Where are we going?'

'You'll see,' she smiled.

'But I only have a robe on.'

'I don't think that will be an issue,' Emily smiled again.

They took the stairs that led to a balustrade-framed terrace on the top floor. There were several doors along the wall beyond the terrace. Emily knocked and to Danny's amazement Madame Nhu opened the door so it was barely ajar.

'Come in please, Danny,' she whispered intensely.

Danny looked nervously at Emily.

'Go on, Danny,' Emily whispered. 'You'll be fine.'

Madame Nhu gripped Danny's hand and guided him through the door and closed it behind him. Madam Nhu stood in her stocking feet wearing a short satin robe. She placed her arms around him and kissed him. Then she led him to the biggest bed Danny reckoned he'd ever seen. Madam Nhu shed the robe in one slinky movement revealing that she was now dressed only in her underwear, reminding Danny of the Gil Elvgren pin-up calendar hanging on the CAT crew-room wall.

To date Danny's sexual encounters had been brief, infrequent and not particularly rewarding, but Madame Nhu was about to change all that. She was intent on seduction and Danny'd fallen under her spell. Who wouldn't? So that night Danny humoured the most powerful woman in South Vietnam. He was in for many pleasant surprises in return.

*

As she turned away from Madame Nhu's suite, Emily's mind was full of misgivings and a little guilt. Diplomacy was so complex. There was no doubt Danny was being exploited, but he was a red-blooded young man, so she could climb down from her moral high-horse. Madame Nhu's husband was fourteen years her senior and spent much of his time away. His wife was a passionate and determined woman by all appearances, so...

Monty met Emily at the stairwell.

'Secret girls business, Em?' he queried, arching his eye-brows. 'What did Madame Nhu want?'

'Youth, I expect.'

'Danny?'

Emily nodded.

'Dangerous game just for a bit of action. Does the general know about this?'

She smiled uncertainly and nodded.

'She's the most powerful woman in Vietnam,' Emily explained as if to justify the point. 'Do we let her have her dalliance and risk a scandal, or refuse and risk her withdrawing her support? Mind you with the amount of money we're pouring into the place, I think she knows which side her bread is buttered on. Remember the embassy is like Las Vegas.'

'What, run by gangsters?'

'Something like that. They don't call it Sin City for nothing. But there's a saying, "what happens in Vegas stays in Vegas". It's just the same here.'

'This ain't exactly Danny's strong suit.'

'He'll be fine. It'll be something to tell his grand kids.'

Monty eyed her uncertainly. Although he had no plans that included grandchildren right then, he was pretty sure it wasn't the sort of thing you told them about.

'Stop worrying,' Emily said taking his arm and leading him downstairs. 'Maybe you can show me what *your* strong suit is..?'

Chapter 4 — Montagnard Territory

Danny may indeed have been playing a dangerous game, but he had little time to dwell on the fact. Madame Nhu discreetly shooed him back to his own room before dawn while everyone was still asleep. Monty mysteriously turned up while Danny was shaving. Major White and Major Black were raring to go and busy arranging supplies for their flight up country. CIA agents were rife in Saigon and Hué, the main cities of Cochin China and Annam, which now comprised South Vietnam. As top operatives, the majors were assigned to the remote mountain regions bordering Laos.

Lightning Joe Collins and Emily bid them goodbye, although Iron Mike O'Daniel was already up and away into the bush with one of his MAAG teams. Madam Nhu remained in her room. She didn't appear to be an early riser. Monty and Emily exchanged a brief nod before he, Danny and the majors bundled their gear into Lightning Joe's Jeep. The general had assigned a marine PFC to drive them to the Tan Son Nhat airport.

Political intrigue and midnight assignations were risky business and it was eminently wise to get Danny as far away from

Saigon and Madame Nhu as possible. As the Jeep was absorbed into the swirling urban mayhem of Hãm Nghi Boulevard, Lightning Joe and Emily breathed a collective sigh of relief. Soon they would be negotiating Vietnam's future with the country's most powerful woman and they didn't want any distractions.

'Y'know it's funny really,' Monty reflected as he was prone to do while they drove to Tan Son Nhat. 'The South is now the *Republic of Vietnam* while the Commies now call North Vietnam *the Democratic Republic of Vietnam.* I mean there's nothing *democratic* about Communism. Does anyone else see the irony?'

'It's an oxymoron,' Major White commented just to sound impressive. 'East Germany calls itself *the Deutsche Demokratische Republik* and what about *the People's Republic of China?* I mean who do they think they're kidding?'

The *Customers* supplied Danny and Monty with *Lambert's Conformal* charts for the Central Highland plateau of Annam. There were no radio beacons in the area, so it was going to be all map-reading from then on. However the flight was uneventful in good weather now that the dry-season was well established. There were certainly mountains to negotiate, but nothing more challenging than those Monty and Danny had previously tackled in New Guinea and Tonkin. Kontum was their first destination. It was an attractive small town surrounded by paddy fields and grazing pasture.

This was the home of the Sons of the Mountains or Degar people as they called themselves. The French had dubbed them Montagnards which simply meant mountaineers. The Khmer lowlanders rather harshly referred to the Montagnards as Moi or savages.

After landing they were greeted by an excited crowd of locals. Planes had certainly used Kontum's rudimentary airstrip during the war, but now the French were withdrawing in droves, aircraft movements were infrequent.

As Danny cut the engines and the two majors put down the boarding steps a delegation approached. They were led by several Montagnard chieftains, a Catholic priest, a rather earnest looking nun and a pretty, petite young woman. There were many dialects and individual languages spoken throughout Vietnam so the CIA agents had recruited a translator, who waited now for them. They were introduced to the chieftains, but Danny found their names impossible to remember. Fr Édouard and Sister Camille ran the local mission and orphanage. There seemed to be no end of orphans in Vietnam, being the tragic legacy of a thousand years of war and pestilence.

Fr Édouard introduced the young translator simply as Sam. Whether it was her Degar name or a western substitute remained unclear. She spoke several major Degar dialects, French and English with a charming accent.

It seemed that the Montagnards were between a rock and a hard place and had been betrayed from all sides. They'd fought the Communists, who they despised, but now the French had lost interest they were often victims of North Vietnamese reprisals. The Southern lowlanders were encroaching into their territory since they realised there was good grazing and agricultural potential in the highlands. The Montagnards were fighting on all fronts to preserve their homeland with very few resources at their disposal.

This was where Major Black and Major White came in. Their job was to train the Montagnards in guerrilla warfare and supply the weapons for them to do so. The *Gooney Bird's* cargo consisted almost entirely of M1 carbines and .30 calibre ammunition. However before any progress could be made, there was going to be a lengthy discussion about exactly who would do what and what they'd get in return.

The Montagnard chiefs had every right to be sceptical. So far everyone they made a deal with had let them down. The majors had some delicate negotiating ahead. It seemed that while Iron Mike O'Daniel's team focused on ARVN, the CIA was left to deal with remote civilian populations on a more informal level. Once the introductions were complete, the Montagnard chieftains led the way to a long house not far from the airstrip. Sam ushered the majors after them.

'You guys make yourselves right at home,' Major White called to Danny and Monty. 'This is gonna be like dealing with injuns and African tribesmen. It takes time just to get the preliminaries established.'

As Danny and Monty were merely the chauffeurs and not involved in the talks, they checked their plane and arranged fuel with Fr Édouard. The majors had insisted that all the weapons remained on board until they were satisfied they'd convinced the Montagnards to play ball.

'I wonder how Major White knows about Indians and Africans,' Danny said.

'I don't think you want to know half the stuff those two guys get up to,' Monty replied. 'C'mon, let's put the plane to bed. I don't reckon we're going anywhere anytime soon.'

Once they'd chocked the *Gooney-Bird,* fitted undercarriage locking pins and pitot-tube covers, Danny and Monty took their ukuleles from their cases, found a shady spot and began strumming. Monty had already shown Danny how to play a 12-

bar-blues progression and rock-turn-arounds. They were now working on a ukulele boogie that really just consisted of a few blues clichés tossed together with a shuffle beat.

In an instant they were surrounded by a crowd of grinning children who just naturally started dancing to the music. The kids squealed and giggled as they pranced around. Soon they were joined by a few teenagers and adults who clapped in time to the beat. Only moments later several young men rolled up, pounding *trong* drums to the beat. And it wasn't long before other musicians playing a *dān nguyêts* and *sáo* which were the Degar equivalents of a two-string banjo and a flute respectively. Another group set up a bamboo xylophone called a *trung*. Even though the traditional Degar music tended to rely on a straight 4-4 beat, they easily adapted to the triplet-style shuffle so common in Mississippi Delta blues.

Nobody knew any words of course, but that didn't matter. Danny and Monty could have played the same tune all day and the Montagnards would have been content. But they did mix it up and played pretty much every song they knew and were pleasantly surprised to see the local musicians had little trouble keeping up.

After a while Danny and Monty urged the town musicians to play some of their own tunes. They tended to use Chinese pentatonic scales, so Danny and Monty joined in where they could. Otherwise they simply kept time by playing what Monty called a 'Z' chord. This meant they muffled the strings producing a drum sound. Monty and Danny added the old time favourites: *Camptown Races, Wreck of the Old 97, Jambalaya, Orange Blossom Special, Bonaparte's Retreat, Deep in the Heart of Texas, Wabash Cannonball* and a brand new song topping the US country music charts, *This Ole House.* That got the crowd dancing

They were having such a good time, a group of mothers decided to put on a spread for lunch. Everyone pitched in to lay out some trestle tables that were soon covered with platters of spiced rice, smoked fish from nearby Lake Ya Ly, vegetables, tropical fruit and tea from local plantations. Palm leaves or wooden bowls served as their eating apparatus.

'Hey, today's not turning out too badly,' Monty observed.

Neither he nor Danny had mentioned how the previous night hadn't *turned out too badly* either.

'Yeah I'm ready for a bite,' Danny agreed. 'I wonder what the local table-manners are.'

'I think we've dispensed with grace, so tuck in and enjoy,' Sister Camille suggested with a smile. 'The Degar people may be isolated and suspicious, but their hospitality is sublime if they take a liking to you.'

'What if they don't?' Danny asked.

'Your head will probably wind up stuck on a spear outside town — we do try to discourage that practice of course.'

Sister Camille had a charming smile, reminding Danny of his old friend Sister Celeste back in New Britain.

'Can I ask you something, Sister Camille?' Danny said as they ate.

'You can ask, I may not know the answer,' she smiled.

'No, I mean, what made you take Holy Orders? You're so pretty, don't you miss a social life?'

Sister Camille blushed. She didn't often receive compliments from young men, but rather liked the experience.

'Do you mean would I like to have a boyfriend?' she asked coyly.

'Yes I suppose.'

'I'm married to God.'

'He's not much of a husband, is He? I mean He's never home.'

'He is always around.'

Sister Camille looked genuinely amazed that Danny was unaware of that particular fact.

'How do you know?'

'I feel Him.'

What you mean is you imagine you can feel Him.

Danny had covered the same ground with Angela and still remained unconvinced.

It seemed that the smell of lunch distracted the Montagnard chiefs from their discussions and they streamed from the long house to join the feast. That must have happened all the time because the Degar ladies anticipated the extra mouths to feed and laid on plenty for everyone.

'What a great idea,' Major Black said as he joined Monty and Danny.

'Are you hungry then, Major?' Danny quipped.

'Hell, yeah. I remember hearing one of them Limey Royals saying, "Never stand when you can sit, never sit when you can lay down and go to the bathroom any chance you get." Same applies to food in my case — you never know when or where your next meal is coming. I mean I've eaten some crap in my time. Have you ever even eaten bugs, Danny?'

'Well yes, actually,' Danny replied smugly. 'An Abo mate of mine got me to try witchetty grubs once. He ate 'em raw, but I had to roast 'em to get them down.'

Danny felt a pang of sorrow as he remembered his chum, Charlie who'd hanged himself when imprisoned behind the stark walls of *St Ursicinus* boarding school. Monsignor Slaughter and Sister Gertrude — *may they rot in hell* — abused the poor boy to the point of despair where suicide was his only option.

'Anyway, if they were really Pommy Royals,' Danny continued lecturing, 'they'd have said "lie down, not "lay down" and "lavatory" instead of "bathroom". Why do you Yanks call a dunny a bathroom anyway? Back at my mum's place in Rockhampton the lav wasn't even inside the house so it couldn't be a room and it sure didn't have a bath in it.'

'Picky,' Major Black said, piling some food into a palm leaf. 'I never took you for an academic. I thought you hated school.'

'I did, but I like to read and, as Monty and Long Li would say, I pay attention.'

After lunch, the Montagnard chieftains rather lost interest in negotiating and started drinking something pretty disgusting from wooden beakers. Danny and Monty were urged to tune up their ukes and dancing resumed with the adults joining their children. The ukes kept time with the local musicians as they played a repetitive, but pleasant enough theme. A group of teenage girls and young women formed lines and performed a flowing, elegant dance that Danny found charming.

In an instant the afternoon festivity was shattered. Afterwards Danny thought he heard a sinister whine just before a mighty explosion obliterated a nearby hut into a spew-ball of tiles and timber. Lethal shards of shrapnel shot in all directions. Danny was sure he heard the next in-coming bomb before it exploded.

'Mortars!' he yelled. 'Everyone get down.'

It was the only real defence until they located the enemy. Lie flat on the ground while the worst of the blast shot overhead and hope you don't cop a direct hit. Not that many people heeded his advice. Children screamed and ran amok in panic while their mothers chased them, scooping them into their arms and scurrying under the cover of nearby buildings.

Danny was appalled to see many of the adult men and boys race into their huts, scattering the trestle and stools in their path. But they weren't fleeing in terror. They emerged bearing an assortment of weapons including a couple of Webley revolvers and one AK-47 rifle, but mostly they were only armed with crossbows and bolts.

Crossbows against mortars! It's not the flaming Middle Ages.

Maybe so, but the Montagnards were set for a fight to defend their homes and families.

'Get over to the plane, Danny,' Major White ordered. 'Unpack one of those weapon-crates. We need rifles.'

Danny didn't need telling twice as another mortar shell crumped not far away.

Bloody hell, it's GONO all over again!

Monty was right behind Danny while the two majors tried to calm the Montagnards. They organised a group of the most likely looking lads who were about to have a crash course in M-1 carbine marksmanship. Fortunately the gun was a ludicrously easy weapon to use. A fifteen round box magazine clamped onto the stock beneath the barrel just before the trigger guard. All the training needed, or available that afternoon was:

- Clip in the magazine.
- Release the 'safety' at the front of the trigger-guard.
- Point and shoot — the semi-automatic function allows single shots to be fired without worrying about a bolt action.

- Oh yes, don't forget to push the butt hard into your shoulder and be ready for the recoil.

That would do for now. The Montagnards were natural hunters who knew how to aim a crossbow. How hard could firing a rifle be? Many of the Montagnards had fought with the French Union forces and were familiar with weapons and knew how to use the M-1 carbines without instructions.

Danny grabbed Monty's ukulele and tossed both instruments into the cockpit. He quickly unpacked the carbines while Monty and the majors showed the group of Montagnards surrounding the plane how to load and aim the weapons. The local men nodded that they understood then quickly raced away to find out where the mortars were coming from.

The attackers didn't have ammunition to spare, because a long interval elapsed before the next mortar shell slammed into town. This time the explosions erupted dangerously close to the beautiful 50-year-old wooden church. The church was much admired by local Christians and other believers alike. The local men were in uproar and out for blood to avenge the outrage. Fortunately, other than a few paint scrapes, the church remained intact.

Once the crate was empty, the majors raced away to try to organise the Montagnards and identify the enemy. Danny kept two carbines and half-a-dozen magazine clips for Monty and himself.

Just then another mortar exploded on the airstrip and Danny spotted a white smoke puff hovering in the afternoon stillness, giving away the mortar crew's position.

'You think there's just one mortar?' Danny asked.

'Looks like it, but we'll need more than the two of us to flush 'em out,' Monty replied.

'They won't be alone either.'

'C'mon. Let's get the majors. This is their line of work.'

Danny remembered that he'd done this sort of thing once or twice during the siege of Dien Bien Phu, but he agreed with Monty. When you want a job done, get the pros into action if you've got 'em.

Chapter 5 — New Kids on the Block

Danny needn't have worried. Major Black and Major White had seen the mortar smoke and were organising the Montagnards into two companies when he and Monty caught up with them. If you were going into battle, Danny could think of no men better than the two majors to lead you. They were battle-hardened and quite fearless.

From what Danny could determine, the mortar crew were under cover in a large jungle patch half a mile from town. The Montagnards had to cross a terraced pastureland and rice paddies to reach the spot. It meant they would be vulnerable targets while they manoeuvred past the grazing buffaloes and then along the dykes separating the paddies.

Monty joined Major White's company while Danny stayed with Major Black. The two groups split up and moved outwards to outflank the mortar position. What they didn't know and had no time to find out, was the enemy numbers. In military terms a mortar squad normally supported at least a platoon or company of infantry with a couple of machine guns.

Sporadic firing broke out from the jungle fringe. One of the Montagnards close to Danny grunted and dropped, splashing face first into a rice paddy. A man close by who was armed with a cross-bow snatched up his fallen comrade's carbine, but kept his ancient weapon strapped across his back. Danny jumped as a slug hit the ground close to his feet, splattering mud over his combat pants.

'Don't sound like a lot of 'em,' Major Black commented. 'No MGs either.'

Thankful for small mercies Danny raced ahead. The jungle was his refuge. The M-1 carbine felt like the ideal weapon for fighting at close quarters. Compact and light you could squeeze off individual rounds in quick succession. Danny remembered something Colonel Ted Serong had said about jungle warfare — fire a quick burst to confuse the enemy and keep their heads down. It gives you the advantage for a few vital seconds to either take cover or move in for the kill.

More shots sputtered from the undergrowth, but no one appeared to be hit. The intermittent gunfire suggested the attackers were conserving their ammunition which either meant they were waiting to get a better shot, or they were low on ammo.

Danny followed Major Black as he plunged into the foliage. The Montagnards streamed after them. The thick jungle slowed their progress and reduced visibility to only a few feet. It was time for stealth, but pushing your way through the undergrowth and sometimes having to slash vines and other jungle flora was a noisy business.

But that was not the only sound. Danny heard men yelling. Although it was incoherent babble to him, Danny knew the voices were from the mortar team and whoever else was with them.

Then muzzle-flashes glinted within yards as more shots rang out and bullets zinged past, snapping branches and shrubbery in their path. And suddenly Danny was in the middle of it.

A black-clothed figure leapt from the bushes and charged screaming towards Danny. If he'd shut up, he'd probably have got the better of Danny, but his yell sounded a warning. Fortunately – or otherwise depending on your point of view – Danny had been in plenty of tough scraps before and reacted instinctively. He swung the M-1 carbine, smashing the butt into his attacker's face. There was a satisfying crack as the butt shattered a jaw and cheek bones in a spray of dislodged teeth.

The enemy crashed to the jungle floor before Danny fired a single shot into the back of his head. During the siege of Dien Bien Phu, he'd learnt you don't give your enemy a second chance.

Major Black had moved on and was nowhere to be seen, but Danny caught sight of other Montagnards spreading out through the jungle. He pressed on. He missed the second attacker who'd climbed into the lower branches of a tree and waited silently. The man, also dressed in what looked like black pyjamas with a bayonet clamped tightly between his teeth, dropped onto Danny's shoulder. He grabbed Danny in a stranglehold and was about to plunge the blade through Danny's eye, when he froze, went limp and slumped from Danny's shoulders.

The attacker lay face down on the jungle floor with an arrow in his back. Danny spun around to see the tiny figure of Sam jogging towards him while loading another bolt. Danny smiled and gave her a 'thumbs-up' sign before retrieving the bayonet – it might come in handy.

The dead man didn't appear to have any other weapons and there was no time to look around. Anyway it stood to reason if he possessed a rifle he'd have used it.

Together Danny and Sam advanced cautiously. They glimpsed several other black-clad figures darting through the undergrowth. Danny fired individual shots and Sam loosed another bolt, but they had no way of knowing if they'd hit anyone. Danny thought jungle fighting was pretty damned frustrating because you couldn't see what was going on.

Another risk was being hit by friendly fire. Shots came from every direction and the grunts, screams and groans of hand-to-hand scuffles were all around. Danny and Sam passed several bodies lying about, but none looked like Montagnards.

They came upon two men locked in a mortal struggle. A black-clad invader and a Montagnard were wrestling desperately. They pitched to the ground and the Montagnard fell awkwardly. The attacker leapt onto him and started throttling him. Danny pulled the bayonet from his belt and took two steps forward. He loomed over his intended victim, dragged him by the hair and plunged the bayonet through his neck. Danny pulled the blade free and a spray of arterial blood spewed from the wound. The man uttered a stifled gurgling sigh and sank to the ground.

Danny and Sam helped the Montagnard to his feet and returned his M-1 carbine that had fallen from his grip. The local man nodded abruptly and charged back into the fight.

The uproar of the confused melee eventually abated. Moments later Danny and Sam burst into a cleared area. Monty and Major White were already there along with about twenty Montagnards. The clearing was small and no one else would fit. Half a dozen black-clad figures lay dead in grotesquely distorted poses. There was nothing peaceful looking about corpses killed in battle. The majors' strategy had successfully rolled up the enemy flanks, although there was no sign of the mortar. It looked like some of the raiders had escaped and taken their artillery with them. There was no sign of Major Black either.

But four of the attackers survived. They were tightly bound and on their knees surrounded by some very bellicose looking Montagnard warriors. Major White was in a heated argument with the locals who wanted to dispose of the prisoners straight away.

'Sam, thank God you're here,' Major White said. 'Can you please explain that we need to question these guys and find out what they're up to?'

Sam conveyed the message which was followed by more heated discussion and gesturing.

'They say these bad men and should die for attack on Kontum.' Sam declared.

'Maybe so, but we've got to see if there are any more of them,' Major White pleaded.

More discussion.

'OK,' she finally said. 'You question then Montagnard kill.'

'Fair enough.'

'Hang on...' Danny began.

'Their backyard, Danny,' Major White whispered in his ear, 'their rules.'

'How many do you think there were?' Danny asked.

'Hard to tell,' Major White replied. 'Looks like about twenty dead and maybe the same number took off. Major Black and his guys have gone after them to see if they could pick up the trail.'

The captives didn't come quietly. They'd heard what the Montagnards had in mind for them. Mind you who could blame the Montagnards? A bunch of complete strangers had lobbed mortars into their peaceful town for no known reason, what did they expect? The prisoners kicked, wriggled, bucked, swore — at least Danny assumed they swore — until they were subdued by a sound beating. Danny had to admit they were tough little blokes, and he'd seen first-hand just how tough the *Bo Doi* could be when he fought them at Dien Bien Phu. Anyone else who'd received the beating the prisoners got would be dead by now. But who were they?

Before anyone got down to the serious business of questioning the prisoners, Major Black's group of Montagnards returned. They reported they'd killed a couple more raiders, but gave up the chase when the retreating men regrouped and began shooting through the jungle. The Montagnards were keen to fight it out, but Major Black wisely chose discretion over valour and headed back to Kontum.

Danny and Monty chose not to witness the interrogation. They both knew it wasn't going to be pretty and they had no wish to see the final outcome. So they grabbed the *Gooney-Bird's* first aid kit and toured the town to see if they could help.

Fr Édouard and Sister Camille ran a sick-bay close to the wooden church, which seemed to Monty and Danny like a good place to start. Several people had already been admitted. Most of the injuries were superficial, but a couple of children lay on cots in the tiny ward.

'They will recover,' Sister Camille reported.

'Do you need anything for the pain? Those two kids in there look pretty cut up.'

'Thank you, but we have our own supply.'

Danny stared at her.

'We don't generally sanction its use of course, but didn't you notice all those poppy fields around Kontum.'

'So?'

'You seemed to have led a sheltered life, Danny,' Sister Camille smiled.

'I wouldn't say that...'

'He's just a bit slow,' Monty piped up.

Danny glared at him.

'Poppies equal opium around here, Danny,' Monty explained. 'Not flower arrangements or Armistice Day button-holes.'

'So you have your own morphine?' Danny asked.

'Hardly,' Sister Camille said. 'We mix opium cakes with distilled rice spirit to produce home-made laudanum.'

'You'll need some antibiotics. Some of those cuts might get infected.'

'Yes, thank you, Danny.'

There was little else Danny and Monty could do. Sister Camille ran the infirmary with efficient calm. So after handing over the drugs, they headed back to see what the majors were up to.

They weren't hard to find. A crowd had gathered around the four captives who knelt in the centre. One of the Montagnard chiefs was conducting the interrogation while Sam interpreted. So far the questioning wasn't going well. Fortunately Fr Édouard was preoccupied with the wounded otherwise he'd surely have felt a need to intervene on humanitarian grounds. The Montagnards' blood was up and getting in the way was bound to be risky. At least the majors were armed and dangerous.

Monty and Danny reached the crowd just as the interrogator lost his patience. Sam still held her cross-bow. He took the weapon, ordering Sam to hand over the bolts. Without hesitation, he loaded a bolt and shot the nearest prisoner in his thigh. The bolt went straight through the leg so only the fletching stuck out, most of the shaft protruded from the other side.

The man screamed. His agony must have been acute because Danny had seen Vietnamese troops endure great pain in stoic silence. The interrogator didn't hesitate. He reloaded the cross-bow and shot the bolt through the screaming man's other thigh. By then the victim was beyond any comprehensible speech, but the other three started talking. Shutting them up was going to be problem.

The conversation was fragmented and confusing at times. The three captives all talked at once and the majors had to intervene to restore order.

'Rules of debate here, gents,' Major White insisted. 'One at a time, please.'

Sam had trouble getting that message across, but they settled down in the end. Although the wounded prisoner writhed and moaned close by, no one felt disposed to remove him to somewhere more comfortable. His condition was an incentive for the others to co-operate. Sam explained the gist of the conversation went something like this:

Interrogator — *Where do you come from?*

Prisoner — *North.*

Interrogator — *How far?*

Prisoner — *Red River Delta.*

Gulf of Tonkin, Hanoi maybe..? Danny estimated.

Interrogator — *Why did you bomb Kontum?*

Prisoner — *Hoi are traitors who fight for the French imperialists.*

He got slapped around for the double insult.

Interrogator — *How many have come with you? What do you want?*

Prisoner — *Want? To unite Vietnam into a glorious socialist republic. We are many — countless.*

Interrogator — *Bullshit!*

That got the spokesman going. He'd been indoctrinated for years and it was highly likely he'd fought against the French during the 1946-54 war. He began to extol the virtues of their wonderful leader, Ho Chi Minh and his brilliant politburo. Thousands of small guerrilla cells were being formed and their mission was to terrorise the south into submission. Soon Vietnam would be united as it rightfully should be.

Ho Chi Minh had good reason for wanting this outcome. The Chinese behemoth to the north was the greatest threat to national security. Oh yes, they'd been a great help when it came to military logistic support during the fight against the French, but cagey old Uncle Ho wasn't fooled for a minute. Chairman Mao had Vietnam firmly in his territorial sights. China coveted Vietnam's rubber, tin and rice, not to mention the opium trade.

The prisoner said tens of thousands of guerrillas were being trained by Russians and Chinese experts. Many promising guerrillas destined for leadership were sent to those countries for extra attention. Soon South Vietnam would be swarming with communist insurgents. Towns and villages would run red with blood. On a more personal level, this particular terrorist group had planned to lay landmines around Kontum to create panic and fearful doubt whenever the townsfolk ventured into the countryside. Fortunately the plan had been foiled — this time.

'That's new,' Major White observed. 'We've seen all sorts of factions sprout up and take pot-shots at anything that offended them, but these guys seem to be disciplined and organised. Right now the ARVN is in no shape to combat a co-ordinated invasion of that massive scale.'

'They call themselves National Liberation Front,' Sam spat vehemently. 'They liberate nothing in Vietnam. They Communist traitors. *Viet Nam Cong San!*'

'New kids on the block, eh?' Major Black said. 'Viet Cong.'

'Monty, crank up the plane's radio. We need to get a message to General O'Daniel. I reckon he'll want his MAAG boys up here and give these people a helping hand. Big trouble is coming.'

Chapter 6 — The Road North

General Iron Mike O'Daniel turned up the following morning. He arrived in a Sikorsky S-55 chopper, identical to the one Danny had flown in Korea. He had to admit he rather missed chopper flying, but Danny's life had moved on for the moment. The general was accompanied by a team of tough looking MAAG specialists. Each man bristled with weapons of every description. There appeared to be no standard issue. Although Iron Mike's troops worked as a tightly knit team they were nevertheless individuals and chose their armament accordingly. The majors' assessment of the situation caused enough concern for Iron Mike to investigate personally.

The majors briefed Iron Mike, who sensed that his men would need to move further afield than Kontum. All the Montagnard highlanders needed to learn how to protect themselves if the threat of a mass guerrilla incursion was credible. And it appeared that the general did believe the danger was real.

With Fr Eduardo's help, the majors had managed to persuade the Montagnards not to kill the prisoners until Iron Mike at least had a chance to interrogate them. The Montagnards weren't happy about it, but consoled themselves by making the Viet Cong terrorists' captivity as miserable they possibly could. The general said his men would take responsibility for the Montagnards and ordered the majors to expand their investigation further into Indochina.

Danny and Monty's pal, Lieutenant Colonel Ted Serong was taking an interest in Burma and would soon be helping with that country's military training. Although ultimately responsible to the Australian Government, Serong kept in close contact with the CIA, so the agency reckoned that area was covered.

Thailand seemed to be stable while the Brits and Aussies were responsible for the Malayan Peninsula. There was some sabre-rattling from Indonesia that was causing enough concern for ASIO, MI-6 and the CIA to station agents in Djakarta to keep an eye on the place. But resources were spread thinly throughout Southeast Asia which had developed into a fomenting hotchpotch of post-colonial discontent.

Cambodia was the most secure realm in the immediate area. Prince Norodom Sihanouk was keeping a firm lid on his country's affairs. By Southeast Asian standards Cambodia was doing fine. Their woes were still over a decade away. But Laos was a different story.

'Fly on over there and check it out,' the general said as if he was talking about a Sunday drive.

CAT manned an office in Vientiane, so that was as good a place as any to start.

Danny, Monty and the majors bade farewell to the good father, Sister Camille, the village children, Sam, the chieftains and their women-folk. They boarded the plane and took off for

Vientiane, which lay beside the Mekong River on the southern Laotian border.

Navigation was simple. Danny flew the *Gooney-Bird* slightly north of west until he reached the Mekong. From there he turned right and followed the river northwards until it meandered west. The Mekong now formed the border of Thailand and Laos. They were hardly likely to miss Vientiane and the airport was just west of town right beside the river. Vientiane Airport was the only sealed strip in the country and that was a PSP surface. It was also the only airport with a radio beacon that worked when Air Laos employees remembered to switch it on.

When they landed Danny also observed a C-46, several C-47s and a number of Sikorsky S-55 helicopters parked beside the runway. He later discovered the choppers were supplied by the Thai Air Force to aid the Royal Lao Air Force whose resources were seriously limited now the French had withdrawn their support.

The city was very much Saigon and Hanoi's poor relative. It spread in a vast, sprawling cocktail of ancient, crumbling imperial palaces, temples, occasional French colonial edifices and rambling oriental shanties. Vientiane was originally known as the *City of Sandalwood,* which was indeed the most popular building material. There was certainly no shortage of pagodas. Temple building was a favourite pastime of bygone kings, nobles and warlords.

There was significantly less motor traffic than Saigon, but cone-hatted cyclists, livestock, buffalo-drawn carts and street hawkers packed the city. Market stalls and food stands lined the avenues and alleys where shop fronts squeezed together in rows fronting tumbledown terrace buildings. In Danny's opinion personal space wasn't greatly respected in Southeast Asian cities while the now-familiar cooking smells and wood-fire smoke filled his nostrils.

The go-to guy in town was forty-seven-year-old Ambassador Charles Woodruff Yost, who'd set up an American mission only a couple of months earlier. He complained the roof leaked and the place was infested with rats — which also meant cobras, who liked nothing better than a fat rodent for supper. Yost's staff was modest, but growing now that the US was taking an interest in the area. CAT had been flying in personnel and supplies to support Yost's mission since its establishment.

So the CAT agents were able to refuel and service the *Gooney-Bird* while Danny, Monty and the majors cadged a ride into town. Charles Yost greeted them warmly and arranged for accommodation at a nearby hotel which still bore its French title, *Le Touresol,* which meant 'The Sunflower'. The ambassador suggested the hotel's restaurant provided better fare than his lowly mission, so he said he'd join them for supper to explain as much of the local situation as he'd discovered so far.

Le Touresol was one of those Southeast Asian buildings that made luxury out of very little. Danny loved the open verandah-style lounges and bars where ceiling fans spun languidly. A cool evening breeze drifted in from the Mekong River while waiters sped efficiently between tables. The other patrons were a potpourri of disillusioned French colonialists, up-and-coming Indochinese entrepreneurs, elegant ladies and stylish courtesans.

It was a cold beer atmosphere. Danny and his companions were enjoying their first thirst-quencher when Charles Yost arrived. After ordering a drink, he wasted no time briefing the majors about what a perilous task they were about to embark upon.

He explained that right now Laos was in a power vacuum. Lacking the rice, rubber and tin of Cambodia and Vietnam, Laos' one significant cash crop was opium and everyone wanted a slice of that action. Chinese and Viet Minh raiders boldly invaded the Plain of Jars to grab a slice of the opium pie. Local warlords were continually at each other's throats. Bloody territorial wars were rampant with the local peasants usually winding up as collateral damage. But there were new sinister players insidiously creeping into the opium trade.

'Yeah right,' Danny chipped in, 'more sinister than warlords, river-pirates and several varieties of commie bad-arses. I bet you've left out crocodiles, poisonous snakes, tigers and rogue elephants.'

'I was coming to them,' Ambassador Yost grinned, 'but I'd thought I'd break it to you gently.'

'OK, apart from Danny's list, who else is of interest?'

'There's an emerging export trade,' Yost continued. 'The Chinks and Viet Minh had controlled the traditional opium route into China, which is still the number-one customer. Orientals smoke the stuff in the traditional way, but some bright spark has decided it's more profitable to refine opium into heroin and sell it further afield.'

'Further afield, where?' Major Black asked.

'Well, that's why I'm so interested,' Yost said enigmatically. 'I've been receiving more and more reports that the dope is finding its way down the Mekong to the coast.'

'Why should we care?' Major Black asked.

'Because it doesn't stop there.'

All four men simply stared at the Ambassador.

'As you are well aware,' Yost continued, 'the US Government is concerned about the situation in Indochina now that the French are out of the picture. We have initiated a huge logistic programme to assist the Diem Government in Vietnam and other pro-democratic Indochinese governments. Diem wouldn't have been my first choice. He has tunnel vision and is out of touch with reality, while his influential family are a bunch of rascals. Drug smuggling, illegal imports, gun-running, prostitution, and organised crime — you'll find a member of the Nhu family involved somewhere. I guess he's better than the commie alternative.'

'So America is prepared to support anyone, provided they're not red,' Danny suggested.

'Sometimes you have to live with the lesser of two evils,' Yost acknowledged. 'Maybe we can influence things for the better later on.'

'But what has that got to do with heroin?' Monty asked.

'Simple market forces,' Yost said. 'We have ships arriving at Saigon Port with their holds full of relief supplies. Sometimes the skippers can arrange for a return cargo — maybe rice or other raw materials, but it's small fry and often they return with no cargo at all.'

'Uncle Sam is footing the bill,' Major White suggested.

'Sure, but you can see how tempting it would be to supplement your income on a voyage back Stateside.'

'A little drug running..?' Danny said.

'Precisely, but not a little. I have information that the quantity of semi-refined heroin leaving Laos is doubling every week.'

'You're sure?' Major White said.

'As sure as anyone can be about anything in Indochina?'

'Surely that's out of CIA jurisdiction when it reaches the States. It's a job for the FBI.'

'They'd be happier if we could nip the poppy in the bud so to speak.'

'I never heard of dope being a problem,' Monty said. 'Booze yes, and I come from Black Alabama.'

'It's a problem alright,' Yost said. 'FBI reports suggest the most lucrative market is the arty-farty crowd. You know — musicians, actors, those modern artist fellas and the like. LA, Chicago and New York mobsters are making a packet,'

Yost's expression left them in no doubt how he felt about the *arty-farty crowd*.

'So anyone without a proper day-job,' Monty offered.

'Blueblood Ivy Leaguers and rich college kids are starting to experiment as well,' Yost shook his head. 'God knows, they have the dough to supply their habit. And women too. It's not just hookers who have developed a taste for dope. Rich New York lawyers and bankers, bored trophy-wives are experimenting with the stuff. The alarming aspect is how quickly the market is burgeoning.'

Yost didn't paint a pretty picture, but it was an accurate one. Jazz saxophonist Charlie Parker, blues singer Billie Holiday and film actor Bela Lugosi were just a small sample of the rich-and-famous who'd fallen victim to heroin addiction.

'I still say it's an FBI job, the bureau is always complaining we step on their toes anyhow. Let 'em do their job,' Major White insisted.

'It's not quite as simple as that,' Yost sighed with a careworn expression that suggested nothing ever was. 'With opium being syphoned south the supply north is drying up, or at least diminishing. That will make the players on the Plain of Jars more desperate and competitive and, frankly more likely to butcher one another for what's left.'

'And the US doesn't want that because it would dearly love to see anti-Communist stability in Northern Laos.'

'Absolutely.'

'But what can four blokes do about it?' Danny asked.

'You can take these gents on a fact-finding mission north along the Mekong to the Plain of Jars, Danny. I want to know who's doing what to whom and when. I want information on the warlords and the guys smuggling opium south. Once I have that I can arrange for a battalion of RLA lads led by our MAAG guys to sort out the villains and maybe destroy the crop at its source.'

'Haven't you forgotten that the peasants who grow the poppies rely on the harvest to make a living?' Danny asked.

'We'll just have to see if we can supply sufficient incentive for them to cultivate something else. We get rid of the market middlemen, we destroy the trade. I have college boffins on my staff ready and willing to advise the local people on agricultural alternatives.'

'Got any ideas who's involved in the Mekong trade?' Major Black asked.

'French renegades,' Yost shrugged, 'local gangsters, ex-colonial Limeys and even some of our own Yankee boys who've been drifting around Indochina since WWII ended. There're any number of guys who've been in-and-out of trouble just looking for a fast buck.'

They went on to discuss the terrain and facilities they were going to face on their mission. The CIA and Ambassador Yost were developing a series of LSs which was simply an abbreviation for Laos Stations that acted as support bases and fuel depots for any further 'in-country' activity. Danny and Monty wondered whether these outposts were suitable for C-47 operations or 'Dakotable' as the French would say. They'd studied the charts and knew they'd get as far as Luang Prabang, a provincial centre at the confluence of the Mekong and Nam Khan Rivers. Beyond that lay several abandoned French airstrips, but their condition was unknown.

'Now if we had a chopper,' Monty suggested. 'Danny, you still remember how to fly those things don't ya?'

'Like riding a bike, Monty.'

'I don't think my influence stretches to the RLAF,' Yost looked doubtful.

'Leave that to Major Black and me,' Major White said. 'It's what we do.'

They discussed the situation and logistics well into the night. Eventually Ambassador Yost bid the company goodnight and left. Danny, for all his youth, had learnt there was a fine line between going to bed mellow and heaving your guts out on the stairwell. Tomorrow was Christmas Eve although Vientiane did not appear particularly prepared for the event. Danny viewed Christmas with mixed feelings. Last year he'd frozen in the battlefields of Korea, but in the company of true friends and colleagues like Major Vic Armstrong, Long Li and fellow chopper crewmen.

*

Nights in the tropics were not particularly silent events. Insects, birds, bats and goodness knew what else seemed to want to manifest their nocturnal presence with chirps, clucks, whistles and other undefinable sounds. But after a while the cacophony blended into a background white-noise that became restful and eventually lulled you to sleep.

Danny had just reached that stage when for some reason he sensed a movement or sound that wasn't part of the purring background. At first he thought it might be Monty shuffling his way from his room next door to the bathroom along the hallway, although Danny hadn't heard a door open or close.

He remained as still as possible. If someone was indeed skulking around they weren't going to find much. Danny carried some spending money in a mixture of Laotian kip and French piastres that were duel currency used at the time. He had enough to buy drinks and food from street stalls, but Major White and Major Black were the imprest-holders, who covered all main expenses.

So if a night stalker was looking for cash, he was out of luck. But a little money went a long way in post-colonial Laos and who knew what lengths desperation would drive people to?

There it was again — just the slightest movement from the far side of the room. Danny froze. His 1911 Colt lay on the bed stand, but it was still holstered and attached to his military-style webbing belt. Did the intruder have a knife or a gun? The former seemed most likely. Guns were noisy and that was the last thing a stealthy burglar wanted.

Minutes passed while Danny's eyes adjusted to the darkness. Just enough moonlight streamed through his balcony window for him to start defining details. The window was open, as Danny had left it to take advantage of any night breeze, which was probably the intruder's way in. He couldn't be sure but he sensed the burglar hadn't moved, but sat on the only chair in the bedroom.

Sitting! Burglars don't break in just to rest their legs.

Danny eased the mosquito net aside and swung his legs out of the bed.

Even though Vientiane enjoyed its coolest season, temperatures rarely dropped below 16° Centigrade so Danny slept naked, which psychologically wasn't the best way to confront a prospective assailant. However, he was left with no choice. His room did boast the luxury of a bedside reading lamp, which Danny thought of switching on. The hotel generator still operated. He heard it chugging away amid the background sounds.

He dismissed the idea. Surprise in the dark was his best strategy. Danny launched himself across the room. In one bound he tackled the stranger, trapping him in a bear hug. The small body wriggled and kicked in his arms. The chair clattered across the room, smashing into the far wall. The intruder let out a frightened squeal, but Danny's burly arms were firmly clamped around the diminutive torso.

Him?

No, Danny knew enough human anatomy to know when he was holding a girl.

'Hold still, dammit,' he hissed, without really expecting to be obeyed.

With his captive tightly secure in one arm Danny reached for the overhead light switch and flicked it on. After blinking for a couple of seconds the forty-watt bulb illuminated the room sufficiently to reveal a naked brawny six-foot young man embracing a young elfin Laotian girl.

Or at least that was Monty's impression when he burst through the door.

'I heard a commotion, Danny. What's going on..?'

Chapter 7 — Beyond the Mekong

'I'm not interrupting anything am I?' Monty grinned evilly.

'Let go, you monster,' the wriggling figure hissed.

'Oh good, you speak English,' Danny said, but still held onto her. 'Now you can explain why you're sneaking around my room in the middle of the night.'

Monty cleared his throat.

'I know we're buddies and all that,' he said, 'but you might want to put on some pants first.'

'Yeah, right. Hang onto this little spitfire.'

Monty had arrived accompanied by his 1911 Colt automatic, which he pointed menacingly at the girl. She gave a resigned sigh. It seemed the fight had gone out of her. Danny pulled on a pair of shorts and picked up the fallen chair.

'Take a seat,' he invited.

She accepted although not particularly graciously.

'OK. You speak English don't you?'

She nodded.

'Let's start with you name.'

'Kekiokolanee.'

'Pleased to meet you. I'm Danny and this is my mate, Monty.'

'I know who you are,' she eyed them suspiciously. 'But you two are mating? This I do not understand.'

'Yeah...oh, I see...no not like that, we're pals, chums, friends, *amis*.'

'Now we have got our human relationship settled,' Monty said. 'How do you know who we are, Kek-i-o-ko-lan-ee?'

She smiled for the first time.

'Maybe you call me Kekio.'

Monty smiled back at her and the atmosphere relaxed considerably.

'Vientiane is a town not so big. Words move fast,' Kekio said. She spoke English with a soft Gallic lilt and often used adjectives following nouns in French style.

'So what brings you here?' Danny asked.

'I need job with you.'

'You don't even know why we're here.'

'You think waiters have no ears? Man who like me works at bar.'

'You'd better tell us the whole story,' Monty suggested.

It turned out that Kekio was born in a village called Ban Bat along the Mekong to the northwest of the Plain of Jars. Her family, who'd originally migrated from Thailand, still lived by subsistence farming as they'd done for countless generations. They'd endured almost constant war, but had managed to survive and, if not prospered, at least avoided starvation. Actually by Laotian standards their life had been pretty good. They cultivated rice, fruit and vegetables while chickens, pigs, goats and river-fish provided all the protein required for a balanced diet.

The Mekong was navigable for many miles beyond the village, so traders often stopped by to provide the villagers with a few modest luxuries when they could afford them. French missionaries had stayed for a while, but were gone now. However they recognised Kekio as a sharp-witted child with a talent for languages and mathematics. She won a scholarship to study in France and finally at the University of Strasbourg.

She'd secured a job as translator with the UN and had worked during the Geneva peace talks for a few weeks. She sent money home to help her parents pay their bills.

'So you're back for a holiday?' Danny asked. 'You know, to visit the family.'

Kekio's eyes reflected a profound sadness that both Danny and Monty recognised, wondering whether one of her loved ones was sick or had died.

'Is everything OK at home?' Danny asked. Considering he was often forced into warlike situations, he could be a right old softy at times.

Kekio explained that life at Ban Bat was fine until a local drug-lord decided he needed extra territory and manpower to expand his business. The village lay right on the eastern fringe of the Golden Triangle, an area that extended into Thailand, Burma, and Laos. The remote, lawless region was the largest opium poppy producer outside Afghanistan. Without sufficient resources or resolve, local law-enforcers didn't feel obliged to interfere. Most drug-lords knew the price required for the police to turn a blind eye anyway.

The particular warlord bothering Ban Bat was Dahm Daw. Kekio said his name roughly meant 'Dark Dave', but didn't really have a literal translation. However the approximation was appropriate, Dahm Daw was a quality villain, backed up by a gang of thoroughly despicable bloodthirsty cut-throats.

Ban Bat was now a forced labour camp. The community's traditional cultivation was quickly being converted to poppy growing. Food production had dropped to near-starvation levels and, as the drug gangs kept all the profits, the villagers suffered appallingly.

'How do you know all this?' Danny asked. 'I wouldn't have thought the bad guys had put out a news bulletin.'

'Word travels down Mekong River. Everyone knows. Each day worse than day before.'

'Why haven't the police done anything?'

'You joking me, yes? Police and RLA bribed easy — do nothing. I need to get there,' Kekio pleaded. 'I know you go up country. I Thai girl. Speak French, English, Khmer and Tai-Kadai and Hmong-Mien dialects. I help you get around. Talk to local people.'

'You know it's the majors' call,' Monty said to Danny, 'but it's a good place for them to start.'

'Let's go and talk to them.'

If Major White and Major Black resented being awakened, they showed no signs of it. They listened to Kekio's story without comment.

'It fits into our brief,' Major Black conceded.

'Sounds like it falls into the *Heart and Minds* category, if you ask me,' Major White agreed. 'We certainly have authorisation.'

'OK, here's what we'll do,' Major Black said. As the majors were equal in rank, there was no visible chain of command, but both men seemed to always be on the same operation page. 'We leave the *Gooney-Bird* here and dry-lease an S-55 from the RLAF.

We'll fly up to Luang Prabang. That's as far as we can guarantee a fuel supply.'

'What about further up-river?' Danny asked.

'We'll just have to suck it and see,' Major White replied. 'Right now let's get some sleep. It's gonna be a long day tomorrow.'

'I stay with you Danny?' Kekio asked coyly.

Monty rolled his eyes.

'What is it with you and babes, Danny?'

'Shaddup, Monty.'

'I sleep on floor,' Kekio announced darting onto the balcony and retrieving a small canvas bag. 'These all my things.'

Her belongs seemed pitifully little.

'No you won't, Kekio,' Sir Galahad McAlister insisted. 'I'll bunk in with Monty tonight and you can have my room.'

'Mates,' Kekio smiled cheekily.

'There are *two* beds,' Danny stressed.

Danny was amazed how readily the majors had agreed to such a random venture. They may have simply been grateful for somewhere to start. Their brief was frustratingly nebulous after all. Maybe they were just itching for an opportunity to get back into action and Ban Bat was an ideal location to find it.

*

Kekio proved her worth the following morning. Leasing a service aircraft might have seemed unusual to people used to rigid military discipline and security, but the CIA's influence was far reaching. US aid to Laos came with strings attached especially in a say about how things were run. Even so it took all morning to wade through a mountain of Laotian red-tape to secure the chopper.

Kekio navigated them past the pitfalls, knowing instinctively whose palm to grease and by how much. The upshot was Danny was now flying an S-55 northwards along the Mekong River towards Luang Prabang. He had been issued with RLAF vouchers to obtain fuel wherever he wanted. Mind you fuel dumps were limited, but the RLAF representative also supplied a list of locations where he was most likely to find some. Danny hoped that the chopper was well maintained because there was little chance of instant repairs once they reached more remote locations.

Of course the S-55 was limited to a smaller payload than the *Gooney-Bird*, but the majors, Danny and Monty travelled light other than their arsenal of miscellaneous fire-power. Kekio didn't take up much weight or space. She'd travelled by ship and train to Europe and this was her first flying experience. After the initial unsettling experience of the rotor vibrations, she soon relaxed and enjoyed riding in the chopper, skimming along at tree-top level. Danny flew with the fuselage doors open and held in place by locking pins. The rushing slip-stream and rotor-wash made very effective air conditioning.

Although well into the dry season, the Mekong still flowed, wide, brown and muddy. River traffic was plentiful and even over-crowded at times especially as they approached Luang Prabang.

The town was an ancient capital whose main features were countless temples, pagodas and hordes of orange-robed monks. After landing, the majors and Kekio headed into the central market district to see what the locals thought was happening up-river. Danny and Monty remained at the airstrip to arrange refuelling the chopper. In a mixture of school-boy French, grunts, improvised sign-language and pointing, they'd refilled the chopper's fuel tank by the time the majors returned.

It seemed everyone knew things were not well at Ban Bat and beyond, but no one was prepared to do anything about it. Dahm Daw and his crew were notorious and occasionally ventured into Luang Prabang. However no one knew exactly how big and well armed his gang was.

'What's the plan?' Danny asked.

'Recon, I guess,' Major Black replied blandly.

'They'll hear the chopper a mile off.'

'They sure will. I thought of that. What we need is a boat. Now here's what we're gonna do...'

*

Danny gently lifted the collective pitch lever and with a roar from the engine the S-55 lifted to a hover. Slowly Danny raised the chopper higher until the cable attached to its fuselage pulled taut. An eighteen foot hull dangled in a sling attached to the cable. Danny felt the resistance as the hull became airborne, its weight straining the chopper's engine and airframe.

'How's it looking?' Danny asked Monty who stood at the cabin door in the crewman's role.

'Yeah, steady and secure,' Monty replied with a 'thumbs-up'.

Other than the extra weight the main problem with a heavy load swinging under the chopper was pendulum oscillations that caused controllability problems. Danny eased the cyclic pitch lever forward and the chopper slowly picked up speed. The hull trailed smoothly in the slip-stream. Nevertheless Danny restricted his speed to thirty knots.

Major White was riding inside the hull. The weapons and ammunition boxes also lay in the hull.

Kekio and the majors had proven successful negotiators when it came to obtaining the boat equipped with paddles, sails and a tiny 4 hp outboard motor. It certainly wasn't going to win any races, but made very little noise. Although it was unmarked, Kekio identified Ban Bat's position on Danny's map. She remembered the country well, so they were always aware of their exact position.

Who says girls can't read maps?

Danny was surprised how the river traffic had reduced to a few long-tailed boats and sampans until finally the river was entirely empty. Dahm Daw and the drug gangs had deterred upriver commerce.

'Looks like people are steering clear of the area,' Major Black observed.

'Sensible. Keeping out of outlaws' way,' Kekio suggested. 'We only maybe ten miles to go.'

'OK, time to find a spot to put her down, Danny,' Major Black said.

Danny brought the S-55 to a hover and descended until the boat touched the water surface. Major White scrambled into action and released the winch cable before paddling to shore. Danny located a clearing between the jungle and a series of rice-paddies.

I hope it's gonna be firm enough to take the chopper's weight.

The LZ proved adequate. The area was deserted except for a herd of grazing buffalo who eyed the landing chopper suspiciously. Danny didn't know much about buffaloes, but this group had formed a defensive circle to protect their calves. Their formidable horns bristled outwards, forming a menacing barrier. They certainly looked skittish.

Remind me not to mess with buffaloes, Danny thought.

There were no signs of human beings, which wasn't unusual. Although South-East Asia in general and Indochina in particular were over-crowded, Northern Laos was sparsely populated by comparison.

With a weather-eye on the buffalo herd, Danny slid the chopper's side-door shut before Major Black led the way to the river. Danny brought up the rear, constantly looking over his shoulder, alert for a buffalo charge. Although no stampede ensued, there was a lot of snorting and hoof-stamping.

They reached the riverbank without incident and boarded their boat. Major White pulled the engine lanyard and four horse-power spluttered into life. The diminutive motor barely conquered the mighty Mekong's current, but they edged ahead at a few knots. Occasionally they passed basking ten-foot Siamese crocodiles. Danny had a healthy respect for crocs, especially the giant salt-water monsters that frequented Northern Australia and New Guinea coastlines.

'They trouble you not,' Kekio said, 'if you stay clear.'

In fact the crocs were in more danger of humans than the other way around. They were being hunted into extinction and their numbers were dwindling rapidly.

Even with paddle-augmentation, the boat's engine made pitifully slow progress, seemingly content to putt-putt along with steady patience. By nightfall they still had not reached Ban Bat.

'We have maybe to go a kilometre,' she whispered at last.

'Good,' Major Black said. 'We'll have the cover of darkness.'

Major White manoeuvred the boat towards shore where the current slackened. He cut the motor and they relied on paddle-power. As they approached Ban Bat, the jungle had been cleared to allow livestock access to the river. The bank was steep in places, but had been eroded at points where animals came to drink. They beached the boat at one of these spots and crept along the riverbank to a jetty that marked the village position.

Major White led as they clambered onto the jetty and advanced towards the town. Fishing nets hung out to dry on trestles while miscellaneous fishing tackle was scattered around. Ban Bat was less of a village than a random group of shanties made of bamboo, palm fronds, corrugated iron and other found material. It was hard to make out details in the fading light.

The majors were both tense, holding their carbines at the ready. Danny and Monty, sensing the CIA agents' concern, did the same. Kekio was unarmed and stuck close to Danny. He had that comforting effect on girls when danger lurked.

What bothered Major White and Major Black was the total lack of lights or village activity. Ban Bat may have barely been a village unconnected to any electric grid, but even remote villages had one or two diesel-powered DC generators. You'd also expect to see people about their business — it wasn't that late. Pigs and chickens should be scratching around the place and where were the dogs? There were always dogs hanging around Indochinese communities. The only poultry were ducks and geese that'd taken to the water and were paddling nervously around the jetty.

'Where is everyone..?' Danny whispered, but Major Black raised his hand urgently.

Danny got the message and shut up.

And then a sound seared through the night. It was the most terrifying thing Danny had heard, and that was saying something. It was a roar, bark and howl bound in one horrifying thunderous bellow.

'What the blue blazes..?'

Danny was unsure who'd spoken, then realised it was himself.

Suddenly the village erupted in chaos. Once barred windows and doors slammed open and folk poured outside brandishing flaming torches, machetes, crossbows, knives, clubs and metal pots they clashed together. Everyone yelled and screamed for all they were worth although initially they kept close to the buildings. A pack of dogs yapped close by.

The majors thought they were under attack and raised their carbines.

'No!' Kekio shrieked, pressing her palms to her cheeks. 'Don't shoot!'

Whether the majors heard Kekio's warning was problematic. They both fired warning bursts into the air, which didn't seem to make any difference. The screaming continued.

Kekio screamed again as an enormous shadow bounded through the village. The spectre growled and snarled as it loped past leaving the rank stench of death in its path. Danny stood riveted to the spot as the creature leapt towards him. He felt his feet buckle as Monty tackled him around the knees. Danny crumpled to the dusty ground as the shadow flashed inches above him and disappeared a second later.

In moments Danny and his companions were surrounded by a chattering, yelling, and outraged crowd. Men, women and children all stood in confusion, babbling at once. Some jumped in agitation as they stared at where the shadow had vanished. Dogs snapped and snarled at the strangers.

Suddenly another shot rang out from Major White's carbine. This time the crowd *did* take notice, but only to become more agitated. Then Kekio was calling for calm and quiet.

'What was that flaming thing?' Danny stammered as he rose to his feet and dusted himself down.

'That, Danny, if I'm not very much mistaken, was a bloody great tiger,' Monty replied as he gasped for breath. 'If it had been a few inches lower, it'd have taken your head clean off.'

Chapter 8 — Tiger — Tiger!

Kekio suggested that Major White should stop firing warning shots. They only scared everyone even more than runaway tigers. Finally, after what seemed ages, the villagers calmed down. Unfortunately it didn't take much to start them chattering again. Once in the confusion Kekio asked where her family was, but no one listened. As time went by and there was no sign of the tiger reappearing, the villagers eventually stopped talking and became curious about the strangers in town.

When Kekio explained who they were, the locals cheered up considerably, but when she asked about her family again they eyed her sheepishly and said nothing. Finally an elderly man who Danny took to be a chief or counsellor spoke to Kekio. She was visibly distressed when the old fellow finished.

'What's up?' Danny asked. 'Where are your mum and dad?'

'They not here,' Kekio wailed. 'Dahm Daw takes them.'

'Where?'

The villagers seemed to understand and all started pointing towards the north, away from the river.

'Maybe we should find somewhere quiet and find out what's going on,' Major Black suggested. 'We need to talk to this old guy without any interruptions.'

The village elder led them to his home. The only other occupant was an ancient woman who Danny assumed was his wife. A small fire glowed in the room where she brewed tea and offered small cups all round.

Good old tea, it always does the job, although I wouldn't mind a spot of milk and sugar.

Other villagers gathered around the old couple's home, peeking through the open windows and crowding the veranda. Soon there was a sea of faces peering into the room. Then the old boy began to outline their woes.

Ban Bat was in the grip of a double-whammy. True enough local drug-lord Dahm Daw had taken over the town, but the tiger had also turned up a few days earlier. So far it had killed a buffalo calf, a couple of pigs and goodness knew how many chickens, ducks and geese. Luckily, there were no known human victims to date. The villagers hoped it might take out a few of the drug gang, but doubted it.

'Isn't that unusual?' Danny asked. 'I mean the tiger doesn't kill more that it can eat. They wouldn't bother to waste their energy hunting something they don't want to eat.'

Monty and the majors eyed Danny with renewed admiration. Danny read a lot which probably came from hanging around with Angela.

'It's gone rogue, professor,' Major White opined, acknowledging Danny's input. 'I've heard of wolf packs back in the Yellowstone. In the 20s the government culled 'em out of the National Park to appease the farmers. Now some boffins wanna reintroduce them to balance what they call the "food-chain".'

'No wonder those buffalo were so jumpy back where we landed. It wasn't the chopper that worried them. They knew the tiger was in the area.'

'So where are Dahm Daw's boys? They should have the fire-power to deal with one mangy tiger.'

More conversation between Kekio and the elder couple followed. The petite interpreter listened intently for several minutes, nodding occasionally, but saying nothing. The gang was holed up in an ancient Angkor temple about half a day's walk from Ban Bat. The temple had been abandoned for so long it was now almost enveloped by the encroaching jungle. Dahm Daw had conscripted local peasants to hack a clearing in front of the temple.

The drug lab was inside while a shanty-town had emerged at the rainforest edge to accommodate the forced labourers. A bamboo barricade surrounded the buildings, not only to keep marauding wild-life out, but more importantly to prevent the occupants escaping. The poppy fields were several miles away and could only be reached via a narrow trail through the jungle.

The gang were well armed with Chinese made AK-47 semi-automatic rifles. The old man believed they possessed at least one Jeep that just squeezed through the trail and was the main means of transport to carry the poppies from the fields to the jungle hide-away. Right now it seemed that Dahm Daw was having trouble shooing rivals away from his patch which was why he hadn't visited Ban Bat recently. No one knew when he might return.

Finally Kekio turned to her companions and explained the situation to them.

'All Dahm Daw men gone back to drug camp now,' she said with obvious relief. 'My family they are taken for hostages and workers.'

'That's bad, isn't it?' Danny suggested.

'They live,' Kekio replied. 'They work in poppy fields and process factory.'

'Process factory?'

'I think she means where they turn the poppy pods into opium,' Major White said.

'No, just opium,' Kekio said. 'They refine morphine to heroin number four. Make smaller and easier to smuggle down Mekong.'

'That's quite a set-up,' Major Black said. 'Chemicals, technicians, people with know-how. Number four grade heroin is volatile stuff. One wrong move and — poof!'

Kekio nodded.

'So they bring the dope to Ban Bat for transportation downriver,' Danny surmised.

'They store heroin number four in bags here. Move south when shipment big enough.'

'You mean they just leave it here. Who's guarding it?' Monty said.

'Who need guard? No one dare steal from Dahm Daw. He find dope missing. He take ...?'

'Reprisals,' Monty prompted and Kekio nodded once more.

'OK, it looks like we have a double challenge,' Major White announced. 'We have a bunch of rogues and one rogue tiger to deal with. What do you think, Major Black?'

'We didn't come here to tame tigers, but we sure did come to sort out bad guys,' Major Black said, rubbing his chin and considering his options. 'But just maybe we can use one problem to help solve the other.'

'What's the plan?' Danny asked.

'First we're gonna check out that heroin store and see just how much they've stashed there.'

The dope store was probably the most notable building in Ban Bat. It boasted a corrugated iron roof and was raised several feet above ground level. Steps led to a veranda surrounding the building. The interior consisted of two rooms, roughly partitioned by a bamboo screen. Metal ammunition containers were stacked on pallets. The ammo boxes made ideal, water-proof storage for the grade four heroin.

The dope was refined to a beige-coloured powdery substance somewhere between the consistency of flour and sugar. Each single kilogram was individually packed in Saran Wrap, an emerging plastic product.

'There must be a hundred *kis*, here,' Major White said, whistling through his teeth. 'It's worth a fortune. I bet this stuff is bound for the French Connection.'

'French Connection?' Danny stared at the majors.

'Looks like it, Danny. The dope normally comes from Afghanistan and Turkey across the Med to Marseilles, then onto the US through Canada. French-Canadians and Corsican mafia gangs run the show. The Golden triangle was also a good source of supply while Indochina was a French Colony. Exporting the stuff might be more difficult now.'

'What are we going to do about this lot?' Monty asked. 'Not to mention Dahm Daw...and...the tiger.'

'The first things we need are syringes,' Major White said.

'How many?'

'As many as we have in the first aid kit.'

'There are two packs of a dozen when I last checked,' Danny said, all business and professional. The chopper's medical kit contained its own supply of morphine. The majors followed a hazardous vocation where injuries were common and pain relief essential.

'Get 'em.'

'Sorry, Major. They aren't in the boat — they're still in the chopper.'

'I didn't ask where they were, I just told you to get them,' Major White said evenly. 'You and Monty take the boat downstream. Danny, you might as well fly the chopper back here. There's no need for stealth with the bad guys out of town. Monty can bring back the boat now and use the motor all the way.'

At the height of the dry season, the sky was clear and there was enough moonlight to ensure Danny and Monty didn't get lost along the way. After scoping out an LZ for the chopper, they instructed Kekio to get the townsfolk to light torches so Danny could re-locate the Ban Bat LZ. The lack of electric lighting around the place was most inconvenient.

Danny and Monty pushed the boat off and leapt aboard, letting the current sweep them downstream. Both men wondered what the majors had in mind, but were well aware that they'd be told when there was a 'need-to-know'.

They found the landing area with ease and moored the boat to a nearby tree stump that had long ago succumbed to a water-logged death. Keeping a weather eye out for crocs, they headed the short distance from the riverbank to the chopper, which stood as they left it. Monty offered to help Danny with the preflight, but Danny declined.

'You head back, Monty,' he whispered. 'It'll take you longer to get upriver to Ban Bat. I'll be fine, this will only take a few minutes.'

'OK, see you back in town, buddy,' Monty said in equally soft tone. 'Why are we whispering?' he added before heading back through the bush.

After Monty left Danny inspected the chopper by torch-light. He removed the pitot covers. He noticed the buffalo herd still bunched in a tight circle close by. They were just visible in the moonlight, standing knee-deep in paddy field water. Danny could clearly hear them shuffling and lowing. Once again he thought his presence was distressing, but he was wrong.

Seconds later he heard the tiger snarling while it harassed the herd. The buffalo dropped their heads exposing an impenetrable wall of horns. The tiger darted forward in more attempted attacks, but was deterred on every occasion. Suddenly the tiger caught Danny's scent. Its snarl became a growl that grew to a roar as it turned from its original prey to what looked like easier pickings.

Oh shit!

Danny scrambled for the side door, but there was no time to slide it open. The tiger was only yards away and poised to pounce. Suddenly the door burst open. A hand reached out, grabbed Danny by the collar and yanked him into the chopper's cabin. The shadowy figure inside the fuselage slammed the door shut just as the tiger slammed into the side of the aircraft, rocking it violently.

'Blow me down, Danny,' a very familiar voice said. 'Can't you ever stay out of trouble?'

'Long Li!' Danny exclaimed, embracing his old mate with very uncharacteristic emotion. 'How the blue blazes did you get here?'

'Long story, I'll tell you later.'

'You could have opened the door sooner.'

'Sorry, I've been here for a while. I knew you'd be back and I was also aware that a tiger was prowling around, so this was the safest place. I must have nodded off.'

'Shit, the ruddy tiger. Monty's out there in the open!'

Danny raced to the cockpit and opened the side window. He squeezed through and clambered onto the roof, clinging to the rotor hub. The tiger still paced around the chopper. Seeing Danny, it bounded towards him, once again slamming into the fuselage with such force that Danny was nearly toppled from his perch. The tiger leapt again, but its claws couldn't pierce the metal. They did leave deep scratches as it slid down the chopper's side with a screech worse than a thousand finger nails on a black-board.

The tiger prowled around the chopper looking for a way to reach Danny, but there seemed be none. It snarled and roared in frustration.

Right you bastard!

Danny drew his 1911 Colt automatic, cocked the weapon and aimed. Even in the dimness he couldn't miss at such close range.

Blam!

A micro-second before Danny fired the tiger lost interest and bounded away. Danny's first emotion was absolute relief until he realised the big cat was on Monty's trail.

Oh shit again!

Danny fired another shot after the tiger, but knew he hadn't hit it as it leapt from sight.

'Monty!' Danny yelled at the top of his voice. 'The tiger's here. Run for it, mate. Get to the boat. I'm OK!'

*

Thank heavens for still night air. Monty heard the tiger's roar. He had no idea where the animal was but at least Danny was safely inside the chopper. He was running at full tilt when he heard the shots and Danny's warning. As he reached the river he drew his knife and slashed the mooring rope with a single slice. He clambered over the gunwales just as the tiger caught up. The tiger stopped for a second as if the presence of water had interfered with its prey's scent.

But it only paused for a moment, pacing back and forth over a few yards while Monty desperately hauled on the boat-motor starting lanyard.

'Ha, ha, beat ya, you dopey pussy,' Monty muttered as the engine spluttered into life. 'Thought you could bushwhack me, eh?'

Monty should have shut up because the tiger latched onto the sound of his voice. Homing in, it plunged into the river with a gigantic leap.

'Shit, cats don't like water,' Monty addressed the tiger that was now swimming purposefully towards the boat.

It reached the side, slapping one great fore-paw over the gunwale. The boat rocked alarmingly and Monty knew he was done for if he fell overboard. The tiger seemed to sense that it could not get aboard, but it also appeared to know it could tip Monty out if it tried hard enough.

Monty yelled and madly waved his arms, but rather than intimidate the tiger, he only enraged it further. All the time they drifted further into midstream. As Monty was preoccupied with the tiger, he neglected the rudder and they floated randomly.

'All right you sorry son-of-a-bitch!' Monty screamed at the tiger. 'I gave you every chance! I've had enough of this shit.'

He drew his hand-gun and would have shot the tiger right between the eyes, but he didn't fire.

Just as he took aim a light blazed onto the boat as the night erupted into a mini-hurricane. An eighty-mile-an-hour wind swept across the Mekong, accompanied by a deafening roar. The gale buffeted the boat and Monty was pitched over, landing unceremoniously on his back in the bilge. The tumult was too much for the tiger. It released its grip on the boat, turned and made its way back to shore, shaking itself dry as it padded onto dry land. It had to run the gauntlet through a group of irate Siam Crocs who'd been disturbed by the commotion. After much snarling and jaw-snapping the tiger finally slunk back into the jungle unharmed, still hungry but mostly — angry.

Danny banked the chopper away from the boat, reducing the rotor-wash effect and allowing Monty to recover. Once he saw his friend was safely steering the boat back upstream, Danny switched off the chopper's landing light and followed the river back to Ban Bat. He knew they had to do something about the rampant tiger. The problem wasn't going to disappear all by itself.

Chapter 9 — A Trap is Set

Danny landed the S-55 at Ban Bat in a swirling flourish that woke everyone and brought them running to meet the vociferous monster. He couldn't hide his excitement. His pal Long Li was safe and well against all odds.

'I can't believe you got away,' Danny marvelled.

'No sweat. Remember I dodged the Japs for a couple of years, didn't I? Do you think a pack of amateurs like the Viet Minh are going to be any trouble?'

Danny eyed him uncertainly.

'Tell that to the French Union blokes at GONO.'

The majors, who didn't appear to sleep very often, had already devised a plan and were now making preparations. By the time Monty arrived everything was well under way. As the scheme required considerable logistic support, most of the villagers were involved in one way or another.

Therefore, the reunion with Long Li was necessarily brief, but he filled Danny in broad-brush style.

After Danny had been evacuated from Dien Bien Phu, Long Li had slipped into the bush and worked his way westwards before veering south through Vietnam and into Laos. He knew Communist patrols were looking for survivors straggling eastwards, trying to make it to Hanoi. All those were either captured or killed. Using his jungle skill, Long Li avoided Viet Minh patrols, bandits and wild animals. He took shelter in friendly villages when he came across them, working for his keep for a week or two before moving on. In that way he weaved his way through Laos knowing that once he reached the Mekong, he could cadge a lift all the way to Saigon and back to Singapore.

Some local farmers had pointed him in the direction of Ban Bat, but he'd missed his mark and wound up further downriver. He heard the chopper land, but was too late to catch up with Danny, Monty and the majors as they headed up stream. So, waiting in the chopper was the best option. To his delight he found charts and a navigation bag bearing Danny's name along with the latest James Bond adventure. Long Li knew Ian Fleming was one of Danny's favourite authors which was more evidence to support the fact that Danny was the pilot.

He knew Danny would be back before long and when he heard the tiger he was glad he'd made that particular decision.

But the rest of Long Li's story would have to wait. Right then there was work to be done.

Men ranged deep into the rainforest to cut vines. Another gang armed with spades and picks headed to a small clearing several hundred yards from the village and began digging a deep pit. They toiled all day until their backs literally flooded with sweat.

The majors needed some heavy weights as part of their plan, but large rocks were in short supply. So they organised a group of women to rapidly weave palm-frond sacks which were stuffed with coconut shells filled with saturated mud from the riverbank. Monty was in charge of the work detail, but was uncertain about the result.

'You know those bags ain't gonna hold that weight for long,' Monty observed.

'We only have to use 'em once,' Major White replied, hefting one of the sacks and nodding with satisfaction. 'They'll do fine.'

He then disappeared into the hut where the heroin was stored and stayed there for hours. Some suspiciously evil smells wafted from the hut all day, but when Major White reappeared he seemed well pleased with himself.

Kekio and Long Li, along with dozens of villagers, were put to use chopping long bamboo poles and weaving heavy rattan ropes. Long Li was particularly good at using natural materials and gave instructions with Kekio's help.

The hustle and bustle lasted all day while Major Black took several guides inland towards Dahm Daw's lair. He wanted to check that the drug gang wasn't heading back to Ban Bat. Leaving several scouts to keep an eye on Dahm Daw's movements, the patrol returned at nightfall to report they'd reached within a hundred yards of the temple and it appeared to be business as usual there. They'd heard distant gunfire, but couldn't make anything of it. Maybe the drug-thugs were driving off enemies or discouraging escaping slave-labourers who were slogging it out in the poppy fields.

'Did you see how many bad guys we're dealing with?' Danny asked.

'Hard to tell, but my guides reckon there are at least forty or so.'

'Oh, well that's no problem then. Odds of ten-to-one, a piece of cake.'

The majors showed no sign of being fazed by the odds. Being out-numbered was a normal day at the office for them. It was the sort of challenge they relished.

'Yeah, but we've got technology on our side. You still got plenty of fuel in that chopper, Danny?' Major Black inquired cheerfully

'Yep, no problem.'

'And don't forget our secret weapon.'

'We don't have a secret weapon,' Danny insisted.

'Not yet,' Major Black said with a wink.

The majors were insufferable. They were working on the narrowest of margins and there were more 'ifs' in their plan than actual certainties. It was almost as if the majors wanted the odds stacked against them to make the challenge worthwhile. In Danny's opinion there were no certainties in the plan at all, but he pitched in enthusiastically, because it was in his nature.

Monty was as sanguine as ever.

'Heck Danny, we've been in tougher spots than this,' he said cheerfully. 'And it's not as if you had anything else planned for today anyway.'

'A cool swim in the river, followed by a massage, a cold beer and a hot curry,' spring to mind,' Danny replied.

'You can't swim in the river, the crocs will eat you.'

Danny was going to mention he'd seen the local kids splashing about and having a great time. The crocs didn't seem to bother them. But he merely shrugged and went back to work.

By evening everything was ready. Danny got part of his wish. He cooled off in the river before Kekio organised food for everyone. She especially paid attention to Long Li to whom she'd taken an instant fancy. The Singaporean didn't mind the attention either. The pair chatted and laughed together like old chums. Danny would have liked to monopolise Long Li's company and catch up, but he figured there'd be plenty of time for that later. Danny wasn't really the jealous type except perhaps when it came to Angela, but as they'd spent more time apart than together, that particular emotion probably hadn't had time to develop either.

As darkness fell the waiting game began.

At first the delay was tedious, but Danny must have nodded off after a while. Around midnight, he was awakened as the night erupted into bedlam and the majors' plan sprang into action.

*

A goat was tethered to a post in the clearing close to Ban Bat and initially was content to munch on anything that came within range. Soon it had cropped the grass and vegetation in a four yard diameter around the post. However the goat grew more nervous throughout the night. Soon it was bleating pitifully.

And with good reason, the tiger was edging closer to the clearing. The predator smelt the fear of its prey. Of course the tiger didn't know the goat was incapable of escaping, so stealth was still needed although it couldn't resist a purring growl in anticipation.

The tiger reached the clearing edge and stopped. Its every sense was alert. Even the jungle's alpha-predator wasn't blasé to danger. The beast's night-vision eyes easily identified the goat, which grew more agitated by the second. The goat obviously sensed the tiger's presence, yet still failed to bolt for safety. The tiger didn't make any connection now it was totally focused on its prey. Two rough palm frond fences formed a pathway leading to the goat, leaving the tiger only one line of approach. What did it care? One way in was enough and there was nowhere for the goat to run.

With a horrendous roar the tiger pounced, landing only a yard from the goat, now frozen in fear. To the predator's dismay the grass below its feet gave way and it plunged right through the earth's surface. It howled and clawed at the edges of the pit, but was unable to hold on. Its claws raked the earth as it slid onto a bamboo grid at the base of the pit. The opening was large enough for the tiger to fall cleanly, but gave little room for the animal to struggle free.

Moments later the scent of man filled the tiger's flared nostrils. It snarled menacingly as the villagers peeked nervously over the pit. The tiger tried to crouch and leap from the trap, but could not move sufficiently. The staring villagers all breathed a sigh of relief when they saw the tiger was securely trapped.

A group of men and women grabbed the giant net they'd been building all day and tossed it over the tiger. The mud-filled sacks weighted the net down, holding it firmly over the struggling tiger preventing it from swinging its claws or snapping its teeth.

And then both majors moved in. With no weapon other than three syringes each and a rope around their waists, they leapt into the pit, landing squarely on the tiger's back. The animal writhed and protested, but the net held it securely. With slick speed the majors plunged the first two syringes and ejected the full contents of cloudy grey liquid into the tiger's rump. With seemingly practised ease they tossed the syringes aside, took another and once again injected the tiger. They repeated the process with all six syringes.

'OK!' Major White called, 'Bring us up!'

A team of villagers holding the rope-end hauled the majors from the pit.

'It shouldn't take long,' he said. 'We stuck half-a-dozen doses of grade four heroin into the big cat's ass. Hopefully that'll settle him down. Good quality stuff too. I spent all day brewing it myself.'

'Is there no end to your talents?' Danny sighed. 'But of course you have no idea how much dope it takes to neutralise a tiger, do you?'

'True, but you gotta use your intuition at times like this.'

'We've got extra syringes if we need 'em,' Major Black added.

However no more heroin was required. In moments the tiger's roars diminished to what could only be described as a contented purr. Shortly after that Danny was sure he heard the beast snoring.

'Time to cage the bugger,' Major White announced.

The villagers were reluctant to drop into the pit, but the majors merely shrugged and jumped back down.

'Right, let's have the ropes,' Major Black called.

On command, the villagers lowered eight ropes into the pit. The majors tied the ropes to the bamboo grid on which the sleeping tiger lay.

'I hope we haven't *O-Deed* him,' Major Black said.

'Hell, no. He must weigh four hundred pounds. It'll take a jerry-can full of dope to knock him out permanently,' Major White replied, although what gave him the authority to make that judgement was unclear.

Then came the tricky part and Danny, Long Li and Monty squeezed into the pit to lend a hand. All the men were armed with hunting knifes or bayonets, not for protection, but to slash the weighted bags free from the net. Once the extra weight was removed Danny, the majors et al scrambled from the pit. They helped the villagers man the ropes and slowly raise the grid, tiger and all. It reminded Danny of a coffin being lowered into a grave, only in reverse.

Once the tiger reached surface level another team led by Kekio placed long bamboo poles under the grid. This was a tedious process because the poles had to be lodged one at a time. Several men dropped into the pit, forcing poles below the grid and the tiger's weight made this no easy task. Once that job was done, everyone pitched in to push the grid from the pit until it rested on firm ground.

The next job was to lower a cage over the tiger and secure it to the base. This was the most critical piece of equipment, which had to be tough enough to withstand the tiger's rage. The cage builders had judged the dimensions well, giving the tiger very little room to move. The more confined it was, the less likely it would be able to do any damage with its giant paws.

Once the cage was in place Major White scrambled over the tiger's back and removed the net, which despite losing its tie-down weights was still heavy and cumbersome. Danny was amazed how nonchalantly the majors moved around the tiger. Other than a few grumbles the tiger made no other protest or appear threatening in any way. Once the tiger was free of the net, Major Black lowered the trap door at the one end of the cage, securing it with a locking pin. The tiger was now neatly confined inside.

'Right,' Major Black said, 'that's the easy bit done. Now let's see what happens when this bad boy wakes up.'

Everyone relaxed now that the tiger was truly caged and by all appearances in a benign frame of mind. The goat thought it'd had a lucky escape, but what it didn't know was that the villagers were planning a curry feast to celebrate the night's work.

Unfortunately that would have to wait as the majors' timeline was thrown into disarray.

Major Black's scout hustled back into Ban Bat, just after the tiger had been caught. They had bad news. Dahm Daw's men had indeed been shooing rivals off their patch, hoping to wipe out an entire neighbouring gang, steal their heroin stash, and to bring it to Ban Bat in the morning.

'That's not part of the plan,' Danny complained.

'Maybe not,' Major White said, 'but like I said, we gotta be flexible. This has just narrowed our window of opportunity a mite, is all, so we'd better get the lead out.'

'OK, I'll get the chopper ready. It's a pity we can't take everyone with us, but we'll be lucky with just you guys, Long Li and Monty with the extra load. Maybe we can fit an extra couple in.'

But when it came to local volunteers for the task ahead, the villagers had returned to peasant-mode and were reluctant to the point of downright stubbornness. Now the euphoria of tiger-hunting had waned, no one was inclined to put themselves in danger again.

Kekio was outraged.

'They are your families Dahm Daw's holding captive. Don't you want to help them escape?'

A few uncertain nods acknowledged her point, but no commitment followed. They could always hide in the forest until the drug gang headed down-river with the dope.

'The problem won't go away by hiding,' Kekio insisted.

There was still no response other than sheepish looks and shuffling feet.

Kekio gave up with an exasperated sigh.

'I'm coming with you,' she announced to Long Li.

'Danny isn't going to like it,' Long Li replied.

'We're not going to tell him, are we?' she said slyly. 'He won't see me slip aboard when he's at the controls. Now show me how to work that little rifle-gun,' she added indicating one of the M-1 carbines.

'OK,' Long Li conceded with a shrug. He knew when it was pointless to argue with a woman. 'You know you remind me of another girl I know, but she's a bit younger.'

'You think I'm old crone.'

'No, of course not. You're a little corker.'

'I look like bottle stop?'

'No. It's an Aussie expression. I've been hanging around Danny too long. But it's not a bad thing. It's a really good thing.'

'OK,' Kekio said with her most engaging smile. 'A "corker" I do not mind when you say it is good thing.'

Chapter 10 — Temple of Dreams

Predawn, just moments before sunup and things would be stirring in at Dahm Daw's hideout. The slave labourers were still asleep. They'd developed a habit of treasuring every precious moment of blessed slumber before being jarred awake by yelling guards who were over-fond of using their rifle butts as encouragement. The captives would hardly be given sufficient time to splash water on their faces and gulp a cold meal of rice and tea before being herded at gunpoint to the poppy fields.

A lone patrolman guarded the hideout. Dahm Daw saw no reason to bother with more sentries. No one dared to escape. He knew where they lived and, more importantly, he knew where their families lived. The rest of the gang snored inside the temple in their usual state of opium-induced semi-consciousness.

But it wasn't the guards who woke the labourers that morning. Initially no one really noticed the soft chug-chug in the background of the jungle morning chorus. Monkeys, parrots and other birds all added to the day's overture. The chug-chug slowly grew in intensity until it became a thundering roar that scared the labourers witless as they leapt from their sleeping mats. The night fauna's chorus increased to frenetic volume as every bird and beast fled the oncoming monster. Then a brilliant white light blazed into the clearing, illuminating the entire area in front of the ruined temple.

Not only was the noise deafening, but a swirling gale swept through the camp, flattening most of the shanties and scattering debris in every direction. Danny brought the S-55 to a hover right above the centre of the clearing. Jungle foliage swayed dramatically as leaves were wrenched from their branches. Dust, twigs and other light material all added to the maelstrom that now consumed the camp.

A cage descended into the midst of that confusion. None of the labourers noticed the cage held a tiger, which was probably just as well as they were already quaking with dread. Another threat might have caused them to drop dead in fright.

Major White stood on top of the cage, hanging onto the cable attached to the chopper's under-fuselage. He waved directions to Long Li who'd resumed his duties as Danny's crewman. Long Li in turn relayed instructions to Danny. From his precarious position Major White also identified the sentry, who'd frozen in stunned fear, and dropped him in a short burst of lead.

'Forward ten feet...' Long Li called over the intercom. '...Yep, that's it...Steady...Steady...Take her right five feet...Hold your height for the moment...Ease her forward...'

Major White, who seemed to enjoy dangling from the bottom of helicopters, had ridden on top the cage from Ban Bat. The pendulous cage had slowed Danny's progress. Nevertheless they had enough time to reach their target just as streaks of sunlight laced over the horizon, giving enough light for Danny to detect the temple's pagoda-style silhouette. As he edged the chopper closer to the temple spire, Danny worried that the main rotor might clip part of the building or the jungle that partially engulfed it. Long Li and Major White's attention was focused on simply placing the cage as close as possible to the pagoda's front entrance.

'That's it,' Danny finally announced. 'Sorry boys, I can't get any closer. The main rotor's already shredding leaves off the trees.'

'It'll do,' Long Li reported. 'Major White's giving the "thumbs-up". Take her down slowly, Danny...Slowly...'

Danny lowered the collective pitch lever and the S-55 gradually sank earthwards.

'Spot on,' Long Li said as the cage gently nudged onto the ground.

Major White quickly unhooked the retaining straps that held the cage to the chopper's under-fuselage cable. Once the load was released Danny eased the chopper backwards, giving himself space to land the aircraft. The clearing was small, but there was just enough rotor clearance to put the chopper down. As soon as the wheels touched solid ground, Monty, Long Li, Kekio and Major Black leapt from the door with their weapons at the ready.

Danny shut down the engine and followed them.

Meanwhile Major White raised the cage door and tossed it aside. The tiger was awake, but disinclined to move. The animal felt content to rub up against the bar as if relieving some irritating itchiness.

'Come on, you dumb feline,' Major White urged. 'Get out and go scare the living b'Jesus out of those bastards in there.'

The tiger merely eyed him with indifference.

'What's the problem?' Monty said.

'It's still doped to the eyeballs. I think it's actually smiling,' Major White replied.

'What did you expect? You gave it enough to sink a battleship.'

'That's a mixed metaphor, isn't it?'

'Whatever.'

Monty pulled his hunting knife from its scabbard and jabbed the tiger's rump and that did receive a reaction. The tiger didn't actually roar, but gave a malevolent growl, before lurching out of its cage. It hadn't reached bounding potential yet, but rather ambled into the temple. Even when ambling, the tiger still possessed a flowing, sinister grace.

'It looks a bit shaky to me,' Monty said.

'Those buggers in there don't know that,' Major White replied.

By then 'those buggers' inside had scrambled to life. They were still mostly bleary eyed and recovering from a hard night of substance abuse. The noise from the arriving chopper should have been enough to rouse them, but the temple was solidly built of stone that acted as an insulating barrier.

The bandits soon became aware enough to know that a tiger was prowling into their accommodation. Access to the temple was via a narrow passageway that led to a small chamber. The main feature within was an altar where a large somewhat jaded Buddha statue sat in corpulent decline.

As the tiger strolled towards the Buddha, the gang members dashed for cover behind pillars or squeezed against the wall, hoping to become invisible. Whether that was the case didn't really matter because the tiger simply passed apathetically. Those who could bolted for the entrance, only to be waylaid by Monty, Long Li and the majors.

Most of the gangsters had left their weapons behind in their haste to escape. Those who put up any resistance were quickly subdued with a rifle butt slammed into their teeth.

It was only when Danny jumped from the chopper that he discovered Kekio had stowed away. He just glared at Monty and Long Li, shaking his head. His two friends merely shrugged and grinned sheepishly.

'Go and check out the hostages, Kekio,' Danny ordered, thinking it would take her further from any potential danger. She didn't complain, but simply gave a brief nod and obeyed.

What puzzled the majors was the fact that there were only half a dozen gang members huddled in a forlorn group at the temple steps. They eyed the temple entrance nervously while Long Li tried to interrogate them.

'What are we gonna do about the tiger?' Danny asked.

'Go and check on it, I guess,' Major Black said cheerfully.

The thought of entering a confined space with a man-eating mega-cat didn't appeal to Danny, but didn't appear to bother the majors at all. Leaving Long Li to guard the prisoners, Major Black and Major White cautiously entered the temple entrance passage with their carbines at the ready. Danny and Monty followed although they had no idea what they'd do when they came face-to-face with the tiger.

The temple's main chamber was dimly lit with kerosene lanterns and candles, but the majors' eyes had already adjusted in the pre-dawn darkness. The place was littered with human bric-a-brac. Sleeping mats were scattered across the floor and on ledges around the temple walls. Cooking pots and rice bowls were stacked here and there although it looked as if the actual food preparation was done outside. A rank smell of opium fumes, cigarette smoke, stale sweat and unsanitary humanity filled the chamber. A large area was set aside for a long bench which was stacked with chemicals and equipment for heroin processing.

The tiger crouched a foot or two in front of Buddha's statue. A lone gang member stood petrified against the altar, pinned between it and the tiger. Actually 'petrified' was the wrong word to describe the gangster. He trembled uncontrollably and voided his bladder as the tiger eyed him inquisitively.

The smell of urine interested the tiger. Just as Danny and Monty crept into the altar chamber, the tiger stretched its head forward and sniffed the gangster. Its tongue slobbered from between its teeth and the cat began to lick the gangster from head to foot.

'Ugh, that's just gross,' Danny muttered.

'Keep the cat covered,' Major White whispered.

He inched forward until he was beside the tiger which ignored him. Major White grabbed the gangster by the scruff of the neck and slowly pulled him aside, before leading him to the entrance. The tiger mumbled a sinister growl, turned and followed.

The tiger padded past the other men in the tunnel without a sideward glance. As they reached the entrance, Major White dragged the gangster around the cage, pressing him against the bamboo bars. Following the bait, the tiger simply re-entered the cage. Bringing up the rear, Major Black slammed cage-door shut before the tiger realised its mistake.

The tiger gave no indication of distress at being trapped once more. After licking the gangster through the bars, it lost interest, laid down and promptly fell asleep.

'Some secret weapon,' Danny said.

'It worked, didn't it?' Major White insisted defensively.

'To a point,' Long Li said as he left the prisoners in Monty's 'care'.

'Whadda ya mean?'

'Was there anyone else inside?'

'Nope, not unless there's a secret passage or room.'

'We have seven men here,' Long Li sighed.

'Oh shit.'

'Precisely.'

By then Kekio had released the forced labourers. Her family was among the very relieved group.

'Everyone accounted for,' she reported, giving the majors a salute.

'The prisoners maybe,' Major Black said. 'But where are the rest of the gang? Where is Dahm Daw?'

None of the villagers knew the answer. They explained that normally half the gang guarded the fields at night to discourage poppy poachers, but right then only a skeleton-crew remained at the temple.

The prisoners also proved unhelpful. They claimed they knew nothing of Dahm Daw or the other gang member's whereabouts. It was almost if they felt it was safer to feign ignorance. There may have been some wisdom in that tactic, but the majors thought it was time for an attitude adjustment.

Major White nodded to Long Li who arbitrarily selected one of the sullen gangsters.

'He'll do,' Major White said. 'Ask him where his pals are, Kekio.'

A babble of vitriol followed. The prisoner spat at Major White, but refused to give up any information.

'Open the cage,' Major White said to which Major Black complied.

The prisoner struggled, but was no match for Major White who shoved him into the cage. It was a tight squeeze, made even tighter when Major Black slammed the entrance shut.

'Tell him I dunno when the tiger will wake up, but it'll be climbing down from a gigantic case of withdrawal,' Major White said. 'That tiger's gonna be mean as a snake by then.'

Instantly frantic babbling issued from the cage.

'He ready to talk, Major,' Kekio announced.

So they retrieved the prisoner just as the tiger was stirring. The gangster's colleagues all started yelling at him at once. Obviously they thought he should keep his mouth shut, but they weren't the ones who'd been in the tiger's cage, were they? Major Black heaved a pained sigh, aimed his .45 automatic at the group and put a bullet through a random knee-cap.

The victim screamed and writhed in agony until Major Black shot him in the forehead. No one protested after that and information was forthcoming.

What the prisoner said wasn't quite the same as Major Black's scouts had reported either. Dahm Daw had indeed led the majority of his gang against another bunch of cut-throats who planned to muscle into his territory. They had taken the Jeep, most of the weapons and ammunition. But Dahm Daw hadn't annihilated the rival gang and stolen its stash of dope as he'd threatened to. They'd made a deal to combine forces with Dahm Daw in top-dog status. Now the gang's manpower had increased by an unknown number of men.

Dahm Daw had been away all that time brokering the deal. He'd taken the majority of his henchmen for backup and to see that negotiations went the way he intended.

'So what are we going to do about it?' Major White asked somewhat rhetorically because he always managed to dream up a plan.

'Two choices, I guess,' Monty ventured. 'Fight or flight. We either defend or evacuate Ban Bat.'

'There is a third choice,' Major Black said, 'but if it fails there's no plan *B*.'

*

Dahm Daw was pretty full of himself. He'd just pulled off a significant coup against a bunch of bandits who'd been a flea in his ear for some time. Not that it been particularly difficult, it was just a matter of being decisive. When the gangs met, Dahm Daw had simply drawn his Japanese Model 14 Nambu 8mm automatic pistol and shot the rival leader through the heart. No one was expecting that, were they?

While his opponents stood open-jawed, Dahm Daw's men got the drop on them. There was something about staring down the business end of massed AK-47s that was quite persuasive. Changing sides was not only pragmatic, but business-as-usual for the bandits who weren't the brightest individuals and only functioned well under stern leadership.

Right then Dahm Daw rode in his Jeep back to the temple at the head of his gang, now fifty strong. He'd also acquired fifty kilos of grade four heroin that his rivals had planned to transport down the Mekong to Saigon where they had a buyer waiting. The operation had all been too easy in Dahm Daw's opinion, but that was the way he liked it.

His Jeep chugged some distance ahead of the main column. There appeared to be no friction between his original crew and the new recruits. That wasn't surprising as they were all ignorant peasants without the ability for any original thought whatsoever.

Dahm Daw always felt a sense of wellbeing when he left the open poppy field and entered the narrow jungle trail. Open spaces bothered him, especially in broad daylight and it was now mid-morning. The security of a rainforest canopy reassured him. Certainly he had his team of thugs around him, but he often wondered whether the RLAF and police would ever become organised enough to land a helicopter flight of troops nearby. A cramped jungle scrap was one thing, but an all-out battle in open terrain was quite another.

So as the shadows enfolded his Jeep, he relaxed, contemplating a river trip to Vientiane or maybe even Saigon if he sensed the heroin market was right. The Jeep was now well ahead of the foot-slogging gang who trailed single-file along the jungle track. Dahm Daw was ready for breakfast and chivvied his driver to get a move on. The Jeep exhaust coughed as the driver floored the accelerator, but the ill-maintained machine was restricted by mechanical asthma and the track's condition.

About then a niggling, uneasy feeling prickled the hairs on the back of Dahm Daw's neck. Where was everybody? The peasants should be at work by now, but the poppy fields were deserted. Dahm Daw had been so smug he'd failed to pay attention, which was not a good thing for an outlaw. Not only were the fields empty, but they'd met no one along the forest track. Something was wrong ...

And then he heard the first grenade explode.

Chapter 11 — Vengeance Trail

Like most of Major Black and Major White's plans, the one they cooked up to foil Dahm Daw was spontaneous, roughly sketched, hazardous, flawed in detail and considered contingencies *and* fraught with any danger. Just as the majors liked it.

This time when Kekio was asked if they could count on the captives for support, she said they'd already agreed to. Major Black divided the Laotians into four roughly equal groups to be led by Monty, Major White, Long Li and himself. There were about twenty-five people in each group. They armed themselves with the gangsters' guns, machetes, knives and clubs. Danny had to admit they'd been transformed from timid vassals to a fighting force to be reckoned with.

Nothing like a little harsh treatment to put you in a shit-faced mood, eh?

The majors exchanged their carbines for Tommy-guns, giving the single-shot weapons to those they thought most capable of using them effectively. The majors also bristled with hand grenades clipped to their jungle fatigue belts.

As no one knew precisely when Dahm Daw would return the war-party took food and water with them, leaving Danny and

Kekio to deal with the remaining gang members. Kekio protested that she should go with her parents (actually she wanted to go with Long Li), but Danny assured her that she would have an equally vital task.

Once armed and provisioned, the four platoons set off along the jungle path towards the poppy fields. They planned to get as close to the jungle edge as possible. How far that was depended on when Dahm Daw returned.

In the meantime, while Danny covered the gang members, Kekio bound their hands behind them, trussed their ankles and drew the ropes tight so their spines arched backwards and their hands almost reached their feet. It was an excruciatingly uncomfortable position and virtually escape-proof.

'Where did you learn to do that?' Danny asked.

'From the Viet Minh during the French war.'

'OK, I don't reckon they're going anywhere. You are right for this, aren't you? It's going to be risky.'

'I right for this,' she replied earnestly. 'I do my duty.'

'Good for you. Let's get this cage hooked up to the chopper then. We'll have to be quick when the action starts.'

Once the tiger's cage was secured Danny carried out the chopper's pre-flight checks ready to start the engine in seconds. He sent Kekio along the forest path to keep a lookout.

'Don't go too far. Only a few yards — metres — You have to be able to get back here quickly.'

Then Danny waited. Initially the bound bandits wriggled and cursed, but as their discomfort increased and several of them wet themselves, their protests were reduced to whimpering moans. They cried out pitifully. Danny assumed they wanted water, but he had no time for distractions, they'd just have to wait.

Kekio squatted at the edge of the path and waited patiently. After nearly two hours she heard the distant explosive popping of grenade and small arms fire. She sprinted back to the temple. Danny had also heard the explosions and was already starting the chopper's engine. The chopper's fuselage door was pinned open, but Kekio didn't jump aboard. Instead she scrambled onto the cage roof just as Major White had done earlier.

She knew Danny had seen her arrive. He'd given her a 'thumbs-up' sign from the cockpit window. Now all she had to do was hang on tight with one hand while clutching her M-1 carbine in the other as the chopper inched skywards. The cable drew taut and lifted the cage to just above the jungle canopy. This was left to Danny's judgement, because without a crewman at the chopper's side door he had no way of communicating with Kekio. He made a fine job of it with the cage only occasionally brushing the treetops. Danny had estimated his height on the flight from Ban Bat and he was usually good at that sort of flying anyway.

Danny turned the chopper north and flew towards the poppy fields.

*

All students of military history should know that a bottle-neck can spell either success or disaster in a battle depending how it is managed. At Thermopylae in 480 BC and the Alamo in March 1836 a small number of determined defenders held a small area, killing large numbers of the vast forces opposing them. In truth the outcome wasn't totally rewarding for those out-numbered heroes as they were eventually overwhelmed and slaughtered, but not after inflicting huge casualties.

The Battle of Agincourt in 1415 was an even greater success when King Henry V's puny army defeated the far superior French horde by luring a mass of heavily armoured knights into a narrow field that turned into a quagmire under the weight of their chargers' hooves. Seven thousand stout English longbow men had a lot to do with it as well.

The point was that the majors understood the narrow forest path could turn into an efficient killing ground if handled properly. The majors wanted to deploy their people as close to the poppy fields as possible. Fortunately they reached the path end before Dahm Daw arrived, but they spotted his gang in the distance.

The majors quickly hustled everyone back along the forest track. This caused some confusion as the people behind bumped into those retreating from the fields.

'OK,' Major White called. 'My people stop here.'

Long Li had picked up enough of the local dialect, and with the help of his rudimentary French he was able to act as interpreter.

Major White's people melted into the jungle on the right side of the path. Monty's group moved a few yards further back towards the temple before taking cover on the left. Long Li led his team just past Monty's and gestured for them to hide to the right. Finally Major Black called a halt several yards further on where his people disappeared to the left. The trap was set and ready to spring into action.

The villagers were now strung out over more than one hundred yards with no verbal communications, but the majors explained that the signals would be very clear indeed. It was a matter of everyone holding their nerve, which was a big ask as the gang approached the path entrance.

They were a vicious looking bunch and certainly out-gunned the villagers. As the forest canopy cast its shadow, the gangsters needed a few moments to adjust their eye-sight. In that initial gloom they had no idea that the villagers lurked just feet away.

It was about then that Dahm Daw first became anxious, although he didn't have much time to think about it. As soon as the last gang member trudged past Major White he pulled the pin from one of his grenades. There was a slight click as the arming mechanism sprang open. Major White stepped onto the path and lobbed the grenade at the feet of the trailing gangster. The major dived for cover just as the bomb exploded, blowing the gangsters legs from under him. Shrapnel sprayed to more villains as more grenades pitched into their ranks.

The majors, Monty and Long Li each tossed four grenades into the bandits' line in quick succession, decimating them in seconds. The majors insisted that was all the grenades they'd use to avoid injury during the next phase of the attack.

Major White stepped onto the path and sprayed it with a short Tommy-gun burst. Major Black followed at the front of the line and blasted several bandits as they milled around in confusion. Monty was next and then Long Li. In this way they had riddled the enemy with red-hot lead without risking shooting each other in the cross fire.

Then it was time for the villagers to strike, which they did with attitude. They fell onto the surviving drug-gangsters with knives and machetes, making short work of anyone left standing – and several who weren't. The gang was caught in total disarray. The element of surprise was complete. Half a dozen of the trailing bandits made a bolt for safety during a brief pause while Major White replaced his Tommy-gun's magazine.

They raced to the end of the path only to be met by the tiger which was now wide awake and probably nursing a gigantic migraine. Whatever its physical state, the tiger was in a foul mood and went about proving it. With a roar it pounced and ripped the leading bandit to shreds with its fore paws before driving its teeth into its next victim. After mauling a third bandit, the tiger, having had enough of the bellowing and gunfire of battle, bounded from the path and vanished into the jungle.

*

Amid the clamour of exploding grenades, small-arms fire and screaming humanity, no one had heard Danny's S-55 roar overhead. He positioned the chopper at the pathway entrance before lowering the cage to the ground. He sensed when it touched as the engine suddenly required less power to hover the aircraft now the extra weight had been removed.

Then came the risky part for Kekio. Her job was to release the tiger and there was no guarantee how it would behave. As they flew from the temple, she noticed that the tiger was indeed recovering. It was very much awake and extremely agitated when they touched down.

Without a second thought, she yanked the cage door open and held her breath. Fortunately the tiger was not only disorientated, but spooked by the rotor's downwash. An eighty-mile-an-hour wind accompanied by the engine's racket was an extraordinary and startling experience. The tiger simply wanted to get as far away as possible from it all. It took the line of least resistance and raced along the pathway towards those fleeing gang members who'd escaped the carnage along the path.

As soon as the tiger was free, Kekio released the cable that connected the cage to the chopper. This enabled Danny to land without the risk of toppling the cage on its side. Not that that really mattered now the tiger was gone, but Danny was unsure whether Kekio was still perched on top of the cage.

Danny left the engine running in case he needed to make a quick getaway, but that proved unnecessary. Only four bandits reached the poppy fields. They emerged just yards from Kekio. Without hesitation, she fired her M-1 carbine, killing the leading bandit with her first shot. She fired again, winged another in the shoulder.

She thought the other two might surrender, but that wasn't the case. They both raised their AK-47 assault rifles and Kekio knew she had no chance of getting them both before they shot her.

Above the S-55 engine she heard two sharp cracks and the two bandits crumpled lifelessly to earth. She spun around to see Danny at the chopper door with his Colt 1911 army pistol held shoulder high at full arms length. The barrel was still smoking.

'Good job,' Danny yelled and Kekio smiled back, feeling pretty pleased with herself.

'Where's the tiger?' he added.

'Down path. Gone.'

They waited for a moment and as no more fugitives appeared Danny decided to save fuel and shut down the chopper's engine.

'I guess we'd better go and see what's happened,' Danny suggested.

'Major White say stay put,' Kekio reminded him.

'Aren't you even a little bit curious? I mean it's all quiet now.'

'What about tiger?'

'It'll be long gone by now. Wild animals don't like hanging around when humans are making a racket.'

'Why tiger frightened of tennis bat?'

'No, Kekio. A noise.'

She eyed him with a puzzled expression.

'English puzzlement,' she sighed. 'I mainly interpreter French. Only little English I know.'

'Don't worry, you're doing fine. My French is pretty ropey. I keep putting the adjectives in the wrong order.'

At that point they saw a movement in the shadows at the path entrance. Danny and Kekio aimed their weapons.

'Don't shoot, it's me,' Major White shouted. 'It's OK, the show's over.'

Danny and Kekio followed Major White back along the path, which was now littered with dead outlaws. The villagers had come off pretty well, with no one dead and only a few minor wounds. They now armed themselves with captured AK-47s. Surprise and determination had won the day.

Danny and Kekio ran into Monty and Long Li who'd done the lion's share of killing. There was no substitute for experience. About ten bandits survived and were herded into a cluster by some bellicose villages who were disinclined to show any mercy. However when they reached Major Black's position, he wasn't quite as satisfied with the outcome as the others.

'Dahm Daw got away in the Jeep,' he reported. 'He was just too far ahead for me to hit him with a grenade.'

'We'd better get after him then,' Major White said evenly, showing no indication of his disappointment.

'Do you want me to look for him in the chopper?' Danny asked.

'It'll be difficult to spot him under the jungle canopy. You'll just waste fuel if you don't know which way he went.'

'He'll head for the river surely,' Danny said.

'Possibly, but he may cut back to the hills.'

'How about you take Monty, Kekio and Long Li back to Ban Bat. They'll need some fire-power if he shows up there,' Major Black suggested. 'We'll head for the temple and see if we can pick up his trail. The Jeep should be easy to follow. If Dahm Daw abandons the vehicle and goes bush then flushing him out will be a bitch.'

So while the majors and villagers made their way to the temple, Danny's group returned to the chopper and flew back to the Mekong. When they landed the usual welcoming committee was noticeably absent. In fact the village was deserted.

Danny cut the engine as Monty and Long Li jumped from the fuselage door with their guns ready. The village was eerily silent other than clucking, quacking ducks and chickens and grunting pigs. The local livestock seemed to have quickly forgotten the tiger and scratched around the village as normal.

Where the blue blazes is everyone?

'Do you reckon they all decided to hide out until the trouble is over?' Monty asked.

'Seems likely,' Danny said. 'They were pretty frightened of Dahm Daw's crowd.'

'Or didn't have much confidence in us,' Long Li said cynically.

'What do we do now?' Kekio asked.

'Wait, I guess,' Monty said. 'Maybe we can rustle up some grub. I'm starving.'

Dahm Daw didn't have time to worry about the disastrous ambush. He was unaware whether his gang had been destroyed or not. All he knew was that he had the getaway vehicle and the drugs. His men were eminently dispensable. He could recruit more low-life at any time. Right now his priority was to gather any refined dope from the temple and take it down-river to Vientiane.

It was a shame about the stash at Ban Bat, but caution told Dahm Daw to let that go. Whoever had attacked his gang may have set a trap for him at the village as well. He realised it was time to cut his losses for a while. His two remaining lackeys were also expendable and Dahm Daw had no intention of sharing his reduced profit with anyone. He'd take care of his henchmen once they'd served their purpose.

When they reached the temple clearing nothing stirred. That was odd. There was no sound from the jungle. No birds, no monkeys – nothing. Whatever. He shrugged and ordered his men to grab the entire heroin stash from the temple and place it in the Jeep.

The two men moved to obey when Dahm Daw heard a whooshing noise through the still jungle air. Both his men stood rigid for a second before sinking to the ground. They were both riddled with crossbow bolts.

Dahm Daw stared in horror because right then he also noticed the guards he'd left at the temple lying hog-tied in a group. They too had been impaled by darts and were all dead. It was then that Dahm Daw wished he'd learnt to drive the Jeep, but he'd always had someone else to do that. Leaders weren't chauffeurs, were they?

Nevertheless he shunted over to the driver's seat and pressed the starter button. Unfortunately the Jeep was in gear and only jolted forward once before the engine stalled. Then figures moved ominously from the jungle and temple. Dahm Daw estimated there were around fifty people surrounding him. They were armed with primitive but effective weapons. At least a dozen crossbows covered him.

Dahm Daw now trembled in terror as the crowd of men and women closed in. He reached for his pistol and took aim, but before he could fire a shadow flashed from behind him as a machete sliced his hand from his wrist.

After Danny's chopper flew away with the tiger, it seemed the good people of Ban Bat had regained their courage and dignity. After reflecting that Ban Bat was *their* village and it was up to *them* to protect it, they'd quickly armed themselves and headed towards the temple and now they'd exacted their revenge.

Part 2 — Stateside

Chapter 12 — The French Connection

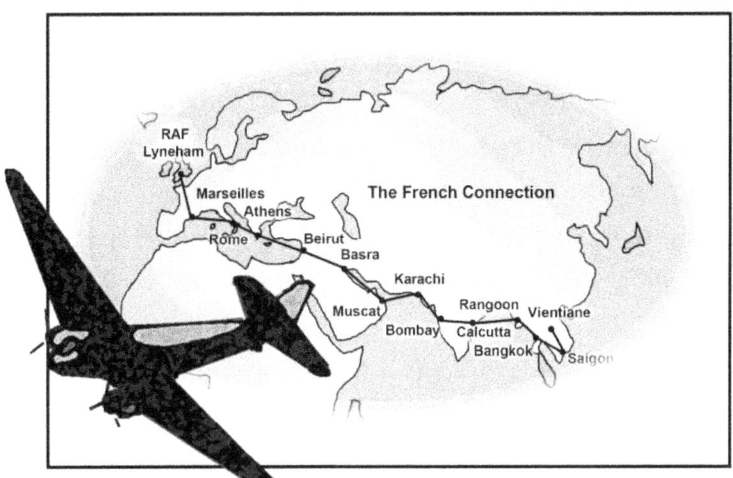

The majors arrived at Ban Bat in late afternoon along with the villagers and their few remaining prisoners. Dahm Daw's stump was bound and Major White had administered a hefty dose of anti-biotics with a grade four heroine chaser. Even so, the bandit boss looked very unwell indeed. His skin was almost transparently pale and he suffered from a fever that left him dripping with sweat. The other gang members were in better shape, but eyed the villagers nervously. They weren't expecting any mercy.

Several of the women disappeared down-river and returned half-an-hour later with the children who'd been left under the care of several teenage girls and those too old or frail for combat.

Dahm Daw and his boys were corralled in the tiger cage, which Danny had brought back for no other reason than he couldn't think what else to do with it. They were pretty cramped, but no one cared.

Ban Bat was in a mood for celebration and the villagers partied long into the night. Once again Danny and Monty added their music to the festivities. Everyone went to bed with full bellies and their heads woozy with too much rice wine and beer.

The following morning with Kekio and Long Li's help, the majors interrogated the prisoners. Dahm Daw was the main source of information as his gang members were simply minions and didn't have a clue about the business end of their operation. Dahm Daw actually knew the dope went to France in a stage of relays, but his link in the chain only reached as far as Vientiane. From there the heroin went down river to Saigon and then by air or ship to its destination which was often Marseilles. At each stage the heroin's price inflated and its quality reduced with added ingredients to make it stretch further.

Under extreme duress Dahm Daw finally told the majors the name of his Vientiane contact.

'We have to warn the local police and customs officials,' Danny said.

'That's already been done, but all the local cops do is take their cut and let the dope move on down the line,' Major Black replied gloomily.

'So what are we gonna do? We're sitting on a fortune of seriously illegal merchandise. We can't push it. We're supposed to be on the side of law and order.'

'How would you like to help us flush out the dealers ourselves?' Major Black said.

'We aren't cops,' Monty reminded him.

'Leave that bit to us, we just want you to get us around.'

'We're still on the CAT payroll and you guys are still paying the bills.'

So began a six month odyssey across Asia to Europe.

The following day they bid Ban Bat's citizens goodbye and boarded the chopper. Danny was disappointed when Long Li said he'd remain behind. Long Li and he'd been a team for so long Danny hoped they'd pick up where they'd left off. But Long Li was adamant. Kekio certainly had a lot to do with it and it looked like the couple was about to become an item.

'Someone has to hang around in case the tiger comes back,' Long Li said.

So with great regret Danny flew the S-55 back to Luang Prabang to refuel. Danny and Monty later discovered the tiger was never seen in the area again so the villagers had simply dragged the cage – including Dahm Daw and his men – into the Mekong River where it drifted a little way down-river before sinking without trace.

On reaching Vientiane, Ambassador Charles Yost arranged for the US to buy Ban Bat's poppy crop and ship it to Saigon where the opium would be purified into morphine for medical purposes. The gesture was part of a huge aid programme to Indochina that President Eisenhower had authorised to deter Communism from spreading its viral tentacles throughout the region.

New Year came and went. So did Danny's twentieth birthday as time flashed by in a blur. As the majors promised, he and Monty were merely chauffeurs. They started at Vientiane and while Danny and Monty relaxed in their hotel, the majors sniffed out Dahm Daw's contact and persuaded him to divulge the next link in the dope chain, before eliminating him.

The majors swapped the S-55 chopper for the *Gooney-Bird*, explaining they were in for a long trip. From Vientiane, they followed a trail to Saigon, Bangkok, Rangoon, Calcutta, Bombay, Karachi, Muscat, Basra, Beirut, Istanbul, Athens, Rome and finally to Marseilles. At times the stopovers were brief, but often lasted weeks. Tracking down drug dealers was easier in some places than others. The majors certainly didn't delay in Palestine which had been partitioned to accommodate Jewish refugees after WWII. The Palestinians were justifiably incensed at having half their country arbitrarily confiscated by the UN while the Jews simply didn't appear to be happy about anything. In any event puffing cannabis through bongs was about as illicit as drug-taking went in the Levant.

In other regions, although the majors were ridding the world of some of its vilest scum, they often acted beyond the law. They would occasionally rouse Danny and Monty to fly them out of town without delay with the local authorities or mobsters hot on their heels.

Monty suggested that it was probably best not to ask too many questions when the majors were in full-scale *spook* mode. Danny's anxiety was tempered by the fact that for most of the time he and Monty lounged around expensive hotel pools, waiting for the cocktail hour. In many ways Danny enjoyed the break. Other than convalescing from his Dien Bien Phu wounds, he hadn't really had a holiday for five years. To make matters even better, he was still officially on CAT duty and therefore the CAT payroll.

Whatever dark, sinister business the majors conducted, they kept it strictly to themselves.

To avert the inevitable boredom – you can have too much of a good thing – Danny and Monty spent much of their spare time exploring their exotic surroundings. There were many spectacular highlights although Danny and Monty had to wade through masses of seething squalor to get there.

Once they reached Marseilles that all changed. Although the French still sulked over the disaster at Dien Bien Phu and the loss of their Southeast Asian colonies, no one could stay depressed along the *Côte d' Azur* in late spring.

Their sojourn ended abruptly when the majors returned to their hotel, informing Danny and Monty that the operation was over. The majors had been ordered to the London Embassy for debriefing. It was the height of the Cold War and Danny discovered later the majors were assigned to East Berlin to perform dirty deeds either side of Check-Point Charlie.

'What about the dope?' Danny asked as that was the whole point of the expedition in the first place.

'We're to take it to Lyneham RAF base in Wilshire, England,' Major Black said. 'We're gonna be met by a bunch of Scotland Yard heavies who will destroy the stuff.'

'What about catching the bad guys? That's why we're here as well, right?'

'We've eliminated a lot of bad guys already and put up plenty of names to the local cops along the French Connection trail. What they do with the information is up to them, but I think mostly they turn a blind eye in exchange for kick-backs.' Major White explained sadly. 'Unfortunately the position is just as bad or even worse here in France. The *Unione Corse* and *Le Milieu Corso-Marsellais* are the two biggest mobster gangs and they've got cosy deals going with the French Government.'

'They control the docks and longshoreman unions,' Major Black continued. 'They've got the whole business sewn up tight. We ain't going anywhere with that side of the investigation. It's disappointing I know, but right now our bosses have decided we have bigger fish to fry with the Ruskies.'

'What about us?' Monty asked suspiciously.

'You still work for CAT and they'll want their plane back. I should imagine you'll be ferrying it to wherever it's needed.'

'Well, I know what I'm going to do when we get to England,' Danny said resolutely.

'Oh, what's that?'

'I'm going to visit Angela.'

The majors raised their eyebrows, but made no objections. As both Monty and Danny still had some leave remaining, they thought a week in the English countryside would be most efficacious.

The following morning they took off at first light and flew north along the beautiful Rhone Valley with the majestic French Alps rearing skywards to the east. They refuelled at Paris's Orly Airport where the USAF leased tarmac space as part of its Cold War strategy. With the amount of contraband they were carrying, the majors liked to stay in American territory if they could, thus avoiding any embarrassing questions from alert customs officials.

Danny was amazed at the size of Paris and arranged ATC clearance for a scenic flight over the city before setting course northwards. They crossed the Normandy coast where Major White pointed out the D-Day invasion beaches, especially Omaha which he described in detail - Dog Green, White and Red: Easy Green and Red: Fox Green.

'Easy — now there's a misnomer if ever I heard one,' Major White said. 'Two thousand dead in a day.'

'You were there, weren't you?' Danny said.

'Yep, from the start — Second Ranger Battalion.'

And that was the most intimate piece of knowledge Danny ever learnt about Major White.

As they crossed the Channel, clouds appeared ahead, but they were broken and as RAF Lyneham was equipped with a radio beacon and GCA radar letdown, navigation was a doddle. Monty had of course flown over Europe during the war, so there were no surprises for him, but Danny marvelled at how civilised British aviation was compared to Southeast Asia and how many services were available to make flying easier.

Lyneham was the home of 99 Transport Squadron which was equipped with Handley-Paige Hasting planes that looked rather like large C-47s with two extra engines. Lyneham was a massive base and the main transport hub for resupplying personnel and matériel to British bases in Gibraltar, Cyprus and the Middle East.

Yet again Danny was impressed by the majors' communication network when a contingent of red-caps, civilian policemen, and secret-service agents were there to greet them. While Danny and Monty secured their plane and discussed its maintenance needs with RAF engineers, the majors were deep in conversation with two men in civilian clothing. After their brief discussion, Major White and Major Black shook Danny and Monty's hands.

'This is it, guys,' Major Black said cheerfully. 'We gotta go. Thanks for the safe trip. See you around.'

The majors were not ones for teary goodbyes. One of the civilians, who Danny assumed worked for the *Customers*, handed Monty a large envelope.

'These are your instructions from CAT,' the stranger said without introducing himself. 'Keep these papers with you at all times. They include your diplomatic clearances, travel authorities, fuel vouchers and your visa, Mr McAlister.'

Nothing like good ole Yankee 'can-do', eh?

The package also included enough sterling currency and green-backs to tide them over.

'Your orders are to ferry this plane to the Douglas plant in California for a complete refit.'

'The plane looks fine to me,' Monty said, looking a little hurt.

'Maybe so, but there are other roles in the pipeline and this plane is destined to fill one of those.'

'But I wanted to see Angela since we've come half way round the world.'

'I presume you mean the young lady from Dien Bien Phu,' another civilian spoke with an urbane English accent.

'How do you know..?

'MI-6, old boy. It's our job to know. I was one of the chaps who spirited Miss Holyman out of Vietnam. Could have been a bit embarrassing having one of ours swanning around someone else's war zone, what?'

'I don't recall she did much swanning around,' Danny said bitterly. 'She saved a lot of lives – including mine.'

'Yes, we know all about that. You Aussies may think you're an independent lot, but we've been keeping a close eye on you too. We like to know what our Commonwealth cousins are up to.'

Danny glared at him.

Toffee-nosed, arrogant Pommy git!

Danny was sure that his animosity must have shown, but the MI-6 agent wasn't particularly bothered. In fact he gave the distinct appearance that nothing bothered him.

After a brief discussion with the CIA team the MI-6 agent was satisfied.

'It seems you have made quite an impression with our American friends,' he said. 'You still have quite a few brownie-points to your credit. It appears the plane is not due for servicing until the end of June. Take some time off just as long as you arrive in California on time. That should give you a couple of weeks. I'm sure these RAF chappies will take good care of your crate.'

'Why the hell y'all want to be here,' one of the CIA agents added, looking skywards as drizzle started to form. 'I'd take Sunny California anytime.'

Danny used the officer's mess phone to call Guys Hospital and was soon connected to Angela's extension.

'Oh, Danny how wonderful,' she gushed. 'You must come and visit. I'd just die if you didn't.'

It was all classic Angela. She'd finished studying and had graduated in record time with a first (of course – nothing else would have satisfied her). She planned to go home for the holidays before taking up her initial position, but she 'simply must' show Danny the sights of London before that.

So within a couple of hours, after Danny convinced Monty he couldn't take his .45 with him, they sat comfortably in a first-class compartment behind a Great Western Main Line steam locomotive as it pulled out of Swindon Station bound for Paddington.

Chapter 13 — Angela

'I didn't expect it to be so grey,' Danny remarked as the soft English countryside rolled by. 'I mean all the houses are made out of stone and all the tiles are grey and squished together,' he added as they passed through Reading.

'You've gotta remember that fifty million people live in a country the size of New Guinea. Australia has less than ten million in a whole continent the size of the US,' Monty reminded him. 'I know it's a bit bleak right now, but when the weather clears up, you'll see the place in a different light.'

'When will that be?'

'Sometimes it doesn't stop raining for a month. That's the problem actually. Well, that and the beer.'

'What's wrong with the beer?'

'You'll see. It's sort of an acquired taste.'

Angela met them at the platform. Danny's first impression was that she was no longer a girl, but a woman of exquisite elegance and beauty. She wore an immaculate Danby outfit with a tailored jacket, fitted blouse and tight-waisted skirt that engulfed a host of petticoats. She rushed into his arms and kissed him ardently, although Danny had long since realised that Angela was the master of mixed signals. Nevertheless he hugged her tightly, making the most of her intimate mood.

Monty cleared his throat to gain Angela's attention.

'Oh, Mr Montgomery,' she said and shook his hand formally after disentangling herself from Danny's embrace.

Monty grinned and embraced her.

'Come here and gimme a kiss,' he said.

To Danny's surprise she obliged Monty with a light peck on the cheek. Their past relationship may not have been exactly a rollercoaster, but certainly undulating. However it looked like they were prepared to bury the hatchet.

Clutching Danny's arm, Angela immediately launched into chatter mode. She was so excited about graduation and *actually* having a job straight off. Taking extra classes during holidays had fast-tracked her through the course and now she was the youngest graduate that anyone at King's College could remember. She was delighted to hear Long Li had survived Dien Bien Phu and that it looked like he'd found a girl-friend.

'What's the job?' Danny asked.

'Oh, I'll tell you later,' she replied. 'Right now we have to get you settled then I'm going to show you around the city. It's so beautiful.'

Danny looked around the grey station doubtfully, but didn't say anything.

Kings College was conveniently situated close to Temple Underground Station. As Danny and Monty only carried light grips they took the tube there. Danny found the experience claustrophobic, but he was distracted by Angela. She lived in digs close to the college, so she knew her way around.

'My flat is tiny, it'll be a squeeze and I only have one couch, 'she lamented.

'No sweat,' Monty said. 'Danny can have the couch and I'll book into a hotel.'

'Hotels are so expensive in London.'

'That's OK, it looks like Uncle Sam is bank-rolling us.'

'I know a pub that's close by that should do nicely.'

'You know a pub?' Monty wondered.

'I do indeed, Mr Montgomery. I do enjoy a Babycham occasionally, but that does not mean I'm a lush.'

'Who's a big girl then?' Monty said. 'Babycham, now that sounds like potent stuff.'

Angela ignored him.

Babycham was sweet perry bottled in miniature champagne bottles with a saccharine fawn logo. A Somerset brewer had introduced the drink a couple of years before and it was proving very popular, especially with young women.

The pub was called *The Jolly Hangman* and turned out to be cramped, but comfortable enough.

'This is London, Mr Montgomery,' Angela said. 'Space is at a premium.'

After leaving his grip in his room, Monty accompanied Danny and Angela on the short walk to her digs. Her place was pretty cramped too. It was no more than a bed-sitter cluttered with assignment-papers and reference books. The flat's amenities were a single-ring gas cooker and a minute bathroom with a bath that Danny could use if he sat upright.

'Like I said – London is expensive,' Angela said defensively. After all this had been her home for four years. She'd won just about every scholarship on offer, but rents were still exorbitant close to the city centre so her accommodation was modest.

'Look, I'll leave you love-birds to get re-acquainted. I reckon I'll head for Soho to check out the action.'

'Soho!' Angela eyed him with one of her most severe looks. 'Why that's just a den of iniquity and vice.'

'Just how I like it,' he grinned, slapping Danny on the arm and winking at Angela. 'Enjoy your sight-seeing, buddy. I'll check back with ya in a couple of days. Maybe a week, it all depends, but we've got plenty of time to get to California. You can always leave a message for me at *The Hangman.* '

'California?' Angela's eyes widened.

'Yeah, we're ferrying a Dak to the Douglas plant in California for a refit and major service.'

Angela gave Monty her parents' Dorset address and phone number in case they decided to visit and he needed to contact them.

So while Monty rode the tube to Soho and what sinful delights lurked there, Angela spent the next three days showing Danny the sights. He had to admit that there was a lot to see in a very small area. The Underground and red double-decker buses were cheap and regular. Angela was an excellent guide and as always, seemed to be well informed about everything. She even relished in the gory details of Traitors' Gate, the Tower of London, Tyburn Gallows Tree Memorial and Jack-the-Ripper's Whitechapel.

'It's just like a Monopoly board,' Danny observed. 'We had a set in the 77 Squadron crew-room after Wing Commander Hubble press-ganged me from Major Armstrong's chopper unit. We played when the weather was too crappy to fly.'

Danny enjoyed the Imperial War Museum, Saint Paul's Cathedral and the Natural History Museum. When Angela commented on how studious he was, he shrugged.

'Yeah, I like to learn stuff too, you know,' he said.

She smiled and took his arm. Danny liked it when she did that.

'C'mon, let's get lunch,' she said.

London restaurants were exorbitant so they usually ate pub-grub, at fish-and-chips shops or Lyons Corner Houses, where Danny especially enjoyed the hearty soups.

As usual, Danny was still unsure where he stood with Angela. She was certainly friendly and returned his goodnight kisses, but he sensed that was as far as she was prepared for now. He cursed the fact he was such an idiot when it came to women. He could never judge a girl's thought process, especially Angela's. They weren't teenagers any more, but Danny was uncertain whether Angela's idea of intimacy had developed beyond a school-girl level.

So Danny decided just to enjoy her company and see where things led — if anywhere. He noticed the white laundry pole Angela always carried around after their first adventures in New Guinea was propped beside the front door.

'In case of intruders,' Angela said.

After three days of intense tourism, Danny'd seen enough urban high-lights to be going on with.

'You know London is great, but I'd like to get out of town for a while,' Danny said as they strolled past Horse Guards Parade along the Mall towards Buckingham Palace. 'I'd like to see some of that English countryside I keep reading about, especially as it looks like the weather's clearing up a bit.'

'Then why don't we go and see Mummy and Daddy tomorrow,' Angela suggested. 'There's plenty of countryside down there and I know they'd love to see you again.'

'The last time I saw your mum she wanted me to fly her to *Torri-Rouge* and drag you kicking and screaming out of Dien Bien Phu. Long Li said he'd kick her off the plane if she tried to get on board.'

'I wished she'd done it,' Angela reflected, 'especially on those last days. I was scared out of my wits.'

'Weren't we all?'

So they enjoyed their final night in London with a performance of *Kismet* at the Stroll Theatre. It was only a short walk back to Angela's digs for a cocoa nightcap, and hopefully a cuddle.

The flat was on the ground floor of a four-storey building. There was a small front yard engulfed by bushes. She was about to turn the key when she heard garden foliage rustling only feet from her.

'What took you so long?' Monty hissed as he stepped from cover. Surprisingly he was carrying his grip.

'We saw a West End show, if that's OK with you, Monty,' Danny said unable to hide the fact that he was peeved and it didn't look like any cuddling was likely now. 'What are you doing here anyway? I thought you wanted a few days to get a good taste of sin.'

'I'm sorta in a bit of a jam...'

'Sorta?'

'Yeah, well I met a girl.'

'And I'm sure she was a right little scrubber ...' Angela sighed

'It's no time to be judgemental, Angela. Two guys are after me.'

'Who?

'As far as I can make out, some guys called Ronnie and Reggie Kray.'

'Oh shit,' Angela gasped. Danny knew she was ultra-prissy when it came to swearing, so something was terribly wrong. She was forever admonishing him for even saying 'damn'.

'You know them?' Danny asked.

'All London knows the Kray brothers,' she replied. 'They're a couple of street-thugs whose gang terrorises half the city. You read about them in the paper just about every week.'

*

Monty had indeed set out to enjoy himself. His love-hate relationship with Angela was certainly more love than hate. Although a little bit of Angela went a long way, especially when she mounted her muscular-Christianity charger on some soul-saving crusade or another. And Soho had everything to tempt a red-blooded, wayward man. Strip-clubs, pubs, snooker-halls, brothels and gambling dens were included in the smorgasbord of delights, and Monty was feeling lucky.

He started out by finding a bar that served cold German lager and not flat dark British sudsy ale. Later he discovered a Wimpy Bar at the Lyon's Corner House on Coventry Street where he ordered a cheeseburger, fries and a *Coke*. Once his hunger was satisfied, he headed for a gambling club and did moderately well at the roulette table, broke even at blackjack which the British called pontoon. He also won a sizable pot at the poker table.

In his home town of Montgomery, Alabama, Monty would never have been permitted to frequent bars alongside white patrons, but while the British called him 'nigger' or 'golly-wog', they tolerated him. His money was as good as anyone else's. Monty also visited several gambling clubs, and enjoyed a winning streak at the pontoon and roulette tables, much to the casino managers' dismay. Monty wasn't losing his money as they considered only right and proper. Now his pockets bulged with several hundred pounds of their 'readies', which was bound to attract unwanted attention eventually.

Mind you, it gave him daytime spending money. He was fitted for a bespoke suit at Chester and Barrie of Savile Row. He ordered Tiffin at Claridges in Mayfair, which was a bit of a letdown because he was indifferent about tea and cucumber sandwiches. The original Indian idea of curry and chapattis would have suited him much better, but he enjoyed the luxurious poshness of it all.

By the third night Monty had frequented enough strip-clubs and realised his fortune would turn at the roulette and pontoon tables, so it was time for a change. Feeling well pleased with his luck so far, he decided to revert to skill. He found a seedy smoke-filled snooker parlour. The entrance was guarded by a bouncer who looked like a championship wrestler. The doorway opened into a narrow stairwell leading to the second floor, which for some crazy reason the Limey's called the first floor. There were four tables and a bar, so Monty ordered a scotch while he waited for a vacant table and checked out the competition. He wasn't particularly impressed in what he saw, so he challenged a first winner who was willing to bet a quid on each game.

His game of choice was eight-ball pool, but the principles of snooker were the same and for the next couple of hours he took on all comers. As his opponents thinned out and drifted to the bar or other tables, a lone woman was left standing beside Monty. She'd been following his progress with interest and, although he'd certainly noticed her, she hadn't put him off his game.

The woman was dressed in a satin skirt that clung so tightly to her thighs and hips that she could only walk in short struts. Six inch stilettos didn't help to steady her either. Her skin hugging halter top barely covered anything at all.

Slinky as a cat on the prowl...hmm..?

'Wanna buy a girl a drink,' she whispered with a cockney accent that was desperately trying to emigrate to Knightsbridge.

'I'm having scotch,' Monty said, 'want one?'

She nodded. Monty knew you didn't give bar-girls a choice or they'd order faux-champagne at ten quid a bottle. She slinked behind the bar and reached for a bottle of Johnny Walker Black and two glasses.

'It's OK, Bert,' she said to the bartender. 'I'll sort this.'

'Right you are, Miss,' he replied leaving her to pour the drinks.

So she owns the place, or knows someone who does.

'My name's Doris,' she said as she poured the drinks.

'Monty – pleased to meet you. Nice place you've got here.'

'Oh, I don't own it, ducky. Let's just say I'm on *really* friendly terms with the bloke who does.'

'I'm sure you are.'

'And I could get right friendly with you too, Monty. I like a bloke what wins.'

'I presume you'd like me to redistribute some of the wealth.'

'I can show you a ruddy good time. My place is close by.'

That was all the encouragement Monty needed. He'd been through a dry patch, so he probably couldn't be blamed for what happened next. Monty was also unaware that Ronnie and Reggie Kray thought of Doris as their personal property and, while they weren't averse to pimping her out to high-rolling customers, they discouraged freelancing.

Ronnie and Reggie were totally unstable and their normal method of dealing with anyone who displeased them was to beat them to pulp. You couldn't really blame Doris though. She was a feisty girl who didn't mind being associated with the toughest mobsters in town. The trouble was the Kray brothers preferred boys. So she was under-utilised, bored and wantonly restless. Monty just happened to be in the wrong place when she was feeling frisky.

Unfortunately for him most of the snooker hall patrons all owed the Krays in one way or another and letting the boys' main-squeeze strut out with a Yank darkie wouldn't go down well with Ronnie and Reggie. And when things didn't go well with the Kray brothers many people paid the price. The best option was to nip Doris's indiscretion in the bud.

'Hey nigger,' one of the patrons yelled. 'You don't wanna be foolin' with Ronnie and Reggie's bint.'

Monty turned.

'You talkin' to me?' he hissed through clenched teeth.

'I'm just warning you. The Kray brothers don't take kindly to no one layin' their 'ands on their property.'

'Who's gonna stop me..?'

Monty had been around long enough to have a second sense for danger. He caught a flicker of movement in the corner of his eye and ducked just as a billiard cue swished over his head, striking Doris a hefty belt on her shoulder. She squealed and fell to the floor while Monty fluidly somersaulted across the room to the cue-rack. Grabbing the nearest stick he smashed it across the nearest man's face and slammed the end into another patron's gut.

The thing that Monty knew about fighting was you didn't hesitate. He saw Doris was still on her knees and crawling clear of the melee while she swore like a wharfie. Other than nursing a bruised arm for a week, she'd be fine.

The snooker-hall patrons all snatched cues from the racks. They out-numbered Monty six-to-one. He swung his cue into an advancing man, smashing him in the ribs and splitting the stick in half. Monty grabbed the fallen man's cue and bolted for the stairway. He barged straight into another fellow standing at the door, shunting him backwards so he tumbled down the steps, colliding with the bouncer.

As the two men struggled in a writhing tangle, Monty leapt down the stairs and, using the bouncer's back as a stepping stone, he bounded into the street. The snooker room mob quickly came to their senses and clambered down the stairwell baying for Monty's blood.

Meanwhile Doris staggered upright and descended the stairs with as much dignity as she could muster. When she reached the door, the bouncer was struggling to his feet and dragging the man who'd landed on top of him aside. He was still stunned, so Doris wisely decided to hail a taxi and head for her mother's place. It was time to lie low until all the fuss was over.

Chapter 14 — London by Night

Monty was on the run with Reggie and Ronnie Kray's mobsters combing Greater London for him. The Kray brothers were beside themselves with rage when they heard the news that Doris had been assaulted by a Yank, and a golly to boot. You'll notice the story had escalated by then and Doris wasn't about to gainsay anyone. Being the victim suited her fine. Receiving Ronnie and Reggie's sympathy was better than the thrashing she'd get if they even suspected she'd been soliciting.

'It wasn't my fault,' Monty insisted as Angela eyed him with her practised look of disapproval. 'If Danny hadn't talked me out of bringing my gun, I'd have shot my way out of this mess. A bit of hot lead flying around can sure be discouraging.'

'This isn't Tombstone, Mr Montgomery,' Angela admonished in her usual fashion. 'You can't gun people down in the streets of London.'

'From what you say, the Kray boys ain't too fussy about that,' Monty replied.

'Never mind what the Kray brothers think, we've got to get you away from them, which means we have to get away from *here*,' Angela said.

'Why? I'm safe now I got away. I can hole up here and they're not going to find me.'

'Don't be so sure. It's not just the Kray brothers' gang we have to worry about. They may control the underworld, but legitimate business people, including local shopkeepers, all pay protection money to the mob. I bet my butcher, baker and green grocer do. It's nothing personal, but they'll sell you out if it means staying in the Krays' good books.'

'Like I said,' Danny added, 'it's time for a trip to the country.'

'All right, but I'm coming with you,' Angela insisted. 'You'll need someone who knows their way around.'

It only took minutes for Danny to repack his grip. Angela wasn't much longer. She exchanged her dress for a pair of rolled-up jeans, check shirt, bobby socks, plimsolls and leather jacket. Her hair was tied in a neat pony-tail

'Nice *Wild One* look,' Monty commented.

Angela bobbed a pert curtsy and smiled. She'd packed a rucksack with a change of underwear, socks and a jumper. Danny noticed she also included cash, chequebook, passport and driver's licence.

'I don't know when I'll be back, do I?' she said, brandishing her white laundry pole in one hand. She hefted the rucksack onto her back and nodded with satisfaction.

'Lucky I had this back-pack. I used to go hiking in the Peak District with some other students last year. It's beautiful up there in...'

'Yeah, tell us later, Ange,' Danny said. 'I think it's time to get cracking.'

After ensuring the essential services and lights were turned off, Angela bolted the windows and locked the door behind them before they ventured into the street.

'Our best plan is to get to Paddington and catch a train west,' Angela said. 'We can take the tube, but there aren't many trains this late.'

'Taxi?' Danny suggested.

'If we can find one. Right now, let's walk and get as far away as possible.'

It was four miles as the crow flies to Paddington Station and even then they had no idea of the train timetable, but they thought it would be as safe as anywhere. They clung to the shadows of the tree-lined Embankment, but the path was well lit by a string of elegant lights along the river wall. Fortunately the Embankment was deserted, but Monty, Danny and Angela kept their eyes peeled and hurried on. Running for a minute – walking for a minute.

Their main problem was that the word was out and the Kray brothers were baying for blood. It may well have been that the mobsters were not so incensed about Doris, but simply in the mood to do someone harm.

Of course there wasn't a bobby in sight when the fugitive trio ran into trouble. Four men approached as they neared Waterloo Bridge and turned right into Regent Street. Monty was just under a street light when they approached.

'Gor-blimey,' one fellow said. 'Innat the golly what gone an' raped Ronnie an' Reggie's bird?'

'Oh, puleease,' Monty sighed. 'No one raped anyone. I didn't even get out of the pool hall before I was bounced by your buddies.'

'We'll see what Ronnie an' Reggie sez abart vat. Grab 'im!'

The four men pounced, wrestling Monty to the pavement, but they'd reckoned without Danny and Angela. Danny swung a punch and clouted one of the attackers in the ear while Angela landed a stunning blow with her stick. Monty flung off one of his assailants and kicked the other in the groin.

Two men were temporarily out of action, but the remaining duo both drew flick-knives. The blades flashed open, but Angela was ready. She smashed the laundry pole across one man's wrist. He screamed but was silenced when Danny slammed a right fist into his nose. There was a satisfying crunch of broken bone as blood gushed over the fellow's mouth and jaw. Danny kicked him in the belly as he fell just to make sure he stayed down. Monty put in the boot savagely to ensure the other two men did the same.

Angela was left facing a flick-knife blade, but as Danny and Monty finished off his cronies and turned to join Angela, the last attacker fled towards Covent Garden.

'He's gonna raise a hue-and-cry,' Danny said. 'Let's get going.'

They figured the escapee would head for Soho to muster reinforcements. It was less than half-a-mile away, but he only went a couple of hundred yards before running into a bunch of his mates. With a collective yell, they charged back into action.

'Oh, goodness,' Angela whispered under her breath. 'This way!'

She led Danny and Monty along the Strand to Trafalgar Square where more trouble was brewing.

A bikie gang had parked their motorcycles in a neat row in front of Nelson's Column. They really weren't planning anything other than hanging around looking cool in their leather jackets, jeans and Johnny Strabler peaked caps. Most had cigarettes dangling from the corner of their mouths. They were just bored teenage lads with a couple of skanky bikie molls who'd come along for the thrills.

Unfortunately a mob of teddy-boys with their judies had been kicked out of several Soho pubs and now roamed the West End streets in a sulky mood. These dandy gangs fancied the look of long frock coats, stove-pipe trousers, junky suede shoes and jelly-roll hair cuts that they combed repeatedly. They weren't necessarily looking for trouble either, but they didn't try to avoid it. Running into a bikie gang was just what the teddy-boys needed to liven the night up.

For no other reason other than a testosterone-fuelled confrontation the two groups squared off and stood their ground. Nothing was said and no argument had occurred, yet the challenge was undoubtable and could not be ignored by either side. Next came a little pushing and shoving followed by a little elbowing and nudging and then a few shoulder barges. A final head-butt was all that was need to start fists flying.

The scrap was in full swing when Danny, Angela and Monty raced into Trafalgar Square with Ronnie and Reggie's henchmen only a hundred yards behind them. The trio were panting for breath by then. They'd run over a mile with their grips slung over their shoulders and knew they couldn't keep up the pace for much longer.

'Do you see what I see?' Monty gasped.

'Too right,' Danny nodded with a grin.

Without a second's hesitation they dashed around the street brawl, hoping to avoid any wayward fist and boots. They reached the line of bikes without the owners noticing. The bikies were fully occupied with the teddy-boys while the girls from both sides had joined the stoush. Just then a dozen Kray mobsters raced into Trafalgar Square. The last thing they expected was a full-scale teenage brawl. They lost sight of Monty and his friends for an instant, which was all the time they needed.

Monty leapt astride a Triumph 650 Thunderbird and stomped down on the start pedal. He plonked his grip onto the petrol tank as the engine roared into life.

Danny did the same, choosing a BSA A7 500 twin.

'Jump on behind, Ange!' Danny yelled as he kicked-started the engine. Laundry pole at the ready, she straddled the pillion seat and clung to Danny with her spare hand. Neither Danny nor Monty was an expert motorbike rider and it was months since either of them had ridden George's Indian on along the dirt tracks of *Kago Ailan*. However, adrenaline and desperation made them both *Isle-of-Man TT* champions.

'Just like riding a bike. Ha! Ha! Ha!' Monty yelled as he released the clutch and revved the Triumph over the cobblestones.

He's flaming stark raving mad, Danny thought as he roared after Monty with Angela clinging around his waist. Yeah, but it felt good tearing away on a powerful machine with a little cutie holding you tight. Their gear changing was rugged at first, but Monty and Danny soon got the hang of it.

'They're getting away!' one of the mobsters yelled. 'Get after 'em!'

Of course, the only way the gangsters would, 'get after 'em', was to commandeer some motorbikes themselves. By then the bikies were aware of the larceny and those who could, disengaged themselves from the teddy-boys and scrambled to protect their property. They tackled the mobsters and brought some down, but teenage lads were no match for the vicious street thugs.

A bloody scuffle followed. The mobsters held the bikies off long enough for two of them to jump onto another BSA and a Norton 490 Café racer and charge after the escapees.

Oddly enough the teddy-boys joined the bikies to defend their rides. Now the mobsters were outnumbered ten-to-one and would have been pummelled to within an inch of their lives, but the shriek of police whistles grew closer. Within minutes dozens of truncheon-wielding bobbies stormed into Trafalgar Square.

Meanwhile it didn't take long for Monty to realise he didn't have a clue where he was going. He slowed up, allowing Danny to take the lead. Angela yelled in Danny's ear and used her laundry pole to point out which way to go. As neither Monty nor Danny was expert bike riders, there were some near-spills as they hurtled along Regent Street in an adrenaline-pumping frenzy.

'Go left!' Angela yelled as they came to the Bayswater Road intersection.

Danny turned sharply while Monty was hard pressed to follow and swung wide across the road right into the face of an on-coming police-car with its siren blazing and blue light flashing. Monty managed to steer the Triumph onto the pavement just missing the police car's front bumper. The copper driving slammed on the brakes, skidded for fifty yards before spinning round in a full three-sixty degree doughnut with the stench of burning rubber hanging in the air.

The police car was originally bound for the melee at Trafalgar Square, but now the coppers saw other fish to fry. They radioed to

Scotland Yard that they were pursuing runaway felons and called for backup. Unfortunately the other units were already converging on Trafalgar Square where it looked like they needed all the help they could get. Nevertheless the squad car was given permission to chase the escaping bikies.

As the police accelerated after Danny and Monty, a pair of unnoticed motor–cycles with headlights switched off, followed a hundred yards behind.

After a few wobbles Monty regained control of his bike and powered after Danny and Angela. The front wheel reared as he cranked the accelerator. Danny glanced back and saw Monty was quickly gaining, but he also saw the following headlights and flashing blue light.

'Bugger, we're being chased!' he yelled to Angela who managed to nod, but was mostly just trying to stay in the pillion seat.

But they needn't have worried. The squad car was an early model Morris Minor with a mere 800cc engine. There was no way even an experienced driver could keep up with the motorbikes. Soon Danny and Monty were powering away at over eighty miles an hour and still accelerating. The bikes would easily do *a ton* and undoubtedly had done so in the past.

Bayswater Road was long and straight and soon the pursuit car dropped behind. The coppers radioed Scotland Yard to inform their controller that they were abandoning the chase and returning to Trafalgar Square. The police driver slammed on the brakes to perform a snappy U-turn in the deserted street. As the car swung across the road a motor cycle slammed into the driver's side. The rider was pitched straight over the winking blue light before splatting onto the ground twenty yards away.

Another bike veered across the road and flashed past the police car.

The two policemen were shaken but unharmed although the Morris' right-hand doors were so badly dented they were unusable. While one of the Bobbies scrambled out of the passenger side to check the motorbike rider, his colleague radioed for an ambulance.

The good thing about hurtling through London in the wee-small hours of the morning was very little traffic got in Danny and Monty's way and the suburbs simply flashed by. Under Angela's guidance they turned left at Notting Hill, down Shepherd's Bush Road to Hammersmith Bridge. They streaked through Richmond and Kingston in no time, heading southwest along the A303.

They stopped at Basingstoke, which was only fifty miles from Central London. Neither Danny nor Monty had any idea of the motorbikes' range so they unscrewed the petrol caps to check how much remained. Although they heard fuel sloshing around when they rocked the bikes, how far it would take them was problematic. After a brief discussion they pressed on to Andover. If they topped up the tanks there, they were confident they'd reach Dorset.

The problem was Andover, and indeed most of Great Britain, had closed for the night. There was nothing for it but to park at a petrol pump and wait for the garage to open. Monty suggested they break the padlock protecting the pump and help themselves, but Angela was having none of it. Stealing motorbikes was sufficient larceny for one day.

'I can't believe we stole these motorbikes,' Angela wailed, full of remorse and guilt.

'What did you want us to do?' Monty challenged. 'What do you think those gang-bangers had in mind for us?'

'Had in mind for *you* actually.'

'I think we'd have copped it by association, Ange,' Danny suggested.

'It still doesn't change the fact that we stole someone else's property.'

'Don't worry, we'll return them.'

'I don't see how.'

'I'll think of something,' Monty said.

'It'll be another one of your hare-brained schemes no doubt, Mr Montgomery.'

They were in for a long, cold and frustrating wait if this kept up.

'Look there are some park benches across the road,' Danny said. 'Let's try and get a couple of hours kip.'

'We'll probably be arrested as tramps,' Angela muttered, but she snuggled next to him and let him put his arm around her. Monty lay on a separate bench and to Danny and Angela's surprise was snoring in a few minutes.

'How can he do that?' Angela wondered. 'It's so cold and uncomfortable, not to mention that we're fugitives from the law.'

'Monty's been on the run before and he knows how to prioritise. Anyway, we don't actually know we're wanted by the police,' Danny said in an effort to be comforting.'

'I guess we're outlaws on the run from outlaws,' Angela giggled.

After a while Angela dozed off although Danny couldn't sleep. It was a nice feeling to have her close to him anyway. The night passed uneventfully. Only one car and several haulage lorries drove by. Danny thought he heard a distant motorbike engine, but saw nothing and no other vehicles came through Andover.

At dawn Danny hailed a horse-drawn milk-van and bought three half-pint bottles of milk. Early morning was the best time to drink milk while it was still cool. A paperboy cycled by and Monty stole a morning edition from a front garden. The Trafalgar Square melee had made the late news dead-line, but was only a brief article with no mention of any stolen motorbikes. Monty was more interested in the page-three Sabrina pin-up.

Just after eight-thirty a craggy-faced man dressed in oil-sodden dungarees showed up and filled their petrol tanks. A corner shop opened shortly afterwards and Angela bought Melton Mowbray pork pies all round with three bottles of Tango orangeade to wash the pies down.

'Let's be off,' Angela said. 'I know just the place to enjoy a healthy breakfast like this.'

Pulling up ten miles west along the A303, they parked the bikes, strolled across an open field and stood in the midst of the most famous cromlech of all time – Stonehenge. They sat on what Angela believed to have been a sacrificial stone in the shadows of the mighty sarsen stones. She passed round the pies and soft-drink bottles and they tucked in.

Monty and Danny were unimpressed by the cold stodgy pork pies, but they were hungry and ate them anyway. Monty lamented the absence of hamburger joints in the UK although Burger-King had opened an outlet in London just that year.

After breakfast the trio headed for Dorset. At the time they were totally unaware that a lone motor-cyclist still clung doggedly to their tail. They were also unaware that the rider had stopped at a telephone box in Andover and made a call to London.

Chapter 15 — Kidnap

Cerne Abbas was a picture-postcard Dorset County village half-way between Yeovil and Dorchester. Its narrow main street was flanked by a pub, church, bakery, butchery and a corner shop, tea house, quaint cottages and not much else. It was a tranquil place that sometimes closed down for no apparent reason other than a lack of sufficient interest to keep commerce going.

Angela's mother's family had been village dignitaries for so long they were mentioned in William the Conqueror's Doomsday Book. After a roaming evangelic practice in New Guinea, Doctor Holyman had bought the village general surgery because it was where his wife wanted to be.

As they rode into town, Danny could see the appeal. The soft greenness and gentle rolling country was so serenely charming he felt relaxed just being there. It was exactly how he'd envisaged the English country-side would look and feel.

Dr Holyman had bought a thatched cottage on the outskirts of town where he'd established his country practice. Right then he was justifiably proud of Angela who'd just graduated. He hoped she might have joined him as a partner, but she had stubbornly insisted she would find her own way in the medical world. So he was delightfully surprised when she turned up on the back of a high-powered motorbike. Mrs Holyman fussed over Danny and Monty who she'd only met briefly in a Hanoi bar when they were flying relief missions into Dien Bien Phu.

'I'll make tea,' she announced, 'and coffee for you, Monty dear. I know you Americans prefer it.'

Dr Holyman joined them once he'd cleared his waiting room.

'How great to see you chaps again,' he said, vigorously shaking Monty and Danny's hands. 'What have you been up to lately?'

'Oh nothing much,' Danny said blandly. 'Just barely escaping a mob riot in Saigon, fighting a new band of commies called Viet Cong in Vietnam, chasing a tiger and drug-lords in Laos and more recently running from London gangsters.'

'Oh dear, so nothing has changed much,' Dr Holyman said. 'You'd better tell me the details.'

After Danny and Monty explained their London adventures with frequent interruption from Angela, Dr Holyman gave a resigned sigh and shook his head.

'Wouldn't it have been smarter to leave the bikes at Yeovil police station and called me to come and pick you up?' Dr Holyman commented. 'Now we have to find a way of returning those machines to their rightful owners and keeping you three out of gaol.'

'We can still do that,' Monty said. 'Tonight after everything has closed up we'll drop 'em off with an anonymous note. We'll have to rub our finger-prints off as well.'

Dr and Mrs Holyman raised their eyebrows. They were scrupulously honest people, but recognised they owed Danny and Monty when it came to getting Angela out of tight spots in the past. So after Mrs Holyman made up spare beds for her unexpected guests Angela, Danny and Monty crashed for the afternoon. They'd had little sleep all night and were exhausted.

Danny woke at around five in the evening. Although Mrs Holyman was a fine cook, they decided to eat at the Royal Oak Inn on Long Street, the main road through town. This time Danny and Monty both appreciated the beef-and-ale pie which lived up to their expectations. They even enjoyed the locally brewed *Badger Ale*.

So the evening progressed merrily with more than a little reminiscing and playing catch-up. After a few drinks and a hearty meal even Angela didn't notice that a lone figure had checked into the pub for the night and now sat nursing a pint in a corner where no one paid him any attention. His motorcycle was out of sight in the pub's guest car park at the rear of the building. No one noticed when he dropped coins into the pay-phone in the snug and started talking earnestly for several minutes before hanging up.

At midnight Danny and Monty rode the stolen bikes along the A37 to Yeovil Police Station at the intersection of Queensway and Lysander Street. The station was quiet with only a desk sergeant on duty. Although constables patrolled their beats, they were all across town at the time. Danny and Monty cut the engines a hundred yards from the station and pushed the bikes to the curbside under the blue-lamp.

Dr Holyman pulled up in his Wolseley 4/44. Danny and Monty climbed aboard and they sped away. Taped to the

Triumph's petrol tank was an envelope containing a carefully written apology.

Dear Bike Owners,

We are truly sorry for taking your bikes from Trafalgar Square two nights ago, but we really needed to get away from some bad people who meant to harm us. We've returned the bikes without any damage and we filled up the petrol tanks.

Thank you for helping us out of a scrape and once again we're sorry for inconveniencing you.

Kind regards from two grateful people.

p.s. Your bikes are really fun to ride.

The licence numbers and road-tax discs would easily identify the bike-owners so Danny and Monty were confident they would be promptly returned to their owners. They were back in Cerne Abbas in half an hour and turned in with the knowledge they'd wake up with clear consciences and Angela's approval.

The following morning Mrs Holyman let the boys sleep late then treated them to a classic English fry-up breakfast.

'You know my people have lived here since Saxon times and maybe even before that,' Mrs Holyman announced. 'There are parish and village records that are all still intact at St Mary's Church.'

Danny eyed her quizzically, wondering where this was going.

'I found something that might interest you, Danny,' Mrs Holyman beamed. 'Quite a coincidence actually.'

Danny couldn't think of anything about a church that would interest him, but merely nodded politely.

'Oh Mummy, please don't tease poor Danny so. He's such a non-believer. He's worried you're trying to convert him.'

'You take him up to St Mary's then, darling. You know where all the documents are.'

After Danny finished his cuppa, Angela took his hand and led him to the church hall, which reminded Danny of a dusty schoolroom. Many of the parish records were stored on shelves. Angela sifted through a surprising number of tomes that held registries of births, marriages and deaths along with other church records and several private diaries of clergymen who'd served the parish over time.

'Here we are,' she said at last. 'You know these particular records go back to 1653. There are others in adjoining parishes that go back even further.'

'That's very interesting, I'm sure,' Danny said with no enthusiasm whatsoever.

She ignored him and opened a dusty black ledger that seemed to flop to a place that had been viewed many times before. The book was entitled *Marriages 1800-1815* and was just one of over a dozen marriage registers.

'When Mummy found this, she was intrigued.'

The entry was dated 30th March 1809:

Marriage solemnized at St Mary's Church in the Parish of Cerne Abbas

Jonathan Hamish McAlister (Bachelor) to Christina Anne Jenkins nee Proud (widow)

The groom's father was Colonel Sir Arthur McAlister and the bride's father was Reverend Cornelius Proud, the local vicar who'd conducted the ceremony.

'You'll notice they don't bother naming the mothers,' Angela snorted. 'I suppose they were prone to dying young and being replaced.'

'Oh, come on, Ange,' Danny protested. 'Just because this bloke's name is McAlister doesn't mean we're related.'

'Mummy thinks he could be your ancestor. She's studied Reverend Proud's personal diary which says Jonathan and Christina sailed for New South Wales soon after their marriage. Just think this is where you could have come from. The same as me!'

'Yeah, right,' he said and kissed her on the cheek. 'Thanks cousin.'

'Of course that doesn't mean *we're* related, silly.'

'It'll take a lot more than this to convince me I'm descended from a lord or an earl or a duke or something.'

'Sir Arthur wasn't a lord. His was awarded a non-hereditary knighthood for service during the American War of Independence. Anyway leave it with Mummy. She's so good at digging things up. Genealogy is her hobby – well more of an obsession.'

'Good for your mum.'

'OK, that's enough dusty books. I'm going to show you something that I know will appeal to you.'

They walked along Duck Street, turning right into a laneway that led past the village hall and over the Cerne River. There right ahead on the hillside stood – or lay depending on the angle – the Cerne Abbas Giant.

'What the blue blazes is that?' Danny asked

'Isn't he magnificent?' Angela giggled.

That was true enough. A naked, enormously endowed, club wielding warrior was etched into the chalk hillside.

'Now who would have taken the trouble to carve that bloke right there?' Danny wondered. 'He must be nearly two hundred feet tall.'

'No one knows,' Angela admitted. 'It's a bit like Stonehenge really – shrouded in mystery. People say it's a fertility symbol and brides wishing to become mothers take their husbands up there.'

'Yeah, I can see how they came to that conclusion. I wonder if it works. You wanna give it a try?'

'I have no wish to become a mother yet, thank you. Let's go back now. I don't know why I brought you here in the first place. I should have known you'd just get ideas.'

Danny found Angela emotionally daunting at times, and once again she was proving enigmatic. He certainly would have liked to take their relationship further, but didn't really know how to go about it. Once again he reflected how his previous sexual encounters had been brief and confusing. In those cases his lovers were predatory and he'd found himself swept along by events beyond his control.

Angela was really the only girl he'd ever been interested in. He valued her friendship and didn't want to risk that by forcing his attentions where they may not be wanted. He regretted their physical relationship hadn't developed beyond the petting stage.

Perhaps if they'd spent more time together – who knew..? He certainly wasn't going to get lucky sharing the spare room with Monty under the Holyman's roof, so it was better not to think about anything remotely lustful. He wondered why she'd even brought him to see the Cerne Abbas Giant at all. Maybe she just wanted to tease him, you could never tell with Angela.

That night was a repeat of the previous one. Danny was not a heavy drinker, but he enjoyed the English pub atmosphere. The blackened oak beams, low ceilings, horse-brasses, slate floor tiles and glowing fireplace gave a cosy, comforting permanency about it. He could understand how the *John Bull* empire-building ethos stemmed from such a solid foundation. He was even getting used to English ale.

'We're not going to make a habit of this,' Angela admonished. 'You'll just turn into a drunkard, Danny. Although Mr Montgomery is probably a lost cause, you're not beyond hope yet.'

'Why thank you, Ange,' Danny said, 'that is most comforting to know.'

He was perhaps a little unsteady on his feet at closing time, but it was only a few minutes' walk back to the Holyman home. Danny flopped into bed and was instantly asleep.

*

'Wake up, you lump!' Monty hissed in Danny's ear, shaking him urgently. Danny was only half awake with a dull headache and slow reactions.

'Bloody hell, Monty. I've only been asleep for ten minutes.'

'Four hours actually, it's two-thirty.'

'Bugger off then.'

It made a change for Monty to be waking Danny from a drunken stupor. It was usually the other way round.

'There's someone prowling around outside,' Monty whispered.

'Probably a fox.'

'Foxes don't talk to each other.'

It appeared that whoever were outside made careless burglars. As Danny came to his senses he heard whispers through the open window, but he couldn't make out what was being said. The sounds were the faintest mumbles. Monty was normally a sound sleeper, but having drunk more beer than usual, his bladder's need had woken him. It was a warm night and all the cottage windows were ajar.

'Who do you reckon it is?' Danny asked.

'Haven't got a clue, but we'd better find out.'

The choice of weapons was limited and remote. Danny was sure he'd seen a cricket bat somewhere and there was always the fire-place poker or Mrs Holyman's rolling pin, but he had to get to them first. Barefoot and dressed only in singlet and boxer-shorts made him feel vulnerable too. Then the sound of glass smashing at the kitchen door leading to the back garden gave him no time to dress. Danny and Monty dashed downstairs, barely able to see as there was little moonlight, but they made out an arm poking through the broken glass to release the door latch.

Danny flicked on the kitchen light, revealing three figures dressed in black and wearing balaclavas – and they were armed! The leading intruder levelled a Webley service revolver and fired just as Danny flicked the switch off again. He and Monty dived to either side sending kitchen bric-a-brac clattering onto the slate floor. Glass and chinaware smashed into razor sharp shards. The room plunged into darkness and the shot went wild. The roar of gunfire was deafening in the confines of Mrs Holyman's small kitchen. Muzzle flashes illuminated the dark figures for microseconds.

Danny heard Mrs Holyman scream from the upstairs bedroom. Angela bounded down the stairs in her fashionable baby-doll pyjamas and pink pom-pom slippers with her laundry stick ready for action.

As Danny and Monty regained their feet, the intruders advanced towards the stairwell. Angela swung her stick and struck human flesh. She heard a grunt so she struck again and this time the man slumped to the floor and was badly cut up by broken glass. Danny tackled one of the shadowy forms, dragging him across the kitchen table.

Meanwhile Monty swung blindly and landed a punch, but he had no idea where. All he knew was that his knuckles hurt like hell. Dr and Mrs Holyman rushed down the steps to the passageway leading to their kitchen. But just then the front door crashed open and three more thugs barged in, quickly over-powering the couple.

The extra intruders joined the frantic melee in the kitchen blackness. The room fell into total confusion for less than a minute while Danny, Monty and Angela desperately struggled to overpower the home-invaders. Suddenly the light blazed on again and a shot-gun blast sprayed plaster onto the table as pellets ripped into the ceiling.

'Right, that's inuff,' yelled a cockney voice. 'You lot pack it in, or I start killin' people.'

Danny, Monty and Angela saw that the shotgun barrel was now firmly levelled at Mrs Holyman's temple.

'Mummy!' Angela screamed, rushing towards the man holding her mother, only to receive a sharp back-hander that sent her reeling back onto the kitchen table. Danny just managed to catch her in time to prevent her cracking her head against the table top. Mrs Holyman screamed again. Dr Holyman was about to move, but the intruder's blazing eyes warned him off.

'Dun even fink abart it, sunshine,' the man snarled, pressing the shot-gun right against Mrs Holyman's skull.

Monty staggered to his feet only to be beaten to his knees by a rap on his shoulder from the Webley gun butt. Danny quickly assessed the situation and didn't like what he saw. There were six intruders including the one Angela had belted who was recovering. The revolver (Danny was unsure how many live shots remained in the chamber) and sawn-off shot gun (only one slug left, but that could do plenty of damage at close range) were the only firearms evident, but the other four men all brandished flick-knives.

'We come for that Yank nigger,' the leader said indicating Monty who was on his knees rubbing a lump on the back of his head. 'Now you lot can be bleedin' 'eroes if yer wanna be, but we'll blow yer to bleedin' smivverines if yer try summat.'

No one moved. Danny weighed his chances of jumping the shotgun bloke and assayed them to be zero. Also he couldn't risk Angela and Mrs Holyman if bullets started flying again.

'Get him on his feet and tie the others up,' the shot-gun holder ordered the gang. He seemed to be in charge.

'What's this all about?' Dr Holyman demanded. 'How dare you invade my home and threaten us?'

'I dare just fine, yer blivverin' idiot.'

Danny knew perfectly well what it was all about. These were Ronnie and Reggie Kray's bully-boys. Somehow they'd discovered where Monty was. About then Danny remembered the bloke in the Royal Oak bar who wasn't drinking with the regulars. He must have followed them from London. Danny had to admire how he stayed under the radar, but admitted they'd been careless and given no thought to pursuit once the police car had dropped out of the chase.

Danny reckoned it was better to stay mum, Ronnie and Reggie mightn't want any witnesses if they thought someone could connect them to Monty's abduction. It was most likely that Monty was destined for a watery grave somewhere in the North Sea held down by 'cement-wellies'.

Monty was manhandled to his feet while Danny, Angela and her parents were forced to sit on the kitchen chairs. The intruders ransacked Dr Holyman's surgery for bandage rolls which made first-class restraints. Danny, Angela and her parents were tightly bound with their hands behind them and their feet tied securely to the chair legs. They weren't going anywhere. The intruders also slapped surgical plaster over their captive's mouths, effectively gagging them.

The thugs dragged Monty through the kitchen door, switching the light off behind them.

Chapter 16 — Death in Dorset

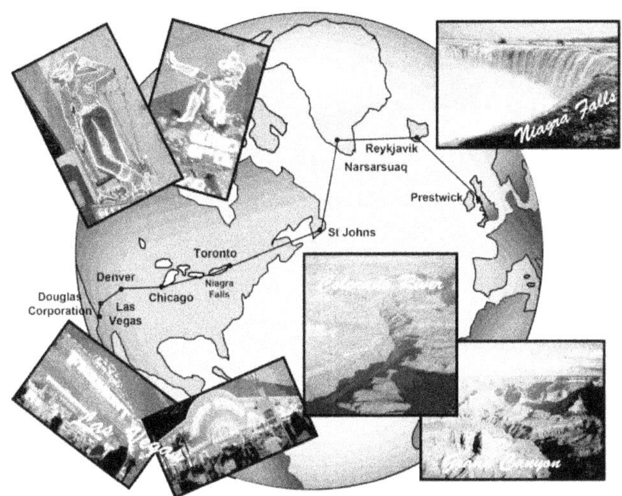

You had to give it to those London mobsters, they were experts at tying people up. They'd had plenty of practice. Not only were their victims' ankles firmly secured to the kitchen chair-legs, they'd also drawn a line tightly from their wrists and tied it to the horizontal cross-bar joining the rear chair-legs. Danny tried to struggle free but only risked toppling over for his trouble. They couldn't even call for help.

The mobsters were only gone seconds when Danny and Angela's predicament became academic. Two dull thuds — more like pops really — sounded from just beyond the kitchen door. One of the mobsters staggered back into the kitchen, collapsing across Angela's lap before slumping to the floor leaving her dainty baby-doll pyjamas drenched in blood.

There was the sound of a scuffle accompanied by numerous thumps, grunts and yelps of pain. The rumpus was all over in a couple of minutes and then a sinister figure edged cautiously through the door. He was armed with a Webley service revolver so Danny assumed it was the gun-toting mobster who'd baled them up previously.

With a flick of the switch the kitchen came to light. The captives all squinted as their eyes adjusted once more.

'Oh dear, dear me,' a plummy voice clucked. 'I say you do look uncomfortable. Hang on a jiffy while we get you sorted.'

Blow me down, it's the toffee-nosed Secret-Service joker from Lyneham aerodrome!

Sure enough it was the MI-6 agent who never revealed his name. Now there was no obvious danger, he confidently strode into the kitchen. He was followed by two uniformed policemen, one of whom rummaged through the cutlery drawer and found a pair of scissors. He soon cut through the bandages, asking if everyone was OK. The policemen were most attentive when it came to Angela. Danny had to admit she looked very fetching even after her ordeal, blood stains and all.

While Dr Holyman comforted his wife and Angela raced to her room for some clothes, Danny tried to assess the situation. He had to admit he was never more pleased to see the pompous MI-6 agent, even if he didn't like him.

'What happened? Where's Monty?' Danny asked urgently.

'Come and take a look for yourself, old bean.'

Danny walked slowly outside. The back garden was crowded with uniformed and plain-clothed bobbies. They were all armed. The shotgun mobster lay on the ground while the remaining four were now hand-cuffed and being led away to a black-Maria. Over the garden hedge in the street Danny saw several other police cars parked randomly with blue light flashing.

Monty stood among the policemen seemingly little the worse for wear. Flanking him stood Major Black and Major White who were lighting a cigarette each. Although they wore their camouflage army fatigues, there was no indication that either CIA man was armed.

'Boy, am I glad to see you blokes,' Danny said.

'Not half as glad as I am,' Monty added.

'I thought you were going somewhere so secret that you'd have to kill us if you told where it was,' Danny addressed the majors. 'How the blazes did you find us?'

'We were about to leave, but having buddies in the right place changed our plans,' Major Black said with a nod towards the MI-6 agent. 'When we got word of what was going on, we delayed our departure.'

Tracking down the would-be kidnappers was a testament to admirable international co-operation, goodwill and communication. Once the Met coppers had settled the Trafalgar Square riot and began questioning those involved they quickly realised they'd scooped up a couple of Ronnie and Reggie's bad lads in the mix. When they discovered the mobsters were out to get a black Yank, the police decided to notify Special Branch who in turn passed the word onto MI-6 that an American citizen might be in danger.

MI-6 notified the American Embassy as a courtesy. As Major White and Major Black were yet to leave for Germany, they had a pretty shrewd notion who that American citizen might be. In any case it was worth investigating. Although still in ICU with several cracked ribs, a broken leg and suspected concussion, the mob's bike rider who'd slammed into the squad car confirmed that he was chasing two getaway bikes with his mate who'd somehow dodged the police vehicle.

'We knew you'd either head for Lyneham and your plane — which would have been the smart thing to do,' Major Black said, 'or come down here to the Holyman place.'

'The "smart thing to do" doesn't seem to be an option for these two,' Dr Holyman said from the back doorway where he comforted Mrs Holyman who was lamenting the blood splattered corpse on her kitchen floor. 'And my daughter isn't much better,' he added, glaring at Angela as she stepped over the dead gangster into the garden. She was now dressed in jeans and a t-shirt. Having endured the bloodbath at Dien Bien Phu, Angela coped better with violent death than her mother who was a bit of a delicate English rose when you got right down to it.

'Once we discovered you weren't at the RAF base, we got down here as quickly as we could,' Major Black continued. 'The cops at Yeovil confirmed our suspicions when they contacted Scotland Yard because the bikes you stole were registered to London lads with some minor form.'

So it all fitted into place and the cavalry arrived in the nick of time with guns blazing. Well not actually. The two majors were merely observers during the shoot-out. Not that it was *the gunfight at the OK Corral.* Special Branch marksmen only needed to fire two shots from their silenced rifles to neutralise the armed villains. The other four surrendered after a short scuffle against an overwhelming force of truncheon-wielding bobbies.

'Ronnie and Reggie Kray are in big trouble then?' Angela said.

'Regretfully I rather doubt it,' the MI-6 agent replied wearily. 'This lot will do time for GBH, breaking and entering and attempted kidnapping. We've got them dead-to-rights on those counts, but they won't grass up the Krays. They'd be dead within a week of going inside if they did. They'll take the fall and do their time.'

While an ambulance was summoned from Yeovil to carry off the two dead men, the other crooks were whisked away in a paddy-van. The toffee-nose MI-6 agent used the police radio to get a clean-up team at the crime scene to erase any evidence of the entire operation. The inspector leading the police team thought it was most irregular and voiced his opinion, but was promptly informed it was a secret-service matter on a strictly need-to-know basis. Everyone, including the police officers, were all solemnly reminded of their obligations under the Official Secrets Act and that was pretty well that.

One matter did remain however, which the MI-6 agent was quick to point out.

'Now what are we going to do with the pair of you?' he muttered, facing Danny and Monty. That seemed to be an ongoing dilemma for authorities worldwide.

'Aw, come on,' Monty protested. 'This wasn't our fault. We didn't do anything just because a couple of crazy gang-bangers got the wrong idea.'

'True enough,' the Secret-Serviceman agreed, 'but I think it would be a grand idea if you two disappeared.'

Danny and Monty exchanged nervous glances.

'No, nothing like that, you dopes,' the MI-6 agent actually smiled as he took out his pipe and lit up.

'It's time to finish the assignment we're paying you for,' Major White said. 'Tomorrow you fly that plane to the States. That should keep you out of trouble for at least a week.'

Danny was disappointed that he'd be leaving Angela again, but realised the majors' plan made sense. They needed to get Danny and Monty far away from the British justice system. Ronnie and Reggie's boys' trial would dredge up all sorts of problems for trans-Atlantic relations, not to mention Anglo-Australian technicalities.

Everyone knew the risks witnesses faced against the Kray brothers. Luckily the Secret-Service could invoke an *in-the-national-interest* clause or DORA where the statements of all five victims would be sufficient for a conviction. Although the case was essentially a police matter, the fact that CIA agents were involved allowed MI-6 to take over proceedings and circumnavigate considerable legal red-tape. The lawyers would just have to sit this one out. As mere spectators, it was probably a bit of a stretch for the majors to be implicated although they'd called in some favours to stay out of the limelight. Nevertheless the four surviving mobsters found themselves doing hard time at some remote, undisclosed location awaiting Her Majesty's pleasure.

The following morning the cleanup team arrived and restored Mrs Holyman's kitchen to its pristine state, including replacing the broken glass panes and removing every trace of blood. They were quick, efficient and remarkably cheerful considering the task in hand. After two hours they bid every one goodbye, climbed into their van and vanished as mysteriously as they'd appeared.

Where Major White and Major Black spent the night was anyone's guess, but they turned up freshly shaven and immaculately dressed in dark suits, spit-polished black shoes, trilby hats and sun-glasses. Mrs Holyman laid them both a place at the breakfast table where they tucked into toast, bacon and marmalade. It wasn't Danny's choice as a taste-combination, but he'd learnt from Monty that Americans were gastronomically unique.

'Now I must say that was an interesting night,' Dr Holyman said, dunking toast soldiers into his boiled egg, which Angela had prepared. Danny recalled the very first meal he'd eaten with her. She'd boiled eggs over an open fire on a tropical beach beside the Fly River in New Guinea five years earlier. Funny how he remembered those details.

'It was just so ghastly,' Mrs Holyman sighed. 'I don't know how I'll ever cook in here again.'

'Oh Mummy, don't be such a baby, of course you will. Everything has been cleaned up just like new. That fellow the police shot was a thoroughly bad chap. Just think what those men wanted to do to poor Mr Montgomery.'

'Thank you,' Monty grinned.

'Umm, I wonder if it had been better to let them kidnap you.'

'Ange, I know deep down you really love me.'

'Love has never been a word I would associate with our relationship, Mr Montgomery,' she replied with one of her most engaging smiles.

'Don't be so smug, young lady,' Dr Holyman said. 'You and I shall go straight up to London and pack your things. You will have to prepare for your first real job.'

'How can you say that, Daddy,' Angela pouted. 'I worked as a waitress all through university to add to my pocket money.'

Danny liked the way she said 'pocket money' and not 'allowance'.

Angela had used the cash to fund extra classes during university breaks. She'd barely taken a day off in all her time at Guy's. Her beauty and charm along with dedicated and intensely focused study had ensured she was never short of tutors ready to help her towards academic success. Angela was King's College's darling and brightest undergraduate star, so shrewd staff members were happy to be associated with her ascendancy. Major Paul Grauwin, the senior medical officer at Dien Bien Phu had written a long and glowing report detailing Angela's work there, for which she was awarded a large number of additional credits. Effectively she'd completed a six year course in four. Of course she was never short of romantic advances, but rejected them all.

Where on earth she got the time was a mystery to Danny.

'You worked damned hard at Dien Bien Phu,' Danny added. 'I seem to remember you saying something about wanting my help on your new mystery project.'

'Well yes, Danny,' she replied sheepishly.

'I don't like the sound of this already,' Monty added.

'Let me explain,' she replied. 'I've been offered a grant to do post-graduate research into tropical diseases, which is where I hope to specialise.'

'Good for you,' Monty cheered.

'Oh do be quiet, Mr Montgomery. I shall be going to East Africa to assist my mentor, Professor Geoff Winslow in field research including a mobile clinic. The project has several sponsors including the WHO.'

'Super!' Monty said with the poshest English accent he could manage.

Angela ignored him.

'It seems you've got it all covered, 'Danny said. 'Where do I come in?'

'The area assigned to us is huge. We'll need someone to fly us around and I immediately thought of you and Mr Montgomery, just like in our old New Guinea days. We're starting on the first of September. We have a plane — a Lockheed Model 10 Electra, I understand. Unfortunately we've been unable to find any pilots so I thought of you two.'

'Well I'd be delighted, it's the same type of plane Amelia Earhart disappeared in,' Danny replied.

'That's supposed to be reassuring, is it?' Angela giggled.

'We won't be flying over endless miles of ocean I presume. We can get back from the States in plenty of time after delivering the Dak, can't we Monty?'

'Sure, no problem.'

'There's just one thing,' Angela said softly, lowering her eyes.

'I knew it! I knew there'd be a catch,' Monty said.

'OK, Ange. What's the deal?'

'All the grant's travel funds have been allocated to lease a plane, so we don't actually have any money left over to pay you.'

'Well no wonder you can't find any pilots. They have to eat, you know,' Danny said.

'We'll feed you of course and put a roof over your heads...and it's only for three months until Christmas.'

I wonder what happens to the tropical diseases after that, Danny thought cynically, but shut up about it. Monty merely shrugged.

'I'm in,' he said, 'but here's something you haven't considered, Ange.'

'Oh..?'

'We're still employed by CAT the last time I checked. Dunno what Bob Rousselot will have to say about it.'

'Tell ya what,' Major Black said with largesse. 'It seems to me you guys are mighty fond of this little lady, so we'll square things with CAT management. After you deliver the *Gooney-Bird,* how's about you take leave-without-pay until New Year then report back to Hong Kong and start work again.'

Monty and Danny exchanged glances, nodded. What Angela thought about being called a *little lady* remained unknown.

'How do we get back east after the job?' Monty wondered. 'In fact how do we get from California to wherever we start in Africa?'

'Easy,' Major White said, 'the CIA can issue travel passes on any US military aircraft. I'm sure we can persuade MI-6 to do the same with RAF Transport Command. You can hitch a ride on any of our planes. You can't ask fairer than that.'

'It's not what you know, it's who you know,' Angela observed.

'These guys have done us plenty of favours in the past,' Major Black explained, 'and they'll probably do us some more in the future. I'd say that's *quid pro quo,* wouldn't you?'

So the deal was struck. Angela hinted she would like to go to California, but Major White and Major Black firmly refused. She had no entry visa to the States, and even they didn't have time to process one. The majors wanted Danny and Monty out of Great Britain that day. Dr Holyman said that Angela would have enough on her plate preparing for the expedition if she was to make a thorough professional job of the project.

Danny regretted leaving Angela of course. As always he felt that, although she could be a right pain-in-the-arse, she was irresistible most of the time. As soon as breakfast was over, Danny and Monty clambered into the majors' Jeep and headed for RAF Lyneham.

The majors arranged for Danny and Monty's CAT back-pay to be transferred to the Chase Manhattan Bank with access through Wells Fargo and AMEX agencies, so they'd have sufficient access to funds while Stateside. The Dak was serviced and fully fuelled. So with their flight plan and diplomatic clearances approved, rations on board, fuel authorities and cash imprest in hand, they soared north.

Their flight took several days via Prestwick — Scotland, Reykjavik — Iceland, Narsarsuaq — Greenland, St John's — Newfoundland, Toronto where Danny and Monty took time to visit Niagara Falls, Chicago and Denver. Monty insisted they make a dawn departure for the leg through the Rocky Mountain passes to the Grand Canyon. Of course he couldn't resist flying well below the rim and the view was awesome in every sense of the word. It was a turbulent ride until they crossed Lake Mead and Hoover Dam. The vast expanse of water cooled and stabilised the air above it. Nevertheless, the temperature was unbearably hot when they landed at McCarran Field, Las Vegas.

'What do you reckon is mankind's greatest invention?' Monty asked as they entered the terminal building.

'I dunno — the wheel: internal combustion engine: electricity: penicillin maybe?'

'None of the above — aircon!'

After arranging fuel for their final flight to California, Monty and Danny took a cab for a tour around town. The infinite flashing neon signs and casino lights including the Golden Nugget Casino on Fremont Street, El Dorado and Pioneer Club were breathtaking. Danny had never imagined such glitter and glitz. The world's top entertainers vied for lucrative gigs at the casinos. Endless billboards proclaimed that Liberace was playing at the brand new Riviera Hotel-Casino on the Strip.

After a while Danny and Monty decided it was time to find accommodation and get the feel of the city on foot. Their cab driver wisely suggested they book into the Moulin Rouge complex on West Bonanza Road.

Las Vegas, like much of the USA, still clung to segregation whatever the official position might be. The strip was predominantly a white paradise although they permitted mega-stars like Sammy Davis Jr, Nat King Cole, Lena Horne, Harry Belafonte and Louis Armstrong to perform as long as they came and went via the tradesman's entrance. West Las Vegas was a black domain, while Bonanza Street was located between the two districts and the newly opened Moulin Rouge catered for all comers.

Inside the rattle at the roulette wheels, the clatter of dice at the crap table and the endless clinking cacophony of slot machines were all mesmerizing.

'It's just as well Ange didn't come,' Danny said, eyeing a cocktail waitress in a cleavage-enhancing satin leotard, fishnet tights and red patent-leather stilettos. As long as you gambled, the girls ensured your glass was always full.

'Yep, she'd disapprove alright,' Monty agreed. 'Look at all these folks having fun. That would never do.'

Monty was right about all those folks. The place was packed. In fact they checked into the last room at the Moulin Rouge. All the hotels on the recently established, rapidly developing Strip south of Fremont were booked out.

'This sure is a popular place,' Danny observed to one of the busty cocktail waitresses.

'Why, you ain't from around here, are ya honey?' she observed sagely.

'No, I come from Australia.'

'My, that musta been a long trip on the Greyhound.'

'No, there's too much ocean between here and there to come by bus. I flew. My friend and I are aviators.'

'Well, lordy and you being so young,' she said wide-eyed. 'Are y'all here for the bomb?'

'Bomb..?'

'Why sure, sugar. Most of these folks have come to see the atomic-bomb test over Mohave Desert tomorrow.'

'I saw enough bombs in Korea and Indochina, thanks,' Danny said. 'I reckon I'll give it a miss.'

It was a wise decision as Americans were still mysteriously succumbing to all sorts of cancers for decades afterwards. Finally someone made the link to the atomic fallout absorbed by bomb-watchers.

Monty was not as successful at the tables as he'd been in Soho and soon got tired of losing. So he and Danny took in one of the burlesque variety shows, which were some of Las Vegas' prime attractions. Why wouldn't they be, with dozens of long-legged, high-kicking show-girls as eye-candy and world-class artists to entertain the punters?

The clubs were mainly run by Chicago and Los Angeles organised crime cartels using shady Salt Lake City bankers to launder their winnings. Fortunately Monty stayed out of trouble with the local mobsters who made the Kray boys look like choir boys.

Danny and Monty took off in the dawn coolness when flying conditions were smooth. They also needed to be away before Nevada and Arizona airways were closed for the atomic-bomb test.

Next stop — the Douglas Corporation, South California.

Chapter 17 — Green Book

The best way to describe the Douglas Aircraft Corporation Field was 'overwhelmingly busy'. Danny had flown in and out of hectic airports before. *Torri-Rouge* immediately sprang to mind, but Douglas Field was like a hornets' nest of activity. And it needed to be. Douglas was vying with Boeing, Lockheed, Fairchild and Convair for military and civil contracts. Right now the race was on to produce long range jet airliners to replace Britain's ill-fated De Havilland Comet, which had stolen a march on its American rivals until three disastrous mid-air structural break-ups saw the pioneer jet plane removed from service.

The Americans knew it could be done and the race was on to get their planes operational. It looked like Boeing was leading the pack with their B 367-80 making its maiden flight the previous year. So Douglas was in a frenzy to catch up.

But civil aviation wasn't the only game in town. Although most US military commanders were focused on the Cold War with Russia, other shrewd planners were well aware of the dangers of guerrilla warfare in far flung places.

A CIA operative met the *Gooney-Bird* when it landed and Danny was delighted to see his old comrade Lieutenant-Colonel Ted Serong was with him. In the past Colonel Serong had helped Danny and Monty out of a couple of tight scrapes in New Guinea. Although he was technically Danny's boss, he was also a good friend.

'Hello Colonel,' Danny greeted him, shaking hands. 'It's great to see you again, but I thought you were in Burma.'

'I get around,' was all Serong said. 'I heard you two were coming and I'm interested in what the military has in store for your plane.'

'We have another unit already converted, Colonel,' the stony-face spook said. 'You wanna check it out?'

'Too right,' Serong replied. 'Do you mind if these two gorillas tag along?'

'Not if you vouch for 'em, sir.'

'They might be a bit feral, but they're not hostile,' Serong grinned.

The spook led Serong, Danny and Monty across the tarmac to a parked C-47. A USAF captain and second-lieutenant already occupied the pilot and co-pilot's seats, running through the pre-engine-start checklist. Approaching from the starboard side there was nothing remarkable about the plane, but when they walked around the tail they saw the rear paratroop door had been removed along with the two side windows just aft of the wing-root. Sinister black cylinders protruded from the breaches.

'Are those what I think they are?' Serong asked.

'Sure thing, Colonel. Heavy-duty AN/M2 rapid-fire machine guns designed to concentrate fire into an enemy position. It's ex-WWII and Korean ordnance, Colonel, but that's all the brass will let us play with. We hope to land a round every three or four square yards.'

'How exactly does it work?'

'Wait and see the demo,' the CIA agent said, indicating the buzz of human activity around the plane. 'These guys are just itching to take her up and try it out. There's plenty room for y'all.'

They clambered aboard to be confronted by a metallic jumble of high fire-power hardware. The machine guns were bolted to the fuselage superstructure and supported by a clutter of ammunition bins and bullet feed-belts. Seats had only been fitted for the gunners on that prototype aircraft, so it was a case of hang on tight as the plane rumbled skywards.

After about half-an-hour the C-47 reached the firing range. One of the gunners pointed out the target area, a chequered marker spread across the desert over about thirty square yards. Dozens of plywood cut out figures had been erected on the target standing several yards apart.

'That's it, sir,' the gunner yelled.

'It's not very big,' Colonel Serong observed.

'That's kinda the point, sir. We're supposed to eliminate small enemy pockets of resistance.'

Serong nodded as he looked sceptically at the target. Just then the gunners all seemed to be communicating with the pilots at the same time. An orange smoke marker puffed skywards beside the cut-outs as the squad of grunts who'd prepared the target scurried for the cover in a concrete bunker a hundred yards away.

The pilot banked the plane at about thirty degrees which was particularly dramatic until the fuselage suddenly burst into utter thunderous mayhem.

The three gunners simultaneously launched into action. The machine guns erupted in a deafening blaze of rapid fire as bullets streamed from the plane fuselage. Hundreds of spent shells spat from the gun ejector mechanisms peppering Danny, Monty and Colonel Serong with red-hot cartridges. As Danny peered through the cargo door he saw the target being ripped to shreds while the wooden figures were vaporised into sawdust. Being on the receiving end would have been terrifying and almost certainly fatal.

However, after only seconds, two of the machine guns stopped as spent rounds wedged in their breaches. The gunners were armed with hunting knives which they expertly used to whip the offending shells free, before re-cocking the weapons and continuing the onslaught. Almost immediately the third gun jammed. The demonstration only lasted five minutes – barely enough time for the plane to circle the target twice, but the target was reduced to a smoking ruin even though each gun jammed three or four times.

Once the ammunition was expended the gunners reported to the pilots that it was all over. The plane circled while the ground crew inspected the target, confirming it had been totalled.

'Impressive,' Serong commented although he was concerned by how prone to jamming the guns were. Military high-command must have agreed with him because, although the project wasn't shelved, it took almost another decade to be brought into operation. Danny thought the idea of turning a transport plane into a firing platform was pretty cool, but considered the C-47 vulnerable to enemy fire. He still harboured an idea of converting choppers into gunships which he'd included in his report to Colonel Serong after a tour-of-duty in Korea.

When they landed at Douglas Field, Serong seemed absorbed with the firing test and strode off to the operations building deep in discussion with the CIA spook. Although still officially under Australian direct command, he liaised closely with the CIA with the primary brief to investigate and develop anti-guerrilla jungle warfare tactics. Danny and Monty tagged along, but it appeared the colonel would be otherwise occupied so they'd have to fend for themselves.

That wasn't any particular problem and Monty made an announcement.

'Y'know, buddy,' he said draping his arm over Danny's shoulder, 'we've got six weeks before Ange wants us, so tell ya what we'll do.'

'I'm all ears as long as it doesn't involve risk, bloodshed or any danger to me whatsoever.'

'Nosirree. We're gonna hire us an automobile and drive right across to Alabama. I ain't been home for years and I'd like you to meet my folks.'

'You're not going to ask me to marry you, are you?'

'Well maybe later, but when they write me they always ask after you.'

'They know who I am?'

'Sure, you're my partner, I've told 'em all about you.'

Danny said nothing.

'What d'ya reckon. We'll live the all-American dream and have a road-trip to remember. It'll be fun and I'd like to show you my home town.'

'I thought *Kago Ailan* was your home.'

'I kinda got deported, remember.'

Danny had secretly thought he'd get back to spend more time with Angela, but the majors had ordered him to lie low for a while.

'Yeah, why not?' he said. 'I'd love to meet your folks. Let's go and say cheerio to the colonel.'

*

Danny and Monty rode the bus to LA where they hired a 1953 Chevrolet Bel Air convertible to begin a road trip east. Luckily Avis had a car they wanted ferried to New Orleans so the rate was reduced considerably. Danny and Monty figured they could use public transport the rest of the way to Montgomery. The car was big and flashy, including white-wall tyres and ample chrome trim. Danny loved it.

They drove out of LA, following the legendry Route 66. Although the song had been recorded by several artists for nine years, it was yet to attain its iconic status. They experienced some great sight-seeing on the way and hanging out in dingy smoke-filled bars where quality local musicians turned up randomly to play for beer and tips was fun.

In some ways America reminded Danny of Australia because of the wide expanses of boring landscape punctuated by moments of sheer magnificence. The most notable difference was the surging feeling of confidence and prosperity. The mighty highways were superb compared to the rutted roads of Northern Queensland or the muddy tracks in New Guinea and Asia. Numerous oil-rigs along the way made novel if not picturesque scenery. Somewhere in New Mexico they passed a sign-post that read:

McALISTER RANCH
PRIME RANGE FED LONGHORN BEEF
GUARANTEED TO TURN
VEGETARIANS INTO CARNIVORES

'Kinfolk of yours?' Monty suggested.

'You're worse than Angela's mum. Just because we have the same name doesn't means we're cousins or anything. McAlister is a pretty common name you know.'

Towns like Flagstaff and Albuquerque were spreading into sprawling suburban metropolises where TV was king. It was the American wonder of the age with three major networks providing almost nation-wide coverage. There was even a set in some of the more up-market motels where Danny and Monty stayed. Although motels were emerging in Australia, Danny had only yet experienced the colonial austerity of country pubs. Even the cabins they stayed at were comfortable, well appointed and clean.

As automobiles were part of the New American prosperity, Travelodge, Harlan Sanders and Best Western motel chains had made family road trips universally popular. But as they travelled further east Danny noticed Monty referring to a green-coloured book when they selected their nightly accommodation.

'What's the book for?' Danny finally asked.

'It's just an accommodation guide,' Monty replied defensively.

'How come we need it? We just drive up. There is always somewhere to stay.'

'Not for long.'

Monty reluctantly passed the book to Danny.

'We're gonna have to face it sooner or later.'

The book was entitled *The Negro Motorist Green Book* published by Victor Green. It was the latest 1955 edition and listed all the hotels, restaurants, motels and other travel amenities that accepted coloured patrons.

'You're joking, right?' Danny said incredulously.

'Nope. You gonna see the Jim Crow laws in operation real soon now.'

It was then that Danny realised the situation was much the same or even worse for Australian Aborigines. The White-Australia Policy kept Australia neatly insulated from the need to face racial challenges. In truth Danny had seen very few Negroes, as Black Americans were then known before political-correct idealists found that term (along with pretty well everything else) offensive.

Danny wanted to see Texas.

'I can't come to the States and not see at least a bit of Texas,' he insisted.

So they turned off the highway at Santa Rosa, New Mexico and took the road through Clovis on the state border to Lubbock, Texas. Not that motoring through the Panhandle flatlands was particularly inspirational, but Danny was able to say he'd been there. Now as they entered cotton-country, the black population increased and prosperity decreased noticeably. Until then music hadn't exactly blasted from the radio, but rather crooned its way over the airwaves. Now radio stations were playing more country and blues, notably KLL broadcasting out of Little Field in Lamb County.

When they reached the town they decided they'd driven enough and called it a day. They checked into a 'green-book' motel and set out to explore Little Field although there wasn't a great deal of sight-seeing to be had. With nothing better to do, they found a downtown bar and stopped in for a beer. A group called the *Texas Longhorns* had set up in the corner. The bar stretched across the entire room with a small dance floor and several tables. A kid of about eighteen with a smooth baritone voice, playing a Harmony Silvertone electric guitar fronted the band. They played some pretty slick music that blended blues, country, Cajun and bluegrass. The band was first class, but the place was virtually deserted other than a group of rednecks on stools lining the bar.

Danny ordered the drinks which the bartender sullenly provided while the red-necks looked positively hostile.

'Hey, Benny,' one of the rednecks hollered to the barman above the music. 'You sure about this situation developin' here.'

'What situation would that be, Phil?' Benny replied softly as the band had suddenly stopped playing. The musicians sensed the tension and looked on nervously.

'You thick or somethin', Benny? You know we don't want no niggers in here.'

'Now y'all know I don't hold with no Jim Crow rules,' Benny answered.

'Maybe you don't, but we're payin' customers and we say kick the nigger out.'

At this stage the 'we' appeared only to be Phil, but his cronies nodded in agreement.

'Hey you, kid,' Phil addressed Danny. 'How about you and your boy there hightail it outa here?'

Danny slowly turned to Phil, glaring straight into his eyes.

'Firstly Monty isn't "my boy" as you so crudely put it. He's my friend. Secondly it's stinking hot outside and we'll stay here until we've finished our drinks and cooled off. I suggest you do the same.'

'Well, listen to mister la-de-da Yankee, won't ya?' Phil jeered. 'C'mon boys, let's show this here nigger and his fancy-dandy buddy some good ole Texas hospitality.'

'You don't want to do that,' Monty warned.

'I ain't talkin' to you, nigger,' Phil snarled, 'but I sure as hell am gonna give you the whuppin' y'all deserve.'

Without further warning the three men charged. Maybe charged wasn't entirely accurate. They'd been at the bar downing shots and beer chasers all afternoon so they were a little unsteady on their feet. While they didn't actually stagger, they were less than impressive and they'd chosen the wrong two individuals to mess with.

As Phil came within range, Danny didn't hesitate. He slammed his foot into Phil's crotch, clouting him on the nape as he went down. Monty smashed his beer glass into the next redneck's face then pummelled his midriff with his left fist before kneeing him in the groin, which was Danny and Monty's target-of-choice in a close fight.

The third redneck wisely bolted for the door and fled into the street. The brawl was over in seconds leaving two men groaning and rolling on the floor, nursing their privates. Then Danny heard a familiar click-click and turned to stare down the barrelled of a Colt .45 Peacemaker revolver aimed between his eyes.

'I aughta blow your brains out,' Benny hissed with menace.

He held the six-shooter at arm's length although his hands trembled with uncertainty.

'Now hold on there, hoss,' the band's lead singer drawled easily. 'You ain't no born killer, Benny and these fellas were just defendin' themselves. Phil and Alan there are hurtin' sure, but it ain't fatal and I opine they had it comin'.

'Hell Waylon, they're my regulars,' Benny complained.

'Yeah, it's a classy joint, but I like the atmosphere most of the time,' Waylon grinned. He appeared extremely confident and obviously carried some local clout considering he was so young. In any event Benny un-cocked and lowered the pistol.

'I think it might be a good idea if you two fellas skedaddled anyway,' Benny advised.

'Yeah,' Waylon agreed. 'Folks around town are kinda clanny and I reckon Phil's kin'll be boiling in here pretty soon. That don't mean y'all ain't welcome from my point of view, but that ain't necessarily universal.'

'We're getting run out of town?' Danny said.

'Better than bein' tarred-and-feathered.'

'No one does that anymore,' Monty said.

'You ain't from around here, are ya pilgrim?' Waylon grinned. 'Tell ya what, we're all done reheasin' for today. Me and the boys are headed into Lubbock for a show tonight. How about you good ole boys tag along? Howdy, my name's Waylon Jennings and I do a regular slot on KLL with these guys.'

Waylon introduced his band members, Emil Macha and JB McShan. It turned out that JB was KLL's owner and manager who'd scrounged tickets for the show. As the boys were between girlfriends at the time they had a couple left over including back-stage passes. Waylon accompanied Danny and Monty back to their hotel while JB and Emil took their pick-up truck and drove on ahead. Waylon said he'd ride with Danny and Monty to show them the way.

Danny and Monty hadn't unpacked so it was no trouble loading their grips into the boot that Americans called a trunk. Waylon indeed showed his influence when he convinced the motel owner to refund Danny and Monty's money as they hadn't used the room although Danny left him five dollars for his trouble. Waylon noticed the ukuleles with interest. He'd played one as a kid.

'You fellas any good?' he asked casually.

'Yeah, not bad actually,' Danny replied truthfully. 'Monty has been teaching me how to play the blues.'

'The kid's a natural,' Monty added.

'Blues on a uke, this I gotta hear, maybe we'll jam some later.'

'Love to,' Danny replied. 'Last serious session we had was in a Vietnamese village.'

'Ain't never heard of the place.' Waylon said.

'And I hope you'll never have to. We'll tell you about it on the way,' Monty said with a grin.

'It ain't in Texas that's fer sure.'

Waylon was impressed by the Bel Air and was pleased he'd decided to ride along with them. Although the amps and electric instruments remained in the bar-room for the weekend show, Waylon always carried a Stella acoustic guitar wherever he went and was likely to spontaneously burst into song at any time. He slung the guitar case into the back seat and clambered in beside it.

'OK, fellas,' he said once he was comfortable and had checked out the car's furnishings. 'Let's go. Lubbock's about thirty miles down the road a piece.'

With Monty at the wheel, the Bel Air sped off with both he and Danny having few regrets about leaving Little Field never to return.

Chapter 18 — Jammin' with Elvis — Roadhouse Blues

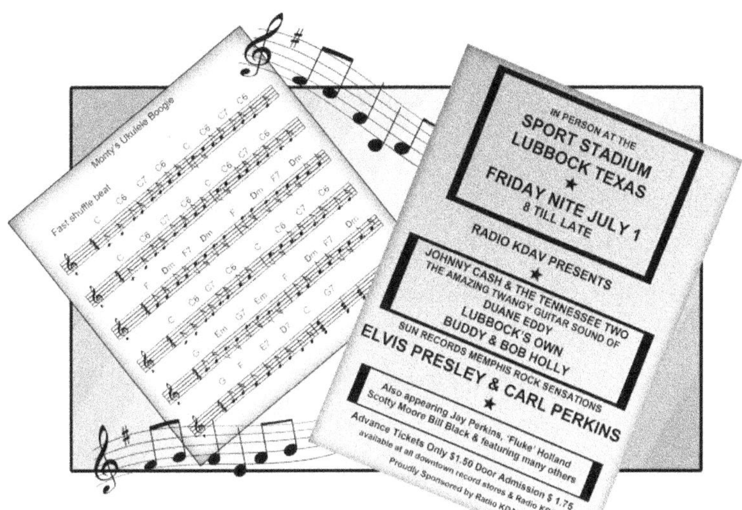

'You buckaroos sure know how to handle yourselves,' Waylon observed as they cruised towards Lubbock. He lounged across the back seat with his arm around his guitar case as if it was his sweetheart, which it was in a way. His mother had encouraged him to sing since he was a toddler and bought him a guitar. He'd been playing and singing publicly since he was eight years old.

'Yeah, we sort of get into tight spots sometimes,' Danny replied.

Did he really say 'buckaroos'?

'You kinda sound like them British fellas in the movies,' Waylon observed. 'You from Maine or Vermont or one of them Yankee states?'

'Australia actually.'

As Waylon was a high school dropout who concentrated on music and pretty well nothing else, it took a while to sort out where Australia was and even then Danny was uncertain whether Waylon understood fully.

'Who're we gonna see tonight?' Monty asked.

'A bunch of out-of-towners, but a couple of my buddies from Lubbock are playin' the lead act.'

Waylon pulled a flyer from his jacket pocket and handed it to Danny. The show's line-up was impressive. You got your money's worth when it came to concerts in those days. Often as many as a dozen top performers would tour together on a star-packed bill. On this occasion Sun Records' master mind, Sam Phillips had unleashed his emerging rock-a-billy talent on a whirlwind tour of Mississippi, Arkansas and Texas. Local boys Buddy and Bob Holly were getting their big chance as supporting artists.

Most of the performers were younger than Danny, clean cut white kids who all hungered for a black music sound. Monty had to park some distance away as streams of automobiles surrounded the stadium because the car park was full. Emil Macha and JB McShan waited for them at the gate. As they filed through the turnstile, Danny was surrounded by hundreds of excited teenagers pouring into the arena where a stage had been set in the centre of the ground. Monty was not only one of the few black men in the crowd, but other than the security officials, he was several years older than everyone else. No one cared or gave him a second glance.

The show started right on the dot by an out-of-town DJ called Lee Hazelwood who was encouraging seventeen-year-old Duane Eddy, an Arizona kid playing a Les Paul guitar and supported by a four-piece band. Hazelwood yelled through the mike to be heard above the roar of screaming girls. The amplifying system was booming at full volume as Eddy took to the stage.

He was shy-looking youngster who almost looked afraid of the crowd. He certainly had the looks to attract hordes of screaming female fans who went wild once he settled in and started belting out grungy guitar instrumentals including *Sugarfoot Rag, Dixie* and a rocky version of *My Bonnie Lies Over the Ocean.*

The Holly brothers followed performing a set of country and bluegrass standards to an enthusiastic home-town reception. Then came the lanky gravel-throated Arkansas baritone Johnny Cash. He was accompanied by upright bass-man Marshall Grant and guitarist Luther Perkins who played in a distinctive clickety-clack rhythmic style. Among Cash's offerings were country rock numbers *Hey Porter, Folsom Prison Blues* and ballads including his first Sun Records hit *Cry, Cry, Cry* and his latest song due for imminent release entitled, *I Walk the Line.* The crowd loved Johnny Cash and roared for more.

Danny had never seen anything like the mass hysteria revved up by thousands of teenage girls, unless of course you counted fanatical Korean, Chinese and Viet Minh troops charging straight at you, baying for blood. Right then Danny wasn't sure which was the most terrifying, but there was still more to come.

Monty, who was a blues man at heart, wasn't sure what to make of it. He enjoyed the music, but he preferred the smoky atmosphere of bar-rooms and pool-halls. Massed crowds were OK for ball games, but right now he found this situation particularly daunting.

As they ate hot-dogs and popcorn and drank soda during the intermission, Danny noticed there was no animosity towards Monty at all. Even though the crowd was virtually entirely white, they accepted Monty without question. It was as if music had levelled the racial playing-fields.

Carl Perkins (who was no relation to Luther) once again sent the crowd into uproar. He sang *Blue Moon of Kentucky, Wabash*

Cannonball and *Cotton Fields* with an up-tempo, rockabilly beat. His songs mostly followed a twelve-bar blues chord progression formula, but he sure made the most of it. His finale was a rocking number called *Blue Suede Shoes* that Perkins had recently composed and Sam Phillips intended to record in his Memphis studio.

But Danny was caught completely by surprise when Elvis Presley exploded onto the stage. Although his voice was remarkable, it was the way he moved that sent the crowd into raptures. Presley gyrated for over half-an-hour. Who knew what he actually sang. The screams from the crowd overwhelmed even the stadium's powerful PA system. The tremor and noise reminded Danny of the Viet Minh artillery bombardment on Dien Bein Phu.

The performance ended in one final pulsating, hip-swinging chorus of *That's Alright, Mama*. Presley and his band were ushered from the stage by a contingent of Lubbock's finest, who then turned their attention to dispersing the crowd. To Danny's surprise the crush of squealing, giggling high-school cheer-leaders, future prom-princesses and homecoming queen hopefuls, college freshmen and sophomores filed out of the stadium without incident. Although they were obviously still buoyed up in a hormonal euphoria, they were just good-natured, law-abiding kids with no axe to grind with anyone or anything. Although many of the girls were driven home by boyfriends, as often as not they were picked up by their parents. Lubbock adults may not have approved of performers such as Elvis Presley, but at least they'd see their daughters arrived home safely.

A pack of autograph hunters crowded around the stadium exits, but the artists were escorted to awaiting buses and driven off to their undisclosed motels. Of course Buddy Holly had told his friend Waylon Jennings where the after-show party was, so that's where the boys headed as well.

The bands' buses were parked by a hotel on the very edge of town. When Danny and the others arrived the party was in full swing. As it was a steamy night, everyone had gathered around the pool. Many of the musicians smoked while beer and *Coke* were the beverages of choice. A group of local girls who'd been carefully vetted by Lee Hazelwood for their party-spirit danced to record music blasting from a stereo unit plugged into an outside power point.

Danny was delighted to discover the burgeoning stars were unaffected by their newly found fame. In fact they were mostly reserved and impeccably polite, especially Elvis Presley who addressed Monty as 'sir' when they were introduced. Being black and a proficient blues musician, they were all interested in his opinion. Soon he and Elvis were jamming away as if they'd known each other for years.

Presley was right at home with the blues as he'd spent much of his teenage life hanging around Beale Street clubs and juke-joints, enthralled by the music. Although Elvis had the voice, he wasn't a great guitar-picker, but most of the others were and took their playing very seriously. Buddy Holly and Luther Perkins were in a deep discussion about the merits of fender Stratocaster and Telecaster guitars which they both favoured. Duane Eddy and Scotty Moore, Elvis' lead guitarist, preferred the sound of Gibson guitars which only led to more discussion about their tools of the trade. Eddy was hoping to earn enough money on tour to buy a big red Gretsch 6120 guitar with a Bigsby tremolo arm he's spotted in a Tucson music store.

Carl Perkins was by far the most exuberant of the performers and led them in a grand version of a rappy little number called *Maybelline.* The song had just been released by a Negro rocker called Chuck Berry for the Chess label in Chicago. The windy city had recently become a Mecca for black musicians. Soon the entire group were singing along. Nobody minded when Danny and Monty joined in with their ukes while Waylon Jennings strummed along too. Johnny Cash and Waylon seemed to hit it off and indeed became life-long friends.

It was one of the most wondrous nights of Danny's life that would remain fondly in his memory for ever. They played until dawn, but then, as with all things, the dream came to an end. The show had to move on. Danny, Monty, Waylon and the local boys helped pack the instruments, amplifiers and stage equipment into a couple of trucks.

Everyone said goodbye as the performers piled into their buses. They'd take turns driving so they'd all get a chance to sleep on the way to the next gig. JB and Emil climbed into the pickup while the Holly brothers and Waylon jumped in the back. As they sped away in a cloud of Texas dust, Monty and Danny exchanged glances and shrugged.

'Now that's something you don't do every day,' Monty said.

'You said it. I wonder how they'll go. I mean show-biz is a hard nut to crack I should imagine.'

'Hard to tell, but I hope so. I mean the music's new, ain't it? Sorta raw and edgy. We'll have to wait and see. So whatcha wanna do, book in here for twenty-four hours or just hit road?'

'I don't reckon I can sleep anyway, Monty. How about we keep going? We can always stop if we get drowsy. There are plenty of motels. Don't worry about your green book, I'll check us in and no one will notice.'

Danny was to reflect later how a simple decision could alter their lives so dramatically.

*

They filled the Bel Air's petrol tank and took the highway to Abilene, Fort Worth and Dallas. As the day wore on, both temperature and humidity rose to an unbearable level. Sure Monty and Danny were used to tropical heat, but somehow the vast openness of the South Texas Panhandle intensified their discomfort. Finally Monty pulled over and they raised the hood before driving away with the aircon on full cold. The Bel Air's V-8 engine was a gas-guzzler at best, but now the fuel gauge could have been mistaken for the second hand on the clock.

Texas gas was cheap and service-stations plentiful, which was fortunate because they took the wrong road out of town and found themselves en route to Seymour. As they were in no hurry it wasn't a big deal especially as Monty stopped at every roadhouse diner for a caffeine fix. As a result they found themselves ambling eastwards rather than carving up miles.

What Danny and Monty were unaware of was the reason for the extreme weather conditions. A cold air mass streamed in from Alaska and butted into the hot, moist prevailing south-easterly wind from the Gulf of Mexico. Normally this would simply herald a cool change, but Central USA had one massive geographical feature that exacerbated the situation – the Rocky Mountains. This range hemmed in the conflicting air masses leaving them only one way to go and that was upwards. The result was thunderstorm build-ups that were not only numerous, but monstrously severe.

In this case a line was forming from Alberta through Montana, Wyoming, Nebraska and Kansas. By early afternoon the first tornado touched down somewhere to the north. As Danny surfed the radio frequencies, stations started broadcasting the first weather alerts. Danny unfolded their road-map and plotted the touch-down points.

'Hey Monty, there are tornados only fifty miles from us,' Danny declared.

'Don't sweat it, kid,' Monty replied in his usual nonchalant way. 'Take a look outside, there ain't a cloud in the sky.'

That was true to a point. The air was hazy and a sheet of high-level cirrus overcast was rapidly enveloping the upper atmosphere. As yet there was not a breath of wind, but a wall of thunderstorms was hammering in from the northwest. It was possible that the Bel Air could have out-run the storm front, but the thunder-heads were now so numerous and building up ahead.

And then Danny saw his first tornado. The swirling grey spiral of destruction was almost mesmerising as it uprooted trees and ripped fence posts from the ground, sending them gyrating randomly skywards. To Danny's relief, the first tornado dissipated as quickly as it had appeared, but others took its place.

'We gotta find shelter and ride this out,' Monty declared as he peered ahead through the rain lashing the windscreen.

They came to a road house on the outskirts of Seymour and Monty swerved the Bel Air off the highway, screeching to a halt by the petrol pumps. Forty-mile-an-hour wind gusts were already blasting sand that felt like a thousand needles. The Bel Air's beautiful paint job was about to take a hammering.

Danny braved the weather and raced into the diner where the owner and his family were bracing for the storm.

'Hey fella, you better stay inside till this is over,' the owner yelled.

He was about forty and his family appeared to consist of his wife and four children aged from about six to fourteen.

'We've gotta get our car under cover,' Danny said.

'Y'all ain't from around here, are ya?'

Danny'd heard that before.

'No sir, but my buddy and I have rented an expensive car and this dust storm's gonna wreck the paintwork.'

'That's the least of your problems right now, son,' the station owner said as he finished hammering boards across the windows. 'C'mon, we'll get yer automobile into the barn, but I don't guarantee nothin'.'

As they went outside Danny almost staggered against the wind blast which had increased noticeably. The roadhouse windows were all fitted with outside shutters that the kids were now slamming closed and securing with slide-bolts. The shed door was open so Danny waved to Monty to drive the car inside. They slammed the door shut and hurried back to the road house. As they raced for cover, Danny looked in horror beyond the roadhouse. A tornado swirled ominously less than a mile away and looked like it was heading straight for them.

When they were safely inside the roadhouse, the roadhouse owner's wife gathered water and food which she stashed in their cellar.

'It's time,' she called. 'C'mon you kids, get down them steps.'

Three of the children dutifully obeyed, but one was missing.

'Annie-May, where are you?' the mother wailed. 'You get over here or you'll feel the back of my hand, girl.'

But Annie-May wasn't anywhere to be found in the diner and the tornado was only a few hundred yards away.

The wind now howled like an express train. The shutters shook so violently it looked as if they'd be ripped from their hinges. Dust swirled as thick as soup, clogging any crevice in its path.

'Get down into the cellar all of you,' Monty yelled.

'My baby's still out there!' the woman cried.

'Danny, you make sure everyone stays here,' Monty yelled, barely audible above nature's bellowing.

He didn't wait for an answer, but forced the door open and staggered into the storm. The door was immediately ripped from its hinges and flung away. Air and sand blasted through the opening forcing Danny and the Texan family backwards. They had no choice but to clamber into the cellar and slam the trap door closed because the maelstrom was about to smash into the roadhouse.

The tornado took an eternity to pass. As wind, hail, dust and debris, slammed into the building, the Texan family could only lament the loss of their youngest member who'd obviously become disorientated and unable to find her way back to shelter. The owner's wife was distraught and wept uncontrollably. The tumult above continued unabated accompanied by thunderous crashes as the corrugated roof was ripped away sheet after sheet. Now unprotected, the furnishing and even the heavy commercial stove was wrenched from its mounting and hurled through one of the walls which collapsed instantly. Without support the other walls disappeared in seconds.

Anything left within the walls also vanished. In moments that felt like hours the roadhouse had been totally flattened.

But tornadoes don't linger. In due course this particular one passed, meandering away to destroy whatever else lay in its path. The storm left an eerie silence in its wake that Danny later described as a *sound-vacuum.* A pile of debris covered the cellar trap door which took both Danny and the owner's strength to shift before finally forcing the door open.

They emerged into filtered sunlight as nothing of the road house remained except the petrol bowsers which miraculously survived intact. As the grey wall of meteorological hate drifted away in the distance, they surveyed the devastation.

The shed was another of the tornado's victims. It appeared to have been lifted bodily and vapourised into thousands of wooden slats and metallic shrapnel. Yet amidst the wreckage and looking apparently unscathed, the Chevrolet Bel Air stood steadfastly rooted to the ground.

There was no sign of either Monty or Annie-May and no amount of calling her name induced her to appear. That was until the Bel Air passenger door eased open and a tiny figure skipped from the front seat and raced into her mother's arms. Monty appeared second later grinning as he swept away the coat of dust covering him.

'Are you alright, child?' the girl's mother wept.

'Sure mama,' Annie-May replied. 'This here nice nigger found me.'

'No offence intended,' the roadhouse owner said, eyeing Monty sheepishly.

'None taken,' Monty replied as the little girl prattled on about her adventure.

'...and I was so scared...and then we got in the car...and the barn roof blew off and everything...the noise was crazy and...'

Chapter 19 — Deep in the Heart of Texas

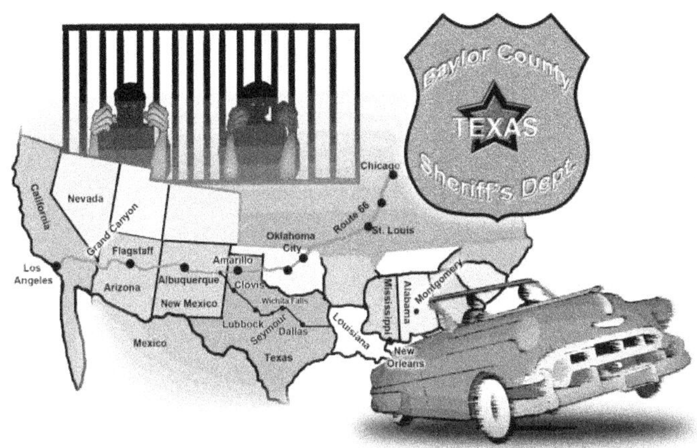

No one was sure what to do next. The roadhouse owner's pickup was lying on its side about fifty yards away. Monty, Danny and the Texan family managed to pull it upright, but the two front wheels were so badly damaged the vehicle was undriveable.

'Do you think we can all squeeze into the Bel Air?' Danny wondered.

While they pondered their situation, a Baylor County sheriff's department patrol car drove up. A bulging, deputy sheriff stepped out of the car and surveyed the damage.

'Shoot, Errol,' he addressed the roadhouse owner, 'you sure as hell was outta luck. Why that danged twister flew right on by town with nary a busted window-pane. We'd better get you folks outa here. You wanna go over to your sister Ellie's place? Sheriff Penny's out chasin' the storm to see what damage it's done so I thought I'd come and check on you folks.'

Errol merely nodded. The enormity of what had happened was finally sinking in.

'We can give someone a lift in the Bel Air,' Monty offered.

'I weren't talkin' to you, boy,' the deputy snarled.

'Fine, just trying to be helpful is all, but as you seem to have everything under control...'

'Don't sass me, boy. I don't need no uppity nigger tellin' me what I know or what I don't know.'

'I can see you *know* an awful lot, deputy,' Monty couldn't help himself.

'You back-talkin' me, boy?'

'Just standing up for myself. I don't hold with bullying and I don't take crap from anyone.'

'Oh, you don't, do ya? Well I reckon I ain't takin' no lip from no nigger, neither. A night in the county gaol's gonna teach some respect.'

'I ain't committed a crime.'

'You want to make a felony outta a misdemeanour?'

'What misdemeanour?'

'Showin' disrespect to a peace-officer. Now turn around and put your hands behind your back. I'm takin' you in.'

'This is ludicrous...' Danny said, taking a step forward.

That was all it took for the deputy to draw his .38 revolver and aim straight for Danny's heart.

'Back off, ya nigger-lovin' Yankee,' the deputy snarled. 'One more step and I'll blast you where you stand.'

'Hey Josh, this guy didn't mean nothin' by it,' Errol said, indicating Monty. 'Why he saved our Annie-May from gettin' blowed away.'

'Sure did, deputy,' Annie-May piped up. 'He hid me in his car.'

'You don't say?' the deputy oozed. 'Sounds a mite like attempted abduction to me. You some sort of kid-molester, boy? Now turn around before I put a bullet through your skull.'

'You're barking mad,' Danny said.

'Let it go, Danny,' Monty sighed, realising there was a real risk of the deputy opening fire at any second. 'This guy obviously ain't in charge. We'll sort it out downtown.'

Monty complied. The deputy holstered his gun while Monty allowed his hands to be cuffed and meekly submitted to being hustled into the police car. The deputy whose name-tag declared 'Bodine' returned to face down Danny.

'An' just who might you be, Sonny-Jim?' the deputy demanded, jabbing Danny in the chest. 'It ain't normal for white boys to be hangin' out with no niggers. You some kinda pervert or what?''

'My name is Danny McAlister and I don't take kindly to some trumped up public official manhandling me.'

'Don't take that fancy Yankee tone with me boy.'

'I'm not a Yankee,' Danny protested, pushing Bodine's hand aside. 'I'm Australian.'

'A goddamn Nazi. We done fought your kind in the War and now you're here stirring up your commie, nigger-lovin' ways in Baylor County.'

It seemed that communists and fascists were tarred with the same brush in Baylor County — at least in the deputy sheriff's view.

'What the hell do you mean?'

'Hitler was one of the Australians and you have the goddamn gall to come bustin' into my county.'

'We're just taking a road trip in that car over there. We got caught in the tornado.'

Deputy Bodine eyed the Bel Air suspiciously then turned and stared slyly at Danny.

'I wanna know what y'all are doin' with a nigger and how come you're drivin' that fancy automobile. You own that car, boy?'

'No...'

Before Danny could tell the deputy the car was hired, Bodine redrew his weapon and Danny found himself once again staring down the business end of a Colt .38 revolver.

'Thought so. You thought you were pretty smart hijackin' that fancy vehicle. Well you reckoned without Deputy Josh Bodine. Turn around and place your hands behind your back. I'm gonna cuff you too'

'You're an idiot. We...'

You had to give it to Bodine. For an over-weight buffoon he was quick. Danny felt a suddenly shooting pain across his temple as his vision blurred and he sank to his knees.

'That'll teach y'all to sass me, boy!'

When Danny came to his senses, he was sitting next to Monty in the patrol car. His head throbbed and his vision was still hazy.

'Good one, Danny,' Monty murmured as they sped away. 'Now we're both gonna wind up behind bars.'

'Sorry.'

The tyres screeched as Bodine stomped on the brakes and the patrol car skidded to a halt in front of the sheriff's office on Washington Street. Bodine had radioed ahead so his fellow deputy was waiting at the door. Danny and Monty were frog-marched into the station and finger-printed before being shoved into the single gaol-house cell – no phone call, no lawyer, no bail.

And that's where they sat for an hour or so, which was how long it took for Danny to recover from the blow on his head. He gloomily surveyed the bare cell that contained two bunk beds, blankets and an ablutions pail.

Of all the deputy-sheriffs in the state of Texas, we have to run into this donkey!

Shorty afterwards Errol turned up with his wife, Nadine. She carried a tray with two plates of beef stew, fresh bread, salad and greens with ice water and coffee.

'I thought you fellas might be hungry,' Nadine said. 'Deputy Bodine will probably only get y'all a burger, fries and *Coke.* This here's some good Texas home-cookin'.'

'Thank you, ma'am,' Monty replied and tucked in after she'd passed the tray trough the serving hatch in the cell bars.

'You saved my Annie-May and we're all rightly obliged to you fer that, mister.'

'Call me Monty.'

'We gathered what we could and drove your fancy rag-top car to my sister Ellie's place,' Errol said. 'Deputy Bodine done impounded it right off. What's he charged you with, anyhow?'

'Right now it seems Monty's in here simply because he's black and I'm here because the good deputy's too pig-ignorant to know the difference between Austria and Australia. He said he didn't fight Nazis to have them tramping around his town.'

'Hell, Bodine didn't fight no Nazis,' Nadine snorted. 'He ain't never been no further than Wichita Falls. I should know 'cos my Errol here joined Big Red One with some of the Comanche boys.'

'You saw plenty of action then?' Danny said turning to Errol.

'He don't talk about it much,' Nadine replied, 'but them boys fought in North Africa, Sicily. Done went ashore on Omaha Beach and copped a right whuppin' at the Battle of the Bulge. Errol got hisself shot up at Remagen Bridge when they crossed the Rhine. He still got a limp from it.'

Errol might have been reticent about his war service, but Nadine was proud of his achievements and happy to tell people about her heroic husband. And justly so.

'You boys ever been in the military?' Errol asked.

'Fly boy for the Tuskegee Red Tails,' Monty said. 'Danny's seen plenty action in Korea and Vietnam.'

'Vietnam?'

'French Indo China,' Danny said. 'I kinda got caught up in the wrong place at the wrong time.'

'If you don't mind my sayin' that's kinda where you're at right now. This sort of thing often happen to you fellas?'

'Yeah, it does a bit,' Danny admitted, 'but at least now Deputy Bodine has the Bel Air he can check with Avis in LA and they'll confirm we rented the car legitimately.'

'I don't reckon the deputy's in any hurry,' Errol lamented. 'Right now he's ridin' around town with the top down tryin' to impress Betty-Lou Coleman on account of he's sweet on her.'

'He can dream on,' Nadine smiled. 'Betty-Lou's got more sense than to hook up with the no-good likes of Deputy Bodine.'

'Sorry about this mess. Bodine's a goose. He won't listen to me,' Errol said. 'Trouble is his daddy's a big man in town and I reckon that got him the job.'

'Maybe, but why doesn't Sheriff Penny do something about it?' Monty asked.

'The sheriff's more of a politician than a lawman and he's got elections comin' up. He don't want to rock the boat. He's kinda gotta play a cagey game.'

'What are you gonna do now?' Monty said. 'All your stuff is gone.'

'It' just stuff,' Nadine said philosophically. 'My family's safe and that's what matters. I stashed Errol's war medals, family photos and such in the cellar, so our precious things are OK. Folks down at our Baptist church will pitch in and before you know it, the place'll be up and runnin' again. The pump's still working so we filled the car before we skedaddled.'

Deputy Bodine returned for a few minutes, smirking about what a smooth ride the Bel Air was and how he might just hang onto it for a while. When Danny asked what the charges were, he was appalled to hear Deputy Bodine rattle off:

- Disturbing the peace.
- Violence towards a police officer.
- Resisting arrest.
- Attempted kidnapping.
- Inciting civil unrest.
- Grand theft auto.
- Child abuse.

It was all nonsense of course and Danny told Bodine what he thought in no uncertain terms.

'Now you listen up, kid,' Bodine snarled. 'You and that thar nigger's gonna stay put till the circuit judge gets here. But I reckon y'all goin' down for five misdemeanours and that's gonna get you six months hard-time on the road-gang.'

'Bloody hell, you're flamin'-well joking.'

'Watch yer mouth, kid. There's a lady present. This here's a good Baptist community and we don't take kindly to cussin'.'

Blimey, he's worse than Angela.

'When's the judge getting here?' Monty asked.

'Don't rightly know – depends how busy he is. Maybe a week, maybe two. Maybe the twister's gonna delay him some. Looks like you're right comfortable where y' are.'

Danny threw up his hands in despair.

'That guy's a lunatic,' Danny said when Bodine had left to continue pursuing Betty-Lou Coleman.

'He's a lunatic with a gun and law on his side,' Monty said. 'You think we need a lawyer, Danny?'

'I think we might. What do you reckon, Errol?'

Errol reported dismally that it was unlikely that either of the town's two lawyers would feel obliged to defend a Negro or an alien citizen. Ninety percent of Seymour's population was white, so no one bothered much with other ethnic groups which included a few hundred Comanche Indians, Mexicans and Orientals. Also the moderate Sheriff Penny was still following the tornado front to assess its damage and no one knew when he'd return.

'Y'all gotta get out of there,' Errol said to Danny. 'I don't like the look of Deputy Bodine. He just might decide to give Monty a bashing just for fun.'

'You think?'

'Wouldn't be the first time. '

'Get out and then what?'

'First you gotta get over the county line and outta Bodine's jurisdiction. Then you gotta get outta the state and the Texas Rangers' jurisdiction ... and you got just the automobile for the job.'

'One problem. We're locked in this cell.'

'Yeah, we gotta work on that,' Errol said. 'Meantime I'll see if I can rustle up a lawyer.'

He left to try to find one.

Nadine stayed until Danny and Monty had finished their meal, then she took the tray and left too, promising to return with coffee and supper. Bodine didn't return, but his fellow deputy drifted in and out as his duties demanded. The deputy was a rather uninspiring young man who went under the equally uninspiring name of Arty Pitts. At least he allowed Danny and Monty to use the gaol-house toilet and shower, albeit individually at gunpoint. However their grips were still in the Bel Air's boot, but neither Danny nor Monty were in any hurry to get their bags which contained their 1911 Colt Army automatics and spare clips. Hopefully Deputy Bodine was so busy trying to impress Miss Betty-Lou that he hadn't bothered to inspect the car too thoroughly.

It was nightfall before Nadine returned with coffee and their supper. She seemed cheerful enough and chattered randomly.

'Now you boys just relax,' she said. 'I'm sure everything will work out just fine.'

She smiled enigmatically, leaving Danny and Monty wondering whether she was up to something or just trying to reassure them.

The night dragged on.

Fortunately Josh Bodine was the senior deputy and didn't bother with night duty. The graveyard shift fell to Arthur who seemed resigned to the dirty jobs. He didn't appear to be the sort of guy with a boisterous social life anyway. Nor was Seymour that kind of town. By eight pm, other than a faint glow from the corner drug store the place was dead.

Finally after a bathroom visit, Danny and Monty turned in. In truth they were both dog-tired. Neither man had slept for forty-eight hours. Danny took the top bunk and instantly fell asleep. Monty wasn't far behind him. As all was in order, Deputy Arty Pitts pushed his chair back, swung his cowboy booted feet onto the desk-top and started reading an edition of *Marvel Comics.* Soon he pulled his Stetson (no one seemed to take their ten-gallon hats off) over his eyes and dozed off.

What the blue blazes..?

Danny jerked upright, slamming his head into the wooden ceiling boards. He'd just recovered from the Deputy Bodine inflicted migraine. Another head-ache was the last thing he needed. Right then he was unsure what had woken him as he dropped to the cell floor still disoriented in the darkness. Then he heard what could only have been an explosion in the distance. Seconds later a small shock-wave rattled the objects on the sheriff's office shelves. Monty was now awake too.

'What the..?' Deputy Arthur Pitts mumbled as he jerked out of his drowsiness, fell off his chair before scrambling to his feet and drawing his .38.

Right then Nadine burst into the office and she was pretty lucky Deputy Pitts didn't shoot her in his confusion.

'Arty, you gotta come quick,' she cried. 'I reckon them Comanche boys have got all liquored up and are runnin' amok.'

Arty grabbed his gun-belt and followed Nadine into the street. They hardly left when Errol peeked around the door. He entered lugging two paper-stuffed burlap sacks.

'Wake up, boys,' he said cheerfully dropping the sacks for a moment and grabbing the cell-door key from a hook behind the sheriff's desk. 'Time to vamoose!'

They placed the sacks on the cots and covered them with their blankets. Errol ensured the cell door was relocked and replaced the key on its hook. To their delight Danny and Monty saw their precious Bel Air parked a few yards down Washington Street. Having pointed Arty in the opposite direction, Nadine now stood beside the car keeping a lookout.

'That dope Bodine left the keys in the dash and parked right outside his place. He's asleep with a belly full of beer, so we just drove off,' Errol said.

'Now you boys high-tail it,' Nadine hissed. 'Take Route 82 to Wichita Falls and right across the state line to Oklahoma.'

'Hopefully Josh Bodine won't notice you're gone till morning. We'll tell him you've headed back through Lubbock to New Mexico on your way back to California,' Errol said.

'Your bags are still in the trunk and I've put sandwiches and a flask in the car,' Nadine said. 'You boys take care now.'

She reached up and kissed them each on the cheek.

'We're sure in your debt, ma'am,' Monty said. 'Thanks.'

'Ain't no debts between friends,' Nadine smiled. 'Now get goin'.'

They shook Errol's hand, leapt into the Bel Air and sped north out of town as another stick of dynamite exploded in a vacant lot. The entire town was awake including alcohol-befuddled Deputy Bodine.

Chapter 20 — B Company HQ

Deputy Bodine dressed and dashed outside to find the Bel Air missing. His first instinct was to think the Comanche boys had taken the car. He headed for Washington Street as quickly as his bulk allowed. Bodine ran into Arty Pitts who'd been patrolling the vicinity close to the sheriff's office.

'What the Sam Hill's going on, Arty?' Bodine demanded.

'Dunno, Josh. Nadine burst into the office and said the Comanche boys were blowin' stuff up, but I don't see no damage.'

One of the good (or bad depending on your POV) aspects of American social philosophy is the ease in which you can obtain guns and other weapons of moderate destruction. It was not unusual for farmers, tradesmen or even normal householders to have an arsenal worthy of a small military unit. Indeed in Texas, amongst other cowboy states, it was almost mandatory to have at least a shot gun, Remington repeating rifle, several handguns, a thousand rounds of ammunition and maybe a few grenades and dynamite sticks thrown in.

If you didn't have these household essentials, it was simply a matter of heading over to your local hardware store and buying them across the hunting counter. Errol's sister Ellie's family was no exception. Although child-infested, there was still a choice of lethal weaponry at their disposal.

Most of the hard-working, predominantly white Seymour residents had been brought up through the depression when jobs were scarce and most of the mid-west had been reduced to a dust bowl. Now in the fifties they may not have been wealthy, but they were no longer starving. Universal government health-care was never the American way, so if you visited a doctor you paid for it. As a result people were selective about heading for the surgery and many illnesses went undetected. Infant mortality was still high so every child was precious. Monty had just saved one and that was no small matter for Errol, Nadine and their kin.

Generally the town was racially tolerant. Citizens had little time for Deputy Bodine and the idea of bringing him down a peg or two was tantalising. The rub was that more than a few townsfolk had previous run-ins with the law. Their offences may have been trivial, but for Texas' 'three-strikes-and-you're-out' policy. That meant if you were convicted of three offences, the state deemed you impossible to rehabilitate and could consign you to the chain-gang for an indefinite sentence. So although Errol's kin sympathised with Monty, they were reluctant to help, so it looked like the draconian deterrent worked.

'It ain't numbers we need anyhoo,' Errol had told Nadine. 'Stealth and cunning are the go and believe me -- I got a bunch of those fightin' krauts.'

So armed with a few sticks of dynamite and a case of *Lone Star*, Errol approached the Comanche boys who were loafing around the all-night drug-store. It was just a matter of a simple decoy to get Danny and Monty safely out of gaol. After setting off the dynamite in a vacant block, the Comanche boys jumped into their pickup and sped out of town to enjoy their beer where the law couldn't find them.

Meanwhile Deputies Bodine and Pitts drove back to the sheriff's office. They were hailed by townsfolk who'd been woken by the explosions and wanted to know what was going on. As Bodine had no idea, he could only ask people to stay calm and he'd let them know as soon as he found out. Already rumours of gas-explosions, UFOs and communist invasion were emerging.

When they reached the gaol, Bodine and Arty found the door unlocked, but everything appeared in order.

'You lock up after you left, Art?' Bodine asked.

'Didn't think to. Nadine was in a right state. You think someone's broke in here?'

'Everything looks OK,' Bodine said, but drew his .38 just in case. 'Go check them two losers in the cells.'

Arty was gone for only a moment and reported that both prisoners were still asleep in the bunks. At first Bodine seemed satisfied, but then a prickling, uneasy sensation crept over him.

'Shoot, Arty! The whole town's awake by them explosions. Y'all heard 'em right enough, right?'

'Sure did, they woke me up too...'

Bodine glared at Arty and shook his head. He grabbed the keys, unlocked the cell and flung the blankets aside.

'Them varmints have skedaddled!'

Leaving Arty to broadcast an APB to all law enforcement agencies to apprehend the drivers of the Bel Air, Bodine rushed to his patrol car. Quite a crowd had gathered in the streets where the deputy spotted Errol and Nadine. Then it struck him that it was Nadine who'd roused Arty only seconds after the explosions. What the hell was she doing out in the middle of the night?

Bodine pulled up beside the road-house couple and rolled down his car window.

'OK, where'd they go?' Bodine demanded.

'Who?' Errol asked.

'That goddamn Yankee and nigger of course.'

Both Nadine and Errol gave Bodine their best *how-would-we-know* stare.

'They ain't gone nowhere, Josh,' Errol said. 'Ain't they locked in your cell?'

'No they ain't. They busted out.'

'You don't say,' Nadine said. 'Maybe they went back to LA. Seems that things didn't work out too good for 'em here in Texas.'

Bodine gave her a shrewd sideways glance.

'I don't reckon so,' he said. 'They'll head for the nearest state line f'sure.'

Bodine had wasted enough time. He planted his foot, the engine roared and tyres squealed as he sped off to Route 82 in hot pursuit.

*

Meanwhile Danny and Monty felt pretty pleased with themselves. They'd got clean away and doubted whether Deputy Bodine had the common-sense to work out where they were heading. The only obstacles in their path were wayward armadillos that regularly scuttled across the highway. So far Monty had managed to avoid contributing to the Texas road-kill. He nearly hit a pronghorn buck. The prolific antelope-like animals roamed throughout central USA from Canada to the Mexican border, posing a constant threat to night traffic.

At Wichita Falls they pulled into an all-night gas-station to ask for directions. While Monty topped up the tank, Danny entered the kiosk to pay the bill and buy some gum for Monty.

An extremely bored attendant was listening to Hank Williams lament *Your Cheatin' Heart* over a local late-night radio station. As Danny handed over a five dollar bill, an announcer cut into the song.

'OK, here's a heads-up for all you truckers out there on Interstate 277. An alert just in says the Highway Patrol is settin' up a road block on the state line. You folks headin' for Oklahoma might be in for delays.'

'What's that all about?' Danny asked.

'Shoot, how I would know, man?' the attendant drawled in reply. 'Probably a breakout from Rolling Plans, Dickens Correctional or Fannin County. That's why I keep this baby handy.'

The attendant, took a long-barrelled Colt .45 Peacemaker from under his serving counter. 'Ya never know when it might come in handy. Y'all know what I'm talkin' about, man?'

'Sure,' Danny said, instinctively raising his hands. 'I'm not looking for trouble. Just came in for gas and gum.'

'You cain't be too careful, 'the attendant eyed Danny menacingly.

Danny backed to the door.

'Hey man, you forgot your change,' the attendant called after him.

'Keep it,' Danny called over his shoulder.

'What's the problem?' Monty asked as Danny slammed the car-door.

'Dunno for sure,' Danny replied. 'The cops have set up a roadblock at the Oklahoma border.'

'No sweat,' Monty replied with a grin. 'We'll just head in the opposite direction. Now gimme a piece of that gum.'

And that would have worked well, except an APB meant just that – *all points*. Monty navigated his way back to Route 82 then turned south on the road to Fort Worth and Dallas.

'This may not be the best automobile for the job, but if you wanna get lost,' Monty explained, 'there ain't nothing better than a big city to do it in.'

'Do you think it's us they're after?' Danny asked.

'Dunno, but we can't take the risk. At least this way we'll be heading the right direction for New Orleans.'

Monty was in no hurry as they motored into Dallas just before dawn. He certainly didn't want to attract any state troopers' attention by speeding. Road traffic was sparse, but cars and trucks still flashed past. Generally motorists kept below the speed-limit, but occasionally a speedster would overtake the Bel Air and disappear ahead. So Monty wasn't surprised when an unremarkable car pulled out beside the Bel Air. That was until the occupants activated a siren and beacon. The unmarked car pulled in front of the Bel Air. With the road now effectively blocked, Monty had no choice but to bring his car to a halt.

'Oh shit,' Danny whispered. 'What the hell do they want, we weren't speeding.'

'No sweat,' Monty said, much too cheerfully in Danny's opinion. 'It might just be routine. There's hardly any traffic this late, they're probably just bored.'

Two men stepped from their car and stalked towards the Bel Air. They were lean and athletic and wore immaculate tailored cowboy shirts and stove-pipe jeans. Sun glasses were the eyewear of choice and of course cowboy boots as standard footwear.

'Who are they?' Danny whispered. 'They aren't wearing police uniforms.'

But it was their pristine Stetson hats and Lone Star badges stamped from Mexican dollar coins that had caught Monty's attention. Both men wore gun-belts, but neither had drawn his weapon – yet.

'They don't look like cops to me,' Danny hissed.

'Nope,' Monty replied. 'Ten times worse — Texas Rangers.'

'Well howdy there,' the guy-in-charge greeted civilly. 'My name is Lieutenant Virgil Delaney and this is my colleague Sergeant Bill Waddy, B Company Texas Rangers. We're surely proud to make your acquaintance. Now I'd take it as a right kindness if you'd cut that motor and both step out of your vehicle.'

Danny and Monty had no choice. Their 1911 Army Colts were still in the boot and a shoot-out with Texas Rangers wasn't really an option. Both men appeared relaxed, but something told Danny that they were alert and knew their business.

'Now sir,' Delaney continued, 'I'd be mightily obliged if you'd show me your driver's licence.'

Monty obliged.

'And you too, sir, that would be right neighbourly.'

'My stuff's in the glove-box,' Danny said cautious. 'Is it OK if I open it up?'

'Yessir, you go right ahead.'

Danny noticed that the Rangers remained at ease as he opened the glove-box and produced his Australian and international driver's licences along with his passport. It was a measure of Deputy Bodine's incompetence that those documents hadn't been located and confiscated.

'I see y'all not from around these parts, sir,' Delaney observed conversationally.

'No we're just touring,' Danny replied uncertainly.

'And how have you found our Lone State so far, sir?'

'We almost got sucked into a tornado.'

'Yessir, a twister can do that to y'all right enough. Now my guess is that would have happened over Baylor County way.'

Monty and Danny stared at him.

'Mr McAlister, if you'd come with me please. Mister Montgomery sir, I'd be mightily obliged if you'd allow Sergeant Waddy to accompany you in your fine automobile and follow us on to our headquarters.'

So Danny and Monty found themselves in a Texas gaol house for the second time, although now they were held in an interview room at B Company's Garland HQ. Lieutenant Delaney and Sergeant Waddy questioned them briefly, but merely established they'd been in Seymour the previous day. Soon the morning shift Rangers filed into the building. With two-dozen officers, B Company was the biggest Ranger unit in Texas. In military terms it barely rated as a light platoon, but Texas Rangers made their own rules. With less than two hundred Rangers in the entire state, they felt entitled to down-size.

Danny and Monty enjoyed a breakfast of scrambled eggs, bacon, coffee and a white porridge-like mush called grits. Danny didn't fancy the stuff, but Monty wolfed his down before cleaning up Danny's left-overs.

'It's an acquired taste,' Monty said, reading Danny's mind.

It wasn't long before Deputy Bodine waddled into the Ranger HQ. As soon as he'd identified the alleged offenders he demanded that Danny and Monty be transferred into his custody. He could add *escaping from lawful custody* to their charge list. However Lieutenant Delany was having none of it.

'Now hold on there, deputy,' he insisted. 'These men ain't going anywhere until I say so.'

'They're wanted men in Baylor County,' Bodine countered.

'We'll see,' Delaney replied enigmatically.

Danny and Monty were held all day. Everyone they met at Company B was pleasant and courteous. Rangers regularly brought coffee and consequently escorted Monty and Danny to the toilets. The station didn't have much choice in reading material, but it did own a Scrabble board. Once Danny and Monty worked out the rules, the game kept them amused most of the day. There was some discussion about American and British spelling, but it helped pass the time. After lunch Lieutenant Delaney looked in on them, but was evasive when they asked how long they were to be detained or if they were to be extradited back to Seymour.

Bill Waddy turned up during late afternoon.

'Will you gents come with me, please,' he said and led them into B Company's administration area. Rangers manned several desks processing arrests and court paperwork. A hat stand stood beside each work-station each holding one or two identical Stetsons. Lieutenant Delaney sat at one desk and invited Danny and Monty to sit in chairs in front of him. Two bulging files lay on the desk.

'I must say you turned out to be a pair of mighty interestin' hombres,' he said. 'My associates and I have been on the phones all day while the telex has been running non-stop — and here's what we came up with.'

Delaney opened the first file.

'Mr Montgomery: WWII fighter ace: five confirmed kills, six probable: Distinguished Flying Cross, Bronze Star. My, my, sir you certainly kept busy. I have some references of service to the nation with China Air Transport, although my source in that area was a little coy about revealing details. Nevertheless, an impressive résumé.'

'Hey, you never told me about all those medals,' Danny said.

Monty shrugged and grinned.

'Now you, sir,' Delaney addressed Danny. 'You were harder to track down — but not impossible. It seems you're something of a war hero yourself. Two citations for bravery in action during Korea...'

'That's the first I've heard about it,' Danny replied.

'That doesn't surprise me considering where I discovered the information. I started with customs and immigration of course, but you'll never guess where the trail led — Langley.'

Danny stared at him.

'*Spook* HQ, Virginia,' Monty enlightened him.

'Precisely,' Delaney agreed. 'Now they weren't prepared to divulge too much about you either. It's kinda their way, so I expected it and didn't take it personally. It appears you are a pioneer rotary-wing aviator who also served with CAT. Now I don't know much about this CAT outfit, but Langley assures me it's kosher.'

'Amen to that,' Monty said. 'I guess Major Black and Major White said nice things about you, but forgot to tell you, Danny.'

'All in all that makes you both right upstanding citizens. More importantly we interviewed that roadhouse couple who confirmed you'd saved their little girl and hadn't committed any offences. I think we can overlook "escaping from lawful custody" because I'm not sure how lawful it was.'

'Good on ya Errol and Nadine,' Danny said.

'Exactly, so unless you wish to sue Baylor County for wrongful arrest, you're free to go.'

'No, much as we'd like to stick it to Deputy Bodine,' Danny said, 'we have places to go and things to see. We are just on a road-trip after all.'

'Just one thing before you go,' Delaney said, picking up the phone and addressing the operator. 'Can you put that call from Langley through now please, Sherrie-Jo.'

Do all Texas girls have double-barrelled names..?

Soon Delaney was speaking again.

'Yessir...no problem at all...my pleasure...I'll put him on the line...good day to you, sir.'

Delaney handed Danny the phone.

'Hello...'

'Can't you keep out of trouble for one second?' Colonel Serong asked conversationally.

'Sorry, colonel, but we were just in the wrong place at the wrong time.'

'So it's business as usual then?'

'Yessir, but I thought you were in California.'

'Like I said, I get around. You enjoy the rest of your trip. I'm leaving Langley for Burma tonight, but I'm sure we'll run into each other sometime so I can dig you out of a hole again.'

'Yessir. I look forward to it...well not the getting into a hole bit.'

'Have you got a pencil and paper handy?'

Danny found a pad and pencil on Lieutenant Delaney's desk.

'Write down this phone number just in case. It'll come straight through to this office at Langley. I probably won't be here, but the desk is manned twenty-four-seven as the Yanks say.'

'Will I need a secret password or code?'

'Sorry to disappoint you Danny, but if you just tell them who you are, that will do. There is quite a thick file on you.'

'Thanks, Colonel,' Danny said as he carefully wrote the number including its area code. 'Got it.'

'OK, Danny. Say hello to Monty for me. Cheerio, for now.'

Then Colonel Serong hung up. Danny made a copy of the phone number and gave it to Monty.

'Friends in high places?' Delaney suggested.

'Friends in middling places,' Danny corrected.

As Deputy Bodine had blustered back to Seymour once he realised he wasn't getting custody of Monty and Danny, they planned to spent that night in Dallas before making an early start for New Orleans the following morning. They shook hands with Delaney and Waddy before leaving to find a motel for the night. Both Rangers actually looked weary and ready to call it a day, but before they parted Lieutenant Delaney handed Danny and Monty each a Mexican dollar ranger star.

'Y'all said you were touring,' Delaney said. 'So here's a regular Texas souvenir for you to remember us by. Enjoy your trip and drive carefully, you hear.'

'Those Rangers are friendly blokes,' Danny observed as they drove to their motel.

'I guess so,' Monty replied. 'I reckon I'd want 'em on my side when lead started flying rather than the other way around, that's for sure.'

They didn't have to go far to find a motel. After checking in they bought pizzas and a six-pack of Lone Star from the gas-station next door. Even Monty didn't feel like checking out the Dallas night-life, so they were content to watch a networked episode of *Arthur Godfrey's Talent Scouts*. The show was fine, but Danny couldn't understand why Elvis Presley had failed the auditions. He'd been upset, but sanguine when they'd met him in Lubbock. An episode of *Gunsmoke* followed starring James Arness as Dodge City's Marshal Matt Dillon.

While Danny and Monty enjoyed the show, a Baylor County sheriff's department car eased to a halt in the car park. A uniformed figure slipped from the driver's seat. After checking with the reception clerk he stalked along the pathway towards Danny and Monty's room. His cowboy boots crunched softly into the gravel as he stopped uncertainly outside the door.

Maybe it was a sixth-sense or second-sight or whatever you'd like to call it, but Monty just knew someone lurked outside. He dashed to the window and peered through the drapes. The Baylor County car was clearly visible under the motel's neon sign.

'Shit, Danny — Bodine's outside ...'

There was a sharp rap on the door.

Danny gave Monty a *what-do-we-do-about-it* look. Monty grabbed his 1911 Colt automatic from his grip. He stood behind the door and gave Danny a *thumbs-up*. Danny got the message and turned the TV volume to minimum.

'Come in,' he called. 'The door's not locked.'

The handle clicked open and the door eased ajar as a uniformed police officer stepped into the hotel room. Monty slammed the door closed and placed the pistol barrel against the officer's head.

'Hold it right there, Bodine,' Monty hissed.

'Put the gun down, Monty,' Danny sighed. 'We don't want to get into any more trouble with the law.'

'Whaddya mean..?'

'This isn't Deputy Bodine,' Danny grinned although in truth pointing a gun at a lawman was a pretty serious offence. He stared at a rather careworn middle-aged man.

Danny lowered the weapon.

'Howdy,' the stranger said. 'I'm Sheriff Elijah Penny.'

Oh shit!

'Sorry about that, sheriff,' Monty mumbled sheepishly. 'We thought you were someone else.'

'My illustrious deputy, no doubt.'

'Yessir.'

'It's Bodine that I've come to see you about.'

Sheriff Penny accepted a peace-offering of beer and pizza.

'I came to apologise on behalf of Baylor County for my deputies' behaviour.'

'We ain't got no beef with Deputy Pitts,' Monty assured Sheriff Penny. 'He treated us fair and square.'

'I believe you. Arty Pitts may not be the sharpest spike on the cactus, but given the right example, he'll make a half-decent lawman yet.'

'I don't think Deputy Bodine is the right example,' Danny ventured.

'That is true and I have taken steps to ensure he is no longer an example at all. Some folk think I'm a bit lax, but a sheriff has to keep his town harmonious as much as maintaining law and order.'

'Folks have got to get along, I guess,' Monty agreed.

'Josh Bodine's daddy may be the president of the city chamber of commerce and a handy guy to have on your side, but that don't mean his son can run rough-shod over anyone he feels like. I don't reckon I'll fire him though...'

Danny and Monty exchanged glances.

'No sir, I reckon I'll reassign him to another position more suited to his temperament and ability.'

Danny and Monty exchanged glances again.

'Tomorrow he'll take up his new position of City and Parks Sanitation and Disposal Manager,' Sheriff Penny announced grandly.

'Impressive title.'

'Yessir, but still just another name for the guy who picks up the city trash,' Sheriff Penny smiled.

'What about the Comanche boys?' Monty asked although neither he nor Danny had met the mysterious rascals.

'Reckon I'll give 'em a quiet verbal warning. Letting off firecrackers ain't hardly worth the paperwork of arrestin' 'em.'

'Some firecrackers,' Monty observed.

'This is Texas, remember,' the sheriff grinned. 'We like to do things in a big way.'

He finished his pizza slice and skolled his drink.

'Thanks for the beer, fellas,' he said shaking hands. 'I just thought I'd let you know how things stood. Enjoy the rest of your trip.'

The sheriff left and the boys returned to see what Marshal Matt Dillon, Deputy Chester Goode, Miss Kitty and Doc were up to.

Chapter 21 — Alabamy Bound

Dallas to New Orleans was a five-hundred mile journey that took them into steaming bayou country where Spanish moss draped eerily from native oak, cypress and flowing dogwood trees. Monty regaled Danny with tales of southern gothic voodoo until they reached New Orleans.

With some regret they dropped the car at the downtown Avis agency and took a bus to the French Quarter. The weather was hot and oppressive reminiscent of Indochina, while the French Quarter had much in common with Saigon and Hanoi. They checked into a small, modest Dauphine Street hotel. Danny was alarmed that the shower water soon lapped around his ankles. When he contacted the concierge he discovered the town lay several metres below river-level and the Mississippi was only held back by extensive levee-banks. The water eventually drained away.

Danny met Monty in the foyer and they went sight-seeing. Danny thought Bourbon Street was the finest city street he'd been to. Monty agreed that it was even better than Beale Street in

Memphis or Nashville's Broadway. It was bars, beer, gumbo, jambalaya, mega-sized oysters, Creole eye-candy and bands for a week. Jazz was everywhere. Soloists and combos busked in the street, bar-rooms and hotel balconies. There was also plenty of blues action and three new musical genres that sort of stumbled into each other, Cajun, Creole and Zydeco.

The idea of using a washboard as part of the rhythm section reminded Danny of London's emerging skiffle craze. He'd heard kids who'd been forced to learn the piano-accordion at school and felt the instrument was stilted and boring, but in the hands of Cajun masters the sound was sublime.

When they visited the Cajun Seafood House for chowder and oysters, they were enthralled by a new Cajun sensation, *The Zydeco Ramblers*. The combo front-man, rising star Clifton Chenier belted out French vocals while playing the piano-accordion for all it was worth. His brother Cleveland worked the washboard along with the house band's banjo, fiddle and upright bass players. The lively two-steps, locally known as *specials* had everyone on the dance-floor until late.

The following day they cruised the river on a stern-wheel paddle steamer, feasting on lobster while listening to a continuous selection of jazz bands.

Danny always looked back on that week in New Orleans with particular fondness. Although hurricane season was at its peak and 1955 was the costliest hurricane season ever recorded to that date in Southeast USA, Danny and Monty were spared the excitement of another cataclysmic meteorological event.

They caught a Greyhound PD-4501 model Scenicruiser bus to Montgomery. The only stops were Biloxi in Mississippi State, and Mobile on the Alabama border. So the journey was fast enough while Danny and Monty had a good view through the upper deck windows. As Monty was approaching his home turf, he pointed out anything interesting en route. When Danny stepped off the bus at the Montgomery Greyhound terminal on South Court Street, his entire world-perspective changed. He and Monty picked up their grips and ukulele cases before walking from the late art-deco building into the bustling downtown street.

It took a moment for Danny to work out what was eerily strange, while Monty looked on with a resigned expression. Then it struck Danny. Like New Orleans, the population was roughly a fifty-fifty mix of coloured and white people. Unlike New Orleans though, the population didn't mix. White pedestrians walked on one side of the road while coloured folk used the other.

'Welcome to Dixie,' Monty said with mock amusement. 'Now see that bus sign along the street, you go on down there and I'll catch up.'

'Where are you going?'

'My side of the street.'

'You're kidding?'

But Monty was gone, so Danny joined the white surge to the bus stop. When he arrived he noticed that a concession had been made where black passengers were permitted to queue on the white side of the street, but respectfully behind white passengers. When Monty caught up, Danny stood uncertainly to one side. Queue-jumping was against his nature.

When the cross-town bus arrived the white passengers filed on board, but there was an awkward pause while everyone waited for Danny to go ahead.

'Just get on the bloody bus,' Monty hissed. 'It's a dime fare.'

Danny shrugged, feeling very self-conscious as he boarded the bus and paid for his ticket. He was even more confused when he saw the bus was divided roughly in two sections. A sign at the front row of seats was marked 'W' while another halfway down the aisle bore the letter 'B'. Most of the seats behind the 'B' sign were already taken, but several 'W' seats were still vacant. Fortunately Monty had decided to queue-jump and boarded right behind Danny.

'Sit there,' he whispered to Danny, indicating a seat just ahead of the 'B' sign. 'I'll let you know when to get off.'

Danny obeyed. There were no overhead racks on the bus, so Danny nursed his grip and ukulele on his lap. Although there was a spare seat beside him he was surprised that Monty headed for the back of the bus and found the last available seat in the rear section.

The next person to board was a young black woman who didn't take a seat, but remained standing in the aisle.

'We're full up,' the driver called to those still waiting. 'Next bus will be along in ten minutes.'

There was a hiss as the pneumatic door closed and the bus jolted away causing the black woman to lurch and almost lose her footing. She gripped Danny's seat rail to remained standing. Danny shuffled over towards the window, making room. What insanity made the bus-driver turn away paying passengers when there were still empty seats on board?

'Why don't you take this seat here, miss?' he said. 'There's plenty of room.'

The woman looked at him with horrified disbelief.

'Oh, nossir. I cain't do that. I gotta sit in the black section. I ain't gonna cause trouble sittin' in no white seat.'

'That's ludicrous, there're several spare seats...'

Two things happened next. The first was Monty came to the rescue. Seeing the threat of an incident developing he left his grip in the aisle and escorted the black girl to his seat then stood beside her while she sat. The second event was less subtle. A man in the seat ahead of Danny turned to him with a look of pure loathing.

'What game are y'all tryin' to pull, boy?' he drawled in a thick southern accent that Danny found difficult to follow.

'What do you mean?'

'You one of them goddamned nigger-lovin', Yankee, communist homosexuals,' the man hissed.

'Are you always so friendly in Montgomery?' Danny asked blandly.

'Don't sass me, boy,'

'If I hear that one more time in America, I think I'll thump someone.'

'Are you threatenin' me, boy?'

'Take it how you like.'

'You treat niggers different where you come from?'

No, not really, but we don't make such a performance of it.

'Don't you see the stupidity of having spare seats and then forbidding people to sit down? Doesn't that sound like lunacy to you?'

By now other white passengers were turning in their seats and eyeing Danny with open hostility.

'You ain't from these parts,' someone challenged.

If I hear that one more time I think I'll scream.

'Of course I'm not,' Danny retorted.

He was getting pretty fed up with the lot of them by then, but the debate was hotting up. Fortunately the journey to Monty's parents' home was a short one. Montgomery city was divided into wards which were populated on a strictly racial demographic. The inner city wards 1, 2, 4 & 6 were poor or middle-class black suburbs, while the more affluent whites lived in the outer-city wards 3, 5, 7 & 23.

Monty's parents lived in the relatively wealthy (by coloured standards) ward 4 which lay just beyond the City CBD. Monty rang the conductor bell and the bus pulled to a stop at the next street corner. Monty picked up his gear and headed for the front exit.

'Our stop, Danny,' he hissed as he passed.

As Danny rose to leave the fellow he'd been arguing with confronted him, blocking the aisle He was a burly red-neck in a plaid shirt and denim dungarees.

'Looks like you're a nigger-lovin' Yankee, communist, homosexual son-of-a-bitch after all,' the oaf drawled turning to the other white passengers. 'Maybe we can show him our good-ole southern hospitality.'

Some of the passengers nodded in agreement, but Danny noticed others looked decidedly uncomfortable. It certainly appeared that Danny's list of heinous crimes was growing in the Deep South.

'Now let it be, Leroy,' the driver called. 'That fella's entitled to get off wherever he pleases.'

'Maybe I'll just give him somethin' to make him mind his manners...'

The red-neck let out a stifled grunt as Danny's knee slammed into his groin. He doubled over and Danny shoved him back into his seat. The red-neck gasped and cursed between his teeth, but the pain was too intense for him to bother Danny further. Danny had long since learnt the best way to nip trouble in the bud was to strike first and hard, immobilise your enemy and maybe talk afterwards.

'Don't even think about it,' Danny warned as a couple of rough types looked like they might interfere. 'I fought Reds in Korea and Indochina, so I know a thing or two about scrapping and I don't take shit from anyone.'

No one opposed him as he picked up his kit and walked calmly to the exit. As he stepped onto the side-walk the door hissed and the bus drove away. No one had followed him. He heaved a sigh of relief that he didn't have to use his 1911 Colt automatic which lay in the top of his grip, but would have been hard to reach in a hurry.

'Making new friends, eh?' Monty said.

'All that crap about a flaming seat on a bus — give me strength.'

'Yeah, I'd kinda forgotten how it was around here. C'mon, my folks live just around the block.'

Monty's parents owned a neat, three-bedroom house that reminded Danny of a single storey version of his mother's place in Rockhampton which was raised on stilts for ventilation and flood-avoidance. The picket-fenced block contained a colourful garden with several large shade trees. Monty's father had worked hard and saved enough to afford a modest, comfortable home in an all-black suburb where prices were far lower.

Danny and Monty were met at the front gate by a couple in their late fifties or early sixties and a pretty woman a few years younger than Monty. Up until then Danny had never really thought about Monty's relations, but now it seemed he had a kid sister about Danny's age at least.

After much hugging and very *un-Monty-like* emotional outpouring, they all turned to Danny.

'I'd like you to meet my momma and daddy and sister Belle,' Monty said.

'We've heard so much about you,' Monty's mother said, embracing Danny as if she'd known him all her life. Belle did the same while Monty's father shook his hand warmly.

'I'm pleased to meet you, sir, ma'am,' Danny replied genuinely before realising he had no idea how to address Monty's parents. After all this time, he still didn't know Monty's surname. Angela always addressed him as *Mister Montgomery*, but Danny was pretty sure that wasn't his actual name.

'We don't stand on ceremony here, son,' Monty's father said as if he understood Danny's dilemma. 'You just call us Delores and Al and make yourself right at home.'

'He doesn't like grits, momma,' Monty said.

'That's 'cause they ain't been fixed right. We gonna change that attitude, Danny, you see if we don't.'

They spent the rest of day drinking coffee and catching up. It turned out that Monty was a regular correspondent and his family knew much about Danny and Angela's adventures.

'Y'all right sweet on Miss Angela ain't ya, Danny?' Belle ventured mischievously.

'She kinda has that effect on folks,' Monty agreed.

'She can drive you nuts,' Danny said, 'but yes, Belle, I kinda like her a lot.'

Belle looked a little disappointed.

'I reckon Monty's taken a shine to her as well,' Belle said, because she liked to tease her brother. Her other two brothers had moved north to Chicago and Detroit to find work on the car assembly lines. Her sister had married and moved to Florida.

That evening Delores added a plate of grits to the evening meal. She'd baked and fried the corn-meal rather than simply boiling it porridge-style. Then she'd added butter, diced bacon and chopped onions before melting cheese over the dish. The result was more like mashed potato than white gruel. Delores served fried chicken, black-eyed peas and corn cobs with the meal. Belle had fried a poke-salad using boiled pokeweed with onions and bacon.

Danny dutifully bowed his head when Al said grace. The family joined hands. Belle, who'd ensured she sat next to Danny, squeezed his fingers firmly. Of course the subject of segregation and the bus issue raised its ugly head during the dinner conversation.

'I think it's universal,' Danny admitted. 'Australia won't even allow people to migrate there unless they're white. I reckon our Aborigines' position is more like your Red Indians though. When I cut sugar-cane in North Queensland, the old-timers there told stories of Pacific Island people being imported as virtual slave labourers. They called them Kanakas.'

'You cut sugar?' Belle said. 'Ain't no white folks round here gonna be cuttin' no sugar.'

'Can't blame them, it's hard work,' Danny acknowledged with a grin. He knew Monty's family was a devoutly religious unit, so he avoided any 'damns' or 'bloodies'.

This was borne out when Al announced it was early to bed because they'd be attending an early morning service at the Dexter Avenue Baptist Church and Danny was cordially invited to join them. Monty gave him a *just-go-with-the-flow* shrug so Danny said he'd be delighted.

The night was oppressively steamy so Monty and Danny opted for hammocks on the back porch. Running water was by no means available in all Montgomery homes, especially in the coloured wards, but Al had installed a shower in the bathroom. There was no water heating, but that didn't matter. Even at dawn the thermometer inched above 85 degrees Fahrenheit which is close to 30 degrees Celsius.

Danny was pleasantly surprised to find he actually enjoyed the morning church service. He felt a little under-dressed in shirt-and-tie, but no one seemed to mind. There were no other white people in the congregation, but everyone knew Danny was Monty's friend and welcomed him accordingly. Danny loved the music. Catholic and Anglican sombre hymns sounded like monotone dirges compared to the jumpy, rocking gospel music of the southern Baptists. Danny was later to discover white Baptist congregations were not nearly as lively.

Another charming aspect of the service was the immaculate care everyone took in their appearance. Even though the temperature soared, the men and boys dressed in their best suits while the women wore elegant dresses and hats. Little girls all wore delightful multi-coloured hair ribbons.

The minister was a sincere twenty-six-year-old who'd just completed his PhD at Boston University, so he was now known as Dr Martin Luther King. His sermon contained all the usual glory to Godliness accompanied by liberal smatterings of 'halleluiah', 'amen', 'praise the Lord' from the congregation. But once he was fired up he marched straight down the civil rights trail. This of course had been brewing for years since the black day of the 1920s when the KKK had lynched, raped and tortured coloured people with total impunity. Three years ago WAC Private Sarah Keys had defied South Carolina's Jim Crow segregation laws and spent a night in gaol for her trouble. She challenged her twenty-five dollar fine and the case was still bouncing around in the justice system.

After his sermon and before the last rousing encore of *Swing Down Sweet Chariot,* Dr King announced that two special guests from Harlem NY would be speaking at the evening chapel-meeting. Equal-rights activist Bayard Rustin and a young firebrand who called himself Malcolm X were touring the area and eager to spread the message to Dr King's congregation. This caused great excitement and everyone planned to attend.

Chapter 22 — The End of the Road

Danny wasn't sure what to make of it. On the surface the coloured community appeared happy enough, but rumbles of discontent surfaced regularly. Talk of civil rights was nothing new, but the groundswell now grew at an unprecedented pace. The Sarah Keys incident was just the beginning. Danny soon realised that so many things he took for granted were hard to do in the segregated South.

In Danny's opinion the Bible banged on about the Jews being the chosen race which smacked of racism in itself, yet Dr King's congregation were ardent *Good-Book* worshippers. *Go figure* as Monty would say. The more Danny was exposed to faith, the more mystified he became.

After the service Danny suggested that they walk back to Al and Delores' home and take in the sights along the way. The Dexter Street Church was only a block from the Capitol Building which was a grand edifice and worth a look. But of course Monty couldn't openly accompany him. Nannies caring for white children were about the only inter-racial fraternisation permitted under Alabama's Jim Crow laws.

At first Monty had been sanguine about the Montgomery status quo, but a boiling resentment quickly emerged.

'This place is bullshit,' he whispered to Danny. 'We've been around the world together and now I can't even show you around my hometown.'

Danny had no answer. In the end they piled into Al's battered pre-war Ford and drove back to Ward 4. In any event the day passed pleasantly enough. As the temperature and humidity soared Danny was pleased that all he had to do was laze in a porch hammock drinking iced lemonade. They planned to eat lunch under the shade of the garden maple trees. Danny and Monty were given the task of setting a trestle table and finding enough chairs to go around. Belle placed a crisp red-and-white check cloth over the table and set out the cutlery and crockery.

'There's plenty of room for the five of us,' Danny observed.

'The reverend and his friends are coming over,' Belle said, setting extra places.

Dr King duly arrived in a 1953 General Motors Oldsmobile. Another equally grand car pulled up behind the Oldsmobile. Dr King had gathered quite an entourage around him. Foremost among the new arrivals were his wife, Coretta, Bayard Rustin and Malcolm X. They were accompanied by two other women, an adolescent girl and a rather distinguished man in his mid-fifties.

All the new-comers eyed Danny suspiciously as they filed through the front gate and gathered under the maples. Belle brought pitchers of lemonade from the kitchen and served all the guests who turned out to be the very nucleus of the civil-rights atomic-bomb ready to explode.

Once they'd been introduced, Dr King's party accepted Danny who quickly explained that he was a foreigner and in no position to make judgements. Only Malcolm X remained hostile, referring to Danny as a 'fence-sitting cracker'. Malcolm X was slightly taller than Danny, lean to the point of emaciation with the look of a bird-of-prey perched and ready to strike. Danny disliked him instantly from the outset and the feeling was obviously mutual.

Coretta Scott King was pleasant, bright and conversational. The other women were less cheerful. Forty-two-year-old Rosa Parks was a discontented Montgomery local. Betty Sanders, an idealistic twenty-one-year-old had met Malcolm X in Harlem when she moved there as a nurse. She'd been following him around ever since. The middle-aged man was an indefatigable crusader for equal rights called Edgar Nixon, who now worked with Rosa Parks in their quest for equality and justice.

Danny was seated between the teenage girl and Belle at the lunch table.

'Hello,' he greeted. 'I've met everyone else and they've had so much to say, we haven't had a chance to be introduced. I'm Danny McAlister. I come from Australia.'

'Hi, I'm Claudette Colvin,' she beamed as if she didn't get to speak to strangers often, especially white ones. 'You got kangaroos and koala bears and such,' Claudette added. 'I learned about that from school books.'

'Do you like to read?'

'Yessir, I do. But I gotta go to the black library which is small and I reckon I've read most of the books. I bet them white folks got plenty more books I could read if they only let me in there.'

'How did you meet Dr King?' Danny asked. 'Are you related?'

'No,' Claudette laughed, 'I sorta came to his attention 'cos I got into trouble.'

Danny arched his eyebrows.

'Yeah, I wouldn't give up my seat on the bus to no white lady,' Claudette announced with pride. 'Police come an' arrested me.'

'That was last March and they're still fussin' about it in the courts,' Coretta King explained. 'We've taken Claudette under our wing until the case is resolved.'

'It's those wretched buses again,' Danny said. 'Seems to me this town's problems are about who sits where on a stupid bus. It's insane.'

'Easy for you to say, cracker boy,' Malcolm X snarled. 'We have to live, eat, sleep and work with this every day. One day black folk are going to rise up and take what's rightfully theirs. Take it all in the name of Allah!'

That's new, where did that come from?

'So you're not a Baptist then?' Danny smiled.

'People must choose their own path,' Dr King intervened, although in a tone that suggested he was ill at ease with Malcolm X's Islamic leaning. 'It is the inequality of races that is at issue. However we're all believers of Ghandi's non-violent protests.'

Edgar Nixon and Bayard Rustin nodded sombrely, but Danny was still uncertain about Malcolm X.

After that Danny avoided Malcolm X. He knew he'd only wind up embarrassing his hosts if he let the black activist get under his skin. Danny saw the difference between Malcolm X and the others was that he was striving for black domination not black equality. His bitterness may have been justified because his family home had been set ablaze back when he was a kid. He also suspected his father had been murdered by white supremacists who ironically named themselves 'The Black Legion'.

Luckily Monty was able to steer the conversation into safer territory. He mentioned he'd trained as a pilot at Tuskegee and it turned out that Betty Sanders had qualified as a nurse at the Tuskegee Institute while Rosa Parks was born there. Thus the tension was relieved as they reminisced about the town.

After lunch Danny helped Belle clear up and wash the dishes while Monty collapsed and stowed the trestle table. Danny insisted Delores relax as she'd prepared lunch. He didn't mind tidying up. Delores had boiled the kettle and the women drank tea as they chatted in the shade.

'How come Malcolm calls himself "X"?' Danny asked Belle. 'I mean it's not his real name, is it?'

'No, he was christened Malcolm Little, but he renounced it because he says it was a "slave name".'

'Doesn't show much imagination, does it? It's sort of what you sign when you can't write.'

'Maybe that's his point. I dunno. He's a complex man.'

'It seems to me you've got a long road ahead,' Danny observed.

'I guess we'll get to the end sometime,' Belle said. 'I don't see Dr King and them others giving up.'

'Claudette seems nice, and brave too. It took a lot of courage for someone so young to stand up to the Jim Crow laws. I know from what happened on the bus yesterday.'

'She's gonna need a lot more courage in the months to come.'

'Yeah, I suppose with the court case?'

'That and a whole lot more.'

'What do you mean?'

'She's in the family way. I guess you being a fella ain't spotted it yet.'

'No, can't say as I have. She's a bit young don't you think.'

'Maybe she didn't have a choice, but it's another reason Dr King and Coretta are looking out for her.'

During the afternoon Dr King decided they should all walk to the Dexter Street Church and gather the congregation along the way. Hopefully the march would demonstrate coloured solidarity for all Montgomery to see. Belle offered to spread the word around the neighbourhood and Danny went with her to avoid tussling with Malcolm X. Belle seemed happy to take the risk of being seen with a white man.

Dr King's party set off in the late afternoon as the temperature cooled, expecting to reach the church by sunset. He anticipated it would be a lively meeting and suggested his parishioners leave their children at home in the care of those too old to make the walk. So the march began with Monty joining the leaders. Danny followed at a discreet distance. He felt this was one time to simply be an observer. To his surprise he found Belle walking beside him about a hundred yards behind the growing crowd.

She took his arm as if it was the most natural thing to do.

'It's nice to walk beside a white man who ain't ashamed to be seen with me,' she said.

'Who'd be ashamed to be seen with a lovely girl like you?' Danny said.

You old smoothie, Danny. Well done, occasionally you get it right.

When it came to women, he was learning what they liked to hear.

As Dr King passed by, people joined him in twos and threes. It was a peaceful, cheerful procession. Someone started singing *Bringing in the Sheaves* and *We Will Overcome* and soon everybody joined in. The crowd had grown to almost two hundred and fifty people when it approached the Baptist Church on the corner of Dexter Ave and Decatur Street, but they were not alone.

Word may have spread to Dr King's coloured congregation, but the KKK local chapter had got wind of it too. The Grand Wizard was not about to tolerate a bunch of trumped-up niggers running riot in the fair streets of Montgomery, especially when they're stirred up by a couple of Yankee commie blow-ins from New York.

A line of hooded white-robed figures stood across the intersection, blocking access to the church entirely. A dozen Confederate *Stars-and-Bars* ensigns drooped languidly between several blazing crosses that stood erect, illuminating the darkening street. As he and Belle caught up with the crowd, Danny counted about fifty Klansmen. From his position at the rear he also caught a glimpse of something everyone else missed.

He spotted at least half a dozen MPD patrol cars parked down side alleys off Decatur Street. Armed policemen milled around the cars, trying to keep as inconspicuous as possible. Danny saw a commandeered yellow school bus ease to a stop and more policemen poured out to join their colleagues. It looked as if there were now more cops than Klansmen. No one in the crowd noticed the police because their attention was focused solely on the white-hooded figures ahead.

'Good, the cops are here to maintain order,' Danny said, pointing out the patrol cars to Belle.

'Don't count on it,' Belle replied doubtfully.

For a moment it looked like a standoff, but Dr King had planned a church meeting and that was precisely what he intended to have. The Grand Wizard probably didn't give a hoot about Dr King's church, but here were a bunch of uppity niggers who needed taking down a peg or two.

'Why are you blocking our way?' Dr King demanded. 'Please move aside and let us pass.'

'Move aside?' the Grand Wizard jeered. 'You hear that, boys. We just "move aside" on the say so of this nigger. Any of you boys gonna "move aside"?'

'Hell no!' came the unanimous response.

'So how about y'all just slink away back to whatever stones you crawled outa,' the Grand Wizard snarled.

'We're not going anywhere,' Dr King declared and sat cross-legged right where he was.

Coretta promptly joined him before the others sat one by one along the street. Only Malcolm X remained standing as the crowd started a rousing chorus of *Steal Away to Jesus* while clapping their hands in time.

Danny could hardly see the point of what happened next, but who knew what went through a KKK mind. Until then it appeared that the Klansmen were unarmed, but that was an unheard of absurdity in the USA. However the hooded figures weren't armed with guns, they didn't need to be. Each Klansman drew a baseball bat from under their robes. This was an ideal weapon-of-choice for street-fighting.

The Klansmen charged forward swinging their bats. The crowd erupted in panic as they tried to dodge the incoming blows. Danny's eyes darted to the police cars, but the officers remained where they stood.

Monty was at the centre of the melee right in front of a charging Klansman. He knew the first rule of fighting when you're unarmed and your opponent has a dirty great stick is to run away. If that's not possible then turn the tables at all costs. To the Klansman's surprise Monty jumped to his feet and charged straight for him. Monty slid soccer-style feet first so his heels slammed into the Klansman's ankles. The hooded fellow toppled over, dropping his bat. Monty grabbed the weapon and slammed it into the fallen victim's skull. The Klansman grunted, went limp and remained still.

Monty didn't hesitate. He swung the bat into another hooded figure's gut. Contrary to modern pop-culture that insists movie fights go on forever, one decent clout with a baseball bat is enough to put you out of action. Monty knew the second Klansman wasn't going anywhere any time soon.

Danny didn't stand around either. He bounded through the screaming panic-stricken mob as they tried to avoid the swinging bats and escape. He was buffeted from all sides, but managed to reach a Klansman with his bat raised to strike a fallen woman.

Danny grabbed the bat and drove his knee into the Klansman's kidneys. Danny wrenched the bat from the Klansman's grip and struck him behind his ears. Another Klansman was out of action, but there were too many more to deal with. Several of Dr King's congregation lay on the street in pools of blood, but most had managed to run away.

Danny turned to see Belle beside him. He wanted to tell her to run for it, but saw she was helping her mother and father who'd been slightly injured. Fortunately KKK robes were about the worst outfits for street-fighting. They were cumbersome and obstructive, so Klansmen's blows often glanced off their victims with minimal effect.

Although there had been a wanton, unprovoked attack on helpless citizens, the police still made no move to intervene. Danny saw Coretta helping Dr King away. Blood covered the pastor's face. He was relieved to see Belle making her way to safety as she supported her parents. Malcolm X was nowhere to be seen.

Danny and Monty suddenly found themselves alone on the street confronted by an angry mob of Klansmen. They were the only two who had retaliated and now became the Klansmen's target. The Klansmen advanced cautiously even though they vastly outnumbered Danny and Monty. They'd seen what the duo could do.

'It's that nigger lovin' Yankee white-trash,' a familiar voice bellowed from under his hood. 'I'm gonna get even with that son-of-a-bitch.'

Danny was hardly surprised that his bus-riding adversary was a Klan member, but now he wasn't alone.

'Time to bail, Monty,' Danny said.

'What about those people?' Monty yelled pointing to the injured forms lying randomly along the street.

'Nothing we can do. Maybe we can decoy these goons away so Dr King's people can come back to them.'

Danny and Monty turned and ran. With a collective howl of victory, the Klansmen gave chase. But where were Danny and Monty going to run. The police had finally moved away from their cars, but only to herd the crowd away using their night-sticks as encouragement. They made no effort to stop the Klansmen.

As Danny rushed past the patrol cars he notice the school bus driver was still at the wheel casually smoking and looking on with amusement. Danny bounded over two police car bonnets and climbed aboard the bus. He jabbed the baseball bat into the driver's ribs.

'Drive,' he yelled, 'or I'll beat your bloody brains out!'

The driver hesitated for just a second, but the look in Danny's eyes convinced him. He revved the engine as Monty climbed aboard. A Klansman tried to clamber after him, but Monty booted him in the chest. The Klansman tumbled away as the bus door closed. The vehicle lurched forward with other Klansmen hammering on the bodywork as it passed by.

'Where's the nearest military base?' Danny demanded.

'Maxwell,' the driver replied. 'It's just across town, not far.'

'Go there!'

The police were fairly well dispersed by then and either didn't notice or attach any importance to the bus's sudden departure. It took the Klansmen several minutes to get the message across. Police officers raced to their cars and sped off in pursuit. Two patrol cars slammed into each other as the drivers lost control in their excitement. Other cars sped away in different directions to locate the bus. It didn't take long and soon all units with sirens blaring and lights flashing turned into Bell and Day Streets, converging on Maxwell Boulevard.

There was no way a school bus could outrun a fleet of police cars. Fortunately Maxwell AFB was barely a mile away and Danny ordered the bus driver to swing into the main entrance with the patrol cars right on their rear bumper.

'Don't stop!' Danny ordered.

The bus slammed through the main gate, smashing the boom gate to splinters. As Danny had anticipated the police cars screeched to a halt just beyond the airfield fence. Jurisdiction was so ingrained into American law enforcement protocol that the police officers could not bring themselves to violate military property. The bus jolted to a halt at the HQ building steps.

Until recently Maxwell had been a major operational flying base, but those units had been withdrawn and it was now a military training centre. Nevertheless armed air force MPs poured from everywhere. In seconds they'd surrounded the bus with their rifles aimed and ready. A young captain commanded the MPs.

'Come out with your hands up,' he bellowed confidently through a megaphone. 'Now!'

Danny and Monty had no choice but to comply.

'You stay here,' Danny whispered to the driver with a wink, 'just in case they have itchy trigger-fingers. We'll tell 'em you had nothing to do with it – promise.'

Danny knew he must act quickly before anyone had time to think straight.

As he stepped from the bus he waved the sheet of paper with Colonel Serong's telephone number written on it.

'I need you to ring this number at Langley right now,' he yelled with a lot of authority he didn't have. 'Tell them Captain McAlister and Captain Montgomery need to talk to Colonel Serong or his deputy. We're on official business.'

Now there was a nice concoction of fact and fiction for you. Danny had used their CAT titles which the air force guys could well confuse with military ones. Official business was a bit of a stretch, but then they hadn't been formally released from CAT, which was still firmly connected to the CIA.

Meanwhile a heated territorial discussion was developing between the Montgomery PD and Maxwell AFB MPs. The Montgomery police demanded Danny, Monty and the bus be handed back to them, but the MPs insisted the incident had occurred on air force property and they'd handle it. Who knew? It might well be a communist terrorist attack.

The USAF captain delegated a lieutenant to sort out the mess at the gate while he escorted Danny, Monty and the driver into the HQ guard-house. The driver continued to protest his innocence, which in all fairness, Danny and Monty confirmed vehemently. But once again Danny and Monty found themselves behind bars with a squad of severe, crew-cut cropped guards at the door.

'Who the hell are you guys?' the driver demanded. 'What did I ever do to you? What are you playin' at?'

'Sorry, we needed sanctuary and you were the closest transport,' Danny said.

'Sanctuary, you say?' the driver said.

'Yeah, you know like them knights in armour hiding in a church,' Monty added.

'I saw *Ivanhoe* at the drive-in movie back a ways,' the driver reflected, although he probably still didn't really understand the whole sanctuary concept. 'That Elizabeth Taylor sure is one fancy broad.'

'No argument there,' Danny agreed, 'and we're sorry we hijacked your bus. I hope we didn't damage the grill too much crashing through that boom-gate.'

After an hour or so the chisel-jawed guard commander returned, ordering one of his men to open the cell.

'You're free to go, sir,' he addressed the bus driver. 'The bus has a few paint scratches, but looks OK. We're sorry for the inconvenience.'

They're all so polite.

The driver didn't wait for the MPs to change their minds and vanished. Danny heard the motor start and the bus return to civilian territory at speed.

'As for you two,' the captain said. 'You seem to make a habit of this sort of thing.'

Danny and Monty stared at him sheepishly.

'I have to give it to you, Langley answered the number as soon as I dialled and guess what the first thing the operator said – not them again!'

'Sorry about that,' Danny whispered.

'It doesn't matter. I don't know and I don't want to know and Langley certainly ain't gonna tell me. The upshot is we have a civil incident downtown. That's none of my business either and I ain't sending MPs off base to investigate. Maybe the cops will call out the National Guard, who knows?'

Danny and Monty remained silent.

'All I know is Langley wants the pair of you out of harm's way. You guys must be something special because they're diverting a Lockheed P-2 Neptune here to airlift you someplace else. "*Any* place else", were the guy's exact words.'

'Dunno about being special,' Danny admitted. 'An embarrassment might be a more accurate term.'

'The base commander is away for the weekend and all the majors and colonels are at home with their families over at the married quarters. So I want you guys outa here and the front gate fixed before they get back Monday mornin'.'

'I'm staying,' Monty announced.

'What? Not on this base you ain't,' the captain was horrified

'No, I mean I'm not leaving Montgomery.'

Danny stared at him.

'Sorry Danny, it's the end of the road. I've been roaming around the world for over ten years now. I dunno what I was looking for. All I know is that I may find it right back where I started. There's some mean shit going on in the Deep South and I aim to help put it right. My folks are here and that's where I belong too.'

'You mean join Dr King and Malcolm X in the civil-rights fight?'

'That's exactly what I mean. I dunno where it'll lead, but that's what I gotta do. That's what I wanna do. That's what I'm gonna do. You go on back and fly that Lockheed for Angela. It won't take both of us to do that. I'll miss ya kid, you're a hell of a good guy.'

'What about New Guinea? What about the *Goose?* It took you ages to get it going again.'

'Dave Bradley will take good care of it. I'll work something out and write him what to do.'

'I gotta warn you, sir,' the captain said, 'it makes no difference to me if you walk out or fly out, but once you go past that gate I can't help you. You're on your own.'

'I know, captain,' Monty replied, 'and I want to thank you for your kindness.'

'Best I can do is to sneak you out in a covered Jeep anywhere you wanna go in town. We aren't all closed-minded red-necks in the South, you know.'

'I'm much obliged. I'll send your gear back with the driver, Danny,' Monty said.

The captain picked up his office phone and moments later a Jeep pulled up outside the HQ building. There was no time for protracted goodbyes. After a quick handshake Monty climbed into the Jeep and it sped away.

'You guys are pretty thick,' the captain observed.

'Yessir, I just said goodbye to my best friend.'

When the Jeep returned Danny was surprised to see Belle sitting beside the driver. She carried Danny's grip which contained Danny's passport, CIA travel authority and 1911 Army Colt automatic. She also brought his ukulele.

'Thank heavens you got away safely,' Danny said as she embraced him. 'Are your mum and dad OK?'

'They're fine Danny, but several folks were taken to hospital. Luckily the ruckus broke up real quick and no one got killed. I reckon Malcolm X, Betty and Bayard Rustin are half way back to Harlem by now,' she grinned. 'I couldn't let you go without saying goodbye.'

'Thanks. I'm glad you came. I'm sorry my stay wasn't longer and under more pleasant circumstances.'

'I'm sorry too. You're a true friend, Danny.'

She kissed him. The kiss lingered before she turned and walked towards the gate.

'Would you like a ride back home, ma'am?' the captain offered.

'No thank you, captain. I still have time to catch the last bus home and I'll sit where I damn-well please!'

Danny and the MP captain stood on the HQ steps and watched Belle leave to join a short queue of service personnel waiting at the bus-stop just outside the main gate. A repair-team was already hard at work fixing the boom.

'Nice girl,' the captain observed.

'I think so.'

'Chance of what might have been..?'

'Ships that pass in the night I guess, but there's a special girl I know in England.'

Moments later the runway lights illuminated and they heard the mixed roar of Pratt & Whitney radial and Westinghouse turbo-jet engines. The P-2 Neptune growled overhead before banking for its approach to Maxwell Field.

Part 3 — The Dark Continent

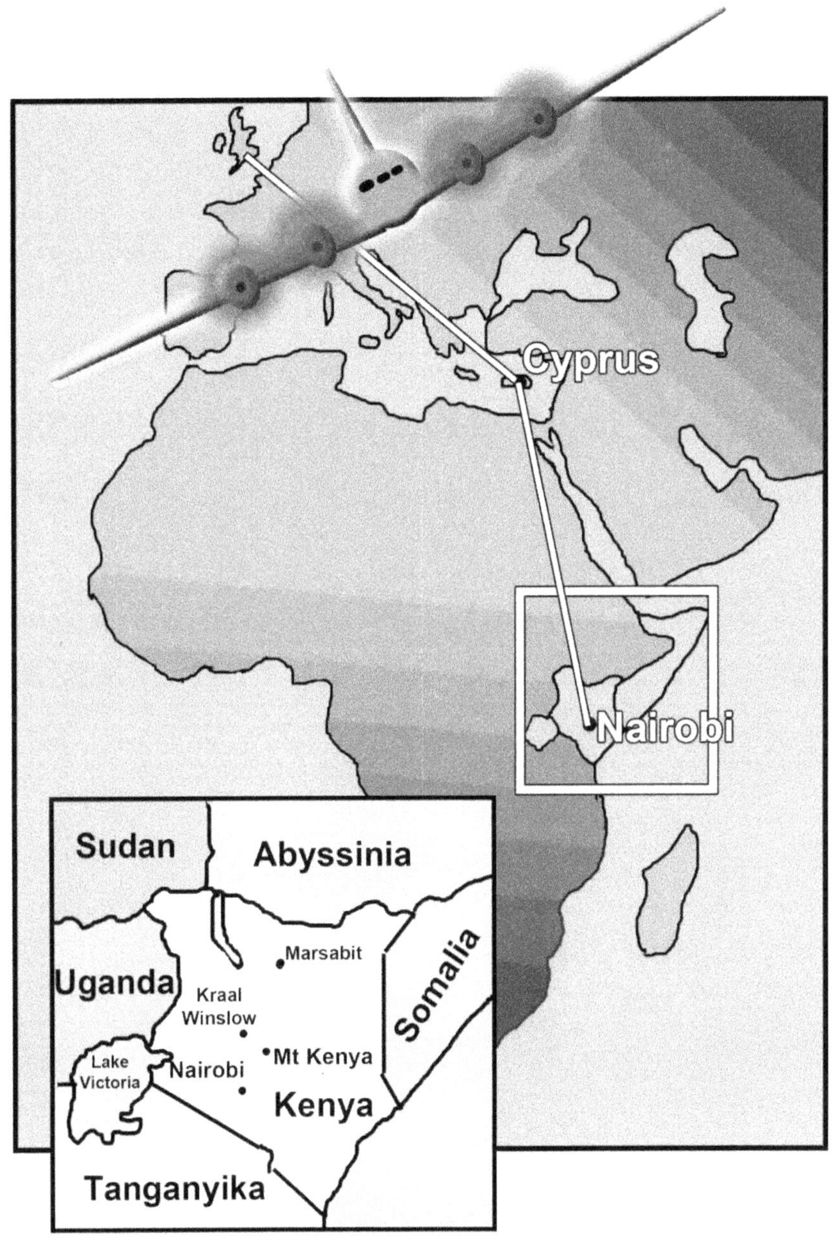

Chapter 23 — Flying Solo

Major Black and Major White's CIA travel documents facilitated Danny's smooth passage back to the UK by an assortment of US and Commonwealth aircraft. The final stage was in a four-engine 206 Squadron Coastal Command Shackleton to RAF St Eval in Cornwall. He rang the Holyman house and was delighted when Angela picked up the phone.

Danny explained he'd catch the bus to Yeovil, where Angela would pick him up in 'Daddy's car'. He was impatient to see her again so it was a tedious bus trip along the A30 through Bodmin, Launceston, Oakhampton and Exeter. Fortunately Danny bought a copy of *HMS Ulysses,* a page-turning naval adventure novel by an emerging author called Alistair Mclean. The harrowing drama of Murmansk convoys and the endearing English scenery, helped pass the time.

What was it about Angela? She drove him crazy, but deep down his heart always ached to see her again. It went far beyond any sexual desire, which was just as well, because so far he hadn't been particularly successful in that direction. His feeling only deepened when she met him at the bus stop. She skipped towards him in neat heels, a crisp blouse, multi-petticoat skirt held tightly with a broad belt around her waist. Her hair bobbed in a flowing pony-tail as she flung her arms around his neck.

'Oh Danny, I've missed you,' she cooed. 'It's been so lonely around here.'

'I can't imagine you being lonely, Ange,' he replied before kissing her.

He made sure it was more than a brotherly peck-on-the-cheek and received a pretty good response for his trouble.

'Where's Mr Montgomery?' she asked when they finally disentangled themselves.

'He's not coming. I'm flying solo from now on.'

'What happened, did you two have a row?'

'Nothing like that. He decided it was time to shoulder his responsibility back home and fight the good fight to end racial segregation. Things are pretty bad in the Deep South. I think it was a wake-up call for Monty.'

'How commendable I'm sure, but what about Kenya?'

'Don't worry, Ange. I can fly the crate by myself. My FAA and Australian licences and instrument rating are all up to date, so there'll be no problems with the authorities. That is if Kenya has aviation regulators of course.'

Angela drove along the A30 to Sherborne before turning south on the A352. Whatever her true relationship with Monty was, Danny sensed she was disappointed that he wasn't going to join them on their African adventure.

'Thank you for the *two* postcards, by the way,' she said in an affronted tone accompanied by a wounded pout.

He'd sent her postcards from Las Vegas and New Orleans.

'Sorry Ange, but in my defence we visited a lot of palaces that weren't much for selling postcards.'

'You don't have to explain to me,' she huffed. 'I suppose those fresh American bobby-soxers and cheer-leaders were all over you like a rash.'

'You know what they say, "what happens in Vegas, stays in Vegas",' he grinned.

'I know no such thing and you're a beastly tease,' she wailed, punching him in the arm.

'Careful or you'll run off the road. Anyway there wasn't much time for that sort of thing. We wound up in gaol twice, you know. Colonel Serong had to bail us out.'

'Now why doesn't that surprise me, but what's Ted Serong doing in America?'

'If I told you, I'd have to kill you,' he said.

She glared at him.

'Honestly, I don't really know,' Danny admitted. 'He just gets around and is in really tight with the CIA. For an Australian patriot he spends a heap of time with the Yanks. But tell you what, when we reach town I'll shout you a Babycham at the Royal Oak and I'll tell you all about our American road-trip.'

'Do you think I'm the sort of girl who can be bribed with the promise of Babycham?'

'I certainly hope so.'

It was still an hour before opening time when they reached Cerne Abbas, so they took a stroll round town. Angela didn't object when Danny took her hand. Mind you the mood was ruined when they turned off Long Street into Piddle Lane.

'I don't believe it. You've got a street called "Piddle Lane",' Danny declared. 'I'm not walking down anywhere called "Piddle".'

'You can't avoid it,' Angela replied. 'We're in the Piddle Valley. There's no escaping it. Anyway it's probably just a misspelling of "Puddle".'

They walked back to the river which was so delightfully quintessentially English. Angela was eagerly anticipating their trip to Kenya but said she was still waiting for news about their transportation from England which was still under negotiation. In such an idyllically romantic setting, Danny would have preferred to keep the conversation on a more personal level, but Angela prattled on so he didn't get to say much other than a few snippets of what he and Monty had been up to.

By the time they returned to the Royal Oak the bar was open. Dr and Mrs Holyman arrived at the same time to greet them. Danny ordered two pints, a G &T and of course a Babycham sparkling perry.

'I have some wonderful news,' Dr Holyman announced, although his wife didn't look so pleased.

'Professor Winslow has organised a deal with BOAC to fly you to Nairobi.'

Danny vaguely remembered Geoff Winslow was the bloke in charge of the project.

'BOAC is taking one of its new Bristol Britannia planes on a route-proving flight to Kenya and they have agreed to fly you for nothing as sort of sponsors.'

'How wonderful, Daddy,' Angela gushed.

'There is a catch,' Dr Holyman said. 'As Professor Winslow is already in Kenya, you'll be expected to do the PR.'

Danny and Angela stared blankly.

'Nothing too bad,' Dr Holyman assured them. 'The BBC wants to do a feature for its *Panorama* programme. I'm afraid it's going to go along the *pretty-young-doctor-heading-for-darkest-Africa* lines and what great chaps they are at BOAC.'

'Daddy, when I think about the stories I had to tell the Viet Minh to get Danny out of Dien Bien Phu, I think I can handle a journalist trying to beat a story out of nothing.'

'You got here just in time, Danny,' Dr Holyman said. 'The flight leaves London next week.'

Danny had hoped for a few more romantic country walks and maybe a picnic by the river, but Angela plunged into preparation mode. So any chance of a budding romance was dashed after that. Angela was too busy ensuring she had everything ready for their departure. Whereas Danny just carried his grip and ukulele case, Angela needed a much greater logistical support. It was not so much personal effects, but her notes and medical paraphernalia that occupied most of her attention. She also packed her trusty white laundry pole.

'It has become quite a talisman, hasn't it Danny?' Angela said as she packed it with her gear.

'You'll be able to beat off black mambas and angry lions with it,' Danny grinned. She'd carried the stick with her since she'd escaped from Frenchy Duval and his cut-throats in New Guinea five years ago.

They drove to Bath to buy kit including shirts, pants, slouch hats and desert boots. Dr Holyman ensured they carried ample supplies of quinine.

'Do you know malaria kills more people than any other disease worldwide?' Angela said.

No, I didn't know that, Ange, but of course you would.

The days flew by.

Dr Holyman drove Danny and Angela to London Airport sited west of the city at Heathrow. Mrs Holyman didn't accompany them although there was room in the Worsley despite Angela's kit. Instead she said a teary goodbye before they left Cerne Abbas. Mrs Holyman admonished them both to take care and stay in the protected areas. That puzzled Danny, but he'd no time to ask questions.

'Your mum seems a bit upset,' Danny observed uneasily as they motored eastwards along the A303.

'Oh she's just concerned about the silly old emergency,' Angela replied, a little too glibly in Danny's opinion.

'She's quite right,' Dr Holyman said. 'You take your mother's advice. You know I'm still in two minds about letting you go.'

'Oh, to be twenty-one,' Angela sighed, leaning across the front seat to kiss her father lightly on the cheek. 'Don't worry, Daddy. I'm a big girl now. I can take care of myself.'

'What "silly old emergency" would that be?' Danny asked cautiously.

'It's just Mau-Mau ruffians stirring up trouble. Don't worry, we have troops keeping order and those Kepenguria Six ringleaders are all safely behind bars. Even General China who was the main Mau-Mau leader had been rounded up and is helping the authorities now.'

In Danny's defence he'd been too busy for East African affairs to appear on his radar, but it was the first he'd heard about the Mau-Mau. Dr Holyman and Angela supplied a broad brush précis of the situation, although Danny was to discover the rest for himself later on.

The Mau-Mau was a name given to Kenyan dissidents who came primarily from the Kikuyu around Nairobi. Their claim was reasonable enough as British colonialists had commandeered most of the country's prime real estate for their own farms and plantations, growing prosperous in the process. The Kikuyu thought it was high time to redistribute the territory and started attacking British farmers. The Mau-Mau took a blood oath to kill as many white people as possible – an oath they took very seriously. Around a hundred white settlers had already been murdered.

Not all Kikuyu agreed with the Mau-Mau and were often beaten or murdered for their opinion. One such unfortunate elder was Chief Waruhui who was shot in his car on the streets of Nairobi in 1952. Newly appointed Governor Evelyn Baring declared a state of emergency, ordering a crackdown. Thousands of Mau-Mau suspects were rounded up over the next couple of years and herded into detention camps. A group of independence (not necessarily Mau-Mau) leaders were also caught in the net at a remote town called Kapenguria and, after a distinctly evidence-challenged trial, sentenced to long prison terms. Among those men who became known as the Kapenguria Six was future Kenyan prime minister and president, Jomo Kenyatta.

Governor Baring requested Military units, which Prime Minister Winston Churchill happily provided. Army and RAF units were quickly despatched to restore colonial order. By 1955 military operations had proved reasonably successful and the RAF squadrons were being withdrawn. Unfortunately the Mau-Mau rebellion had morphed into individual terrorist groups who still hid out in the Aberdare Mountain Range forests. These gangs ventured from their lairs to pillage rape and murder whenever the opportunity arose. Two influential leaders were still at large –

Stanley Mathenge and self-proclaimed Field Marshal Dedan Kimathi.

So although much of the fighting was over, a state of emergency still existed in Kenya and would do for some years. Danny now realised why Mrs Holyman was so reluctant to see her daughter head off into another potential war zone. Maybe Mrs Holyman was being over-cautious, but with a declining imperial power and an emerging nationalist native population, it all sounded a lot like French Indochina to Danny. He realised that he should have done some more research before agreeing to help Angela, but conceded he'd probably follow her into the pits of hell if she asked him to.

Sure enough there was a TV contingent waiting when they arrived at London Airport. A cameraman and sound engineer tussled through the crowd of gawkers. Up-and-coming BBC presenter and *Panorama* anchorman, Richard Dimbleby greeted Angela courteously and introduced her to several BOAC heavies. Angela farewelled her father with a brief hug and dutiful kiss before being ushered in front of the camera. Danny was relegated to baggage-handling status. He shook hands with Dr Holyman who stood rather forlornly watching his daughter embrace the limelight. She posed in front of the giant passenger aircraft while charming everyone around her.

'Don't worry. Tell Mrs Holyman I'll keep an eye on her for you,' Danny assured him, with no idea how he'd actually honour his promise.

'Thanks, Danny,' Dr Holyman smiled, shaking his hand firmly. 'It's only until Christmas and then we'll be able to talk about settling her into a sensible practice.'

Yeah, good luck with that one, Doc.

But Danny merely nodded then watched Dr Holyman slip away to his car and drive home. Danny turned to Angela who was glibly fending questions about her youth, film star beauty and the awaiting danger while gushing all over her BOAC benefactors. He wondered if she'd even seen her father leave.

The Bristol Britannia was a sleek four engine turbo-prop one-hundred-and-twenty seater. It was BOAC's latest acquisition, but due to production delays and technical hiccups it was already out-dated. Indeed if it wasn't for the disastrous De Havilland Comet crashes the year before, it may not have even been considered for BOAC's intercontinental routes at all. Pure jet airliners from Boeing and Douglas were already looming as potential rivals.

The air crew arrived shortly afterwards. They were led by a businesslike captain, first officer and navigator followed by four pert flight hostesses. The pilots were entranced by Angela, although she didn't have the same effect on the cabin crew, who looked overtly hostile, but managed professional, fixed smiles when they greeted her. Danny left their luggage in the hands of a porter and was about to board the plane when he heard a *crump-crump* that he instantly recognised, heralding the arrival of marching troops.

Sure enough two platoons of the Royal Inniskilling Fusiliers strode purposefully towards the plane. Heading the column were a captain, two lieutenants and a sergeant major. At their sergeant major's booming command they crunched to a halt.

'Right turn!'

Crunch! Crunch!

'Stand...at...*ease!*'

Crunch!

Apparently Danny and Angela weren't travelling alone. A half company of British troops were being rotated to Cyprus where trouble had erupted between the Greek and Turkish Cypriots. The Greeks wanted Cyprus to become part of Greece, while the Turks of course preferred to be aligned with Turkey. Cyprus had been bandied around between Greece and the Ottoman Empire for ages until Britain declared the island a Crown Colony in 1925. Now with the real threat of civil war between the Greek and Turkish Cypriots, British forces were committed to yet another quasi-colonial conflict.

Taking into consideration, Malaya, Palestine (half of which was now Israel), Aden, Suez, India – (finally independent – thank heavens), Pakistan, Kenya, Tanganyika, Uganda, Ulster and goodness knows how many other imperial back-waters, Great Britain was paying a high price for conquering half of the known world in the first place.

Fortunately Danny and Angela sat in the first class section with the captain and lieutenants. Angela did acknowledge that the fusiliers were well behaved for Irishmen. In fact since Dien Bien Phu, Angela held a soft spot for common soldiers and spent much of the five-hour flight in the economy cabin aisle chatting to the men. She even charmed the BOAC hostesses by carrying a teapot around and topping up the soldiers' cups.

Meanwhile Danny tried to finish his Alistair McLean novel.

'Nice girl,' the captain commented. 'Quite a little knock-out too.'

'Yessir, she has that effect on most people,' Danny replied. 'I've known her for a long time now.'

Cruising smoothly at twenty-four thousand feet the Britannia glided past the afternoon cumulous build up over Greece. Danny visited the flight-deck which seemed unduly complicated, but the pilots and navigator appeared sublimely relaxed in their pressurised, turbulence-free work station.

It was dusk when they landed at Nicosia. The fusiliers disembarked while Angela took it upon herself to stand at the exit door to bid them goodbye and good luck. A scheduled BOAC DC-4 had diverted to Nicosia with mechanical problems so about twenty passengers from that flight joined the Britannia manifest. One was a middle-aged man accompanied by his forty year-old blonde wife who seemed in a particularly bad mood.

With a crew change, refuel and fresh catering, the plane took off at midnight for the six-hour flight to Nairobi.

The couple were assigned to first class seats alongside Danny and Angela. They didn't introduce themselves immediately. Once the Britannia reached cruising altitude and, while Danny peered through the passenger window at the last lightning flashes from dying heat-storms, Angela struck up a conversation.

'Hello, I'm Dr Angela Holyman,' she said.

The concept of having doctor as a title was still a novelty, but Angela liked using it. And rightly so, she'd worked damn hard to get there.

'Armand Denis,' the man said with a pleasant Belgian accent. 'This is my wife Michaela.'

'Oh, the *Filming Wild Animals* people! I loved your first programme.'

Armand Denis nodded and smiled an acknowledgement. He was a successful film maker who'd moved from Hollywood to capture the raw wildness of Africa.

'Are you making many more episodes?' Angela asked.

'Yes indeed,' Armand replied. 'We are returning to Kenya after talking to BBC's producers.'

'They are such fools,' Michaela Denis spat, 'and as for that upstart Attenborough. He is worst of all.'

'You don't mean David Attenborough, surely,' Angela said. 'I watch his *Zoo Quest* series. I mean he's so dishy and afraid of nothing. I love him.'

'He is an amateur and a thief,' Michaela snorted.

'It is just unfortunate timing,' Armand said reasonably, but Michaela merely sulked.

It seemed that David Attenborough's latest *Zoo Quest* programme had featured a segment similar to one covered by Armand and Michaela in their next episode. They'd flown to London in protest. Armand was satisfied when the BBC, David Attenborough and his production team agreed on a new broadcasting schedule, but Michaela appeared to bear a long-seated grudge.

Fortunately Danny didn't have to deal with the disgruntled Michaela Denis as he was studying a copy of the Lockheed Model 10 Electra pilot's manual until he fell asleep. When he awoke the dawn sunrays streaked through his window outlining the silhouette of Mount Kenya as the Britannia began its descent into Nairobi Airport. Angela was full of excitement and leaned across Danny for her first view of Africa.

Chapter 24 — On Safari

Michaela Denis' mood didn't improve when she disembarked to discover the change of schedule had confused their reception team. After passing customs and immigration, Armand placed several calls over a dubious phone network. He learned their Landrover was still upcountry at the Safari site where they'd been filming.

In the meantime Danny was inspecting the Lockheed Electra and met the chief mechanic, Komotho Mwangi. Danny was pleased to see the plane was well maintained with its airworthiness certificate, operating approvals, weight and balance sheets and service schedules all up to date and in order. The Lockheed Model 10 Electra was a chunky, robust business-like airframe that looked as if it would fly well. Danny remembered Monty's golden-rule of aviation — *if the plane looks good, it'll fly well: if it looks a mess, it'll fly like a brick.*

Komotho explained that he'd travel with the plane along with a tool kit. He also supplied Danny with charts, flight-plan forms and a copy of local aviation regulations.

'Spares may be a problem, boss,' he said. 'If anything goes wrong we'll have to freight spares overland to wherever we are.'

'You'll have to make sure everything goes smoothly then,' Danny replied.

'That's what they're paying me for.'

'You're being paid — lucky you. And call me Danny. I'll introduce you to the *real* boss. Then we'll get the gear stowed.'

Komotho grinned.

When they returned to the terminal, the Britannia was refuelling and already manned by a new crew. Passengers were boarding for the return flight to England. Angela stood next to Armand and Michaela Denis in the shade of the cargo hangar beside their baggage. The two divas were chattering like old chums while Armand looked distracted with his own thoughts.

'Oh, Danny, darling,' Angela gushed. 'I'm so pleased you're back.'

Darling? Blimey Ange, I was only across the tarmac.

'You'll never guess, Michaela and Armand's camp is only a few miles from Professor Winslow's field surgery. They're stuck here because of a beastly mix-up. I'm sure we can take them with us and their boys will pick them up from our site.'

Danny noticed that Kikuyu employees were universally referred to as 'boys' which was reminiscent of Alabama. Angela seemed to have adopted the term without hesitation. Danny shrugged.

Whatever.

'No sweat. The plane seats ten and we should be right for baggage, even with all your stuff, Ange.'

She glared at him while he grinned in return.

'I'd like you to meet Komotho,' Danny said. 'He'll be travelling with us to look after the plane.'

'I'm so pleased to meet you, Komotho,' Angela greeted extending her hand.

After completing the introductions, Danny and Komotho examined the map and discussed the strip at Professor Winslow's site. Armand Denis knew the strip well and had used it previously for his own aerial resupplies. Komotho had arranged for forty-four gallon drums of AVGAS and a hand pump to be trucked to the airstrip.

While Danny, Armand and Komotho loaded the Lockheed, Angela and Michaela took over the terminal ladies' room to change into bush outfits. The boys were ready when Angela and Michaela reappeared looking like cover-girls for *Vogue*. Angela was disappointed when Komotho occupied the co-pilot seat, but understood that he needed to show Danny the plane's technical intricacies. She and Michaela chatted away happily in the rear cabin anyway.

Danny filed a radio flight plan with Nairobi ATC and was cleared for takeoff. Once the plane left Nairobi terminal airspace, the controllers lost interest other than a HF call once they'd landed safely. Danny flew northwest into the Kikuyu high country. Landmarks were no problem here as Mt Kenya's snow-capped peak was always visible.

Snow on the equator, how cool is that?

Danny flew west over the Happy Valley where rich and privileged white gentry had settled from early colonial times. They had notoriously debauched themselves into an infamous corner of Kenya's history known as *The Happy Valley Set* and were a prime target for the Mau-Mau. Next Danny turned the plane north along the Great Rift Valley that stretched from the Tanganyika border all the way into Abyssinia. He didn't have to fly far before the country below became ruggedly isolated.

Just like those halcyon New Guinea days eh, Danny Boy?

The valley floor was savannah while forests stretched away to the highlands towards Mount Kenya. The grassland was often dotted with zebra and buffalo herds. Suddenly Angela squealed from her seat.

'Yes, darling,' Michaela laughed. 'They are elephants. Hopefully they will avoid poachers.'

Danny navigated with ease and an hour later they reached Professor Winslow's camp. They made radio contact. Danny assessed the wind direction and speed from a nearby campfire and chose his landing direction. The strip was rough, but adequate. The Lockheed's main wheels touched down smoothly considering it was Danny's first attempt and at an altitude that he estimated was about four thousand feet. Angela and Michaela clapped theatrically and Danny nodded in mock acknowledgement.

Angela was about to disembark, but Michaela held her back.

'Oh that will never do, darling,' Michaela chided digging a beauty case from her otherwise utilitarian pack.

She produced a compact and several lipstick tubes.

'Darling, we never confront the wild looking like common scrubbers. Now let's see what your best shade in this light is.'

Danny, Armand and Komotho had unloaded the plane by the time Angela and Michaela stepped from the plane suitably cosmetically enhanced. Apparently Michaela Denis was quite prepared to face a pride of man-eating lions or a charging rhino provided she looked her glamorous best.

Professor Winslow was a sixty-something shabby, rather harassed looking fellow with a perpetually worried expression.

'Welcome to Kraal Winslow,' he said and shook hands all round.

His setup wasn't a kraal at all, which was an Afrikaans word anyway, but Professor Winslow was a physician and medical researcher rather than a linguist or anthropologist. He'd dubbed his camp-site Kraal Winslow and the name had stuck.

The camp consisted of half a dozen tents erected in the shade of an acacia grove. These served as a surgery, accommodation, storehouse, canteen and laboratory. The trees were alive with squawking birds and monkeys making Angela wonder about the hygienic aspect of the piles of droppings that coated the branches and area surrounding the trunks. Angela's other issue was with the relentless flies.

'Say hello to Africa, darling,' Michaela said. 'You either get used to it or you leave.'

Michaela Denis was something of an enigma. She'd been a Paris and London dress designer before meeting her Belgian husband in New York. Considering her love for glamour and high society, she appeared right at home in the African wilderness as long as her compact was handy.

Kraal Winslow was situated at the centre of a dozen remote Kikuyu villages. Local folk arrived unannounced for treatment, but who was going to announce them anyway. Subsequently a queue often formed. Those most needing treatment were usually children although there was no shortage of pregnant women who had come to trust Professor Winslow.

Winslow may have appeared an absent-minded professor, but he was right down to business and suggested Angela could start her clinic right away. The good professor knew Armand and Michaela quite well. He'd been an occasional guest at their film safari camp which lay about an hour's drive away along a tortuous bush track. Winslow contacted the Armand camp on his shortwave radio. Armand's foreman assured them he'd send a Landrover right away and, 'sorry about the mix-up'.

And so camp routine began. Angela's duties included clinic work, vaccinations taking blood samples for analysis, thus relieving Professor Winslow to conduct his research. In many ways it reminded Danny of New Guinea when Angela had assisted her father with his roving clinic through the remote highlands and islands.

Winslow explained that he wanted Danny and Komotho to take one of the four-wheel drives and scout out suitable landing strips within a hundred mile radius. They examined a map for likely sites.

'If we get to outlying villages quickly by air,' Winslow explained, 'we can help so many more people and gather a vast amount of data. I want you to go as far north as Marsabit here on the map. It's not big but it's the only place that can call itself a town between here and Abyssinia. There's an airstrip there, but you might want to check if there is fuel available.'

'It's going to take a while to cover all that territory, professor,' Danny warned.

'Take provisions for a week and see how you go,' Winslow replied. 'Concentrate on this north sector. The trails are rough and even the main road to Marsabit is little more than a goat-track for miles.'

Winslow indicated the area west and north of Mt Kenya.

'You can see where I've marked these villages. It takes those people two or three days to walk here. If Dr Holyman and I can fly out there it would be a Godsend.'

Yeah, Dr Holyman, Danny smiled.

'OK professor, we'll head off at first light,' Danny said.

Komotho made doubly sure that the plane was locked and all the windows closed. He paid special attention covering the pitot tubes and engine air intakes. Monkeys and baboons were prone to making themselves at home where they were not welcome while insects were rife. Komotho was going to prove invaluable not only as Danny's interpreter, but he'd been brought up in the Aberdare Ranges and knew his way around.

Michaela and Armand's ride showed up shortly afterwards and they left for their safari camp. Angela and Michaela embraced like long lost pals, promising they'd visit each other whenever possible.

'We girls have to stick together out here in the wilderness,' Michaela said with a wink, waving from the Landrover. '*Ciao,* darling.'

That night everyone sat around a blazing campfire enjoying an impala stew supper washed down with sweet tea. Danny pulled out his uke and began strumming. Soon the *boys* joined in with a guitar and drums. They introduced Danny to a catchy three-chord tune entitled *Wimoweh* written by Natal performer Solomon Linda. Many of the local songs followed the same simple three-chord progression, so Danny had no trouble playing along.

While tapping their feet to the rhythm, Angela and Professor Winslow discussed the scientific wonders of the region. The professor believed that Kenya was the birth-place of mankind and archaeologists had discovered ancient skeletons to back him up.

Despite her fundamental Christian upbringing, Angela was inclined to agree, which left her wondering why the Bible had neglected to mention the fact. Sure, the St James edition was an interpretation of a translation from Ancient Hebrew, Latin and Old English to its present form and had probably undergone some serious editorial input during the process. But you'd think they'd have paid more attention to details like that.

As a doctor Angela was assigned her own tent. Danny's role as pilot also afforded enough status entitling him a tent, although his was so small it was barely big enough for a single occupant. Komotho had wisely brought his own tent with him. If Danny expected any personal time with Angela, he was sadly mistaken. After the all-night flight, they were both ready for bed and turned in early.

The trouble was that nights on the Kenyan savannah were far from peaceful. The myriad of wildlife species all wanted to be heard through the darkness. Monkeys argued, parrots squawked, insects chirped and buzzed, hyenas and jackals howled, elephants trumpeted, a faraway lion pride roared and a leopard growled ominously close by. Fortunately the fire and camp hustle and bustle kept large predators at bay.

You'll get used to it, Danny. Dunno how it'll be out in the Landrover though.

The following morning Angela was up early and busying herself around the camp. Danny and Komotho loaded the Landrover with food, water, rifles, ammunition and jerry-cans of petrol. Danny still carried his 1911 Army Colt automatic and spare .45 clips. Angela was so preoccupied with her new endeavour, she barely managed to wave when they drove off, but that was Angela for you.

In truth Danny enjoyed the days that followed. Komotho was easy to get along with and a wealth of local knowledge. Danny was a pretty handy marksman, but Komotho was a crack-shot. At first Danny thought he was on a veritable big-game safari when they spotted giraffes and several antelope herds, but that was not to say the place was teeming with wild-life every step of the way. They often drove for miles without spotting any game at all.

They passed Kikuyu villages where boys and young men tended herds of cattle, goats and sheep. At each village, Danny surveyed the surrounding terrain, marking any suitable landing sites on his map. Komotho always checked with the village council. Kikuyu tribes tended to rely on a group of acceptable delegates to manage their affairs rather than a single chief. In all cases Professor Winslow was well thought of and they were overjoyed to learn that he'd be coming to them, thus avoiding the long trek to his clinic.

Danny and Komotho were invariably village guests, but they camped out for a couple of nights. On one such occasion Komotho shot a Thompson's Gazelle and Danny had to stand nervously on guard while he skinned and butchered the carcass. A wild dog pack cautiously sniffed around, so Komotho took what they needed and left the rest for the predators. A bunch of hyenas showed up and chased the dogs off while vultures circled overhead.

'Who said nature was peaceful,' Danny said as he watched the scavengers squabble over the gazelle.

'I think we'll drive a few miles away,' Komotho suggested. 'Just in case lions spot the vultures and come looking as well.'

'I'm with you,' Danny agreed.

After a week they'd covered most of the district within a hundred mile radius and found half-a-dozen suitable landing strips. In some cases there were established strips that looked as if they'd been used by previous bush pilots.

When they returned to Kraal Winslow, Angela embraced Danny and kissed his lips.

'I missed you, you big lummox,' she said genuinely.

'Me too,' he replied, although in truth he'd been so fascinated with the African veldt, he hadn't actually given her a second thought. She eyed him sceptically as if she'd read his mind.

That evening at supper time, Professor Winslow explained his work roster.

'Danny, I would like you to fly Dr Holyman to those villages where you have found satisfactory landing fields. Will you have sufficient fuel to reach all the settlements?'

'I believe so, professor, unless we strike bad weather. If not, we'll just return here and refuel. It'll still be way quicker than on foot. I'll need to take Komotho as my mechanic.'

'Absolutely. I shall remain here and continue the blood sample tests and conduct the clinic for anyone who comes in. Dr Holyman I'd be pleased if you would assist me when you return.'

Angela nodded. She was proud she'd reduced the professor's work-load significantly, freeing up his time for research. At last Angela had found another sense of purpose since Dien Bien Phu. She'd qualified as a doctor in record time and now she was ready to put that training into practice.

Chapter 25 — Mau-Mau

The following morning they took off. Danny planned to visit the furthest villages first and work back towards the Kraal Winslow. In that way he'd be able to calculate his fuel requirements accurately. He also wanted to fly in the morning when the weather was at its best. Angela could conduct her clinic in the afternoon so they wouldn't be airborne if storms reared up reducing visibility. With no navigation aids to guide him, Danny had to rely on his map-reading skill and Komotho's local knowledge. Fortunately they'd arrived in Kenya during the lull between the long and short rains which helped weatherwise.

Wherever they landed they were met by a delegation of cheerful bubbling people, who seemed not to have a care in the world. The Kikuyu lived a simple, subsistence life. The climate was mild in the highlands around Mt Kenya compared to the sweltering heat of Swahili coastal towns like Mombasa and Malindi.

Because flight times between settlements were short and the Lockheed spent most of the time on the ground, it burnt very little fuel. Angela, Danny and Komotho were able to stay away from Kraal Winslow for nearly a week.

At night it was party time. The Kikuyu loved to dress up and dance. They wore wonderful costumes adorned with colourful beads as they danced the night away. Angela was dismayed at the volume of beer consumed, but pleased to note that most villagers she met were practising Christians, although they remained non-aligned to any established Western denominations. Kenya was one of the early missionaries' success stories.

After a week, Danny told Angela they'd have to return to Kraal Winslow and refuel the plane. By now word had got around and people were drifting in from even smaller communities for treatment. Ailments included infected cuts, broken bones, a snake bite, a nasty gash from a warthog's tusk and the usual ensemble of pregnant women. Angela had already delivered two babies with the help of local midwives. A line which didn't look like diminishing any time soon had built up outside the surgery hut.

'You take the plane, Danny,' Angela said. 'I'll be at least a couple more days at this rate, and that's if no one else turns up.'

'I don't want to leave you alone out here,' Danny protested.

'That's sweet, Danny, but I'll be fine and I'm certainly not alone,' she said as they dodged a group of children kicking a soccer ball around with no apparent rules other than to have fun. 'I have the whole village to keep me company.'

She laughed as the ball dropped in front of her and she booted it back into the cheering kids.

'Don't look so glum,' Angela chided. 'I'll make a list of the supplies I'll need from Professor Winslow's pharmacy. What is it, less than an hour's flight time? You'll be back in time for lunch. Remember I have my trusty laundry stick to defend my honour.'

Danny still harboured misgivings as he took off, but once airborne he turned his attention to navigating back to Kraal Winslow. After landing he left Komotho to refuel the plane while he arranged for Angela's supplies with Professor Winslow. While they gathered the stores a hubbub erupted throughout the camp. One of the boys rushed into the pharmaceutical tent.

'Professor, trucks approaching,' the young fellow said.

Sure enough a convoy of three open Landrovers lumbered along one of the tracks that led towards the village from the south. The vehicles were filled with uniformed native troops all bristling with weapons. A Bren gun was mounted on each Landrover. At first Danny feared they may be under Mau-Mau attack, but was relieved to see two white officers seated in the first pair of Landrovers — and one looked familiar.

The Landrovers ground to a halt and the troops from the Tribal Police piled out. A lean handsome man in his late twenties stepped from the leading vehicle. The presence of an aircraft seemed to intrigue him.

'Hello,' he greeted with a lilting Scottish accent, extending his hand. 'Ian Henderson, Tribal Police.'

'G'day, Danny McAlister, bush pilot,' Danny replied returning the strangers firm handshake. 'That's my mechanic Komotho Mwangi refuelling the plane.'

'Well, well, well, Danny McAlister as I live and breathe!' the second officer exclaimed.

'Blow me down if it isn't Lord Jeremy,' Danny said

Jeremy Fuller St Chalfont-Smyth was the second son of a British earl whose exact title Danny couldn't recall. They'd met a couple of years earlier in Hong Kong Harbour when Jeremy was seconded from the Royal Navy to the local water police. Jeremy had rescued Danny and Long Li from a Communist patrol-boat while Danny was trying to help refugees escape Red China.

'What the blazes are you doing here?' Danny asked pumping Jeremy's hand. 'You're supposed to be a sailor.'

'Protecting the family interests, old boy. Pater owns a tea plantation in the highlands and cattle property around Nairobi. Ian and I are trying to track down Dedan Kimathi's latest gang. We think he's been hiding out in the desert around the Abyssinian border, but it looks like he's back in town. Apparently the Mau-Mau heard the RAF has withdrawn its aircraft, which has given 'em a change of heart.'

'I guess that would make a difference,' Danny said.

'It certainly does. Last year we had twenty Mau-Mau surrender just because a flight of bally Vampire fighters flew overhead. They didn't believe they'd be able to tackle anything that went that fast. I suppose they had a point.'

'To make matters worse, there was a breakout from Kamiti Prison a fortnight ago,' Ian Henderson added. 'Half-a-dozen guards took the Mau-Mau oath and planned the whole thing. It looks like they've joined up with Kimathi and are out for a spot of mischief. Rumours are that Stanley Mathenge is also active. Luckily he and Kimathi have no time for one another, so they're unlikely to join forces. A regular army patrol got caught in a fire-fight near the Somali border last month. They think it was Kimathi or Mathenge. The rebels took off, but our boys didn't have the numbers to follow and confirm.'

'Talking of numbers, you look a bit short-handed yourself, Ian,' Danny said. 'You're telling me Dedan Kimathi has a few hundred blokes and all I see here is a light platoon.'

'Quite right,' Ian replied, 'and *The Happy Valley Set* agrees with you. They've hired a South African mercenary commando to supplement our Tribal Police Force. One of their vehicles got a flat. They'll fix it in no time and be along just now.'

Happy Valley Set was by now something of an anachronism as WWII had forced most of them to moderate their behaviour. However, the name had stuck to the wealthy British settlers.

Sure enough the mercenary unit arrived shortly afterwards, but to Danny's dismay was only a similar force to the Tribal Police. MG equipped Landrovers appeared to be the transport of choice. The mercenaries rode in three of them. The vehicles were in fine mechanical condition although an attention-grabbing human skull was strapped to each radiator cap.

A dapper man in his mid-thirties stepped purposefully from the passenger seat of the leading vehicle. He was dressed in tailored bush gear with a major's crown insignia on each epaulette. He wore a black beret with a red shield badge, binoculars dangled from a strap hung around his neck while two automatic pistols were holstered to his belt.

'All fixed?' Ian Henderson asked the stranger who merely nodded while eyeing Danny suspiciously.

'Danny McAlister,' he ventured, extending his arm.

'Major Mike Hoare,' the stranger replied brusquely returning Danny's handshake. 'That your crate?'

'It's leased by the WHO actually, but I'm the pilot. Komotho over there is the mechanic.'

'Might be handy for some aerial recon,' Mike Hoare suggested.

'I'm working for Professor Winslow,' Danny replied a little testily. 'I'm doing medical runs with Dr Holyman.'

'Where's he now?' Hoare asked, although in a tone that suggested more of a demand.

'*She's* at a village about a forty minute flight from here.'

Henderson, Jeremy and Mike Hoarse exchanged glances.

'It might by a jolly good idea to buzz over there and bring her back, old boy. Can't to too careful with those bally rebels running around, what?'

'The current situation is that regular troops will be securing this area,' Mike Hoare explained. 'We'll be moving north to locate and engage the enemy.'

Meanwhile Major Hoare's men had disembarked and were idly lighting up awaiting orders. They were the toughest bunch Danny reckoned he'd ever seen. They were dressed more-or-less in standard khaki combat uniforms, but choice of head gear and weapons appeared optional. American GI helmets, berets, WWII German storm-troopers caps, slouch-hats, turbans, Arab keffiyehs were as varied as the small arms the mercenaries carried.

These were men who'd found no solace after the wars they'd endured. Ex-SS misfits from WWII, Guerrillas from Greece, Foreign Legionnaires from Indochina and Algeria and British servicemen who were permanently scarred by war, yet knew nothing else, especially how to fit into civilian life. The pay was good, the risks high and if life was to be short, then what the hell? To date their toughest task had been chasing big-game poachers, diamond smugglers and enforcing apartheid, which entailed ensuring that malcontent Hottentots and Bantus kept their proper place.

'Lieutenant Duval,' Mike Hoare called, 'don't let the men get too comfortable, we're moving out in five.'

'*Oui*, Major,' the lieutenant replied.

Danny's head spun in the direction of the mercenary convoy. Danny hadn't seen the man strolling towards him for over a year, but he'd aged more than that.

'*Bonjour,* Danny,' the mercenary greeted. 'I see you escaped Dien Bien Phu in one piece.'

'Blimey, Frenchy Duval, now there's a turn up for the books. So you got back from Indochina OK.'

Frenchy shrugged.

'Maybe not so OK, but I got back.'

Frenchy Duval was an erstwhile pirate and general all-round bad guy. Danny and Angela had come to blows with Frenchy a couple of times in New Guinea, but then found themselves on the same side fighting the Viet Minh at Dien Bien Phu. Frenchy had been captured after the garrison surrendered and endured four months of starvation and deprivation at the hands of the reds. Over half the POWs died in captivity, but Frenchy'd been tough enough to survive.

He resigned when his battalion was reformed and assigned to Algerian duty. Why fight for a pittance and a government who'd deserted the Legion when he could make ten times more as a hired-gun? Tough, battle-hardened and ruthless, Frenchy was just what 'Mad' Mike Hoare was looking for and was recruited instantly along with several other disgruntled Legionnaires.

'I'd like to stay and chat, Frenchy,' Danny said, 'but I've got to pick up Angela before she gets into trouble.'

'Angela is here..?'

'Yep, and I bet she's just dying to catch up with you,' Danny grinned.

'You two know each other, then?' Mike Hoare said.

'Yessir Major, Frenchy and I go back a few years,' Danny replied.

'You go in the plane then, Duval,' Hoare said. 'Keep a lookout for anything suspicious. Listen out on our radio frequency.'

'Mind if I tag along too?' Jeremy said. 'Extra pair of eyes and all that, what?'

Danny wasn't sure how he felt about Mike Hoare commandeering his plane, but a couple of extra guns wouldn't go astray.

'OK, let's get going. Major, please bring as many jerry cans of AVGAS as you can. I don't want to run out of fuel.'

Komotho had refuelled the plane by then, so they all climbed aboard. A few cumulous clouds were building up towards Mt Kenya, but Danny knew his way around fairly well by then. Provided the weather didn't deteriorate too badly, Danny recognised landmarks especially where the savannah merged into the forest tree line. Danny had drawn all the settlements on his charts and easily pin-pointed them by the smoke from their cooking fires. Trails were also useful because they normally led from one village to the next.

The problem was when he spotted the smoke from Angela's clinic, there was too much of it — far too much of it.

Oh shit, no.

Danny circled the plane to land closely into wind. There was plenty of smoke to guide him. In fact it reduced visibility to a point where Danny wondered if he'd be able to land at all. The huts were all ablaze and the village livestock had scattered into the surrounding bush. Ominously, black dots lay randomly on the ground. Their distorted positions confirmed Danny's worst fears.

'They have been hit,' Frenchy bellowed from the back. 'It is not safe to land. The Mau-Mau may still be around.'

'Angela's down there,' Danny replied. 'I'm not leaving without her.'

There was nothing Frenchy could do, because the main wheels had already touched down. Danny braked and the Lockheed lurched to a stop.

'Keep your engines running,' Frenchy ordered, naturally assuming command.

'What about Angela?'

'If she is here, we will find her.'

With that Frenchy, Jeremy and Komotho tumbled out of the plane and moved cautiously through the village. Some of the huts had already collapsed, while others were blazing so ferociously, it was impossible for the three men to approach them. The flames crackled while sparks shot skywards. The problem with natural building materials was that they burned so very well.

It only took about five minutes to determine the Mau-Mau had gone. Frenchy saw tyre tracks leading away north and estimated there were at least ten vehicles including several trucks and a US ex-WWII half-track. The tracks were fresh, but Frenchy saw no sign of a dust cloud along the trail. He went back to the plane and signalled Danny to cut the engines.

The props had barely clattered to a stop when Danny leapt from the cabin door. He raced to the hut where Angela conducted her clinic, but it was nothing but a smouldering pile of ash and glowing embers.

'Where the hell is she?' he screamed, but of course no one knew the answer.

There were six bodies lying around. They were all men and had been shot except one victim who Danny recognised as one of the village chiefs. His hands and feet had been severed and, from the huge dark stain around his corpse, he'd been left to bleed to death. Two of the bodies suffered back wounds suggesting they'd been shot trying to escape, but the other three had neat entry holes in the back of their skulls and messy exits wounds that took off most of their faces.

These poor buggers were executed.

Danny poked around the smouldering wreck that had once been Angela's surgery. He discovered her white laundry pole lying close by. Perhaps it was an odd choice of talisman, but it was her good luck charm and she'd never leave it if she had the choice.

'*Mon Dieu,*' Frenchy said stepping beside Danny. 'I remember that when Madame Kwok broke my arm with it.'

'It was your own fault for kidnapping her and treating her so badly,' Danny chided. 'You had it coming.'

During his pirating days in the Bismarck Sea, Frenchy had abducted a Singaporean family who Danny and Angela rescued with a little help from their friends. Frenchy regularly kidnapped people back then and even held Angela captive for a while.

'Angela!' Danny yelled. 'Where are you? It's me – Danny!'

At first there was no response. Then Danny noticed a movement about fifty yards away in the bush.

'Over there,' he called to Jeremy who was closest.

Then he saw another black shadow dart through the bush. Other flashes of movement followed. Danny drew his 1911 Colt automatic.

'Take it easy, old bean,' Jeremy whispered beside him. 'I don't think they're Mau-Mau.'

'Got 'em sighted, lieutenant,' Jeremy called to Frenchy who was scouting the far side of the village.

'*Oui*, monsieur,' Frenchy replied with his Sten-gun levelled and ready.

There was no sign of Komotho.

This is no bloody time to go bloody walk-about.

'Hold your fire,' Komotho called from the bushes. 'I've found survivors.'

Sure enough, Komotho appeared herding a group of very distressed villagers ahead of him. They were mostly elderly or very young children although there were a few people of intermediate age among the group. The children were thirsty so the four men handed around their water canteens. Danny was surprised to see that Frenchy showed genuine compassion towards the villagers and offered them some of his biltong.

Who'd have thought it?

It took a while, but Komotho finally pieced the story together.

Chapter 26 — House Call

Dedan Kimathi
the last Mau-Mau chief

Danny's plane had barely departed for Kraal Winslow when the rebels struck. Their trucks growled along the northern trail, lumbering in between the huts. The half-track bulldozed any dwellings in its path, crushing several victims along the way.

At first there was no shooting, but as people started fleeing Mau-Mau riflemen gunned down two men who tried to escape with their families. Rebels leapt from their trucks and rounded up anyone they could find – including Angela. Anyone who resisted was beaten into submission with clubs and rifle-butts.

'What is the meaning of this?' Angela screamed. 'This is a clinic. We aren't harming you.'

The rebels simply stared at her with a perplexing mixture of loathing, amusement and lust. Their pure malevolence turned Angela's blood cold. The Viet Minh were formidable enemies, but she never feared for her safety after they'd over-run Dien Bien Phu. Whereas the Communist Vietnamese had acted with impeccable correctness, the Mau-Mau were a totally different story. These men had butchered innocent women and children without a second thought. Africa was proving to be a savage continent, and the Mau-Mau had done their share. The colonial forces were far from blameless too. Brutality begat brutality in this bitter conflict.

At least The Mau-Mau hadn't raped and murdered Angela out of hand. Although that was something, she still trembled in the clutches of two rifle-toting rebels.

Suddenly the cacophony of shrieks, shouts and bellowed orders became silent as a figure moved through the throng and faced Angela. He was a Kikuyu in his mid-thirties with a broad forehead and hair pulled back in ringlets. He wore military battledress and a pistol belt, but carried a riding crop in one hand and a parade-ground baton in the other. He glared at Angela through piercing black eyes as if he was reaching into the brain.

'You are the doctor, are you not?' the stranger said.

He spoke English perfectly without a trace of any accent in what was known as a BBC voice. Angela simply froze on the spot.

'I asked you a question. My name is Field-Marshal Dedan Kimathi, and as such I expect an answer.'

Dedan Kimathi hadn't raised his voice, but spoke with such authority and menace, Angela dreaded the thought of him doing so.

'Now shall we start again?' Kimathi said. 'Are you a doctor?'

Angela nodded.

'Do you have a name?'

'Dr Angela Holyman. I work for the World Health Organisation. As I said before, what is the meaning of this atrocity?'

Ah, Angela was back to her old self again.

'Don't talk to me of atrocities, English bitch. You colonists think it is your divine right to subjugate the Kikuyu. You don't like it when we poor dumb niggers fight back, do you?'

'I think no such thing. Do not put words into my mouth. I am neither a colonist nor a bitch,' Angela said evenly. 'I am here to help the Kenyan people.'

'Have I not heard that before, but that is precisely what you will do. I have wounded men. You will come with us.'

'So you want me to make a house call. You only had to ask.'

'I am not in the habit of asking and I have other business to attend to here.'

It seemed that Dedan Kimathi needed recruits to bolster his force and replace those killed in skirmishes with the British Army, Tribal Police and local militia. He had a pretty standard way of going about it too. Once all the young men and women were gathered into the village centre he began a tirade. Angela didn't understand a word, but assumed Kimathi was condemning the British to hell and back and they must be driven out of Kenya by any means of which terrorism was the first option.

The villagers shuffled around uncertainly. In truth that particular community hadn't been particularly bothered by British rule. That was not to say others had been so lucky. Also many people believe that colonial rule would only be replaced by tribal warfare just like the 'good old days' before the British arrived. Essentially there was no Mau-Mau support to be found here.

One of the village elders mentioned the fact, protesting that they'd never done anything to harm the Mau-Mau, and yet their huts were being destroyed for no good reason. Kimathi wasn't in the mood for a discussion – he rarely was. The unfortunate elder was bashed senseless with rifle butts before Kimathi ordered his hands and feet severed. Four men armed with simis slashed the elder's limbs. Arterial blood gushed from his stumps as he bled to death. Mercifully he appeared unconscious until he died.

To reinforce his point, Kimathi randomly selected three men. His followers forced them to their knees while Kimathi drew his pistol and shot each man in the back of his head. The villagers screamed in dismay, but obeyed the Mau-Mau instantly from then on.

The Mau-Mau hustled as many men as they could into two trucks until they were tightly packed and then filled another truck with young women. They piled Angela's entire medical supply into a Landrover and bundled her in beside the boxes. Dedan sat beside the driver. There was something about seeing half-a-dozen cold-blooded murders that would subdue most people, but Angela only felt bitter rage and loathing for the Mau-Mau. Whatever their grievance, there was no excuse for such barbarity.

Then for no good reason other than pure spite, the Mau-Mau torched the huts that had not already been smashed by their half-track.

The rebel convoy took a trail that led upwards into the forest. Soon the path became torturously slow and the vehicles bounced and lurched alarmingly. Several of the captives succumbed to motion sickness. Fortunately for their companions the trucks were uncovered and the sufferers managed to vomit over the side. But the rank stench of sickness was infectious and soon there were many more sufferers. Finally Dedan called a halt, allowing a short recovery break.

Everyone settled down after that as the trucks ground further upwards. Finally Angela could contain her indignation no longer.

'Why have you kidnapped these innocent people?' she demanded. 'What have they ever done to you?'

'They allow the colonial overlords to dominate them. That is intolerable,' Dedan replied, swivelling in his seat to face her.

'But a Mau-Mau overlord isn't?' Angela countered. 'Anyway they weren't aligned with anyone. They were just leading independent lives until you showed up.'

'I am of this country as are they. They must learn to fight for Kikuyu rights.'

'I can't see how murder and arson will win them over.'

'They will join our sacred cause to fight the oppressors. No one sits on the fence. Many martyrs have died and must be replaced.'

Angela couldn't help herself. She'd been hanging around with Danny for too long.

'I wondered about that,' she said acidly. 'You don't seem to have a very big army.'

'There are two hundred men waiting at my camp.'

'If you don't mind me saying so, that hardly seems enough for a field-marshal to boss around.'

'My men are *Muruthi-Hearts*. They fight like a thousand warriors.'

Angela cast her eyes around at the gaol-sweepings that made up the majority of Dedan's army and wasn't so sure.

'*Muruthi?*' she said.

'Lion-hearts, the Swahili say *Simba.*'

'I see. So you've got two-hundred thousand *simbas,* well that's altogether different.'

'Don't mock me, *gatumia,*' Dedan hissed.

Luckily at the time Angela was unaware he'd used a title that was roughly translated as *little woman.* Who knew how she'd have reacted to that.

'Dear me, no. I would be foolish to mock you, *Field-Marshal,* I am your prisoner and you have all the guns.'

'You are my guest,' Dedan grinned slyly.

'You still have all the guns.'

They drove further.

'Why have you taken the women?' Angela asked after a while.

'I need the men to be calm in camp and not fight amongst themselves. These women will keep my men happy.'

'Have you considered how they might feel about that?'

Dedan Kimathi turned once again, staring at Angela with a look of total astonishment.

It took several hours of gruelling travel to reach the rebel camp deep in the forest. During the journey the tree canopy thickened until it completely enveloped the trail forming an arboreal tunnel. The Mau-Mau HQ was almost invisible and unlikely to be spotted from the air.

Unlike Kraal Winslow, the Mau-Mau camp lacked any sense of order. Several tents were scattered in a forest clearing, but most of the two-hundred rebels had simply built crude shelters wherever they felt like it. The rebels herded the kidnapped villagers into a tight group and left them to their own devices. Dedan believed the villagers would join him when they got hungry enough.

Angela's first concern was health. The camp already reeked of human effluent as no provisions for personal sanitation had been considered. Angela entered the hospital tent, dreading what she'd find there. A blizzard of flies swarming around the entrance and the overflow of sick men hanging around outside were discouraging. Over twenty men were jammed inside. Some squatted while others were so sick they sprawled haphazardly on groundsheets. A few wounded writhed and moaned in pain but most lay in stoic silence so ill they were past caring.

So this is how Florence Nightingale felt when she arrived at Scutari.

Although many of the patients suffered gunshot and knife wounds, Angela diagnosed a couple of gastric cases that could well be typhoid.

'These men should be in hospital,' she protested to Dedan.

'This *is* their hospital,' he replied blandly.

'The first thing we must do is clean everything — and I don't just mean this tent — I mean the entire camp.'

And then it was Angela in full-on business mode. Even Dedan Kimathi didn't stand a chance. Before she set up a triage ward, she organised the villagers to prepare a latrine well clear of the camp and downhill from the spring that supplied the camp water. Angela visited every group of rebels, ordering them to clean up their mess. Many refused to obey.

'Then die in your own filth,' she said, 'but don't come to me when you get sick.'

She stormed to where Dedan sat at a camp table, studying a map.

'I don't know why I care,' she said. 'If this lot died of their own stupidity, it would be so much the better, but I have taken an oath to try and save life, so that's what I must do. Either you order your men to follow my instruction or you might as well let me go for all the good I'll be able to be in this cess-pit.'

Most of the Mau-Mau had hitherto lived primitively as subsistence farmers where all their materials were organic, so anything they discarded simply rotted back to nature in time. Human waste was used as manure and carefully disposed of. Now that plastic and metal products were available, the litter remained intact becoming a breeding ground for bacteria and attracted vermin.

'Very well,' Dedan sighed, nodding to one of his lieutenants. 'Tell the men to do what she says. Let them know I'll shoot anyone who disobeys.'

Dedan saw extra merit in Angela's notion of putting the men to work. His rebels came from Kamba, Gussii, Embu and Tharaka tribes amongst others. Although they generally fell under the Kikuyu umbrella, they had their differences. Dedan had also recruited a few bellicose Swahilis from the coast along with a group of Communist inspired Congolese malcontents who called themselves *Simbas*. They'd joined the Mau-Mau to learn guerrilla tactics and get a bit of match practice. Idle men drank too much, argued and fought among themselves. Half-a-dozen of Dedan's casualties were results of such disputes.

Keeping the men busy not only improved the smell around camp, but stopped brawls erupting.

'If you want those villagers to co-operate I suggest you take care of them, Field Marshal,' Angela added. 'They won't be much use if they resent you or starve to death.'

'We'll see,' Dedan replied vaguely. 'Now go and care for my wounded.'

Once the cleanup operation was underway, Angela turned her attention back to the sick and injured. She recruited four young women who'd acted as nurses and midwives back in their village. There was no shortage of other volunteers, but any more would simply get in the way, so she used the extra womanpower to bring fresh water from far upstream along the creek.

Despite their feeble protests, Angela stripped the men of their filthy, ragged and blood-stained clothing. Angela instructed her water-gathers to find all available cooking pots and boil as much water as possible. Next she had the hospital tent dismantled and re-erected in a clean spot. She also arranged for the filth to be removed from the campsite. Any salvageable rebel clothing was washed thoroughly while Angela ordered the tattered remainder to be burnt.

Angela once again had to badger Dedan for any spare blankets for the hospital tent. Finally she got down to the messy business of saving lives. She had a small supply of local anaesthetic, but nothing stronger than that, luckily she only needed to probe for half-a-dozen embedded slugs, but here was plenty of painful stitching for the wounded to endure.

Some men tolerated pain courageously while others had to be held down by their comrades as Angela operated. By and large the Mau-Mau bore their suffering in much the same way as the French Union troops at Dien Bien Phu.

Time blurred as daylight faded. Angela worked long into the night with only a paraffin lamp to see by. Eventually she was too exhausted to go on, but all the serious cases had stabilised and the minor casualties were clean and in no danger of deteriorating over night. Before collapsing, she arranged a duty-roster for the village women to make sure the hospital tent remained clean and hygienic.

She ate something that reminded her of porridge although it tasted of very little. Fortunately the meal included a banana and some pineapple, which she ate with relish. It was her first meal since breakfast. The Mau-Mau provided her with a woven-straw mat, a blanket and even a pillow. So after relieving herself, she lay on the mat without a care for scorpions, centipedes, spiders or snakes.

I'd kill for a toothbrush, though.

She was asleep in seconds.

Boom!

Boom!

Blam! Rat-a-tat-tat!

Angela jerked awake to the familiar sound of mortar shells and small arms fire. Then she heard the roar of aero-engines as a shadow flashed overhead at treetop level. By then Angela recognised the Lockheed's motors. Danny had found her and by the sound of it, he'd brought the right kind of help.

Chapter 27 – Reinforcements

The surviving villagers quickly filled Danny and the others in on what happened when the Mau-Mau arrived. The story was a familiar one to Jeremy who'd been fighting rebels for the past year. There was no doubt where the terrorists were heading either. Fresh tyre tracks were clearly visible leading north from the village. It was a frustrating wait for Ian Henderson and the mercenaries to catch up, but they made good time once Frenchy radioed the situation to Major Hoare.

The next move was to locate the rebels, which didn't prove as difficult as it might have seemed. Some of the villagers already had a pretty good idea where their hideout was and pointed out the position on Danny's map. That wasn't surprising as the rebels had been encamped for over a week and word was out to steer clear of the area. Mau-Mau heavy-handedness hadn't made them any friends and the locals were only too happy to have the authorities shoo them away.

The rebels were so confident they'd made no effort to hide their tracks. The mercenaries and Tribal Police encountered no rear-guard or booby traps. Danny flew to the site, but remained several miles away to avoid warning the rebels. Although the forest canopy was thick he was able to make out the track in places and saw smoke wafting through the tree-tops that was either an indication of humans or a forest fire. As the latter didn't eventuate, Danny radioed the news to the column.

Danny arranged a rendezvous by the forest edge at one of the landing sites he and Komotho had used during the week. The strip was only an hour's drive from where Danny reckoned the rebels were hiding out. Ian Henderson and Mike Hoare agreed that a dawn attack was best. It was a tried-and-tested classic tactic that caught the enemy when they were relaxed and vulnerable. It usually worked if executed properly, especially if the mercenaries and police approached with the rising sun behind them.

Danny was concerned that Angela was going to be in the line of fire, but Mike Hoare merely shrugged, saying she wasn't going to be in any greater danger than she was already.

'We're going to need you and your plane for a diversion and aerial recon,' Major Hoare explained. 'If we can confuse the kaffirs, we'll nab the bastards cold.'

The convoy moved out as soon as it was light enough to see the track without using headlights that were likely to alert the Mau-Mau. Danny and Komotho remained with the plane. Danny wanted to go with the mercenaries and Tribal Police, but Ian Henderson insisted he might be needed in an aerial capacity.

What occurred over the next few hours was confusing and had to be pieced together afterwards by those involved on both sides. It went much along these lines.

*

Danny gave the ground force an hour's head-start before getting airborne. Prior to take-off he noticed Komotho lunking a crate onto the plane. It seemed unusually heavy for its size.

'What's that?' Danny asked.

'Insurance maybe,' Komotho replied, taking a hand-grenade from the box.

'Blimey, who did you nick those from? They're going to be pissed off with you.'

'They won't notice,' Komotho winked slyly. 'I only took a couple from both the mercenary and police supplies.'

'And just what do you plan to do with them?'

'I've just got a gut-feeling. I'll explain on the way.'

Once the Lockheed was within the ground force radio range Danny made contact.

'ETA in five minutes,' Danny reported.

'Roger that,' Jeremy replied. 'We'll go in when we hear your engines.'

Although no one expected the plane to do any damage, Ian Henderson hoped it would confuse and unsettle the rebels as RAF aircraft had done in the past. Danny held the Lockheed at tree-top level as he flashed towards the Mau-Mau camp. He saw the first mortar shells hit as plumes of smoke spurted through the forest canopy. Danny banked the plane for another pass over the camp.

'OK, Komotho. For heaven's sake don't drop the flaming things inside the plane,' Danny yelled back into the cabin.

Komotho grinned back at him and took the first grenade from the box. He wedged the cabin door open which took all his strength to combat the slipstream. He pulled the pin and slipped the grenade through the crack in the door. He only had time to drop one more before Danny had flown past the camp. They didn't expect to do much damage, but if the Mau-Mau thought they were being bombed from the air, it might soften them up.

*

Meanwhile on the ground Mike Hoare led half his force to the right flank while Frenchy took the remaining mercenaries to the left. Ian Henderson commanded the Tribal Police in the centre, leaving Jeremy in charge of the mortars.

The initial mortar explosions sent the rebels into turmoil. They rushed from their shelters, grabbing their weapons as they went. They had barely levelled their guns when the mercenaries reached the first rebels. The hired guns blazed away, forcing the Mau-Mau back into a tight perimeter.

The Tribal Police and mercenaries were outnumbered five to one, but the element of surprise gave them a significant advantage. The fact that terrorists didn't make particularly good soldiers was also a factor. They were right at home ambushing and murdering innocent people, but tackling a determined, well trained foe was quite a different story.

*

The Mau-Mau fell back behind their vehicles as the mercenaries and police advanced. Then Dedan took control. He'd seen brief army service, but had been dismissed for habitual drunken brawling before his military training could take any meaningful shape. But he was a natural leader and rallied his men.

344

Dedan ordered his machine guns teams to man their Brownings. Red hot lead sprayed into the advancing police who dived for cover. The rebels then turned their own machine guns onto the flanks just in time to stop the mercenaries overrunning their position.

'Bring up our Landrovers,' Mike Hoare yelled to the man behind him.

The mercenary dashed for the rear, but was cut down by a .50 cal burst.

The mercenaries were now pinned down, hugging the ground or huddled behind trees. Mike Hoare and Ian Henderson had made the mistake of thinking they'd be able to roll up the rebel flank in double-quick time with just Sten-guns, rifles and grenades. Jeremy had ceased firing the mortars to prevent casualties from 'friendly-fire'.

The enemy was secure in its defensive position, and appeared content to stay there. But finally Dedan realised that the mercenaries and police weren't just going to shove off. He'd have to force them to do that.

Frenchy saw that a stalemate had developed. Machine-guns rattled sporadically now, but slugs still sliced through the forest shredding bark and foliage into arboreal confetti. Danny's plane roared overhead once more and was followed by a couple of crumping explosions, which were almost lost in the overall din of battle.

Frenchy had no way of knowing it, but one of Komotho's grenades landed beside the rebel machine guns. After hitting the ground it bounced head-high before exploding. The blast killed one gunner and wounded the other. While Dedan cajoled two men to replace the gunner, Frenchy seized the opportunity during the lull to dash for Jeremy's mortar position. Bullets zinged past him as he sprinted to the rear, yelling for three men to join him.

The four mercenaries reached safety.

'Give them all you have, monsieur!' Frenchy yelled to Jeremy whose view was obstructed by the forest. 'Send one man forward with a spare radio. You will need a range finder to know when we are going to advance again.'

'Righto, old boy,' Jeremy acknowledged and the mortars opened up again.

Now it was time for Frenchy to get down and dirty. The mercenaries leapt aboard their Landrovers and lurched through the forest to the rebel camp. By the time they brought their guns to bear, the rebels were back in action. Tracers streaked through the forest, slicing a swathe of red-hot death in their path.

By then the mortars blasted all around the rebels again and the mercenary MGs opened up throwing the rebels into a frenzy.

*

Angela was right in the middle of the killing ground. The mortars had started only seconds after she heard Danny's plane zoom overhead. She was left with no choice but to dive for cover as the first shots blazed into the rebel camp. When she thought there was a lull, she raced from her sleeping mat straight to the hospital tent. As she flung the flap back the canvas was shredded by another solid blast of .50 cal rounds. The wounded bucked as bullets slammed into them. Limbs were blown to shards while blood fountains gushed from severed arteries. One .50 cal round was enough to tear a human torso into scarlet pulp embedded with shattered bones.

Angela hit the floor. She heard the fizzing as slugs sliced through the air only inches above her prone body.

Dear God, those men were stable, they'd have survived. I'd saved them and now they're dead. Danny I know it's you up in that plane. What have you let these people do?

There was no way the rebels could take this punishment for long. It was Dien Bien Phu all over again on a small scale. Although Dedan Kimathi knew little about Indochina, he felt the same. It was time to head north. There was no way the rebels could take this punishment for long.

He rallied his men, ordering them to board the trucks. The villagers, who'd been held under guard until then, saw their chance. They bolted for the forest cover en masse. No one tried to stop them in the confusion. They were smart enough to run away from the mercenaries and police who poured lead into the camp. The rebels fired a few shots, but no one was hit. The villagers melted into the forest. Unfortunately, much as they may have wanted to, the villagers saw no opportunity to take Angela with them.

But Dedan did.

He quickly surveyed the wreckage that had been his hospital tent and assayed there was no hope for the occupants other than Angela. He spotted her staggering from the collapsed canvas and sent men to seize her. The way things were going there would be other casualties for her to care for.

'Salvage what you can!' he ordered, meaning weapons ammunition, food and medical equipment.

By now bullets flew thicker than a swarm of rampant hornets. The rebels grabbed what they could, including Angela, who was bundled into the back of the half track. Twenty dirty and malodorous Mau-Mau followed her. One rebel slumped to his knees as a slug ripped through the half-track's canvas hood, blasting his head to mush. His comrades simply hauled him to the rear and pitched him over the tail-gate.

As the rebels pulled out forming a convoy, the gunfire stopped while the mercenaries and police regrouped. The Mau-Mau trucks lurched and bumped along a rough track at a speed that tossed the occupants around like ping-pong balls.

*

Danny circled the Lockheed overhead, but other than frequent gouts of smoke stabbing through the forest canopy, he'd no idea what was happing on the ground. Finally after Danny had vainly badgered the airwaves for what seemed hours, Jeremy answered.

'What the blazes is going on down there, Jeremy?'

'We've hammered 'em pretty hard, old boy,' Jeremy's voice crackled in Danny's earphones. 'The blighters put up a fight, but now they're pulling out to the north. Can you see if you can spot 'em when they clear the tree-line?'

'Roger — wilco. Have you found Angela?'

'We're checking the camp now, but no sign so far. It's possible they've taken her with them or she's escaped into the forest.'

Why can't she just stay out of trouble for once!

*

Frenchy, Ian Henderson and Mike Hoare led their men through the Mau-Mau camp. Occasionally a rebel stirred and a Sten-gun blurted to silence him. Although Jeremy disapproved, he conceded the mercenaries were mostly putting the rebels out of their misery. Henderson, Frenchy and Mike Hoare were 'no-quarter' kind of guys. Only four wounded men were still alive in the hospital tent and begged for mercy, but were quickly and efficiently despatched.

'We don't have time for niceties, Jeremy,' Ian Henderson hissed between clenched teeth. 'The courts would hang them anyway.'

Jeremy wasn't so sure, it wasn't the first time he'd found Ian Henderson's methods questionable. In fact he was not the only one with reservations about Henderson's behaviour. Governor General, Sir Evelyn Baring and newly appointed C-in-C East Africa, Lieutenant General Sir Gerald Lathbury wanted a few answers too. Mike Hoare's attitude was clearly to kill all the bad guys and save as many good ones as possible. He wasn't paid to take prisoners.

*

Danny flew north for a short distance when the forest broke into small copses surrounded by farming and grazing land. He spotted some isolated villages that appeared deserted. Obviously the locals were lying low until the Mau-Mau left the area. There were several tracks leading to all points of the compass. The Rift Valley Provinces adjoining Mt Kenya's woodland was fertile and profitable agricultural country, so it was no surprise that people had settled there. The main northern route caught Danny's notice. A dust cloud shimmered a few miles ahead and soon Danny identified a convoy of a dozen vehicles.

'Hey Jeremy, are you expecting reinforcements,' Danny called over the radio.

'We haven't any information on British military units in the area,' Jeremy's voice crackled back. 'The Shropshire Infantry and First Rifle Battalion are up along the Somalia border while the Royal Irish Hussars are in Nairobi as far as I know. I haven't a clue where the Gloucestershire Regiment is right now.'

'Well you've got what looks like a battalion sized force heading your way. If it's a government force, it'll make mincemeat of the rebels down there. They're heading straight for them.'

'That's if they are British troops or Kenyan Rifles.'

'I'll take a look.'

Danny banked the plane to smoothly lose altitude and position himself for a run over the oncoming column. He made out several infantry platoons marching in good order which suggested well-trained regular soldiers, but he also saw a company of men mounted on camels. They wore Arabian thawbs with agals protecting their heads. One thing was for sure, they weren't Kikuyu.

But there were Kenyans marching in front of the vehicles. Unlike Dedan Kimathi's men who rode in trucks, these men marched and it looked as if the transport was for their equipment. In fact the truck drivers made frequent stops, allowing the infantry and camel riders to go far ahead before catching up. In that way they avoided overheating the radiators which would be a certainty by crawling along in the equatorial heat.

As the Lockheed approached the convoy, several men pulled the tarpaulin from a Landrover revealing a Browning machine-gun. Seconds later tracers streamed up towards the plane.

'Time to get out of Dodge,' Danny said, banking the plane sharply and pushing the throttles to full power.

'Hey Jeremy, are you still in range?'

'Receiving you loud and clear, old boy.'

'I don't know who those jokers are coming your way, but they sure aren't friendly.'

'How far away do you reckon they are?'

'An hour maybe – no more.'

'Not our chaps, then?'

'Definitely not, they took a few pot-shots at me with a Bren I think. Funny thing is they've got a bunch of blokes who look like Arabs riding camels with 'em. I dunno what the hell they're doing here or where they came from, but it looks like Mau-Mau have just got reinforcements.'

Chapter 28 — Uncertainty All Round

So far the forest battle had been a confused affair, but there was a brief respite when Dedan's Mau-Mau pulled out. The mercenaries rounded up a group of the former captives who explained they'd all escaped, but the rebels had taken the white doctor woman with them. Soon the other villagers appeared from the bush and started to make their way along the southern track to return home and rebuild the place.

Meanwhile Danny was buzzing in the radio urging the ground troops to get after Angela. Henderson and Mike Hoare checked the units' fuel and ammunition which were still ample. Neither leader was particularly concerned about the large force coming to meet them. In their experience, rebels were hit-and-run merchants and unlikely to stand and fight. The appearance of Islamic cavalry was puzzling, but once again not unduly disturbing.

In their rush to retreat the rebels had abandoned a sizeable cache of arms and ammunition that the mercenaries and police would put to good use. Most of the rifles were redoubtable Russian and Chinese AK-47 semi automatics. The Tribal Police shared these out with relish as they were superior weapons to their out-dated Lee-Enfield bolt-action single shot .303 rifles.

The mercenary commando and police would need all the fire-power they could muster because Danny was right – the reinforcements weren't British. Government forces were miles away, but Dedan Kimathi didn't know that. In fact he assumed he'd been attacked by regular British Army troops as well as Native Police. Admittedly the incoming small arms and mortar fire had been intense, but Dedan had misread the enemy force. Even after several years of guerrilla warfare, his lack of military experience proved a tactical weakness.

Nevertheless Ian Henderson and Mike Hoare's delay in pursuing the rebels gave Dedan his chance to get clean away.

When Danny saw the rebels burst from the forest he expected to see the mercenary command and police right behind them, but to his chagrin, they failed to appear.

'What's going down there?' Danny demanded.

'Sorry, old boy,' Jeremy replied, 'we've just finished tidying up now. We'll be right after the blighters.'

What Danny expected from the mercenaries and police was uncertain. He'd already warned them they were vastly outnumbered, so it was unlikely that an all-out frontal attack was viable.

'Are the new arrivals still advancing?' Mike Hoare asked, taking over from Jeremy.

'Affirmative, major,' Danny replied.

'Roger that, we're moving to the forest edge to set up an ambush. That way we'll stay under cover and the kaffirs will be in the open. Keep us informed of their movements. We shall be in position in approximately three-zero minutes.'

'You'd better get your skates on, major. I estimate the convoy will reach the forest just about then.'

'We'll be ready. Try and contact any other government units in the area. Any help will be appreciated.'

'Wilco.'

'How long can you stay on station?' Mike Hoare asked.

'Another three hours,' Danny replied.

He'd already leaned the engines' fuel-air mixture ratio down to minimum. Engine handling was tricky when flying for maximum endurance. If Danny reduced the fuel intake to the engine too much they might back-fire or over-heat. He reckoned he'd judged the prop, manifold pressure and mixture settings to optimum, but kept a wary eye on the cylinder-head gauges to make sure they didn't creep into the red arc.

Otherwise there was nothing Danny or Komotho could do other that keep their eyes open and report to the ground forces.

Mike Hoare's ambush plan was sound. His men reached the forest edge in good time and discovered ample firing positions behind fallen trunks and other cover. They lined up either side of the track, spreading out for a broad field of fire, but not too widely spaced to create gaps that might prove vulnerable. Fifty determined, well armed and protected men were going to prove formidable indeed.

There was one hitch though.

As their men deployed knowing what to do without supervision, Ian Henderson and Mike Hoare scanned the oncoming track through their binoculars. They'd expected to see the oncoming convoy within a mile or two, yet the track was empty. No vehicles, no men, no camels – nothing.

'Now where the bloody hell are those bastards?' Ian Henderson hissed through clenched teeth.

'Look to your flanks,' Mike Hoare yelled. 'They may be trying to roll us up from both sides.'

'Danny, what's going on?' Jeremy asked through the radio mike. 'We can't see anything ahead.'

There was no answer.

*

Angela became totally disorientated as she was jostled back and forth in the truck. Judging by the increased temperature and diminishing shadows sweeping past, they'd left the forest canopy and emerged into the Rift Valley Plains. As they drove on, rebels would periodically lean around the tail-gate to see what was ahead.

After about fifteen minutes one of the men started chattering excitedly. Moments later the truck shuddered to a stop. The driver hadn't demonstrated the greatest finesse during the ride, grinding the gears mercilessly. The rebels piled out of the truck, relieving themselves on the roadside.

No one objected when Angela hopped over the tail-gate and moved towards the front of the truck. Dedan was engaged in a heated argument with another Kikuyu. Both men were surrounded by their top lieutenants and it looked as if a fight might break out at any minute.

'What's happening?' Angela asked a rebel standing close by.

'That Stanley Mathenge,' the man replied.

Angela wasn't surprised the rebel spoke English. The Raj encouraged its subjects not to inconvenience their masters by having to communicate in a language that had served them perfectly for millennia. In all fairness to the empire-builders, they'd had Latin and Ancient Greek beaten into them from infancy, so they were reluctant to bother with anything other than the 'Mother Tongue'.

Another oddity was that Dedan's rebels showed no hostility towards Angela considering they'd taken a blood-oath to kill every white person they came across. But they'd seen she'd genuinely tried to help their wounded comrades and would have done a good job of it if the hospital tent hadn't been shredded by .50 cal fire. Maybe that counted for something or the Mau-Mau simply believed they might need Angela's help themselves later on.

Stanley Mathenge and Dedan were having the mother of all rows to the point where the lieutenants surrounding both leaders started fidgeting with their trigger-fingers.

'What are they arguing about?' Angela asked. 'Aren't they supposed to be allies?'

'No Miss Doctor, they hating each other long time now. Stanley, he want to know where all Dedan's man are.'

'This *is* all there are,' Angela insisted.

'Yes, but Dedan told Stanley he have many volunteers.'

'How many?'

'Five hundred — maybe more.'

'But all his "volunteers" ran away, didn't they?' Angela said smugly.

'Dedan's telling Stanley that a regiment of government troops ambushed us.'

From what Angela had learnt about military units during her time with GONO she doubted whether the force that attacked the Mau-Mau earlier was anything close to regimental strength. If that had been the case they would have overrun the rebel camp in minutes. She wasn't going to let anyone know that though.

'Dedan wants Stanley to join us and go back and fight the British,' Angela's Mau-Mau interpreter said without enthusiasm.

'You shouldn't have run away in the first place then,' Angela replied acidly while the rebel stared at her in bewilderment.

'Stanley says it might be an ambush,' the Mau-Mau continued.

'Stanley might well be right.'

While Dedan and Stanley continued their heated debate, one of the Arabs joined the discussion. Everyone could see he wasn't a happy man.

'What's happening now?' Angela hissed through clenched teeth, nudging her companion. 'Who is that man?'

'I don't know him. He is Abyssinian. He is leader of camel-men. He speaks Swahili a little. He says Stanley promised many men to fight British. He has called Stanley a liar.'

'That's not good is it?'

'No Doctor White Lady. It is very bad. Not wise to insult Stanley Mathenge.'

Indeed the argument between the three rebel leaders grew to a heated babble and that's when Stanley Mathenge noticed Angela. He'd have sliced her to pieces then and there if Dedan hadn't intervened. Angela guessed she'd only been saved when Dedan told the others she was a doctor.

But that didn't stop the argument raging. Angela's rebel companion continued to interpret as the row continued to escalate.

Dedan was an incompetent idiot.

Stanley was a pompous son-of-a-whore.

Just as the debate looked like resorting to gunfire the Lockheed plane swooped overhead only inches above the trucks. All the rebels dived for cover which was just as well because Danny dipped the plane even lower so the props were only inches above ground level. Angela stood mesmerised as the plane flashed past, but no so bewildered that she didn't spot two black objects tumble from the back door.

She dived for cover as the grenades exploded causing more confusion among the Mau-Mau. Men emerged from the trucks and blazed away after the plane, but it was already beyond range.

Oh Danny, you're such an idiot, but you try so hard.

The rebels now milled around with no direction. Dedan wasn't keen to go back and face the force in the forest. Neither was Stanley who had no idea what he was up against. It was the Arab who finally made a decision.

His name was Hassan al-Wazir and he wasn't an Abyssinian at all. He came from Palestine with attitude and a personal Jihad against all things British, which some would have said was justified. His grandfather had ridden with Lawrence in the Great War and his father and uncles had spied against the Axis during WWII. When the UN arbitrarily partitioned Palestine in 1948 the Arabs felt they'd been sold out and who could blame them? But then the UN had to do something with one-hundred-thousand survivors of the concentration camps.

A bunch of academics from minor UN countries came up with the scheme which the Security Council ratified with a collective sigh of relief. Unfortunately civil war broke out almost immediately the Jewish settlers arrived and had been going on ever since. British forces tried to keep the peace under a mandate they'd held since before the war, but it all got too hard and they abandoned the Levant to its fate.

Although the League of Nations that morphed into the UN after WWII had hinted they'd form a Jewish state somewhere in Palestine, al-Wazir saw it as a purely British sell-out and was out for revenge.

He saw the Mau-Mau rebellion as a perfect chance to rally the Islamic faithful of the Swahili coastal ports and drive the British out. Maybe he'd spread the Moslem word and convert the Kikuyu while he was at it. The trouble was al-Wazir was delayed in Abyssinia at Emperor Haile Selassie's pleasure and didn't reach Kenya until the bulk of Mau-Mau warriors were languishing in detainee camps.

Now it seemed the promised reinforcements had failed to materialise, it looked like al-Wazir's journey was in vain. He didn't plan to stick around and saw Angela as travel insurance home. While the Kikuyu ducked for cover and argued with each other he sent a dozen men who grabbed Angela and whisked her onto a camel before anyone noticed. Angela didn't go quietly, but she was no match for so many men grappling her and not being too particular where their hands strayed.

The Arabs turned their beasts and loped back north. They were half a mile away before the Mau-Mau gathered their wits and fired up their trucks to give chase. The track was so uneven that the motorised rebels were barely able to keep pace with the Arabs.

*

While the rebels recovered from their confusion, things weren't much better for the Tribal Police and mercenaries.

Ian Henderson and Mike Hoare had set up a classic ambush on either side of the track approaching the forest. They'd positioned themselves to pour enfilading fire from the tree-cover into the open where they expected the rebels to advance.

Meanwhile Jeremy's frustration mounted as he waited for word from Danny. The last he'd heard was that the Mau-Mau had been significantly reinforced, but that was all. The rolling hills of Mt Kenyan's lower slopes hid anyone approaching until they crested the last rise about half a mile from the ambush site.

'Frenchy, take a vehicle and a couple of men and scout ahead,' Hoare said. 'We've got to know what those bloody Kaffirs are up too. They should have been here by now.'

It was a measure of the mercenary leader's confidence that he felt he could take on a force that out-numbered his own five-to-one. But they had the cover, the position and the training, so Mike Hoare felt justified. Frenchy beckoned the two closest mercenaries and they trundled away in a Bren-mounted Landrover. Frenchy was at the wheel while one mercenary manned the machine-gun and the other peered ahead through binoculars.

They'd barely reached halfway to the ridgeline from where they could observe the rebel position when Danny's plane roared over the crest straight towards them. It didn't appear that Danny was expecting to meet any obstacles on the track because he pulled the plane upwards sharply. As he did so a small object dropped from the rear door. It narrowly missed the machine-gunner before hitting the track and bouncing several times and coming to rest about a hundred yards behind the Landrover.

'*Mon Dieu,* what is the young fool playing at?' Frenchy muttered.

He turned the Landrover and motored to where the object lay. It looked like a parcel wrapped in an oily rag. Normally Frenchy would have been suspicious of a booby-trap, but he'd plainly seen the parcel fall from the plane so he sent the mercenary beside him to retrieve the object.

What they discovered was a monkey-wrench wrapped in an oily rag and secured with electric tape. More importantly the package contained a hastily-written pencil note.

Sorry. Radio conked out.

Rebels retreating north. Taken Angela.

Meet you at airstrip I know. Map co-ordinates A-7.

Danny

'*Très bien*, we go back to the force,' Frenchy said. 'It is a chase we have now.'

Chapter 29 — Exit North

Danny circled his plane until the rebels passed the rough strip he'd surveyed the previous week. It was close to the track the rebels were taking. Losing his radio was frustrating, but Komotho assured him it was just a fuse that he'd replace as soon as he could get to the circuit-breaker panel in the battery compartment. Unfortunately they had to land the plane for that.

Then Danny got the idea to write a note. They needed to re-establish communications. The operation was already disintegrating with the rebels still in sight.

'Attach this to something so it won't blow away,' Danny said to Komotho. 'We'll head back to the forest and hopefully drop it where someone can see it.'

Luckily Danny intercepted Frenchy's Landrover and they were able to organise a rendezvous. Danny waited impatiently for the column to catch up while Komotho replaced the radio fuse that had indeed burnt out.

'Pity we don't have another set,' Komotho said. 'It could be an internal fault or a power surge that caused the fuse to blow. We'll lose the radio if it happens again.'

'I bet the mercenaries have a spare,' Danny replied. 'If we can scrounge that, we'll have a backup.'

'Will it work airborne?'

'I don't see why not. It's line-of-sight fox-mike. The aircraft fuselage might shield the signal a bit, but I don't think it'll be significant.'

The plane's installed radio didn't suffer from the same problem because its antenna was fixed outside the fuselage. Komotho thought they could attach a cable from the portable set to the exit door to act as an extended aerial.

Komotho had completed the repairs when the column caught up. Although the Lockheed's tank still contained ample fuel, Danny refuelled anyway. The mercenaries had brought enough AVGAS for at least another two top-ups.

'Crikey, Frenchy,' Danny complained. 'This plane is useless when it comes to firepower. Buzzing the rebels wasn't much help.'

'They have turned tail and run,' Frenchy replied.

'But they've taken Angela with them. How do we get her back?'

'We must disperse them and pick them off in small groups, *n'est-ce pas?*'

'But how will we know who's got Ange?'

'We get to her first,' Komotho said.

'They will have to rest sooner or later,' Frenchy said. 'That will be our chance to sneak in and snatch her.'

'You'd be prepared to do that?' Danny asked.

Frenchy shrugged.

'*Mais Oui,* are we not all a little in love with Mademoiselle Angela?'

'By Jove, count me in too,' Jeremy said.

Although he hadn't met Angela he was pretty gung-ho about rescuing damsels in distress.

'It'll be on a voluntary basis from the commando,' Major Hoare warned.

Ian Henderson explained he could not risk his Native Police unnecessarily, which meant no sneaking into enemy strongholds. Chivalry had its limits, but then Danny had an idea.

'That's OK, Ian,' he said. 'We can keep your blokes ready for cleanup ops. You know it's easy for me to keep tabs on the blighters from the plane. Colonel Serong showed me something he was working on when I was in the States. Komotho, I'll need your help to fix the plane.'

'You'll also need a Kikuyu on the ground,' Komotho replied.

It was about two hundred miles to Abyssinia. If the rebels reached the border and crossed out of British sovereignty, then Angela was lost. The camels could cover a remarkable distance under rough conditions and, although vehicles were faster overall, they required a reasonable surface and that wasn't always available. Only one primitive road led through a minute settlement called Marsabit. From there the trail ran north through Chaldi Desert to the sleepy ex-Italian Army post of Mega just across the border.

'We have two days tops,' Danny said.

'Then the sooner the better,' Jeremy said.

'Can you fix the plane by tonight?' Danny asked Komotho, who nodded confidently.

'I've got plenty of help,' he said indicating the Native Police.

Danny explained his plan, but it was vital that the column kept up with the rebels. There were risks aplenty. Ian Henderson was almost fanatical about capturing Dedan Kimathi and stamping out the very last of the Mau-Mau, or he may have shown more caution and waited for British Army backup. He'd made radio contact with a motorised platoon of Irish fusiliers patrolling the border. The commander said he'd keep an eye out for the rebels and try to intercept them before they reached Abyssinia. But there was a lot of territory to cover and a platoon was only a small unit.

While Komotho worked on the plane, Danny secured the spare FM set to the co-pilot's seat. The rebels and pursuing column made good time, which unfortunately meant radio contact faded. Komotho also made good time enabling Danny to take-off by mid-afternoon and with some extra height resume communications with Jeremy.

'We're still on the road, old boy,' Jeremy's voice crackled through Danny's headset. 'The blighters have made bloody good time. Those camels seem to be able to lope along forever. They're camped at Marsabit for the night.'

'Do you think they know you're on their trail?' Danny asked.

'Hard to say. We kept well back, but it's pretty dusty down here. I reckon if they looked back they'd notice. Mike Hoare reckons they're cautious and have set up a decent perimeter.'

'OK. I know there's a strip at Marsabit, but is there anywhere close to your position where I can land?'

'The stretch of road is OK here. It'll be bumpy, but should do.'

'OK, I'm coming in. Mark the section for me, please.'

The rebels followed the Arabs while the mercenaries and Tribal Police trailed behind. At first it seemed there was no problem keeping up and keeping the quarry in sight. However the Arabs' enthusiasm for the enterprise dwindled as did their interest in anyone involved with it. If they decided to leave the tracks, it would become virtually impossible for a motorised contingent to follow.

The mercenary commando parked two Landrovers beside the road indicating the section suitable for Danny to land his plane. As Jeremy had predicted it was bumpy, but nothing worse than Danny had experienced in New Guinea. Mike Hoare had posted lookouts on a rise overlooking the town. The rebels appeared to be content to rest for the night.

Danny accompanied Frenchy to the lookout point and scanned the area through binoculars.

'They're pretty well dug in,' he said. 'It looks like they've put up barriers and deployed their men all over the place. You'd think they're planning an ambush.'

'*Certainement,* they wait for us. They know we are behind them.'

'Then they know how small our force is or they would still be high-tailing it to Abyssinia.'

*

Dedan looked a bit of a goose when the rebels finally unified and caught up with the Arabs. No one knew what to make of the plane buzzing them and Angela wasn't letting on. As the rebels headed northwards through open country where the savannah morphed to semi-desert, they spotted the column although it was still miles behind.

'Where are the others?' Stanley demanded.

'They must still be coming,' Dedan insisted, but as the day progressed, no government reinforcements appeared.

'Stanley Mathenge doesn't sound very happy,' Angela said to her interpreter.

They rode in an open Landrover behind the leading vehicle, in which Stanley and Dedan still argued hammer-and-tongs. The Mau-Mau warrior had taken Angela under his wing. He seemed happy to act as interpreter as if it was a position of some importance, which of course it was to Angela. Despite the afternoon heat she preferred the open ride to the covered trucks which were unbearably stuffy and stank of stale humanity. Her bush hat was secured with a scarf, Michaela Denis style.

'Stanley says we should have stayed to fight.'

'Maybe you will still have to.'

Angela noticed the Kikuyu didn't look particularly happy about that prospect. She wondered just how committed the others were. After all, they were simply gaol-birds with nowhere else to go. One thing that disturbed Angela was that she hadn't sighted the Lockheed all afternoon. Another hour of daylight remained when they rattled into Marsabit.

By then Hassan al-Wazir was sick of the Kikuyu leaders' bickering and decided to take over. His group was largest and owned most of the guns anyway. Angela was able to follow much of what went on because the rebels resorted to English as it was the most universally understood language. Although many of the rebels, especially the Arabs, distrusted Angela, it seemed that Dedan had convinced them she was an asset and should be tolerated. The Mau-Mau blood-oath to kill all white people they came across seemed to have dampened somewhat. The Arabs thought of her as a mere woman and didn't count anyway. Well, she'd find a way to show them.

Angela sat perched in the rear of a rebel Landrover beside her interpreter who now manned the machine-gun mounted on the rear seat.

'My name is Doctor Angela,' she introduced herself, ensuring she mentioned her purpose and usefulness. 'What's yours?'

'Wamite Njonjo,' he replied with a broad grin.

He looked genuinely pleased that Angela had bothered to get to know him. Although it would be another eighteen years before Dr Nils Bejerot was to coin the term *Stockholm Syndrome*, Angela applied the same principle in reverse. Who knew, it might be well worth Angela gaining Wamite's trust.

Al-Wazir, Stanley and Dedan held a council-of-war beside the Landrover right under Angela's nose.

'I am tired of running from these fleas who chase us,' al-Wazir snorted in a dramatic change of heart. 'We know they are few and they will die in the Name of Allah. *Allahu Akbar.*'

'*Ni Ngai arogocwo,*' Dedan replied.

If the Arabs insisted on evoking their deity whenever they spoke, he had a Kikuyu response.

'We are five times their number,' Stanley said, looking pointedly at Dedan.

'How was I to know? They hid in the woods like cowards,' Dedan spat.

'Opposed to running from the woods like brave men,' Stanley smirked.

'It matters not,' al-Wazir cut in. 'They planned to ambush us, but now we have turned the tables. We will wait here and destroy the infidel when they approach.'

The rebels had the guns and other hardware to do it too. So the leaders set about deploying their men and concealing their vehicles. This wasn't easy because there wasn't a lot to hide behind in Marsabit. The rebels were equipped with camouflage netting which did a surprisingly good job of making the trucks disappear despite the lack of natural cover.

Surely Danny and those men wouldn't be silly enough to walk into a trap. Dear God, it's Danny we're talking about here. He's capable of anything. The more rash and foolish the better as far as Danny McAlister's concerned.

At sunset one of the Arabs, who must have been their Muezzin, chanted the *adhān*. Al-Wazir's men and the Swahili Moslems answered the call to the *Maghrib* evening prayer. They knelt, aligning themselves with the *qibla* as best they could estimate, and were completely absorbed for the next quarter of an hour.

It was fully dark when Wamite brought Angela food and water after the rebels had set up their defences. In the meantime, the Marsabit locals had wisely made themselves scarce.

'Field Marshal Kimathi, he wants you to set up hospital in that house over there,' he reported pointing to one of the few shabby mud buildings covered by corrugated iron sheeting.

'I presume he's expecting more bloodshed,' Angela replied acidly.

'Only white men,' Wamite replied with a sigh of regret.

'We'll see. Come on, Wamite, give me a hand with what's left of our medical kit, please.'

One article she carried was a drop-sheet marked with a red cross that WHO representatives had insisted she and Professor Winslow display so their surgery was easily recognisable. Angela made a mental note to ensure it was plainly visible when the fire-fight broke out.

From their vantage point overlooking Marsabit, Mike Hoare and Ian Henderson watched the rebels settle down for the night. Eventually daylight failed and the town oozed into darkness speckled with cooking fires. The mercenary and police leaders appeared satisfied that the rebels were simply bedding down for the night, but expected the town to be well guarded.

They considered a night attack, but with so few men Henderson and Hoare realised there was a chance of such action going terribly wrong. They needed to see what they were doing and precisely where the enemy was deployed. Very pistol flares were an option, but short lasting and it might be a tough, protracted fight. Danny's plan only involved four men — Jeremy, Komotho, Frenchy and himself. Mike Hoare was prepared to sacrifice Frenchy who'd volunteered anyway and Ian Henderson didn't really have any authority over Jeremy.

So leaving the Tribal Police securely entrenched on high ground one side of the road and the mercenaries at the lookout post on the other, Danny and Jeremy were ready to head back to the plane. Meanwhile Frenchy and Komotho began the long detour around town to approach from the north. Additionally both the Tribal Police and mercenaries had mortar and Bren-gun teams in support.

Danny had parked the plane about a mile back along the road. One of the Native Policemen drove them in an open Landrover. By daylight Danny had spied plenty of game although it thinned out as the terrain grew into desert. At night animal sounds filled the air.

'Noisy blighters, what?' Jeremy suggested with an air of bravado.

Danny was sure he identified elephants, hyenas and maybe baboons, but none sounded close by. He knew lions slept all day so he hoped they'd reach the plane before they got into hunting mode. Elephants kept to themselves if they weren't bothered and hopefully Danny and Jeremy could scare off other lesser predators with a gunshot. Further south they might have run into buffalo herds, hippos, rhinos and goodness knows what else, but the road was clear.

'What about leopards?' Jeremy asked.

'I dunno,' Danny whispered without realising. 'You live here. We only have snakes, poisonous spiders and crocodiles in Australia.'

Their progress was slower at night and it took ten minutes to reach the plane. By then the moon had risen sufficiently to give some illumination. All this talk of savage beasts made the driver nervous. He pulled up when he caught the plane's silhouette in his headlights. The Landrover sped away immediately after Jeremy and Danny got out.

Jeremy led the way with the help of a powerful torch. He carried spare batteries in his kit bag and they were both armed with rifles. Danny also carried his trusty 1911 Army Colt automatic.

Guided by torchlight the two men walked around the plane's nose to the port side where Komotho had removed the entry door and stowed it aboard. Jeremy raised the torch light which not only illuminated the Lockheed's under wing and port engine, but four pairs of eyes that reflected in the beam. Danny and Jeremy froze as a low growl greeted them.

'Lions,' Danny whispered, 'and nowhere to run.'

'Whatever you do, don't run, old boy,' Jeremy warned through clenched teeth.

Indeed four lions had settled under the plane's wing for shade during the late afternoon. The pride consisted of three females and a juvenile male, who must have just made a name for himself to have secured a harem at such a young age. This meant he might be tough, but also inexperienced. The lions were restless and continued growling and fidgeting.

Danny drew his pistol and aimed at the young male who was crouched in the centre of Jeremy's torch beam.

'Not yet, Danny,' Jeremy said in a remarkably conversational tone. 'You know we had to be unlucky. They'd probably had shoved off in half-an-hour,'

'Well they're flaming-well here now and they're between us and the door,' Danny said raising his voice unintentionally.

'Let's not kill anything we don't have to. Follow my lead,' Jeremy said.

He raised his arms and started clapping his hands above his head and began singing *God Save the Queen* at the top of his lungs. Danny joined in with *Waltzing Matilda* as both men slowly edged towards the plane. The lions stood their ground until Jeremy was only yards away. The male rose to his feet glaring at the on-comers, but Jeremy held his gaze. Danny was more concerned about the four females who looked older and more experienced and could attack on either side.

The male's mane bristled as he flung a paw forward with claws extended.

'Is that all you've got?' Jeremy yelled. 'Bugger off and find your own plane!'

'Yeah, this is my plane,' Danny roared in support.

It was probably only seconds, but it felt like hours as Danny and Jeremy faced down the lions yelling for all they were worth. The male grew edgy and nervous. He roared once then turned and loped away into the night. His consorts followed with a few parting snarls of their own.

'That was impressive,' Danny said. 'How did you know they'd back down?'

'Pater says they're usually afraid of men and will take off given the chance. Man-eaters are usually too old or too sick to run down their normal prey so they're forced to take out the slower option. The Kikuyu and Maasai hunt lions that attack their herds. Lions and men have lived together around here since prehistoric times. I guess they've learnt to respect one another. The worst thing you can do is run away.'

'Easy to say. Let's get aboard before they decide to come back. We could have just fired a shot at their feet, you know.'

'Now where's the fun in that?'

'You're stark raving bonkers, Jeremy.'

'Yep, others have said exactly the same thing, old chap.'

They clambered through the doorway. It was a tight squeeze past the Bren-gun that Komotho had secured to one of the rear passenger seats with the barrel poking outwards. The plane's interior was a black maw and Jeremy cursed as he bumped into the door, which was jammed between two seats.

'Hang on, Jeremy. I'll switch on the battery and light the place up a bit...'

Danny flicked on the battery master switch and the red standby lights glowed dimly.

'...Oh shit,' Danny whispered. 'What is it about the bloody wild life in this country?'

'What's up?' Jeremy asked from the rear cabin.

'There's a ruddy great snake coiled up on my seat. Thousands of square miles to choose from and every ruddy animal on the continent wants to be in my plane.'

Jeremy edged towards the pilot's seat and froze as he poked his nose into the cockpit.

'Ah, now that *is* a problem,' he whispered.

'It is?'

'Yep. You see that's black mamba and if it senses we're here, it'll get pretty aggressive. One nip from that chap and it's all over in seconds.'

'Sort of like a coastal taipan back home,' Danny said, stepping back to the doorway. 'Right I've had it with this lot — stand clear, Jeremy.'

There was just sufficient room for Jeremy to squeeze behind the Bren-gun. Danny knew the longer he delayed the more chance there was for the snake to slither down into the many hiding places on board the Lockheed. He took his flight jacket from the hook behind his seat and held his breath for a second.

In one fluid movement he leant over the pilot's seat, just as the mamba stirred. Its head shot upwards as Danny flung his jacket over the serpent. Danny had seen snakes handlers with eastern browns and black snakes lying quietly in sacks, so he hoped mambas behaved the same way once their heads were covered. He was still taking a huge risk. If the snake's head wriggled free it would strike without hesitation. Who knew whether mambas acted like Australian snakes?

Danny saw the mamba's tail flipping from under his jacket. He clamped both hands around the rest of the slithering reptile. So far the snake's head was engulfed in Danny's flight jacket. The mamba was an adult and surprisingly heavy. Danny knew he wouldn't be able to control it for more than a few seconds. Before it could pop out anywhere, Danny flung the jacket and snake through the door.

'Stay out of my plane!' Danny roared.

Jeremy flashed his torch beam onto the jacket in time to see the mamba streak from under it. It sliced through the grass right back towards the plane. It was then that Danny realised just how big the snake was. It reared towards the doorway with its head level with Jeremy's and still plenty of snake was left along the ground. Fortunately for Jeremy the snake probably couldn't see him as the torch shone right into its eyes. Its jaws were agape exposing curved teeth that were not particularly large, but looked ready for business.

In the end the point was academic as a slug blasted from Danny's 1911 automatic, ripping through the night air. The snake's upper body evaporated into venomous pulp when a .45 bullet sliced the snake's head off, carrying it away somewhere into the grassland beyond.

'It's your own fault. I said stay out of my plane,' Danny growled blowing the barrel of his smoking gun. He retrieved his jacket which wasn't too badly covered with snake entrails.

'Looks like it's gonna be a long night, old boy,' Jeremy said.

And it was.

Danny and Jeremy took turns on guard duty. They were not troubled by further snakes, but a pack of hyenas sniffed around and a curious leopard, but a flash from Jeremy's torch was enough to deter them and Danny didn't have to fire his gun again.

By daybreak they had rested a little and were ready to get airborne.

Chapter 30 — Decoy at Dawn

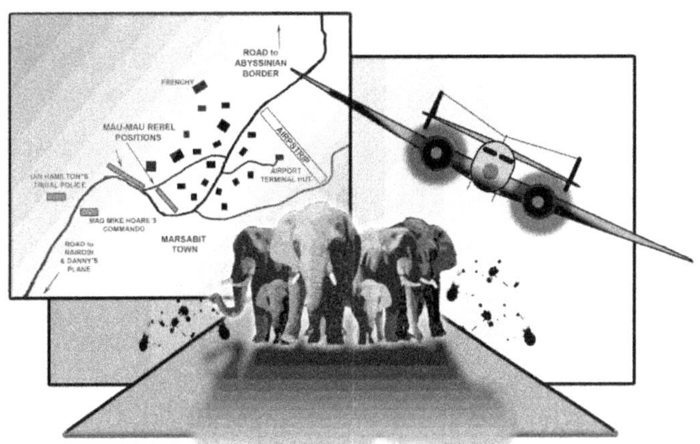

Frenchy and Komotho waited until midnight. Circling around Marsabit took over an hour, but they dodged the Mau-Mau guards. Approaching from the north was clear. The rebels were confident the mercenaries and Tribal Police force were so small they'd never try to surround the town. That was true enough. Ian Henderson and Mike Hoare could only spare two men and one of those didn't belong to either of them.

By midnight the moon had risen sufficiently to see by if you were careful, but still gave cover in the shadows. Frenchy and Komotho stuck to gullies and dry creek beds. While it was easy enough for Komotho to pass as a Mau-Mau warrior, Frenchy needed a disguise. He wrapped a scarf over his head as close to Arab style as he could and hoped it would fool the rebels in the dark.

Both men were armed with Sten-guns, automatic pistols, hand-grenades and Komotho also carried a Very pistol. Other than water they didn't weight themselves down with rations – they didn't expect to be gone that long.

Ian Henderson had suggested they try to set the camels loose so the Arabs would have no means of escape, but the animals were tethered randomly, so that didn't seem like an option. They did find one group of a dozen animals guarded by a lone sentry. Frenchy silently despatched him to Allah while Komotho cut the camels' tether ropes. Unfortunately they didn't appear inclined to move and Komotho had no idea how to stir them without a making a noise.

'Forget it,' Frenchy whispered. 'We concentrate on our primary task, *n'est-ce pas?'*

That task was to locate Angela, which turned out to be simple enough if you had nerves of steel.

As they entered town from the north, Komotho merely asked the first rebel they came across. He pointed to the red-cross banner Angela had draped outside the entrance. Komotho claimed he'd been stung by a scorpion and needed treatment. It was a common enough complaint and the rebel showed no signs of suspicion. The fact that the Mau-Mau formed two groups also meant they didn't all know each other. Komotho was an armed Kikuyu so the rebel thought nothing of it.

Nevertheless Frenchy slit his throat and hid the body behind a rubbish pile just to be on the safe side. In any case it was one less rebel to kill later on.

While Komotho and Frenchy skulked around outside, Angela prepared her surgery as best she could. There was a woeful lack of equipment, but she ensured everything was spotless. Their main source of heat was a kerosene lamp. The building was nothing more than a single room barn. Most cooking was done outside where a stone hearth had been built just beyond the main door. Wamite gathered what fuel he could, which consisted of kindling, some wood and any dried animal droppings that had been stockpiled by the townsfolk.

Once she'd done all she could Angela tried to sleep. Wamite was proving his worth and found her a ground sheet and blanket. Ablutions sites were where you found them and Angela had to walk to the edge of town for some privacy. She thought she might have a chance to escape, but rebel guards were never far away. She returned to the hospital shed and finally she slept through pure exhaustion while Wamite crouched in the corner and nodded off as well.

Frenchy and Komotho crept into the building at around five in the morning. The Mau-Mau guards were concentrating on the outer perimeter without paying attention to the town and the intruders went undetected. Frenchy's disguise appeared to be working well, so no one was likely to pay him any attention while Komotho fitted right in.

They darted through the door into darkness. Angela had lowered the lamp to a minute glow while Wamite was invisible in the corner shadows. Frenchy gently placed his hand over Angela's mouth, using his other arm to hold her tightly around the waist. She jerked a wake, kicking and tried to bite his palm.

'*S'il vous plait rester calme, ma chère,*' Frenchy crooned into Angela ear. '*C'est moi,* Aleron Duval – Frenchy.'

Angela relaxed and Frenchy released her. She turned to face him wide eyed.

'You!' she gasped.

'*Bonjour, mademoiselle.*'

'How did you get here...why..?'

'We are your knights in shining armour – *les chevaliers blancs, n'est-ce pas?* You have met Komotho, I understand. We must go – *allez vite!'*

Just then Wamite stirred. He couldn't have moved at a worse time. Frenchy was coiled like a stalking cat and in a killing mood. In one fluid move he reached Wamite and drove his hunting knife through the unfortunate rebel's ribcage. To Angela's horror, Wamite dropped to the dirt floor and died in a pool of blood.

'You beast,' Angela hissed. 'He befriended me.'

'I have no time for your theatrics, *mademoiselle*. He is an enemy. He dies or we do. We go.'

'So you are my saviour now,' Angela hissed, still smarting from Wamite's murder. 'I suppose it makes a refreshing change from kidnapping me.'

Frenchy rolled his eyes, suggesting he wondered why he'd bothered.

'When you are in the hyena's den, you need a leopard by your side, not a gazelle,' Komotho whispered.

'What I don't need is any home-spun Kikuyu wisdom from you,' Angela replied, glaring through the dimness.

Komotho shrugged. He was used to nagging white women. It was something they seemed to enjoy.

Frenchy handed her the blanket she had slept on and cut as much of Wamite's robe away as he could manage.

'Put these on,' he whispered. 'Cover as much as you can especially your head.'

They crept through the doorway and along the hut wall. Angela had no time to wonder why or how Frenchy had arrived at Marsabit and knew better than to ask. Silence was their only chance of escape. They had to sneak past the two hundred rebels surrounding them. But they planned to return north while the Mau-Mau's attention was concentrated towards the south.

The idea was to use the cover of darkness for concealment, without the risk of being caught in the open at daybreak. Like most of Danny's plans, there was no backup option.

At first it looked as if things were running smoothly. Frenchy, Komotho and Angela hugged the shadows as they crept to the edge of town. Angela still fretted about Wamite's death, but she knew complaining to Frenchy would fall on deaf ears and even she knew right now was the time to shut up.

What they hadn't counted on was the Arab Muezzin calling the *adhãn* once more to announce *Fajr* – pre-dawn prayers. In all fairness to Frenchy, his Legionnaire service had all been in the Far East. Indochina was home to many Muslims, but they had to compete with Buddhists, Hindus, Christians and Jains for God's attention and spiritual elbow-room, so they merged into the rest of the Asia's religious potpourri.

Not that any of that mattered, right then Muslims were stirring in all corners of the rebel camp. Frenchy signalled for Angela and Komotho to flatten themselves against the nearest building wall. Shadows still hid them, but not for long. It wouldn't have been so bad if the Arabs had assembled and prayed in one spot that could have been quietly circumnavigated. Unfortunately they knelt in small groups or as individuals scattered throughout the camp. Also, although they made an effort to face the Scared Shrine of Mecca, it wasn't a perfect science so many of the Arabs pointed in slightly different directions.

'We go now before the others wake,' Frenchy hissed. '*Allez vite!*'

Frenchy led the way towards the airstrip that was their rendezvous point. They had difficulty dodging prostrating figures as they stepped gingerly to safety.

The airport terminal was a mud hut with a tattered thatch roof. The entry door had long since disappeared for firewood. The hut was probably unoccupied other than a home for death adders, but now wasn't the time to be picky.

'We hide inside until Danny lands,' Frenchy explained. 'Then we run to the plane before he flies away.'

He won't leave without me, Angela smiled to herself.

The plan was working well until Angela tripped over an Arab in the middle of his devotions. He was pretty upset about it too. Forgetting his *fard salaf,* he leapt to his feet yelling abuse. Of course Frenchy, Komotho or Angela couldn't understand a word, but it probably went along the lines of:

- What do you think you're up to?
- Why aren't you at prayer (to Frenchy who was still disguised as an Arab)?
- Why is that woman here (obvious it was a men-only area)?

There was probably a lot more the affronted Arab would have liked to say, but his eyes bulged and blood gurgled through his teeth as Frenchy drove his bayonet straight through the worshiper's spleen, dragging it upwards until it pierced his heart. The man dropped silently into the dust, but the alarm had been given.

Even if the Arabs were still confused about disposing of an intruder or continuing their supplications, the Kikuyu had no such reservations. In dawn's first rays, men leapt to their feet and raced to grab their weapons. Soon Ak-47 shots rattled across the camp as slugs zinged through the air.

'Komotho take Angela to the airport,' Frenchy ordered. 'I will hold them off.'

Angela hesitated.

'Allez!'

'What about you?'

'This is what I do,' he kissed her briefly on both cheeks. *'Adieu, mademoiselle.'*

There was no more time. The Kikuyu rebels were massing towards the airstrip. Frenchy fired a burst into them, tossing a grenade for good measure. Komotho grabbed Angela's hand, leading her at a sprint towards the airstrip hut. The problem with Marsabit was that it spread out and there were large open spaces between cover. Angela and Komotho took advantage of the spindly acacia trees and brittle bushes between isolated buildings. Those local inhabitants who hadn't left town glared from their homes as the fugitives fled past.

Frenchy headed away at ninety degrees to Angela and Komotho. He ducked behind an abandoned cart and fired half a clip into the rebel camp. A hail of bullets came in return. The Arabs spotted Frenchy's muzzle-flashes and returned concentrated fire. The cart shattered to splinters, proving no protection for high-velocity lead.

Frenchy moved further to the town edge. There were only a couple of shanties left to shelter behind. Each time he stopped, he ensured he fired a few rounds to lure the rebels away from Angela and Komotho. There was now enough daylight to clearly make out details. Frenchy saw rebels darting from one point of cover to another. He dropped a couple, so the others came on cautiously. Around fifty men were now hot on Frenchy's heels.

*

The mercenaries and Tribal Policemen heard the popping of small arms fire from Marsabit. They sprang into action. Ian Henderson and Mike Hoare knew the plan had been blown because they'd hoped that Angela would be rescued without gunfire.

'No time for secrecy now,' they agreed in unison. 'Let's lob a few mortars in there and see what gets stirred up.'

They raced for their respective lookout posts to give the gunners orders.

*

Al-Wazir was jerked from his devotions. It appeared Allah had more important tasks for him right then. He assessed the situation and spotted a lone figure at the north side of town. Calling for his men to follow, he grabbed his rifle and gave chase. A sharp jet of red-hot slugs sent him diving for cover.

His men returned fire and were met by a grenade explosion. Whoever the intruder was, he didn't lack courage or skill. With sensible respect, al-Wazir led the majority of his men in pursuit. A couple fell to the stranger's gunfire. So far he'd moved with stealth and cunning, but as the sun rose his cover would rapidly disappear.

*

Dedan and Stanley may have been slightly behind al-Wazir to grab their weapons, but not much. They also saw the situation from a different perspective. Dedan spotted Angela and Komotho as they raced for the airport. He had no idea about Frenchy, but noticed the Arabs were pre-occupied moving in a different direction.

'That way! To the airstrip,' he yelled to his men. 'Take them alive!'

The Kikuyu rose en masse and charged towards the airport. Fortunately Angela and Komotho had a good head start. He might have been able to outrun the Mau-Mau, but there was no way she'd keep pace with Kenyans who were acclimatised to high altitude running. The rebels had now broken into two groups – the Arabs who chased Frenchy and the Kikuyu who were after Angela and Komotho.

By the time Angela reached the airport hut, she was gasping and the rebels had closed the gap alarmingly. Komotho darted inside, pulling Angela after him just as the nearest Mau-Mau sharp-shooters fired their first rounds. Komotho glanced back and, to his horror, saw a mass of Mau-Mau heading towards him. He fired a clip from his Sten that stirred a hornets' nest of flying lead in return. Bullets shredded the thatch roof to stalks. Dust and straw poured over Angela and Komotho. Instantly they were coughing and spluttering uncontrollably.

The rebels edged forward over open ground towards the hut. They were aware of enough mysterious bullets flying around for them to be cautious. Just before they could overrun the hut they dived for cover as mortar shells exploded close by. With scant regard for the local townsfolk, Mike Hoare and Ian Henderson's mortar crews lobbed 60mm shells randomly into Marsabit. The mortar spotters were placed too far away for accurate sighting and the shells landed with no effect other than delaying and slightly confusing the rebels.

In any event only two mortar shells landed on Marsabit. Right then Ian Henderson heard the growl of twin 450 horsepower Pratt-&-Whitney Junior Wasp engines. Danny banked the plane from side to side as he flashed overhead. Komotho had heard the plane too. A Very flare shot skywards and burst into an iridescent fireball, which was the signal that it was time for Danny to pick up Angela.

The rebels were not all that the mortars confused. A small herd of elephants had been grazing just north of town. Elephants were a nuisance the good people of Marsabit had tolerated as long as anyone could remember. They caused damage, but also discouraged unwelcome predators like lions and hyenas that weren't prepared to tackle anything as large as a bunch of belligerent tuskers.

Small arms fire popping away close by had certainly alarmed them, but when the first mortar shell crumped to earth spewing clods of dirt and rock into the air, the elephants took flight. In a joint fanfare of pachydermal trumpeting they lumbered across Marsabit's northern perimeter. They rubbed past the airstrip hut reducing it to rubble with Angela and Komotho struggling to free themselves and lucky not to have been trampled to death.

Danny manoeuvred the Lockheed on final approach to the airstrip. Just before touchdown he saw to his horror the elephants charging in panic straight towards him along the landing strip. He had no choice but to slam the throttles forward and lift the plane back into the air, just missing the elephants by inches as they rushed on by.

Chapter 31 — Race for Life

Danny cursed as he regained altitude, but it gave him time to assess the situation below. He was so close to the ground that he easily spotted the group of rebels approaching the wrecked airstrip hut. Although there was no sign of Frenchy, Angela and Komotho, he knew it was the pre-arranged pick-up point and he'd seen the flare, so they must be down there somewhere.

Although the elephants had cleared the strip, Danny doubted if there was time for him to fly back for another approach before the Mau-Mau reached the hut.

'You ready back there, Jeremy,' he said over the intercom system Komotho had rigged from the cockpit to the rear cabin.

'Absolutely, old boy,' came the reply which was a bit too cheerful in Danny's opinion, but that was Jeremy for you.

'Remember, keep clear of the hut although it looks a bit smashed up right now.'

'Will do, old chap. Just like the brief — on your mark or when I see a clear target — shoot!'

Angela and Komotho dragged themselves from the wrecked hut, but now stood in a very vulnerable position. As shots zinged pasted, they ducked behind the remaining wreckage again. The rebels recovered, but then Angela and Komotho were granted another brief respite.

The mortar shells had not only panicked the elephants, but the camels Komotho had cut free during the night also bolted and ran amok among the Mau-Mau before galumphing across the airstrip into the hillside beyond.

As the rebels rose for a final strike on the hut, Danny banked the Lockheed in a tight circle overhead. It was a skilful piece of flying. He needed to fly close enough to stay in range, but keep the bank angle small enough so g-forces didn't make it impossible for Jeremy to operate the Bren. As Danny and Jeremy hadn't practised, it was going to be hit-and-miss – literally.

'Target coming up...now!' Danny called.

Jeremy pulled the trigger and the Bren spluttered into life. He didn't have to aim as Komotho had fixed the machinegun securely. It was a drawback, but they couldn't risk the bullets spraying into the plane's wing or tail if it had been rigged on a swivelling device.

The idea was that Jeremy was to fire at a set position while Danny flew in a circle around it. Jeremy pumped the first magazine into the Mau-Mau warriors. Dirt spurted up at the bullets' impact points. Several men dropped and lay still. Jeremy ripped the empty magazine from the Bren, slammed another into place and resumed firing.

It took three full clips to throw the Mau-Mau into confusion. They were caught in the open and the Bren's fire was deadly. The Lockheed was a handy plane at low speed and Danny held it close to the target. The Bren's recoil proved insignificant. The turning plane allowed Jeremy to pour incredibly dense fire into a small area. One shell could even take out two victims, maybe killing one and wounding another. Soon a dark stain of blood seeped into the ground surrounding the airstrip. Angela and Komotho popped from their cover in disbelief. The rebels had come so close, but now they scrambled back to town in search of cover as the bullets rained down.

Komotho grabbed Angela by her shoulders and pulled her flat onto the ground. He lay on top of her, protecting her from some wayward slugs that smashed into the hut. The bullets then streaked away as Danny banked the plane leaving a trail of still and moaning men in its wake.

Some of the rebels kept their nerve and fired back at the plane. Bullets sprayed through the port-side fuselage and out the starboard just inches from Jeremy's head. He gritted his teeth as he clipped another magazine into the Bren's breech and continued firing.

*

Once Mike Hoare and Ian Henderson saw the Lockheed open up, they realised they couldn't hang back any longer. The mercenaries and police clambered aboard their vehicles and raced forward. The Landrovers roared into town bristling with guns that blazed away simultaneously.

There was some sporadic resistance from the rebels who remained behind cover, but they were quickly flushed out and herded into a bunch under the watchful eyes of Tribal Police. Meanwhile the mercenaries searched each building and shelter with surprising consideration for the remaining villagers they found. Their medic went to great lengths to ensure no one had been hurt and in the end was able to report all the locals were safe and accounted for.

Meanwhile the mercenaries ran headlong into the Mau-Mau who were fleeing Danny and Jeremy's killing ground. One warning blast from the mercenaries was enough for the Kikuyu warriors to toss their weapons aside and raise their arms. They too joined their comrades under police guard.

A group of Arabs reached their camels and bolted north in a hail of pursuing bullets. Most got away and disappeared into the desert. Two Landrovers sped off with the Arabs on the road to Abyssinia. At the time no one knew who was aboard those vehicles, but later it seemed that Dedan Kimathi and Stanley Mathenge had abandoned their men and escaped.

Two Native Policemen were helping Angela and Komotho to their feet when Danny landed the Lockheed and taxied to the ruined hut. The plane pulled up and the props clattered to a stop. Danny finished the shut-down checklist while Jeremy placed the chocks under the main-wheels. Danny jumped from the door with Angela's white laundry stick tucked under his arm like a drill sergeant. Angela raced into his arms and for once was lost for words.

'This belongs to you, I believe,' Danny said.

'Good to see a plan that works — sort of,' Komotho commented.

'Yeah, thanks, mate. Your blood's worth bottling. Ripper job.'

'This was your plan I believe,' Angela frowned, pushing him away in one of her unpredictable mood-swings, pointing to the dead and wounded men all around.

Danny and Komotho exchanged glances and shrugged.

'It's barbaric,' Angela said softly.

'I know, but they started by torching that village and kidnapping you,' Danny replied. 'You're safe now. That's the main thing.'

'I don't think I was in any danger. The rebels needed a doctor. I was more likely to get blown up by your bombs. You destroyed my hospital tent in the forest and killed most of the wounded men.'

Blimey, there's no pleasing her. What does she expect?

'That's what war's all about – dead people! What do you think the Mau-Mau would have done with you when they didn't need a doctor anymore?''

'Frenchy killed my friend,' Angela accused, waving the white stick wildly.

'You had a friend here? Jeeze-Louise, Ange. Where *is* Frenchy anyway?'

'He led the Arabs away from us,' Komotho said. 'He went north-west.'

Ian Henderson drove up in his leading Landrover while Mike Hoare was busily rounding up the last rebels.

'Great, here's the cavalry,' Danny said.

Henderson reported that Frenchy was yet to be located, but Mike Hoare arrived moments later with news.

'You'd better come and have a look at this,' he said.

Danny, Angela and Jeremy climbed into the Landrover, leaving Komotho to inspect the plane's fuselage damage. They followed a trail of dead and wounded Arabs that grew more numerous the further they went. Mercenaries and police were already questioning both Arabs and Mau-Mau captives. Finally the vehicle came to a stop in front of a slight rise with a rough shelter perched on it. Bodies surrounded the shanty. Several had been shredded by grenade blasts while others suffered from multiple bullet wounds.

Two bodies lay inside.

One was an Arab who rested on top of Frenchy. The Arab gripped a janbiya in his lifeless hand. Frenchy's bayonet was buried to the hilt in the Arab's gut with the blade jutting through his spine.

'Looks like Frenchy took a bunch of them with him,' Mike Hoare muttered as he rolled the Arab off his comrade. 'From what we can gather from the Kaffirs, we've caught, he's the Arab leader, Hassan al-Wazir.'

'I wonder what his beef was,' Danny muttered.

'Didn't like the English apparently,' Ian Henderson replied. 'I guess he's not alone there.'

Blood seeped from two bullet holes in Frenchy's torso and he bore several knife wounds. For once he actually appeared quite peaceful, even serene. Angela knelt beside him and examined his body. Tears filled her eyes.

Why am I crying for Frenchy? He kidnapped me and wanted to sell me to some fat heathen layabout. He slapped my face. He...He's...got a pulse...

'Danny, Frenchy's still alive,' Angela gasped. 'We have to get him to hospital.'

'Yeah right, Ange, maybe you haven't noticed, but we're in the middle of nowhere. This place hasn't even got a pub.'

'If we can get him to Kraal Winslow we might be able to stabilise him before taking him to Nairobi.'

*

Danny, Angela, Jeremy and Komotho lost track of the Mau-Mau rebellion after that. They focused entirely on getting Frenchy to an operating table. The mercenaries and Tribal Police had suffered no casualties, while the rebels would have to be satisfied with the mercenaries' medic. Angela also commandeered one of their first-aid units. Frenchy remained unconscious when they laid him on a stretcher. Four Tribal Police carried him to the plane.

There was a frustrating delay while Komotho dismantled the Bren-gun to make room for Frenchy's stretcher. Finally they placed him in the aisle without bothering to bolt the door back onto its hinges. Komotho assessed that the bullet holes wouldn't stop the plane flying.

Angela found no other bullet wounds than the ones she'd already located, but Frenchy'd lost a dangerous amount of blood from his collective injuries.

'I need your blood, Danny,' Angela called as he started the engines.

'You're not supposed to operate heavy machinery for forty-eight hours after donating. Planes are heavy machinery.'

'Special case. Remember your blood is O-negative. It's compatible with everyone.'

It seemed bizarre to Danny, but once they were safely airborne and heading south, Angela found a vein and inserted a syringe into his arm. She half filled the plastic container from the first aid unit. She judged that was enough without running the risk of affecting Danny's performance before transferring to Frenchy's vein. Even so Danny was feeling slightly heady when he landed the plane at Kraal Winslow.

Professor Winslow greeted them with dozens of questions, but there was no time for answers. Frenchy was whisked into the surgery while Angela and the professor gowned up accompanied by a brace of nurses. Winslow fretted that he was a physician rather than a surgeon and Frenchy should be flown to Nairobi.

'We've already wasted too much time, professor,' Angela snapped. 'I don't think he'll make it if we delay further. It's touch-and-go as it is. If you'll please assist.'

Duly admonished, the professor did as he was bid. Angela turned to one of the nurses and ordered Frenchy's blood to be tested and to have any compatible donors standing by.

'Looks like our Ange has taken charge again,' Danny said to Jeremy and Komotho.

Danny radioed Michaela and Armand Denis to let them know the situation and that Angela was safe. They heard the relief in Michaela's voice as she promised to relay the information to Nairobi on their Low Frequency radio set. About half an hour later Armand came on the air. He said a chopper and military medical team had been dispatched from Nairobi, while another unit was heading for Marsabit to deal with the wounded there. Michaela said she was coming right over to see how she could help.

With nothing more to do, the boys sat on camp chairs outside Winslow's tent.

'Fancy a cuppa?' Jeremy asked, lounging in his chair.

'Crikey no, I'd kill for a beer,' Danny said.

'Leave it to me,' Komotho said. 'I'll scrounge up something.'

Sure enough he returned with a bucket containing half a dozen bottles of *Tusker* brew on ice.

'All the comforts of home,' Komotho grinned. 'I raided the old prof's medicine fridge.'

'He'll be mad,' Danny said without sounding particularly sincere about it. 'He'll probably feel like one himself after the op.'

Angela and Professor Winslow were still working on Frenchy when the chopper arrived. A brusque looking medical team disembarked and entered the tent with enough equipment to supply a small hospital including an ambulance gurney. Only minutes later Frenchy was wheeled from the tent and lifted aboard the chopper.

Angela accompanied the gurney with a military doctor who wore a major's crown on both shoulders. Angela's operating gown was stained with blood while her mask now draped from her neck. She peeled off her surgical gloves and shook the major's hand.

'Excellent work, doctor,' he smiled as he boarded the chopper. 'You've done all you can, we'll take it from here.'

The helicopter lifted and disappeared south. Danny never saw Frenchy again.

Angela was exhausted. She didn't want to eat or drink and it was all she could do to wash up. She collapsed in her tent and slept for thirty hours. Danny, Jeremy and Komotho did much the same.

Before she fell asleep Angela smiled.

The British major had said, 'Excellent work, doctor.'

*

The following months rushed by. Danny was so busy he hardly noticed. The Lockheed was used more and more as local people got used to it and discovered how handy it was for getting to surgery. He saw little of Angela who was either tending patients or assisting Professor Winslow's research. She was more reserved and preoccupied and, although friendly enough, seemed to avoid Danny if she could.

Jeremy left to rejoin Ian Henderson in his search for the illusive Dedan Kimathi. Although the fight at Marsabit marked the last major action in the area, it took another year for Henderson's men to finally track Dedan down. He was tried and hanged in Kamiti Gaol a year after that. Stanley Mathenge was never found, but many people thought he was hiding in Abyssinia.

Frenchy remained in a critical condition and was flown to Durban for further surgery. Nothing more was heard of him at Kraal Winslow where life went on in its normal, munificent way.

Danny began counting the days until his tenure was up. He could have left at any time because he was working for nothing, but he stayed on Angela's account. On their due departure date, Komotho and Danny prepared the Lockheed for its final flight to Nairobi. All their gear was stowed on board and they waited to help Angela with her luggage.

When it was finally time to leave, Angela dropped a bombshell.

'I'm staying,' she announced

'You're joking?' Danny replied. 'You said we'd only be here till Christmas. It's time to go home and celebrate with your family. I want to be there too. I've had enough of conflict and wilderness. I'd like us just to be normal.'

'I'm needed here, Danny. There is so much I can do.'

'Angela, I'm twenty years old and I've been fighting for the last five years. I've had enough of it. Don't you want some peace and quiet for a change?'

'This is my work. God has put me here to make a difference.'

'It's where you'll get killed more like. It'll never be different, Ange. There'll always be war and famine. There are just too many people rubbing up against one another to get along. When this war ends another will flare up. It always has and it always will. You're the one who said it was barbaric, remember? Come to Australia with me.'

'And do what?'

'Be a doctor, of course.'

'In some country practice, marry you, have babies and live happily ever after.'

'Right now that sounds pretty good to me.'

'Is that a proposal, Danny?'

She eyed him with acid amusement.

'If you like...yes. They need doctors in Australia too, you know?'

'How very romantic and sweet of you, Danny, but remember I'm only twenty as well. I can't ignore my duty. There's more for me to do right now than just being plain Mrs Danny McAlister.'

'There's nothing plain about you, Angela. What's wrong with being Mrs McAlister and living a peaceful life?' Danny managed a wry smile.

'Nothing Danny, but not for me. I'm not ready for that yet.'

'And that's the rub, isn't it? I'll never be your handbag, Ange. I can never be Mr Dr Angela Holyman.'

Danny turned and boarded the Lockheed. He didn't even kiss her goodbye. Komotho shrugged and nodded to Angela before following Danny onto the plane. Danny started the engines. Minutes later the Lockheed zoomed over Kraal Winslow and vanished from view.

Epilogue — Merimbula NSW

'And that was that,' Grandpa said. 'I'd kinda burnt my bridges. I went back to work for CAT. I'd been away too long and it was time to start earning a living again. I think Bob Rousselot and General Chennault would have sacked me if I'd stayed away any longer.'

We were watching the sunset on Grandpa's verandah while dinner simmered deliciously in the pot. Danny and Angela's story had almost come full circle.

'I wrote to Angela, but somehow it didn't seem quite the same,' Grandpa added vaguely.

I didn't know what 'quite the same' meant, but I think it was Grandpa's way of describing what he couldn't understand himself. Somehow he and Angela had drifted apart. They exchanged a few letters until Angela said she'd found someone new and the correspondence ceased.

'So you never saw each other again.'

'No,' Grandpa replied.

'Yes,' Angela said.

We both stared at her and she smiled.

'It was in the autumn of 1969, Zach. Your Grandpa came to Buckingham Palace to receive his long overdue DFC. Prince Charles presented the awards that day. It was his first ceremonial duty since his investiture as Prince of Wales.'

'You were there?' Grandpa asked.

'Yes, I'd been appointed as physician to the Royal Household for some months.'

'I didn't see you.'

'That was because you weren't looking for me.'

'Why didn't you come and say hello?'

'You were there with your young family and beautiful wife who had eyes only for you. She was so proud and I could see she loved you unconditionally. Who was I to intrude? No, much as I wanted to rush over and hug you, I kept my distance. It was her day with you.'

'Yeah, funny thing about your Nan, Zach,' Grandpa said and I knew he was remembering her fondly. 'I met her when I was on leave from CAT in Sydney. You know what she said to me when we first started going out? "I'm just an ordinary girl, there's nothing special about me." I told her that was the most special thing I'd ever heard a girl say. I quit CAT and started working for Airlines of New South Wales for a while, but then your Nan's folks got too old to manage the farm. I took over full-time after we married and started a family.'

'So you finally settled down here,' I said.

'To a point,' Grandpa replied grimly. 'I remember one morning back in the early sixties. I'd been working the paddocks and mustering all day. I got home and your Nan said there was a bloke to see me. Guess what? It was Colonel Serong. He said he needed my help with his Australian Army Training Team who were preparing Montagnards to fight the Viet Cong. I'd been there before of course. He lured me with a new toy – the Iroquois helicopter. Your Nan was pretty upset about it, but I came back in one piece.'

'I can imagine,' Angela said, but who was she to talk after all the hot-spots she'd been in?

'I ran into Major Black and Major White once,' Grandpa reminisced. 'Although they were colonels by then, they still liked creeping around the jungle and shooting things.'

'They probably ended up as generals.'

'I dunno, but Brigadier Charlie Spry showed up every now and then with jobs he thought I'd be good at here in Australia.'

'What was wrong with his regular ASIO agents?' I asked.

'He said he trusted me. The pay was good and he knew I sometimes needed a little extra cash to keep the farm going.'

'Sort of touchy-feely blackmail,' Angela suggested.

'It was Silent Charlie's style, but that's a whole bunch of other stories.'

I let it go, because I knew Grandpa wasn't going to give anything more away that evening. Although I was intrigued, I changed the subject.

'What about you, Angela?' I asked. 'Who was your "someone else"? Why did you say that?'

'Oh, it was mostly talk,' she replied with a smile. 'I needed to free Danny. My work had taken over my life and Danny'd made it clear he didn't want to follow me around like a lap-dog. There were a few chaps. Jeremy St Chalfont-Smyth even showed an interest...'

'Never,' Grandpa chuckled, 'he was old enough to be you father.'

'He wasn't *that* old, but things didn't work out. I didn't want to be "Mrs Anyone" and by the time I thought I might like to be "Mrs Someone" most of the opportunities had slipped by.'

For a moment she looked away, maybe remembering when she was fifteen and thought she was going to drown in a mud slide. Afterwards she'd told Grandpa that right then all she wanted to do was survive and grow old enough to have babies. Was it regret or just acceptance I saw in her eyes when she turned back to face me?

'Are you still very religious,' I said, not really knowing whether it was impertinent or not. 'Grandpa said you were a real firebrand when he first met you. You haven't asked to go to church since you've been here.'

She smiled again, looking out over the rolling bushland.

'I see his presence in the beauty here,' she said, 'but over the years I've come to believe that God has been watching over me even if I don't pester him for attention all the time.'

If Grandpa disagreed, he didn't say anything.

'You never told me you ran into Long Li again before he returned to *Kago Ailan*, Grandpa,' I said, changing the subject.

'Sorry, I was probably getting to that. There are a lot of details to recall. It must have slipped my mind. He married Kekio you know. He'd lost his first family in the Singapore Sook-Ching massacres during the Japanese occupation. I was happy for him when he started another family.'

'Is he still on *Kago Ailan*?' I asked.

'No one is, Zach,' Grandpa replied. 'The volcano finally erupted so violently that everyone was evacuated from *Kago*,

Daiman and *Nogat Nem Ailans*. The islands disappeared after the eruption and are now just coral reefs. Long Li moved his family to Rabaul. We still exchange Christmas cards.'

I was of course interested to hear about Monty. Apparently he wasn't a very successful civil-rights activist. It took too much dedication and sense of purpose. He left Belle to fight the cause and went back to his first love — music. He joined a moderately successful Chicago blues band, but was offered a job flying float-planes during an Alaskan tour. His group was going through a self-destructive implosion that so many bands succumb to anyway. Monty decided to stay, and started flying again based in Juneau.

He soon secured a regular gig playing at the Red Dog Saloon and met a part-Eskimo girl who sang a tight harmony. She moved in with Monty who settled down happily, judging by his letters to Grandpa. Dave Bradley shipped Monty's guitars to Juneau along with the cash he got for selling up Monty's stuff. Dave also sold *Alabama Airlines* and retired to the NSW central coast as a wealthy man.

'That pretty well covers it,' Grandpa said. 'I think it's time for dinner.'

'There is just one thing left,' Ange said with that wicked grin she sometimes used when she knew she was going to say something smarter than anyone else. 'Frenchy.'

Grandpa and I stared at her.

'He survived?' Grandpa asked.

*

In 1970 Angela was awarded an MBE for services to medical research. It was a singular achievement for someone who was only thirty-five years old. To celebrate, she took her parents on a motoring holiday through France.

'Two weeks of wine and fine food,' Angela remembered with relish. 'I'd come a long way from *Babycham*. We stayed overnight at Roscof before catching the morning ferry back to Plymouth.'

Roscof was a pretty seaside town on the north-western tip of Brittany. It was noted for its fine seafood and rustic cuisine. Angela found a pleasant looking restaurant and studied the menu in the window.

'Look they have a dish named after you, darling,' Mrs Holyman declared.

Sure enough right at the top of the menu, Angela read:

Les Spécialités du Chef
Le plat de Poisson d'Angela

She looked up and saw the restaurant was simply called *Café Duval*. For a moment she stared at the sign, and then shook her head. 'Duval' that was a very common French surname.

'We'd better try it,' Angela said.

They were greeted by a stunning West-African woman who looked a few years younger than Angela. It was early for a meal by Continental standards so there were only a few other patrons although their host explained the place would be packed in an hour or so. Two coffee-hued children sat amusing themselves with colouring books at a corner table. Although Angela spoke fluent

French by then, the waitress immediately recognised her as English and used that language flawlessly.

'My name is Angela, so we'd love to try your chef's speciality.'

'Madame has made an excellent choice. It is my husband's favourite dish to cook.'

When the food arrived Angela gasped with astonishment. It was a simple dish by Michelin Star standards, but cooked to perfection. Grilled white fish fillets, basted lightly with olive oil, herbs, condiments and spices topped with slivers of pineapple, mango and a splash of lime juice.

'It can't be?' Angela said just as the chef emerged from his kitchen.

'*Pardon, Madame,*' he said, looking genuinely distressed. 'You do not care for my food?'

'Frenchy...' Angela stammered.

Then she smiled.

'It's just as delicious as I remember when you barbequed it on *Nogat Nem Ailan* twenty years ago – although I prefer these surroundings.'

For once Angela was dumbfounded, but she sprang to her feet and embraced him. He was perhaps a little stouter, but still fit and muscular.

'You're looking well,' Angela said.

'*Et tu,*' he grinned. 'I have a young wife to keep me fit, *n'est-ce pas?*'

Dr and Mrs Holyman were initially more circumspect. They remembered what a proper villain Frenchy had been, but a lot had changed since then.

He introduced his wife who was born in the Congo when it had still been a Belgian colony.

Frenchy had recovered from his wounds and remained with Mad Mike Hoar's Five-Commando. He'd fought alongside the mercenaries during the Simba uprising in the Congo during 1964 and '65. Frenchy had rescued the girl, her family and their small community from the rebels' savagery. She was to become his wife. After the horrors of Katanga and Stanleyville even Frenchy'd seen enough.

He'd made enough to start his restaurant in a most beautiful part of Brittany. The restaurant was proving popular with tourists and locals alike. Frenchy made a comfortable living.

'Come, let me introduce *mes enfants,* Angela and Daniel.'

'You named your children after Danny and me?'

'*Bien sûr.* Do you not call *votre enfants* after those you admire most?'

It was almost impossible to believe that Frenchy possessed the tenderness and passion to love a woman, let alone father two children. Yet there he was playfully teasing them with his arm proudly around his delightful ebony wife. He looked surprisingly sad when Angela told him she and Danny hadn't wound up together.

*

I'd never heard of the Simba rebellion or Katanga and knew very little about the Congo, let alone when it was called the Belgian Congo. I *Googled* it and leant the uprising was a blood-bath, so no wonder even someone as tough as Frenchy was sickened by it. Rwanda, Nigeria, Uganda and Somalia were all much the same and had also been scrapping viciously for the last sixty years as far as I could tell.

'It's sad you and Grandpa never made up,' I said. 'Especially after mending so many fences with Frenchy.'

'It was silly really, Zach,' Angela replied, 'but remember we were so young and we'd seen too much. I think if Danny had come back and held me in his arms, I'd probably have fought him, but I'd have given in.'

'If only I had gone back and told Ange that I loved her. She already knew that, but I should have gone back and told her again.'

'It seems funny,' I said. 'I mean you're...umm...like...'

'Yes Zach, darling,' Angela said leaving her seat and kissing me on the forehead. 'Your Grandpa Danny and I are lovers. We took our own sweet time getting there, but it's our turn now.'

'C'mon, dinner's ready,' Grandpa said.

THE END

The McAlister Line

The McAlister Line reviews:

'McAlister's Way is a fast paced page-turning read, the kind of read where you lose track of time. Absolutely enveloping! Highly recommended!'

'...Masterfully handled and quite eloquent — Wonderful.'

'With pirates and secrets set amongst the northern tropics, you're in for a delightful read. It has a really good sense of place and from the voice to the detail, it's a fast moving action story that will leave you wanting more'

'*McAlister's Spark* is a fast-paced, action-riddled amazing read you will struggle to put down.'

'*McAlister and the Great War is a* very good and well researched read. I enjoyed it very much.'

Illustrated Books for All Ages

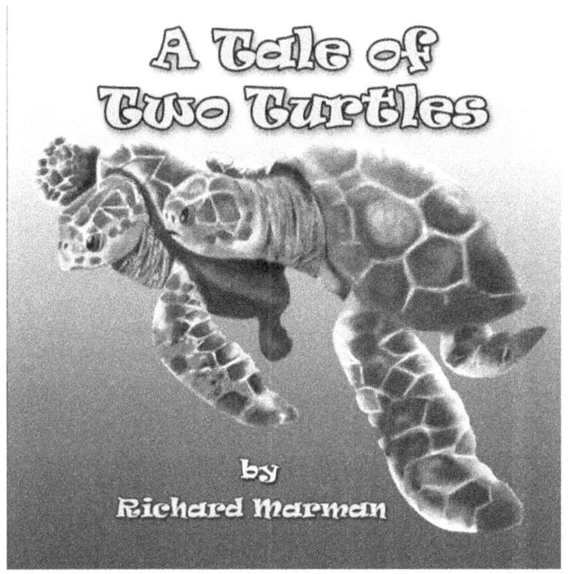

Other Adventure Titles

Approaching his sixteenth birthday, Henry is thrust into a perilous quest when his village chief's wife is abducted. Joined by three companions and his pet wolf, he vows to track down the mysterious kidnappers.

With no magic or special skills, they can only rely on their courage, determination, wits and friendship to survive in a cruel realm which makes no concessions for youth or innocence.

Danger mounts with each challenge until ultimately they face a seemingly unconquerable foe at the gates of a hostile, alien city.

A mighty dragon called Brimstone is terrorising the quiet village of Oak Tree. Prince Roger and his sister Princess Crystal set out to hunt the fiery beast.

They are ably assisted or hindered — as the case may be — by an evil knight, a mysterious good-guy, the local sheriff, loyal men-at-arms, forest brigands, ogres, trolls and Oak Tree's villagers with a bunch of attitude.

There are thrills, spills, romance and heaps of rollicking fun to be had by all.

Illustrations for other Authors